Rose Hanelon had been asleep for hours when the pounding on her door began . . .

Groping for her eyeglasses and then her terrycloth bathrobe, she stumbled toward the door, propelled only by the thought of dismembering whoever she found when she opened it.

"Miss Hanelon?" An anxious Margie Collier, looking as if she'd thrown her clothes on with a pitchfork, fidgeted in the doorway. "Did I wake you?" she gasped. "I mean . . . I thought you writers worked late on your manuscripts."

"No," said Rose between her teeth. "I'm usually out robbing graves at this hour, but it's raining! Now what do you want?"

"I'm sorry to disturb you, but since you are a mystery writer, we thought . . . Oh, Miss Hanelon, there's been a murder!"

"How amusing for you." Rose started to close the door. "These little parlor games are of no interest to me, however."

"No! Not a murder game! A real murder. Someone has killed John Clay Hawkins!"

"That is too bad," said Rose, shaking her head sadly. "He wasn't my first choice at all. . . . "

—from Sharyn McCrumb's
"Happiness Is a Dead Poet"

ELIZABETH PETERS

presents

MALICE DOMESTIC

1

An Anthology of
Original Traditional
Mystery Stories

POCKET BOOKS

New York   London   Toronto   Sydney   Tokyo   Singapore

This book consists of works of fiction. Names, characters, places and incidents are either products of the authors' imaginations or are used fictitiously. Any resemblance to actual events or locales or persons, living or dead, is entirely coincidental.

An *Original* Publication of POCKET BOOKS

POCKET BOOKS, a division of Simon & Schuster Inc.
1230 Avenue of the Americas, New York, NY 10020

ISBN: 0-671-73826-7

First Pocket Books printing May 1992

10 9 8 7 6 5 4 3 2 1

POCKET and colophon are registered trademarks of
Simon & Schuster Inc.

Cover art by John Zielinski

Printed in the U.S.A.

Copyright Notices

Contents

Contents

MALICE DOMESTIC
An Idea Whose Time Had Come

Elizabeth Peters

When the indefatigable Mary Morman first suggested the idea of a "cozycon" my heart sank into my sneakers. You see, I had attended conventions of Mary's, one of them devoted solely to my humble self, and I knew she would not only work herself cross-eyed but would expect the rest of the committee—including *me*—to do the same.

Yet I was strongly in favor of a convention honoring the traditional mystery, for it seemed to me that this part of the genre had not received the respect it deserved. Readers had always been loyal and enthusiastic, but critics tended to dismiss such books as "froth," awards committees considered them frivolous and unrealistic, and publishers weren't publishing them in sufficient numbers or giving them sufficient promotion. Out of pure nobility and a selfless dedication to the happiness of others, I therefore consented.

No one is going to believe that, so I may as well be honest. I agreed for purely selfish reasons. As a reader, I wanted more of my favorite books. Besides, I thought a convention would be fun.

And it has been fun, though there were times that first nerve-racking year when some of us wondered whether we had rocks for brains. We were starting from ground zero. We had no money. We had no hotel, no logo, no teapots. We didn't even have a name. Most important, perhaps, we had no reputation. What if we gave a party and nobody came? There were only eight of us to begin with, and when one member of the committee dropped out, the rest of us had to add her duties to ours. (I inherited the job of collecting and distributing the mail, which I adored, since I like reading other people's letters, and I love sorting papers into little piles held together with paper clips.)

My primary responsibility was to persuade, bully, and intimidate fellow writers to attend. I knew all we had to do was get people like Robert Barnard and Sarah Caudwell, Sharyn McCrumb and Aaron Elkins—to mention only a few—in the same room and let them talk. Readers would flock to hear and see them; publishers would take notice.

They came, and the rest is history. I doubt that even that small, dedicated group who sat around my kitchen table eating my famous soup ("Cook it a long time, till it's done") could have predicted how quickly and dramatically Malice Domestic would catch on.

It is now one of the big events of the mystery year, and the Agatha is one of the most coveted of mystery awards. Malice Domestic is not and never has been a "cozycon," for it celebrates the traditional mystery in all its forms. These forms are diverse and nonexclusive. One of the most exciting developments in mystery writing over the past decade has been the broadening of its boundaries and the breakdown of formerly rigid categories. Would you call Reg Hill's novels "police procedurals"? To do so would be to miss the vitality of Reg's sensitive studies of human and social relationships. If you have categorized Charlotte MacLeod as a "cozy" writer, you haven't noticed her effortless erudition and brilliant plot construction. And they are only two of the fine writers whom Malice Domestic claims as "one of ours."

When people ask, "What kind of mystery *is* a Malice Domestic mystery?" I am tempted to reply with a cliché: I may not be able to define one, but I know one when I see it. "Malice" is a self-explanatory, I trust. If "domestic" confuses some readers and critics, they aren't familiar with the primary meaning of the word. It distinguishes the personal and private aspects of crime from the public and impersonal. Our murders don't kill for the fun of it (serial killers) or for a misguided ideal (assassins and terrorists) or for pay (hired hit men.) They only do in people they know and love (or hate).

As for "traditional," another of the terms we employ to describe our work, its applicability is equally accurate. With the Agatha we pay tribute to a distinguished predecessor of the 1920s, but the tradition goes much further back in time—not only to Conan Doyle and Edgar Allen Poe, but to the great nineteenth-century novelists such as Dickens, Collins, Twain, and the Brontës. The present-day mystery novel is primarily a *novel,* in the classic tradition, and at its best, it is as good or better than any example of so-called mainstream fiction.

I'm proud to have been one of the founders of Malice Domestic, for I believe it is achieving the objects I hoped for in the beginning—greater respect for the genre, greater financial and critical success for the practitioners thereof . . . and a lot of fun. There are no finer people in the world than "our" authors, and no better writers. Enjoy this first of—we hope—many Malice Domestic anthologies. Come up and see us sometime. (But be sure to register early; Malice always sells out.) And if this is *your* kind of mystery, think kindly of that first earnest group of volunteers (including *me*) and their equally dedicated successors. It is to them and to the writers who had faith in the then unfulfilled promise of Malice Domestic that it owes its uproarious success. Obviously it was an idea whose time had come.

The Perplexing Puzzle of the Perfidious Pigeon Poisoner

From the Memoirs of Charlotte MacLeod, Detective

"But damn it all, Charlotte, if you don't take the case, we'll have to go out and *pay* somebody."

I could follow Dolph Kelling's argument easily enough. I had to grant that pigeon poisoning is a despicable practice; poisoning them within the historical purlieus of the Public Gardens amounts, in the eyes of us Bostonians, to something barely short of sacrilege. From a Kelling's viewpoint, having to pay for a service that might, with adequate arm twisting, be got for nothing falls into much the same category.

As a professional private investigator, I knew how to steel myself against blandishments, badgering, and downright bullying. Indeed, I had all too frequently been obliged to do so back when Dolph's Uncle Frederick was alive.

Fred had prided himself on his diplomatic skills, of which in truth he had possessed none whatsoever. Dolph, with his downright foot-in-mouth approach, had often succeeded where Fred would have failed, although he'd never been given any credit for his achievements until Fred at long last had been locked away in the family vault. I had felt in the past, and still retain, a sort of grudging fondness for Dolph. I left the last bite of my crumpet on the plate for Mr. Manners

1

as children of my class and generation had been taught to do, set down my teacup, and groped under the table for my umbrella.

"Very well, Dolph," I told him. "I'll look into the matter."

It would be awkward for me to do so at this time; I was already committed to a potentially more interesting and assuredly more lucrative assignment. This matter was baffling the Boston police and had so far, I confess, also baffled me; although I was confident of ultimate success, since I had never yet failed. I do not boast, I merely state a fact. To fail would result in a waste of time and energy; persons of my ancestry and upbringing deplore waste in any form.

The case I had just accepted involved the recent disappearance of the celebrated Papaver pearls, a long rope of matched India pearls quite improbable in size although in fact quite genuine. The pearls had been handed down to the present owner through a string of ancestresses almost as long as the rope itself. Albernia Papaver (the given name was also hers by inheritance) had worn them to the opera on the previous Friday evening. Somehow or other they had been removed from her person, most probably during that breathless moment when La Tosca was hurling herself from the high parapet to the spring mattress below. Mrs. Papaver, a fervent Puccini worshiper, had not noticed the draft around her neck until Baron Scarpia was taking his third curtain call, by which time many seats had been emptied and the thief had evidently made a clean escape. Here indeed was a pretty kettle of fish, and how might so slippery an eel be hauled up from its murky depths?

It had been, I should explain, not Albernia Papaver herself but her daughter and son-in-law who had come three days since to seek my aid. Albernia the Sixth, I believe she was, had been married to Dr. Kenneth Whittler, a brilliant young brain surgeon, some two years previously; it was now apparent to my discerning eye that their union was to be blessed. Mrs. Whittler had come straight to the point.

"I cannot claim any personal disinterest in the matter of the robbery, Miss MacLeod. The pearls would, in the fullness of time, come to me or to my daughter—" she gave her handsome husband a sweet, secret smile "—and would be treasured for their intrinsic worth and beauty but far more for their familial associations. The thought of losing them forever is thus doubly bitter to me. Bitterest of all, however, is having to observe the dreadful effect this shocking event has had on my dear mama. *Our* dear mama, I should have said, since Kenneth dotes upon her as much as I. Do you not, my dearest?"

"How could I not?" cried the rising star of the intracranial correction. "Mother Papaver is the apotheosis of virtuous womanhood: a model of rectitude combined with grace of manner, steadiness of principles, and warmth of heart."

He did not add swiftness of intellect, I noticed. That was understandable. Such standards of decorum as Albernia Papaver exemplified would not leave much room for brilliance. "Does your mother know you are consulting me?" I asked.

"She does not," Mrs. Whittler confessed. "Mama is naturally distressed at the loss of her cherished heirloom, but far more distraught at having become a target for publicity as the victim of so daring a theft. Scrupulous as she is, she cannot help seeing the incident primarily as an appalling breach of etiquette. She won't even let us allude to it in her presence."

"Much as I feel for Mother Papaver," said Dr. Whittler, "my most serious concern is the strain which this grievous situation is putting on my beloved wife. Albernia the Younger is, as you may have divined, in a delicate condition requiring rest and tranquillity above all things. She desires to be her mother's prop and mainstay, but circumstances prevent her remaining long in such an upsetting situation. Mother Papaver is, of course, never neglected; Father Papaver is always close at hand."

"But darling Papa is, like my dear husband, totally caught up in his work," Albernia the Younger all but sobbed.

"And what is it that your father does?" I asked, mainly to divert her mind into a less harrowing channel. "It was my impression that he, a fourth cousin to your esteemed mother and equally an heir to the vast Papaver fortune, lived the life of a country gentleman insofar as one is able to do so in a Beacon Hill town house."

"Oh, Papa is no idle dilettante," the loyal daughter insisted. "He is an expert maker of miniature ship models, which he puts into bottles. He has already succeeded in assembling the *Niña*, the *Pinta*, and the *Santa María* under full sail inside a Haig & Haig Pinch bottle; his next triumph is to be the fight between the *Bonhomme Richard* and the *Guerriere.*"

"Father Papaver's is a labor of both aesthetic and historic importance, as we well realize," Dr. Whittler added, "but it does leave Mother Papaver too much to herself, and we cannot but fear the worst. Miss MacLeod, only you can save our dear parent from sinking into melancholy and ultimate decline. Will you help us?"

How could I refuse? Immediately I got down to business.

"Very well, I accept your commission. Now describe to me the precise circumstances of that direful night. Where were you sitting?"

"Row C, left center aisle," Dr. Whittler replied with obvious relief. "We had the first four seats: Father Papaver on the aisle, Mother Papaver next to him, my Albernia beside her, and myself farthest in. It would thus have been impossible for anybody else in our row to have reached over and possessed himself of the pearls."

"In fact, we can't see how anyone at all could have removed them without Mama's noticing," said his wife. "Whereas Grandmama always wore them hanging down to her knees, Mama has always preferred to loop them several times around her neck."

"An interesting point," I rejoined. "And who was sitting behind your mother?"

"A man with a beard, I believe."

"I think it was a woman in a mink or sable coat, my dear," the husband objected.

"Might there not have been one of each in adjoining seats?" I ventured, although I do not like to lead a witness.

"That is possible," Mrs. Whittler conceded. "I have only a general impression of furriness."

"And my recollection is, I fear, equally fuzzy," the young doctor added ruefully. "Truth to tell, I always refrain from turning around when I'm out in public, for fear some acquaintance will spot me and start telling me about his symptoms."

"But what of Mr. Papaver?" I asked. "He, it would seem, was best situated to notice those around your party."

Grave as the situation undoubtedly was, Albernia the Younger could not repress a small giggle. "Oh, darling Papa slept through the whole performance. The only parts he likes about going to the opera are the intermissions. His chief recollection is of how long it took him to get served at the champagne bar."

Police interrogation of the ushers and certain members of the audience who had not yet left the auditorium when the loss was discovered had been futile. The furry person or persons, needless to say, had not been found. The only hopeful piece of information my own sources had been able to turn up so far was that the pearls were apparently not yet fenced, either in Boston or elsewhere.

In my mind it was more than likely, indeed quite certain (and, as I mentioned before, I am never wrong) that the priceless strand was still right here in town; hidden until the heat, as we say in the field of detection, should be off. That the rope might have been broken into segments and sold off piecemeal was unthinkable; its great value lay in its being such a truly monumental aggregation of rare pearls all the same size.

I had mulled in vain over the possibilities, and searched not a few likely hiding places without result. Well, the necklace was somewhere, and I would find it. Perhaps turning briefly to a different task, for surely no pigeon poisoner could stay for long concealed from me, would stimulate my keen mind to fresh insights. I crooked my umbrella over my arm, straightened the purple velvet toque which had been an inheritance from my late aunt Elizabeth, and set forth to discover what evildoing columbiphobe had so far successfully dispatched seventeen victims.

How can I pinpoint that number so precisely? First, you

must understand that Boston pigeons are not without friends. That is particularly true of those which frequent the Common and, to a somewhat lesser degree, the Public Gardens. While some residents of the Hill and the Back Bay detest the creatures, others are solicitous for their welfare, and the latter are in the moral majority. Moreover, these wily avians know very well how to work the tourists.

I have no statistics as to what percentage of the popcorn and peanuts purveyed by vendors in the area is bought partly, chiefly, or even exclusively for consumption by the local fauna; but it must be considerable. We must also count those dedicated bird lovers who fetch bags of crumbs from home, not to mention the park-bench picnickers who donate portions of their doughnuts and frankfurt rolls either voluntarily or perforce. Common and Garden pigeons can be as aggressively pestiferous as the late Frederick Kelling, which is saying a good deal.

Some of this largess goes to the ducks and the squirrels, I grant you; but the major consumers must surely be the pigeons, because there are so many more of them. Ordinances against feeding the feathered denizens of our cherished inner-city green acres have been passed from time to time but have always failed of their purpose, which is essentially to starve the pigeons into flying off to deposit their unsightly and unsanitary droppings somewhere else. Our pigeons like it where they are, and Bostonians by and large like having them here. Wherefore then the poisonings? And how did Dolph Kelling, my informant, know the precise number of victims to date?

The explanation is only too simple: Dolph knew because Lovella Burdock told him. Lovella Burdock, I suppose I ought to explain, is a Hillite and a longtime embracer of allegedly worthy causes. When I add that for upward of forty years she supported Fred Kelling in each and every one of his loopy undertakings, I believe I have said it all.

Anyway, Lovella had taken it upon herself to be chief mourner for the slain pigeons. Garbed in deepest black, she now spent her days pacing solemnly along the Garden's paths, a black oilcloth bag dangling from her black-gloved hand. When, as too often had happened during the past five or six days, she came upon a feathered corpse, she scooped it up with a trowel she kept somewhere about her person and laid it tenderly in her bag, to be given a decent burial in the tiny garden behind her Beacon Hill brownstone.

These public paradings were innocuous enough, no doubt; but if the silly woman really wanted to do something useful, why didn't she devote her efforts to finding the poisoner and making him—or quite possibly her—stop it? I had asked that question of Dolph Kelling; he'd replied with his usual bluntness, "But then she'd be left without a cause."

So the upshot was that I myself had a new cause to pursue; I might as well get on with it. The afternoon was salubrious enough to have lured forth plenty of strollers, and also, I noticed, a few extra policemen. Some of these were casting suspicious glances at anybody who happened to be carrying a bag of popcorn; others were shooing moppets out of the flower beds, for this was springtime, when the gardens are at their loveliest if one happens to care for tulips en masse.

I am fond of flowers, but those somewhat military-looking blooms are not my favorites, particularly when planted with geometric precision in large beds next to other large beds of clashing colors. The pansy beds are more to my liking; even as a small child I loved their gentle fragrance and little monkey faces, and still do. After having paid my grudging meed of admiration to the gaudy tulips, I paused to visit for a moment with my friends the pansies. It was then I noticed the pigeon.

The bird was in its death throes, and the reason for its impending demise was all too clear. Nothing but strychnine poisoning could cause those agonized back somersaults; the poor thing was rolling like a hoop. The spectacle was heart-wrenching; my sympathies were at once fully enlisted on the side of the preyed-upon. I even began to think less disdainfully of Lovella Burdock.

Or did I? Here she came, just the way Dolph had described her, sooty as a crow from head to foot, with a voluminous mourning veil draped over some sort of black turban affair and billowing out behind her like the exhaust from an uncleaned engine. Thanks to my middle-aged presbyopia, I could make out the expression on her face well enough. Lovella was by no means cast down at the loss of a feathered friend, she was avid for the hunt.

Perhaps it was the ill-concealed glee that repelled me; perhaps it was the tasteless affectation of the antique mourning veil. Whatever it was, I chose not to indulge her whimsy. I opened my umbrella just enough to admit the by now mercifully stilled form at my feet, scooped it inside with one quick motion, closed the trusty bumbershoot, and sauntered on my way, holding the bulgy side concealed against the ample pleats of my well-worn tweed skirt.

Never much of a runner and far too aware of my position to try, I can nevertheless saunter at a surprising rate. In a matter of moments I had left Lovella searching vainly among the tulips, crossed the ornamental bridge over the pond without pausing to gaze down, as was my wont, upon the graceful swan boats and the lines of ducks quacking importunately after them, and made my way to Charles Street.

In my profession, one learns upon occasion, notwithstanding one's innate predilections, to cast economy to the winds. Steeling myself for an exorbitant fee, I hailed a passing taxicab, directing its driver to take me to the office of a veterinary whose name had best not be given for reasons the perspicacious reader either will or will not understand, as the case may be. Suffice it to mention that this was the same vet who had been so viciously—though, thanks to myself, only temporarily—victimized during the lurid affair of the substitute sealyham. He or she (though I might have said she or he, since so many of our outstanding vets are females. The most apposite term in this context would perhaps be bitches, but unfortunately this formerly innocuous word has gradually acquired a pejorative slant)—where was I? Oh yes, the person to whom I refer greeted me as a valued friend and inquired the reason for my visit since I was unaccompanied by an ailing quadruped, as had customarily been the case.

"It is this." I shook my umbrella on the examining table and snapped it open to reveal the pathetic contents. "I require an immediate autopsy on this unfortunate creature, and I intend to watch you perform it."

"You won't like what you see," cautioned the veterinarian.

"It can be no worse than what I have already seen," I retorted. "Only minutes ago, I stood and watched this pigeon die in agony, a victim of the so far invisible fiend who is turning the Public Gardens into a veritable charnel house."

"Good gad! I had not realized the situation was so dire. Just let me finish clipping this savage Doberman pinscher's toenails—now the other paw, Susibelle, that's my good girl—and we'll buckle down to our gruesome task."

My friend was as good as her (or his) word. To my secret relief, the pigeon did not have to be thoroughly dissected; a mere cursory inspection of the opened crop was enough to expose the kernel of popcorn stuck in its throat. Under my direction, a chemical analysis was done forthwith, and my surmise confirmed.

"It's strychnine, all right," said the vet. "A tiny amount, but definitely present."

"A tiny amount?" I queried. "Would so small a dose be sufficient to effect the demise of so large a bird?"

"Oh yes. As a multitalented Harvard faculty member has reminded us, it requires no more than a smidgen to effect the demise of a pigeon. This kernel was the fatal instrument, you may rest assured of that."

As I gazed upon that small, whitish object, a great light dawned. "Then let us," I said, "proceed to dissect the kernel. Carefully, if you please."

"Very well," the vet replied with a shrug, "though I fail to—great Scott! Will you look at that?"

I nodded. "This is no more than I expected. The kernel has been cunningly hollowed out to receive one superb Orient pearl, indubitably taken from the famous rope stolen last Friday night from Mrs. Albernia Papaver during the final scene of *La Tosca.*"

And I knew where to find seventeen more just like it, but not yet. I must go canny, as some ancestor from the land at which my patronym hints might perhaps have remarked. "I humbly beg that you breathe not even a syllable of this to any living soul, and further that you dispose of this wretched avian's remains forthwith, by whatever means is most expeditious and least detectable."

"It shall be done" was the welcome answer.

I have no doubt that it was, but I did not wait to see. Carrying the pearl with me inside a small envelope of the sort generally used in dispensing worm pills, I made my way back to my modest residence, taking, as always, a quiet pleasure in the aspect of its simple Bulfinch design. Behind the ancestral lavender-hued windows, I exchanged my sensible crepe-soled walking shoes for a pair of fuzzy pink house slippers, for even we private investigators have our frivolous moments, rang for my faithful Florence to fetch in the tea, and sat down to brood.

There was much to brood about. Was Lovella Burdock the innocent though rattle-pated do-gooder Dolph Kelling believed her to be, or was she a witting accomplice of the jewel thief? And who was that thief?

The opera box office had been no great help. Those desirable aisle seats behind the Papaver party had indeed been marked off as sold; the middle-aisle ushers had been sure they were occupied on the night, else the gap would have been noticed. The occupants, however, had gone unremarked, as was only natural in so large an assemblage. There was no record of a reservation's having been made in anybody's name; the tickets must have been purchased for cash at the window, or possibly from a scalper, who would certainly never confess to his unethical practice. The police were trying to track down those elusive occupants; good luck to them. It was clear to me now that the thief and the poisoner must be one and the same.

As to the modus operandi (a technical term of the investigative profession), the lone pearl had told me all. Young Mrs. Whittler had expressed puzzlement as to how those multiple strands could have been removed without her mother's noticing. Quite simply, they could not be and had not been.

A rope of pearls, I reflected, is not like, for instance, a diamond necklace wherein each separate jewel is individually mounted on a chain. Pearls are drilled through their centers and strung on strong thread of gut, waxed linen, or in this day and age, more usually nylon, with a knot tied after each bead to guard against loss should the strand be broken. Careful owners, as Albernia Papaver no doubt was, have their pearls restrung from time to time purely as a preventive measure. Why, then, would it in any way impair the value of the rope to take it apart and smuggle the pearls away one by one, to be restrung later in a safer place?

Obviously this was what the thief had reasoned that night at the opera while snipping through the various twists and stealthily pocketing each separate section in its turn. It must have been done with extraordinary deftness by someone almost preternaturally skilled in finicking little operations. A brain surgeon or a bottler of miniature ship models could have done it; an expert pickpocket was far more likely. I thought of alerting my friends on the force to round up the best of the lot. Then I reflected that really expert pickpockets no doubt would be unavailable; they retain their anonymity by never getting caught!

No, this was a task in which I alone had a better chance of succeeding than all the Boston police force put together. I drank my tea, then paid a brief visit to the ancestral attic, where I easily found such things as would best serve my purpose. That done, I ate my dinner with good appetite, read a few chapters of *Sense and Sensibility,* and went early to bed.

Fresh and rested the next morning, I made my ablutions, did a few push-ups, breakfasted as usual on porridge and stewed prunes, and proceeded to array myself in deepest black from head to toe. Great-grandmother's mourning veil was a nuisance but essential to my scheme; I must manage the thing as best I could. Black oilcloth shopping bags must have been all the rage sometime or other; I had been able to duplicate Lovella Burdock's pigeon carrier as closely as made no matter.

One accessory that Lovella seemed not to have thought of was a black umbrella. I resolved not to be parted from mine, since I carry no other weapon and have never needed any. Fully equipped, then, I set forth betimes on my quest. There was no danger of Lovella's showing up to cramp my style; knowing her voracious sweet tooth, I had sent her a box of chocolates heavily laced with a certain patent remedy guaranteed to promote regularity. To lull her into a sense of security, I had enclosed one of Dolph Kelling's visiting cards. Desperate situations require desperate measures.

This was a beautiful morning to be out and about in the Gardens. The trees were all in bloom—those which in fact do bloom, that is; the tulips were rampant in their splendor. The swan boats were bobbing gently at the dock, waiting for their operators to seat themselves inside the carved wooden swans and activate the foot pedals which are these flat, open barges' sole means of locomotion. Many a time from earliest youth had I sat on their slatted benches and been pedaled over these popcorn-sprinkled waters, under the bridge, around the lagoon, past the little island and back again. It would be pleasant to loiter here awhile, but duty called; I must move on.

It was less than a week since the pearls had been stolen. To have killed seventeen pigeons—possibly eighteen by now, since another could have been poisoned while I was at the vet's—was fast work. I was wise to have come early, for the poisoner must even now be abroad. His foul task was not a simple one; he must make sure his quite possibly unwitting confederate was present on the scene, and synchronize his (I have decided to stick with the masculine pronoun, but in its impersonal sense) fell scatterings, as I was about to say, with the chief mourner's peregrinations. It would not do for a pigeon to expire unless Lovella was close enough to pick up the cadaver before one of the park keepers beat her to it.

Strychnine acts quickly; the poisoner need only stay just far enough and not too far ahead of the woman in black.

Keeping my pesky mourning veil down over my face and forsaking my customary brisk stride for Lovella's pigeon-toed shamble, I meandered along the more secluded paths, every sense alert for clandestine popcorn tossers.

Anybody feeding a feathered flock that contained even one duck had to be eliminated, of course. Boston ducks are so pushy that they easily beat even the boldest pigeon to the popcorn; and surely my quarry would not risk poisoning a duck, for it might take to the water, die there, and become impossible for Lovella to retrieve.

I had a couple of false alarms, then I spotted him. Or her. Baggy flannels and jacket, a shapeless poplin rain hat, hair of indeterminate length, and oversize sunglasses created an effect of androgyneity; the disguise would require closer inspection to penetrate than I dared attempt at this juncture.

I could not have been mistaken; the person had collected only three or four pigeons, not a duck among them, and was doling out the popcorn one kernel at a time, eyeing a certain member of the group with peculiar intensity. Ah, now the first dire symptom was beginning to appear. The person flung the rest of his or her popcorn among the avians to create a concealing flurry, cast one hasty but meaningful glance in my direction, and strode briskly away.

Was he heading for the subway kiosk? No, a meter maid was too close by, tagging cars with the self-satisfied expression of her kind. He swerved back whence he had come, thinking no doubt to cross over to the Common and lose himself there among the loiterers and dog walkers. But the popcorn cart was by the gate, and a policeman beside it, eyeing would-be purchasers so intently that they were all passing up the popcorn and buying pinwheels instead. With an aplomb born, one suspects, of much practice, the poisoner changed course again, hung over the bridge for a few moments, then tripped down the steps to the dock, thrust money at the ticket collector, and hopped aboard a swan boat that was just about to pull away.

So that was the miscreant's little game! Well, two could play. His latest victim safely stowed inside my oilcloth bag, I had naturally contrived to make my way again into his vicinity. His sudden dash for the departing swan boat disconcerted me not a whit; the scoundrel had played straight into my hands. A second swan boat rode idly at the dock, empty of passengers, for business was not brisk so early in the day. I hastened aboard, flashed my private investigator's license at the youth who sat inside the swan, and ordered imperiously, "Follow that swanboat!"

"But I'm not supposed to go till the starter tells me," protested the pedaler.

He was but a rosy-cheeked stripling; I thrust him aside, took his place inside the swan, lashed my mourning veil securely around my neck, and began to pedal for dear life.

The youngster stammered further protests and even attempted to take me by the arm, but I shook him off and kept on pedaling. The gap between the two boats narrowed; unfortunately some of the passengers ahead had noticed what was happening. They were craning their necks in our direction, either cheering me on or urging their own swan-man to greater efforts. The pigeon poisoner panicked, leaped inside the swan, and pressed a pistol to the pedaler's head.

Farsighted as I am, I easily discerned what make of pistol it was. The fool! I do loathe incompetence, even in my adversaries. I beckoned the still dithering youngling back into our swan.

"Here," I ordered, "take my place and pedal your heart out. I must board that boat with all dispatch. Yonder villain with the gun is none other than the infamous pigeon poisoner!"

"But if we keep chasing him, he'll shoot my father, for it is in truth my esteemed parent who propels the craft now fleeing before us," moaned the lad. "How can I take action that may precipitate the demise of a beloved sire?"

"Be of cheer, my boy," I replied. "That's only a water pistol."

"Sheesh! Then hang on to your veil, lady."

Si l'agesse pouvait! I had, I think, performed capably on

the pedals, but that youngster had the feet of a Hermes. He sent us flying across the water, sending up great fans of spray, leaving an angry squadron of hopelessly outdistanced mallards quacking anatinian profanities in our tempestuous wake.

I half crouched in the bow, accurately calculated the short gap between the boats, and sprang. As I landed, I raised my ever-dependable gamp and brought it smartly down on the hand that held the pistol, now pointed waveringly in my direction. Except for one brief squirt, I remained unscathed, as I always do.

From then on it was, as we say in the profession, a piece of cake. I dragged the by now totally demoralized and half-collapsing miscreant aboard my commandeered craft, wished those on the full boat bon voyage, shrugged off the grateful protestations of the father, and tipped the son handsomely to take us back to the landing. En route, I set the prisoner down on the front bench and took my place— yes, beside *her!* Exactly as I had anticipated, the stealer of Mrs. Papaver's pearls was none other than Albernia herself. Who else, after all, could have done it so well?

But why? I refrained from pressing the question until I had got the wretched woman into my house and rung for Florence to bring the tea. After a few sips (Albernia took milk but no sugar), the erstwhile model of rectitude was able to falter out an explanation. She, Albernia Papaver, that apotheosis of virtuous womanhood, was being blackmailed!

"In God's name, how?" I am not easy to astonish, but who could have anticipated a revelation like this from such as she? "What could you possibly have done?"

She swallowed the last of her tea, as if to stiffen her resolve. "I—I was caught sniffing a hallucinogenic substance."

"What do you mean by a hallucinogenic substance?" I demanded. "Was it cocaine?"

"Oh no! No, never. It was—I suppose I must reveal the whole sordid story."

She held out her empty cup. Hers was a gesture of

supplication; neither etiquette nor compassion could have refused her a refill. I performed the time-hallowed ritual of the pot and the pitcher, and waited.

I had not to wait long; Albernia Papaver was no poltroon. "Without trying to make myself sound less perfidious than I am," she began in a low but now firm voice, "I should explain that I had led an even more sheltered life than other girls of my class and generation. I was simply not aware of the pitfalls."

"That is so often the case," I said by way of encouragement. "Please go on."

"It happened at boarding school." Albernia mentioned the name of a distinguished establishment for young gentlewomen, which I shall not repeat for obvious reasons. "We were in the art room. Our instructress, Miss Braque, was an intensely creative person and an inspiration to us all. On this day she had us experimenting with what she termed collage. We were to cut out interesting shapes and arrange them in unusual ways. Each of us was handed a random assortment of materials to cut from and, what becomes germane to my narrative, an individual portion of adhesive."

On this last word, her voice faltered. I pounced on the clue. "By adhesive, do you by chance mean glue?"

"Pray do not condemn me, Miss MacLeod," she cried. "I thought the stuff was just to stick things down with."

"And you therefore proceeded to stick?"

"I stuck. Being neat-handed though by no means vulgarly artistic, I accomplished my task so featly and expeditiously that I was accorded the privilege of cleaning up after class. One of my appointed tasks was to return the leftover portions of—of substance to their original container."

"I see." Oh yes, I saw! "And this container was . . ."

"A large glass jar with a screw-on lid."

"The adhesive itself being a jellylike substance about the consistency of an overcooked blancmange, having a not unpleasant spicy odor?"

"Great heaven, Miss MacLeod, you astound me! How can you have described the noxious substance so accurately?"

I shrugged off the question. "The adhesive had merely been scooped out of the jar in dollops and handed to you on scraps of paper?"

"On small cardboard plates with decorative floral borders," Albernia replied with a hint of asperity. "Violets, I believe they were."

"I stand corrected." I am always gracious when circumstances do not require me to be otherwise. "So as you scooped the remains from the plates back into the jars, you inhaled the aforementioned spicy fragrance?"

"Had I but known, I could have held my breath," Albernia replied bitterly. "Instead, to crown my folly, before screwing the top back on, I leaned over the jar and took a great, heady whiff."

"Did you feel any hallucinogenic effect?"

"I had not time to feel anything but embarrassed. At that moment, a classmate burst into the room and exploded into derisive laughter at finding me with my nose in the jar. Knowing this rude girl's talent at public ridicule of her classmates and being myself a shy child, I begged her not to tell. That was a terrible mistake; she only taunted me further. Desperate at the prospect of being branded by the whole school as Stickynose, I retaliated in the only way open to me. I told her that if she breathed one word about what I'd done, I should go straight to the headmistress and tell her who poured the molasses on the chapel pews!"

"This classmate herself having been the culprit, no doubt," I deduced. "She would have been punished?"

"Oh, direly," cried Albernia. "I should have been believed, and she knew it. Her mischievous propensities had made her many enemies; they would have corroborated my testimony. Even if she escaped expulsion, she'd have been put in Coventry. To one in love with the limelight, being shunned by the entire student body would have been the greatest blow of all. I had her in my power. Grudgingly she yielded. Little did I suspect her grudge would be carried through the years. Or what foul use she would make of it in the end!"

"Were you in contact with her during the long interval?"

"Yes, in a casual way. I could hardly not have been; we both live here on the Hill and have acquaintances in common. One hates to snub an old classmate, and why should one? I had long ago dismissed that distasteful scene from my mind. I honestly believed I'd been guilty of nothing worse than a moment's silliness, and surely my threat to her had lost its power once we were graduated."

Albernia drew a deep breath. "Three weeks ago, this woman solicited from me a large contribution toward the purchase of an island in the South Pacific, to which all the Boston pigeons were to be humanely transported as a means of ending their pollution of the Common and Gardens. This was a scheme the late Frederick Kelling had once proposed but never implemented, since it was just about then that his nephew Adolphus had him declared mentally incompetent; a step which, in my husband's opinion and, I must say, my own, might well have been taken a good deal sooner. Naturally I refused to support such an addlepated scheme."

My prisoner-guest wet her lips with what must by then have been the cold, bitter dregs of her tea. Cold and bitter was Albernia's voice as she drove herself mercilessly on toward the denouement.

"She pounced on me like a lioness on her prey. That is, of course, a figure of speech; although for a moment I actually did fear a physical attack. She said I must pay, and pay handsomely, or all the world should know that I, who had stood for so long as a model of rectitude, was but a whited sepulcher. She would shout from the housetops, she would whisper to the scandalmongering press, that I, Albernia Papaver, had in my youth been a glue sniffer."

"She would actually have done this?"

"Indeed yes! She recalled every detail of that fateful long-ago encounter. She made it sound as though . . . as though . . . Miss MacLeod, I cannot tell you how degraded, how defiled I felt as she poured out upon me the vials of her long-pent hatred. She reminded me with ghoulish glee how easily glue sticks, how ready people are to hear the bad and make it worse. She dwelt upon the effect her revelation would have on my son-in-law's career. What patient, she demanded theatrically, would entrust his cerebrum, his cerebellum, or especially his medulla oblongata, to the son-in-law of a dope fiend?"

"Those were her exact words?"

"She hurled them in my face. She spoke also of the ignominy that would be heaped upon my daughter, the shock and pain that might complicate my Albernia's delicate condition, the cloud that would hang over the newborn, should my darling succeed in carrying it to term. She even hinted that my dear husband might be dropped from his club! For myself, I could have defied her and borne the brunt. For my loved ones, I saw no recourse but to meet her demands, outrageous as they were."

"Precisely how outrageous, Mrs. Papaver?"

"She wanted five million dollars, in cash. I had a dreadful time trying to make her understand that people in our position do not leave great wads of thousand-dollar bills kicking around the house. When she finally had to face the truth about trust funds and long-term investments, she demanded my pearls."

I nodded. "I thought as much. So, to get to the nub of the matter, Lovella Burdock directed you to fabricate a robbery during the opera, then deliver the pearls to her via the pigeons, secretly, one by one, by means of hollowed-out popcorn kernels which she supplied to you. Lovella cautioned you not to handle them without wearing transparent rubber or plastic gloves, did she not?"

"Oh yes, she cautioned me. She had every incentive to keep me alive until I had delivered all the pearls. This was another twist of the knife; Lovella knew full well that I had always been scrupulous about feeding the pigeons wholesome, nourishing birdseed. Each poisoned kernel I tossed was a fresh dagger in my heart."

"No doubt," I rejoined shortly. "Getting back to the adhesive, did it never once occur to you that no conscientious teacher would ever have exposed her pupils' tender nostrils to a hallucinogen of any sort? What you sniffed that fateful day could have been nothing more dangerous than ordinary library paste."

"But—but—" The teaspoon fell from her nerveless hand. "Then I have killed nineteen pigeons for nothing."

"You have indeed. Come, let us go and end this senseless massacre once and for all."

"You will not force me back to the Public Gardens? I could not!"

"Trust me, Mrs. Papaver. I, too, attended a school for young gentlewomen."

"Might I not first rid myself of this loathsome disguise?"

"Assuredly. My faithful Florence will assist you. Do you require a change of apparel?"

"Thank you, but I have everything I need hidden in my popcorn bag."

I knew I could trust Florence to keep Mrs. Papaver from doing anything silly; still it was a relief to see her reappear a few minutes later in a properly unsmart two-piece suit and sensible pumps, with a handbag too small to conceal any weapon larger than a popcorn kernel. I myself was still in my ancient black; I remained so as I led the way out of my house and down Beacon Hill.

I had calculated the dosage perfectly; Lovella answered the door in her kimono, pale and drawn but obviously capable of being up and about. Despite her histrionic inclinations, acting was not the miscreant's forte; she recoiled at the sight of my mourning veil and turned pea green when she spied my companion. I barged straight in, urging Mrs. Papaver before me. This was no time for the amenities.

Nor did I mince words. "Lovella Burdock," I cried, "your perfidy is exposed. I have in my possession a pearl taken from the crop of a pigeon poisoned under your brutal coercion by this traduced and deluded woman. You yourself have eighteen more pearls. Get them."

The silly woman stamped her foot like a child in a tantrum. "No! I won't! I want them."

"What you want is a brain scan," I retorted. "You are about to be arrested, Lovella Burdock. Your lawyer will offer a plea of insanity, as well he might. You will then be examined by a team of psychiatrists. If that's the way you're going to act, they'll put you in a straitjacket and squirt cold water at you. Get the pearls, Lovella."

"They're still in the pigeons."

"Humbug!" I retorted. "You may be crazy, but you're not stupid."

She picked up a bowl of popcorn from a nearby table. "Here," she cried with a mad *ha-ha!* "Have some."

I buttoned my lips, located her telephone hidden under a ridiculous French doll with a hoop skirt, and dialed the police station. "Sergeant Imbroglio, could you please send someone over? I have captured the mastermind behind the pigeon poisonings and the Papaver pearl robbery. Oh, not at all, you know I am always happy to do your work for you."

I suggested to Lovella that she get some clothes on before they came to arrest her, but she refused to believe the thing was really going to happen until two stalwart officers in uniforms appeared at the door. Albernia Papaver had evidently not quite believed it, either; she threw me a look of agonized supplication.

"Just tell the truth," I told her gently. "These gentlemen understand human weakness. You will not find them unsympathetic, except to the guilty."

At last it dawned on Lovella that she was really going to be arrested. Wildly screaming, "You'll never take me alive!" she plunged her hand into the popcorn bowl and crammed a handful into her mouth, dropping half the kernels in her frenzy and making a sad mess of the carpet.

I draw the curtain of decency over the appalling scene that ensued. An ambulance was sent for, of course; but there was really nothing we could do except stand around and watch, aghast. As her terrible throes subsided into the ultimate stillness, one of the policemen shook his head.

"All that from a few kernels of popcorn!"

"It only requires a single kernel, dipped in strychnine," I replied sadly. "The missing pearls are almost certainly in the late Mrs. Burdock's right-hand bathrobe pocket. Mrs. Papaver will elucidate."

The pearls were there. Seeing her duty now clear before her, Albernia showed the stuff she was made of. The police were understanding; there would be no scandal. Again I had been right. But then, when was I ever wrong?

Windkill

D. R. Meredith

Maude Turner walked out of the Senior Citizens' Center on Polk Street when the conversation turned to crime and the younger generation. She didn't intend wasting a perfect windy day listening to her peers repeat comments probably first voiced when men still lived in caves and ate their meat raw. Besides, she wasn't convinced people were any meaner today than they were seventy-five years ago when she was born. To say they were was nostalgia talking and not common sense. No generation had a monopoly on goodness, and certainly not hers. Didn't anyone remember Al Capone and Bonnie and Clyde? Machine Gun Kelly and Pretty Boy Floyd? Prohibition and bootlegging? Certainly young people these days talked as if they had personally discovered sin. Certainly they acted as if they had discovered sex. That didn't make either supposition true. The truth was, folks her age were well acquainted with both sin and sex. They just didn't talk about either one over the dinner table or in mixed company. It wasn't considered good manners.

Neither was Maude convinced that meanness would disappear if only society did this or that. Believing that entailed believing that human nature was perfectible, and she wasn't senile enough yet to swallow that hogwash. In fact, she wasn't senile at all. Forgetting where she laid her bifocals and not remembering her brother-in-law's latest lady friend's name didn't indicate that she was ready to be warehoused in a rest home and checked on hourly by some young snippet half her age and with a quarter of her sense. Anyone could forget where she left her glasses, and if her brother-in-law wouldn't change lady friends as frequently as he changed underwear, she might be able to keep track of their names. It would serve the old goat right if he had a heart attack or stroke one day while trying to prove he hadn't lost his virility along with most of his hair.

She had told him so—several times.

He said the same thing about her kite flying.

"At least I'll be dressed when my body's discovered, Victor," she snapped, paying out her kite string as the Texas Panhandle wind tossed her kite higher and higher into the cloudless blue sky. "No one will snicker at me after I'm gone."

Victor arched his left eyebrow, and not for the first time Maude wondered why it was always his left, and if he dyed his eyebrows or if nature had left them that deep blue-black to compensate for his hair loss. Nature usually balanced things out. Otherwise, why did so many fat women have beautiful faces, and homely men such kind dispositions?

"You don't see anything ridiculous about a woman your age running across the grass pulling a bit of paper and wood on the end of a string?" Victor asked, tipping the brim of his Stetson a little farther over his eyes.

Maude didn't care to be reminded of her age, particularly not by a man five years younger who still had all his teeth. "I don't run, Victor. On practically any given day in Amarillo, Texas, there's enough wind to lift a kite without running. Walking briskly and proper technique will suffice."

He grinned and folded his arms. "I suppose walking briskly is how you ended up with your foot in a cast, and proper technique explains why you pulled the tendon in your elbow."

She wiggled her toes that peeked out the end of her cast.

"Anyone could have stepped in a prairie dog hole at Southwest Park. I blame the city maintenance department for not chasing the little beasts out of the park." She hesitated to address his second remark, but she prided herself on honesty. Never turn away from the truth, even if it did embarrass one. "I do accept responsibility for the pulled tendon. I should have known better than to have tried to fly my stunt kite in a high wind. Stunt kites are quite powerful, you know."

"Actually, I don't."

"They are. All require at least two lines to control their flight. I simply overestimated my strength. Which is why I'm flying a simple kite I made myself out of tissue paper stretched over a bamboo frame. It's light and easy to control, but very colorful. It's also cheap—which on my income is a consideration."

Victor cleared his throat. "If you'd just accept my invitation to move into my guest house, you wouldn't have to worry so much about expenses."

Maude tilted her head back to watch her kite and pretended she didn't hear him. She *hated* to argue when logic was on the opposing side. Victor was rich—or reasonably so—and she was not. He owned a beautifully furnished four-room guest cottage behind a house so large as to be almost vulgar. She owned a tacky four-room house with a leaky roof she couldn't afford to have replaced. He couldn't —or wouldn't—cook for himself, and allowed his cleaning lady to cheat him. She, on the other hand, was an excellent cook, and no hired hand had ever gotten the best of her. Victor was a widower, and she was a widow. Although they were not blood relatives, he had been married to her sister, which made them family. They could watch out for each other.

Victor's invitation made excellent sense.

Her refusal made none whatsoever.

"After twenty years of living alone, I don't intend to answer to a man," she finally replied, her eyes still on her dancing kite.

"I don't expect you to. As I recall, you never answered to

your dearly departed husband either. Why break a lifelong habit?" asked Victor.

"My husband was a fine man," retorted Maude.

"He was that, too," agreed Victor. "He was also the only man I ever knew who bored himself to death."

"He died in his sleep!"

"Exactly!"

Actually he died while watching Monday Night Football, but she didn't notice until Tuesday. Saying he died in his sleep seemed so much easier. "I don't wish to discuss my deceased husband," she said, fighting back a yawn.

"You're afraid of what people might say if you move in with me, aren't you?" asked Victor, leaning back against his 1966 candy-apple red Mustang convertible, a car that in Maude's opinion only emphasized his search for lost youth —and lost hair. She had observed that older men lusted after convertibles in direct proportion to their hair loss.

Lost youth or not, she didn't intend to let him get away with accusing her of cowardice. "I have never allowed public opinion to influence a decision of mine, Victor. I am only concerned with cramping your style. A sister-in-law on the premises would hinder your attempts to seduce your way through Amarillo's female population. At least, those females above the age of sixty. You do have the decency to avoid robbing the cradle."

Victor grinned. "You give me credit for more stamina that I possess. These days I look more than I touch. For example, I enjoy looking at that young blonde over there, but I—"

Maude heard Victor gag at the same time she saw the blonde murder her middle-aged husband.

"Do you want another cup of coffee, Victor?" Maude asked, observing that his face was still the faint greenish color of three-day-old liver.

His Adam's apple zipped up and down his throat as he swallowed. "No, I do not want another cup of coffee. I want a drink—as in an alcoholic beverage. Preferably one made with hundred-eighty-proof rum."

"Don't be ridiculous," Maude said in her best no-

nonsense tone of voice. She found that men with delicate stomachs responded better to a firm voice than to a sympathetic one. Sympathy only delayed their recovery. "I need you in a sober enough condition to drive. I managed well enough for the few blocks from Southwest Park to this fast-food establishment, but driving a standard shift with one foot in a cast is awkward."

"Awkward! You drove my mint-condition 1966 Mustang convertible for six blocks in first gear! My God, that's not awkward! It's irresponsible."

Maude waved her hand as though dismissing his criticism. "It was necessary. I can't easily shift gears wearing a cast. And I had to get us away before one of those well-meaning policemen offered to drive us to the station to give our statements. I refuse to allow that young woman to get away with murder, but I'm afraid I'll have to have some sort of evidence to back up my accusation before the police will listen to me. Collecting that evidence will involve your driving me several different places. Exactly how many is uncertain. Since I've never investigated a murder before, I'm afraid my procedures will be a matter of trial and error."

Victor grabbed both her wrists, an action totally out of character for a man she knew prided himself on gentle charm. "What are you talking about? What murder? That was an accident! I saw it—unfortunately. That poor young woman lost control of her kite, and the string—"

"Kevlar," interrupted Maude. "The kite string was made of Kevlar. The same material of which bulletproof vests are made. It's a new innovation in kite strings. It's strong—almost impossible to break, in fact—so it is ideal for stunt kites. Of course, that is an unfortunate characteristic if one's head happens to become entangled in the string, particularly if the string is attached to a kite moving at a speed of over a hundred miles an hour in a wind of twenty to twenty-five miles an hour. The best that can be said is that the victim didn't suffer. A near decapitation kills instantly. Or I imagine it would. I've not really had any experience in such matters."

She noticed that Victor's color had improved. His face

was now the same yellow-tinted white as a catfish's belly. Or perhaps she only thought so because his mouth kept opening and closing like that particular aquatic creature.

"You are accusing that poor little girl of murdering her husband because she used kite string made of Kevlar? And how did you know that? Did you go check out the kite?"

Maude nodded toward her wrists. "If you let go of me, Victor. You're cutting off the circulation, and at my age I have little enough of it as it is."

He eased his grip, but didn't release her. "You've none to the brain, that's certain, or you wouldn't be imagining such an incredible thing as murder. And I don't intend to let you go until you've calmed down. I've heard that women who live alone too long start believing ridiculous and illogical fantasies as a way to get attention."

"You sound like a pompous male, Victor, and I don't like it. I'm not senile, I don't have Alzheimer's, and I don't sit at home behind locked doors and imagine that Martians are trying to communicate with me on my VCR. I have a large circle of friends of whom you are one. At least, you were. I get out every day, as you should know since you've been driving me for the past six weeks since I broke my ankle—undoubtedly at great cost to your social calendar. Now, will you listen to me, or shall I kick you in the ankle with my plaster cast to temporarily incapacitate you and take your Mustang? Driving it all over Amarillo in first gear will not be good for its transmission, but you give me no choice."

He turned absolutely white, and she was certain she felt his hands tremble. "I'll listen."

Maude smiled. "I rather thought you would."

She glanced around the restaurant, saw that no one was paying attention to them, but lowered her voice anyway. Murder was a secret best discussed in whispers. "I know the kite string was Kevlar because David Knight—the husband and victim—told me."

Victor's expression would have done justice to a father who had just been told that his son was incurably insane. "He told you? When? Just before he lost his head?"

Maude frowned. "There is no need for levity, Victor. It's

inappropriate at the moment. David Knight was a member of our local kite association. I've known him—knew him—for several years. His wife, whose name is Melody in case you are interested, had only recently taken up the hobby. Six months ago to be precise, and I suspect it's best to be precise in a murder investigation. Before that, David's kite flying was the source of many arguments. He spent too much time and too much money on a childish pastime. Pastime is my word. Melody's vocabulary is somewhat more limited than mine."

"I can well believe that," Victor murmured.

Maude gave him a sharp look, but didn't detect a sarcastic expression on his face. "At any rate, Melody finally agreed to share David's hobby and requested a stunt kite with Kevlar string."

"You still haven't told me why you think Melody killed her husband," said Victor, his eyes looking much less dazed and more alert.

Maude debated whether to indulge in supposition or tell the truth. Honesty won out. "I don't know why she murdered him. Sex or money, I suppose. Aren't those the two most common motives?"

"I wouldn't know. This is my first murder."

Maude peered at him more closely. He still looked a little shocked, but his voice sounded decidedly flippant. "But motive doesn't concern me at the moment. I know that she did it, because I watched her. What we need to uncover are the steps she took in preparation for her deed."

Victor turned loose of Maude's wrists and folded his arms. "If you're so convinced she murdered her husband, tell the police and let them investigate. That is how they make their living, after all."

Maude looked at her brother-in-law with affection and frustration. Victor was an intelligent man, but he was, after all, only a man, and thus heir to a man's foibles, including the tendency to argue with a woman who knew better. "I did mention it to a young officer, but he was so busy keeping his back to the body—"

"Understandable," said Victor.

"—that he didn't pay proper attention. He referred me to another officer at the scene, a member of what he called the Special Crimes Unit. I thought it was a very apt name since this is certainly a special crime. However, the officer was impatient with me. He even had the audacity to suggest that I was too upset by the tragedy to be thinking clearly, and did I require a doctor." She leaned back against the booth and pinned Victor with a sharp look. "In other words, his reaction was the same as yours. I'm an old lady, so I must be senile."

Victor rubbed his hand over his face and looked at her with an expression of guilt. "I apologize, Maude. You're the least senile woman I know. It's just no one expects a sweet-faced lady with curly white hair to be bandying about words like 'murder.'"

Maude smiled. "Thank you, Victor. I never thought of myself as having a sweet face, but I'll accept your judgment."

He shook his head. "It's not my judgment. I know you too well. But I suspect it was the officer's judgment since he's going by outward appearances. He should have known you are tougher than you look. You didn't become violently ill at the sight of all that blood—and the look of astonishment on the victim's face." He flushed with embarrassment. "I can't claim any such self-control. I emptied my stomach all over the grass."

She leaned across the booth and patted his arm. "Don't feel too badly, Victor. You lacked my background. I taught first grade for forty-five years. I saw enough terrible things in that length of time to permanently inoculate me against the unpleasantness of a mere decapitation. Children eating library paste—that was before they graduated to sniffing glue—picking scabs and noses, pulling their own teeth behind the cover of a beginning reader and then drooling blood on the desktop. And the vomiting, Victor. You would not believe how easily a first grader will regurgitate. One would think that with all the foul substances they ingest that they would have stomachs of iron. Not true. If I had a dollar for every child who was ill in my classroom during those forty-five years, I would not have any financial worries."

Victor swallowed rapidly several times. "I'll take your word for it, Maude. Can we return to the subject of murder and how that little girl committed it?"

"A ground sweep."

"I beg your pardon?"

Maude drew a deep breath to control her impatience. She hadn't been required to make elementary explanations of events since she retired from the classroom ten years ago, but she supposed one never lost the knack. Rather like riding a bicycle. "A ground sweep means one flies the kite parallel to the ground at a low altitude—in this case, neck-high. It's something which requires practice or one will simply fly the kite into the ground. It is a particularly difficult maneuver with a stunt kite since so much skill and strength are required. I suppose one could have beginner's luck and execute such a maneuver on a first attempt," she said, doubt shaking her conviction for the first time.

Victor covered her clasped hands with his. "Isn't it possible that's what happened, Maude? Isn't it possible that Melody performed one of these ground sweeps by accident and her husband was in the way?"

Maude thought back to the morning's event. Fortunately, she had excellent visual recall, although she had never used it for such a purpose. She remembered Melody and her husband standing side by side and launching their kites. Then Melody had run backward several yards, thus increasing the speed at which the stunt kite rose gracefully into the sky, until it reached the end of the premeasured kite line and became a beautiful, triangular object of crimson and gold ripstop nylon dancing on the wind. Then a quick easing up of tension on one line and the increase of tension on the other line, and the kite plummeted downward, only to make a perfect ninety-degree turn parallel to the ground and sweep across the park like a deadly scythe.

The German word for kite was *Drachen*—dragon—and a very fitting term it was. Dragons were winged reptiles, and in Western mythology, very powerful, very vicious, and very dangerous.

So were kites.

Maude shook her head. "It wasn't an accident."

Victor pulled at his collar and twisted his neck as though he were choking. Then he adjusted his tie and straightened the lapels of his suit coat. "Now tell me again what we're supposed to be doing."

Maude wrinkled her nose as the faint scent of mothballs wafted from Victor's suit. "You are a minister and you've come to visit the sick. I wish you had a clerical collar, though. It would be a authentic touch."

"I'm *not* a minister, so I don't own one of those backward collars," he snapped.

She pursed her lips. Victor simply would not enter into the spirit of this investigation. "You could have borrowed one from your grandson."

"My grandson is a Baptist minister, and Baptists don't wear clerical collars. Even if he did, he wouldn't have loaned me one without knowing why, and if we had told him, he would have locked us in the parsonage study and called the cops. He's a sensible young man with a genuine concern for the elderly."

"I'm not elderly! I'm just not as young as I was. And your grandson is full of deadly homilies about aging, not concern. Even with the best intentions, it's difficult to be concerned unless you know your next change of address will be the local cemetery. Until then the subject is academic."

She grasped his arm. "There's her room," she said, pointing at a door flanked by two men in ill-fitting suits.

"How do you know?" Victor demanded.

"I asked the pink lady at the reception desk downstairs while you were parking the car. I used to play bridge with her before I took up kite flying. She always overbid her hand, so I knew she would tell me what I needed to know. Women who overbid their bridge hands always talk too much. Besides, those hard-faced men with the plastic ID badges hanging out of their coat pockets look like police-men. I feel somewhat better that they accompanied Melody to the hospital. She may have convinced them she was in shock after the murder, but they intend to keep an eye on her until she's coherent enough to recount what happens. They might not be such fools as I thought."

"Then tell them your suspicions and let's leave."

"They don't fly kites. They don't understand the skills involved. Until I have something more, it would be my word against Melody's. If another kite flyer in addition to myself had witnessed the murder, then I wouldn't be obligated to play Miss Marple. But I was the only one, and it's my moral duty to help the police."

"Maude, if she really did commit murder, then she's dangerous. She'll recognize you, and you might wake up some morning dangling from a kite string," said Victor, seizing her arm to stop her limping progress toward Melody Knight's room.

She pulled her arm free. "No, she won't, Victor. I knew her husband, not her. I don't imagine I exchanged a dozen words with her in the last six months. Besides, to a young-ster like her, all old ladies look the same. I doubt she could pick me out of a crowd."

Victor patted his bald head with a handkerchief. "Lord, I hope not."

"Trust me," said Maude, taking his arm and nudging him down the hall.

"I feel like a fraud."

She patted his arm. "You are a fraud—but it's for a good cause. Assume a self-righteous expression, please, and let's go visit the bereaved. And remember—I'm your wife."

"What am I supposed to say?" he muttered out of the side of his mouth as they approached the police officer with the suspicious blue eyes.

Maude held her Bible in front of her chest so it would be in full view. "Mumble platitudes about the hereafter, and leave everything else to me."

"Oh, God!" he exclaimed under his breath.

The police officer stepped in front of Melody Knight's hospital room. "May I help you folks?" His voice was polite, but gruff. What one might expect of a watchdog of the law, thought Maude.

"I am the Reverend Victor Timothy Jamison. I have come to offer comfort to Mrs. Knight. Poor woman. Poor, poor woman," said Victor in an oily tone of voice Maude always associated with television evangelists.

The police officer, whose ID badge identified him as Sergeant Wilson, looked undecided, so Maude stepped around him. Life had taught her to go ahead with whatever plans she had in the face of a man's indecision. "Thank you, Officer. When my husband finishes praying with Mrs. Knight, we'll leave. We do appreciate the police allowing the suspect of a crime the sustenance of religion."

Sergeant Wilson's eyes suddenly focused on her. "Mrs. Knight is not a suspect in a crime, Mrs. Jamison. Her husband was the victim of a freak accident."

Maude opened her eyes as wide as physically possible. Life had also taught her that wide-eyed old ladies looked so innocent. Age did have some advantages. "Oh, how terrible. The gentleman who called us did say that Mrs. Knight had cut off her husband's head with a stunt kite."

"She didn't quite cut it off," began the sergeant before his focus sharpened. "What gentleman?"

Maude's hands fluttered helplessly, an easy gesture after a few minutes practice while Victor was changing clothes. "Heavens, Sergeant, my memory has been slipping recently. The reverend, my husband, is so concerned about it. To be so forgetful is terribly frightening at my age. One is afraid of Alzheimer's." She turned to Victor and batted her eyelashes. "Did I mention the gentleman's name to you?"

Victor's lips twitched, so she pinched his arm just to be certain he didn't laugh. "I don't believe you did, my dear."

She turned back to the sergeant. "If I remember it, I will call you. Is it terribly important?"

The sergeant scratched his jaw. "It might be," he admitted. "If the man is a witness and believes he saw a crime."

"He didn't say Mrs. Knight murdered her husband, but

his tone of voice implied it. And of course, stunt kites are dangerous weapons in skilled hands."

"You know something of kites, Mrs. Jamison?" asked the sergeant, his eyes more watchful than Maude would have liked. She wondered if she should chance telling him her suspicions.

"I know one could commit murder with a stunt kite," she replied.

The sergeant smiled. "With a toy? I can't believe that."

Maude tightened her grip on her Bible. She was tempted to swat the sergeant over the head with it. Willful ignorance always annoyed her. "I suppose you are right, and the gentleman who called was exaggerating. Still, you ought to read a book or two on kites. They're not really toys, you know."

Victor pulled her gently toward the door to Melody's room. "Excuse my wife, Sergeant. She's distraught over this whole affair. Thank you for correcting our faulty information. It would be humiliating for Mrs. Knight if I counseled her to confess to murder when I should be comforting her in her loss." He opened the door and pushed Maude through.

Maude limped toward the figure lying on the bed. "Mrs. Knight, the reverend and I came as quickly as we could."

A tall young man whose muscles rippled under his T-shirt looked up from a chair on the other side of the bed. "Who the hell are you, and how come the cops let you in?"

Maude felt Victor's arm stiffen. He was old-fashioned enough to disapprove of using profanity in front of ladies. "I am Reverend Victor Timothy Jamison, and this is my wife—er—Mrs. Jamison. We've come to pray with Mrs. Knight."

The young blonde—by request, Maude noted—sat up in bed, sweeping her long hair out of her eyes with the graceful motion of one hand. "I don't know any Reverend Jamison."

"My husband was acquainted with David," said Maude gently, noticing that Melody's watch—Rolex, she thought—was far too tight. Its band was so tight as to nearly restrict circulation. Certainly a sign of weight gain.

"David didn't attend church," said Melody. She turned to

the young man and laid a delicate hand tipped with expensive red nails on his chest. "Jimmy, please show them out. I don't want to talk to anyone."

"Surely you'll feel better to talk about it," said Maude. "An accident with a kite, wasn't it?"

Melody jerked her head around to look at Maude. "Yes! I hate kites, but if I wanted to see my husband, I had to learn to fly them. And look what happened. I lost control and David is dead." She threw herself against the young man named Jimmy and began sobbing.

Maude thought it a marvelous performance.

Jimmy wrapped his arms around Melody and glared at Maude. "Get out!"

"Now, young man, we were only trying to help," began Victor.

"Out! Before I call the cops."

Maude observed Jimmy rubbing Melody's back in what she would call a most sensuous manner. "Are you a member of the family, young man, to be giving orders?"

His smile revealed expensively straightened teeth and an ill nature. "I'm her cousin."

Maude nodded. "I see." She did, too. As she had been thinking only this morning, people hadn't changed in seventy-five years. Kissing cousins were not uncommon in her day, and the whiff of incest about such a relationship hadn't changed.

Victor ripped off his tie and unbuttoned his collar as soon as he got behind the wheel of his Mustang. "Just what did we accomplish besides getting the bum's rush by that muscle-bound young man?"

Maude tapped her fingernail on the car's armrest. "He was, wasn't he? And his T-shirt had the logo of a local fitness center. I suspect he spends more time conditioning his body than his mind. And so does Melody Knight. Did you notice how tight her watch was? I thought at first she had gained a great deal of weight, but I was mistaken. Let's visit that fitness center, Victor. A little conditioning of our bodies wouldn't hurt."

He looked horrified, but started the car. "Maude, I have no intention of putting on exercise clothes and jumping around a gym in tune to music."

"Don't be ridiculous. I wouldn't be seen in public in a pair of tights even by my own sex, Victor. I don't intend to enroll in an exercise program. I just want to inquire about them. Now, please hush and drive. I must arrange my thoughts."

He drove while Maude made notes in a small spiral notebook. She always carried one in her purse these days. In spite of her protests to the contrary, she didn't always trust her memory.

When she and Victor were seated in front of a ugly metal desk in a tiny office that smelled faintly of sweat and dirty tennis shoes, she consulted her notebook before smiling at the young woman in the skin-tight leotard. "Mrs. Melody Knight recommended this center. Victor and I feel our age is no excuse to let our bodies deteriorate. We would like a membership, one that includes all the facilities you offer."

The young woman smiled and pulled a membership application out of a desk drawer. It was approximately the length and complexity of a corporate legal document. "If you will just fill this out and sign all the appropriate disclaimers. The center can't be responsible for accidents if you fail to follow the rules. We'll also require a physician's report that you are in good health."

Maude nodded, then tried her fluttering hand trick again. "My, I had no idea it was so complicated. I just wanted to enroll in the same exercise program that Melody and her cousin, Jimmy, take."

The young lady pursed her lips. "Cousin? I didn't know he was her cousin, but he isn't enrolled in an exercise program. He is our weight trainer. Melody is in weight training." She giggled. "I don't lift weights myself. I don't like the muscular look—except on men. I prefer a more lithe figure." She smiled at Victor, and he grinned at her. If he were a dog, his tongue would be hanging out the side of his mouth, Maude thought.

"Melody in weight training! How extraordinary. How long has she been enrolled?"

"Six months," replied the young woman, still smiling at Victor.

Maude sniffed. She guessed some young women preferred their men seasoned. "Isn't that interesting? Six months, you say? And Melody developed all that upper-body strength in just six months. Judging by her muscles, she must be terribly strong."

Reluctantly the young woman turned to Maude. "I guess so. You know, it's really funny. I wouldn't have thought Melody would want to gain all that muscle. She's always so worried about her weight and hair and nails. She practically cries if she breaks a nail in the weight room. I don't know why she's doing it."

Maude did.

She rose. "I think perhaps Victor and I should reconsider our decision. I don't care to lift weights, and I can't imagine what Victor's prostate doctor would say about the rest of your program."

"Prostate!" Victor's voice held a note of outrage that almost gave Maude an attack of guilt. "I don't have prostate trouble!"

Maude led him out of the center. "Really, Victor. I would advise you to stay away from young girls. Not only is it unbecoming at your age, but the young are carrying all sorts of unpleasant diseases these days. I've read about it in *Reader's Digest*. Best stick with the ladies over sixty. I believe most of us can pass our Wassermanns."

"One of these days, Maude," said Victor, forcing the words through gritted teeth. "One of these days I'll lose all self-control and strangle you."

"Whatever you say, dear," she replied. "Start the car, please. I want to visit David Knight's neighborhood."

Victor twisted around in his seat to stare at her. "Maude, I refuse to allow you to break into Knight's house. It's illegal, immoral, dangerous, and prison wouldn't agree with you. No privacy at all, and I don't think you would find the company congenial."

"I don't intend housebreaking, Victor—unless it's necessary. I have in mind canvassing the neighborhood and asking questions about the Knights. Put your tie back on. We'll play the reverend and Mrs. again. It seemed to work well at the hospital."

Victor stuck his tie in his pocket and unbuttoned another shirt button. "I refuse. Have you forgotten you are in a cast? How do you intend to tromp up and down the street? I won't allow it, Maude."

"Don't be a chauvinist, Victor, and start the car."

He folded his arms. "You can call me all the names you want, but I won't change my mind. Not only will the whole exercise be physically debilitating for you, but dangerous as well. I heard what that young woman said. Melody Knight took weight training to build up her muscles so she could control that big stunt kite, didn't she? That means she really might have murdered her husband. I like your head right where it is, and I don't intend to risk it by letting you carry out any more charades. Damn it all, Maude, I'd miss you if anything happened. I loved your sister, but I always *liked* you better. Life always seemed more lively with you around. I want to keep you around—for a long time."

Maude looked away and blinked. My, but she hadn't cried in years. She didn't know she still could. She cleared her throat. "Thank you, Victor. I was always fond of you, too. If you hadn't been my brother-in-law—" She stopped, aghast at what she had nearly said.

She heard the car start and turned her head to see Victor smiling. "But that's neither here nor there. The subject at hand is murder," she said.

He nodded his head, still smiling. "That's *one* of the subjects. I'll make a bargain with you, Maude. I'll drive you to the Knights' and help you question the neighbors if you'll move into my guest house."

"That's blackmail!"

"Do we have a deal?"

She clasped her hands and looked at her brother-in-law and reflected on his proposition. Then she thought of poor David Knight and how life might end without warning and without the company of those who love you. And she made her decision. "I suppose that any gossip about our sleeping arrangements could be considered in the nature of a compliment."

Victor grinned. "I can stand it if you can, babe."

She settled back against the seat. "Drive—and don't call me babe."

Maude sat on a sofa worth more than her home and sipped coffee from a china cup so thin, one could practically read a newspaper through it. Carefully she placed her cup on a table whose cost she couldn't begin to calculate and smiled at Mrs. Biggers, a matron who was fighting age to a draw. As long as cosmetic surgeons existed, Mrs. Biggers would never let a line mar her face. Of course, Maude noticed that her skin did have that tight look about it—like an overstretched rubber band—but perhaps the woman didn't mind her loss of facial mobility.

"I can't imagine why David and Melody suggested that my husband and I would be interested in joining your church, Reverend Jamison."

Victor smiled. He really had the most charming smile, thought Maude. "We always like to share our faith with our best friends, Mrs. Biggers."

Mrs. Biggers made an effort to arch her eyebrows in surprise, but failed. The skin on her forehead hadn't moved in the last decade. "We're not good friends of theirs. In fact, we hardly know them."

"How strange," remarked Maude. "I'm certain Melody told me that the two of you shared all kinds of interests in common—like flying kites. I understand Melody was quite enthusiastic about kites."

"She must have been," said Mrs. Biggers. "She's spent almost every day for the last six months flying a kite in her backyard. A big black and gold one. Heavens, I didn't know they made kites that big. She ought to spend a little more time on her landscaping, though. I've noticed several of her trees seem to be dying."

Maude gathered her purse and rose. "Isn't that interesting? Thank you very much, Mrs. Biggers. I hope we haven't disturbed your morning. Come, Victor. We have another call to make."

"The only call I think we should make is to the police, Maude," he said as he followed her down the sidewalk toward the car. "You've learned that Melody Knight took weight training and practiced kite flying. It's time to let the experts take over."

Maude passed the car and walked toward David Knight's back gate instead, skirting elaborate flower beds and struggling to keep from falling. The grass was wet and slick, and her cast kept sinking into the ground. It was unlike Victor not to be holding her elbow and helping her.

She stopped abruptly and looked around. Not only was Victor not at her elbow, he wasn't even in the yard. He was sitting hunched over in his Mustang with only the top of his Stetson visible. "Victor! Get out of the car. We're not done yet. I want to look at Melody's dying trees first."

He straightened and climbed out of the car, catching up with her and opening the gate. "What difference does it make if Melody Knight's trees have Dutch elm disease? We're trespassing, and in this neighborhood, we'll have the police popping out of manholes."

"You don't have to worry about the police, Mrs. Jamison, or whatever your name is."

Maude wasn't sure which was more shocking: the sound of Melody Knight's voice, or the sight of the gun in her hand.

"I think the old lady's too scared to talk, Melody," said Jimmy, stepping up beside her.

"I doubt you'll live long enough to see that," Maude heard Victor mutter under his breath.

"I expected you to either still be in the hospital or at the police station," said Maude, a little disconcerted, and angry about it. She hadn't been disconcerted in fifty years, and she didn't like it.

Melody smiled. It wasn't a pleasant smile, but then, Maude didn't credit her with any more of a pleasant disposition than she did Melody's cousin. "I gave my statement in the hospital, then my doctor told the police I needed a good night's rest before talking to them further. You see, Miss Nosy, after you left, I remembered you. You're the old woman David was always talking about—the one who knew so damn much about kite flying. I didn't know you were the same woman when I picked you to witness David's accident—not until you were leaving my hospital room and I saw your cast. If you hadn't been wearing slacks this morning, I would have noticed it then. David told me about your accident, and I didn't think there could be two old women with broken ankles who just happen to fly kites."

"It wasn't an accident, was it, Melody?" asked Maude.

"You tell me, old lady," the young woman replied.

"You deliberately ran backward several yards both to build up your kite's speed and to put David in a position to be hit when you executed that ground sweep. That's when I knew it was murder, you see. The first thing one learns when flying kites is never to stand behind someone—always beside them. David would have told you that. Then there was the weight training and the practice." Maude glanced at the nearest tree, a graceful popular twenty feet high. "You practiced on your trees. That's why they are dying. The kite string cut through the bark. You've planned to murder your husband for the past six months. You've trained for it as if it were an Olympic event, all the while living with David in loving intimacy. You're a very cold woman, Melody Knight. I hope you can live with what you've done."

"I think I'll manage. Money provides a lot of comfort—and Jimmy will warm me up." Jimmy flexed his muscles, and Maude considered gagging. Even as a young woman, she had preferred slim, wiry men like Victor.

Melody raised her gun. "All I have to do now is dispose of you two. Too bad you can't have an accident with a kite string, but two in one day would alarm even that idiot of a sergeant."

"So would two harmless, interfering old people with bullet holes, Mrs. Knight."

"Sergeant Wilson!" exclaimed Maude.

"Mrs. Jamison—or is it Mrs. Turner?" asked the sergeant without looking at her. He was too busy aiming his gun at Melody Knight.

"What the hell are you doing here?" demanded Jimmy.

"Good Lord, young man, don't you have any originality? You asked Maude and me the same question at the hospital."

Victor had never demonstrated any patience with repetition, but Maude thought he might have picked a more suitable time to be critical. "I would like an answer to that question, too, Sergeant Wilson," she said.

"I took your advice, ma'am. I read a kite book. Then I remembered one of my officers talking about a feisty old lady with a wild story about kites and murder. There were only two witnesses at the scene this morning: a Mrs. Turner and a Mr. Jamison. I'm not brilliant, but I'm not stupid either. I put out an APB for my two missing witnesses who had failed to turn up at Special Crimes as they had promised, reread Mrs. Knight's statement in light of my new knowledge of kites and kite flying, and was more than halfway here when Mr. Jamison called."

"Called?" asked Maude.

Victor shrugged. "Cellular phone. In the Mustang. I called after we left Mrs. Biggers's house."

"If you want to visit, have a class reunion," snapped Melody Knight. "In the meantime, drop your gun, Wilson."

"Gracious, young woman, you sound like a grade B western," said Maude.

"Mrs. Turner, I appreciate your help, but I'll take it from here if you don't mind," said Sergeant Wilson. He directed his next remark to Melody. "Mrs. Knight, you have a choice. You can try to kill me and these two oldsters and find yourself and your boyfriend charged with capital murder. Conviction means life in prison or the big wienie: lethal injection. Your other choice is to drop your gun, be charged with murder, and hire yourself a good attorney who can argue mitigating circumstances—if there are any other than meanness. You have maybe two minutes to make up your mind. I'm only the first cop to arrive. I won't be the last. What's it to be, Mrs. Knight?"

With a foul curse that Maude recognized even though such a profanity had never crossed her own lips, Melody dropped her gun.

Maude felt dizzy with relief. She hadn't realized how tense she had been, nor how very much she wanted to live at least fifteen more years. There were still so many things she'd never done. She glanced at Victor and smiled. At seventy-five, one shouldn't dillydally around. Seize the moment and do what she had never done before and always secretly wondered about.

She fainted into Victor's arms.

Times hadn't changed at all. Men still liked their women to faint occasionally. It did so much for their egos.

The Cottonwood Creek Caper

Diane Mott Davidson

My name is Arch. Three days ago I sneaked off the Furman Elementary School playground during sixth grade recess. My best friend had yelled at me and pushed me in the dirt. After climbing the fence, I ran to my special place by Cottonwood Creek. Sitting there on the bank, breathing in all the wet, sweet smells of a Colorado spring day, I began to feel better. Then I saw Principal Hicks in the water. He was dead.

Here's what happened.

"Geek-wad, turd-breath, shit-head!"

That's what Todd Druckman, my used-to-be-best friend, yelled at me when I wouldn't give him butts in the tetherball line. I looked around for the teacher to yell at him. When I wasn't watching, Todd shoved me in the chest and I fell into the dirt. The kids in the line laughed.

I stood up. "Hey!" I yelled and glared at him. "What's the *matter* with you?" My face was hot. I didn't want the kids to see the tears about to spill out of my eyes. Gritting my teeth, I rammed my head into Todd's waist. He grabbed me by the shoulders and threw me down again. The kids jeered louder.

I knew better than to keep going. Todd's bigger than I am.

So I scrambled up, brushed off the dirt, and walked away. When I got to the fence, I leaned my back against it and checked out the whole playground. As far as I could tell, no one was watching.

Mr. Jameson, the art teacher, usually had Thursday playground duty. But it looked as if he had switched with Dr. Hoover, who was wiping mud off one of her kids in the fifth-sixth combination.

Mr. Hicks, the principal, wasn't staring out his window as usual because he'd been sick all week.

The kids near the fence were arguing over a soccer game. Eight million tiny swamp frogs were cheeping in the long grass next to the parking lot. Even if someone saw me and yelled, no one would hear.

In the parking lot some parents were standing around. The PTA meeting about who was doing what for next week's sixth grade graduation had just ended. But the parents were still yakking away. Who will bring the punch? (I already knew my mother was bringing the cookies.) What if it rains? Does anybody see a kid escaping? I hoped not.

The person who especially would not care that I was climbing over the fence was Todd.

A fence wire caught my shirt, and the cloth made a terrible noise when it ripped. I pulled the cloth free and jumped to the ground, then stopped and looked back. There was Todd. He was watching me.

I walked quickly around to the front schoolyard. When I was higher than the playground and almost to the road, I glanced over my shoulder. Todd had already gone off with the other kids. That was what he wanted in the first place, wasn't it? That's why he called me those names, right? To be cool? *Shit-head!* Even the frogs had stopped their croaking for a second.

I crossed Colorado Highway 32 calmly. There are houses right across from the school, before you get to the path to the creek. The last thing I needed was somebody to call the school office about a kid running away from recess. I knew I had about half an hour to get to the water, sit for a while, and get back in time for language arts, where we all were going to read the stupid poems we made up.

I shook my head. *How much more of school can I take?*

My feet skidded across the gravel. I had to be careful not to fall. My mother had just bought me some almost new jeans from the Aspen Meadow Second Hand Store. Fear was like a baseball thrown into my stomach. What would my mother do if I got caught?

I opened the gate and trotted up the trail toward the creek. Bright yellow dandelions dotted the meadow's thick, new green grass. The air smelled wet and delicious, as if you could eat it.

As a matter of fact, I wished I could have eaten it, because my mother packed me salmon salad for lunch. Salmon salad! Kept chilled with a cold pack! I traded it for a Twinkie, half a cold burrito, and a dill pickle. It wasn't enough. Now that I wasn't arguing with Todd anymore, I could hear my stomach growl.

The *shoosh* of the breeze in the trees next to the meadow drowned out the sound of the kids yelling and even the frogs. Being in the meadow was like being at the bottom of a bowl. The woods went up the sides of the bowl. When I squinted my eyes at the school, the kids looked like ants. Overhead, fluffy white clouds the shape of giant mouse ears floated by. I sniffed the air and let my eyelids slip shut. I was trying not to think of what used to scare me when I was little. I was trying not to imagine that the knotholes in the pine trees were really eyes staring out.

When I started off again I noticed the trail was muddy. Horses had been through. Then suddenly I thought I saw a movement in the woods. It wasn't a horse. I stared at the trees but couldn't make anything out. Fear snaked down my back, and my mouth went dry. I pushed on, more quickly.

I heard the creek before I got there. The water makes a high, rushing sound over the rocks this time of year, when the snow is melting up in the mountains. Todd and I fish a lot in the summer. Well, we used to fish a lot.

I wondered if he would tell on me. Would he be that

mean? I asked myself. If I got caught, I could just say I was looking for rainbow trout.

The trail ended by a spit of ground tangled with weeds. When I got to the creek's edge I couldn't see any fish at all because the water was too muddy from the runoff. Some trash was clinging to a rock in the creek. That made me angry. Litter would kill the fish. I'd get too wet if I waded in to get it, though. I decided to go farther up the stream where there's a picnic table next to a good fishing spot. It's a place where Todd and I used to stash our backpacks and put our soft drinks in the creek to cool. The creek widens there, and each side has calm pools where the trout like to gather.

When I pushed through the bush branches and weeds I just got that feeling again. Like somebody was watching. My shoes squished in the mud. I sat down and thought about being quieter. This was ridiculous, because the school and town were pretty far away. It was while I was making this effort to be silent that I looked up.

In the creek there was . . .

Suddenly it was like I was frozen. You know, the way it is in a bad dream.

I stared. Then I thought, I know this guy. I couldn't place him; his face was all gray. It was an adult. He was dead, because nothing was moving. The body was on top of a rock. It had clothes on, men's gray clothes all soaked. I kept staring, but nothing moved except the water. It was gushing around the gray rock as if the body wasn't even there.

Oh man. When I looked closer I could see the face, even though it was all bloated.

Principal Hicks.

I whirled around and started to crash back through the weeds. Now I didn't care what kind of noise I made. The killer might still be around! He might be watching me! I had to get back to school. My feet slid and I landed in the mud. I rolled over and climbed back up the trail. I keep telling myself, Go fast! There was a buzzing in my ears. I ran across the meadow. My footsteps made pounding noises *boosh boosh boosh* in the soft ground.

In the distance the bell rang. It was very faint, like a

telephone in another room. The kids-like-ants were streaming back to their classroom doors.

I wished I'd stayed on the playground. My lungs heaved as I ran. *Boosh. Boosh.* My footsteps were slower now as I came through the Furman Elementary yard.

My body whacked the school's orange front door. It was like I was in the movies, where you never know when the bad guys are watching. *Calm down,* I thought, *calm down!* I walked straight into the office, where there were four kids waiting to use the phone. Dr. Hoover, the secretary, and a teacher I didn't know were having this big argument about the art class for fifth-sixth combination.

My breath was pumping, in and out. If I told the teachers or the secretary what I saw, I'd just get in trouble, maybe be expelled right before graduation. Then my mother would *really* have a fit.

"I need to call my mom," I said to the secretary, who suddenly looked at my shoes and pants all covered with mud. Miss Sloan had the kind of even tan ladies get from those tanning machines. Her shiny blond hair pouffed out and held its shape like cotton candy. But when she opened her eyes wide in disgust at how I looked, her shiny light purple eyeshadow went way up her forehead, and she looked like an alien. I said, "I fell."

She told me to wait my turn and went back to the teachers. They were arguing about some art equipment.

When it was my turn I pressed 9-1-1. I knew they'd trace the call right away, because my mom is dating a police officer, and he tells me stuff like that about the equipment.

Someone said, "Sheriff's department."

I said in this low, gravelly voice, "Principal Hicks's body is in Cottonwood Creek, near the trail to the Aspen Meadow." Then I hung up. Now I *really* felt guilty. But when I looked at the secretary and the teachers, they were still yakking and ignoring me. I told the next kid in line to go ahead and use the phone. What else could I do? I had to go to language arts.

I ducked into the boys' bathroom and wiped as much mud as I could off my pants legs. I looked in the mirror. It was a miracle I hadn't lost my glasses in all that running. But I'm not a very fast runner. I wiped the dirt off my freckles and had a terrible thought: *What if someone at the school killed Principal Hicks? What if that person saw me leave and come running back from the creek trail?*

I opened the bathroom door a crack. No one was in the hall. I took a deep breath and walked out. *I need to pretend that I know nothing about what I saw.*

When I slipped into the class, the kids giggled because I was late and my pants were streaked with mud stains. The teacher, Miss Alexander, gave me a disgusted look that was worse than the school secretary's. The skin in her cheeks was like an old, wrinkled-up lunch bag. Her eyes were like little drills. I wanted to say, *It is not my fault that my mother thought used beige jeans would be cute.*

"Arch Korman!" she said in that demanding way of hers. "Do you have your humorous poem?"

You see, she was trying to trip me up because I'd come in late. I wanted to say, *I've just found Principal Hicks's dead body in Cottonwood Creek! And you're worried about some dumb poem?* But all I did was mumble, "Yeah."

"Please do not say, yeah. Say, yes."

I said, "Yesss," drawing it out like a hissing snake, but not too much. I pulled a bunch of stuff out of my desk and tried to avoid Todd's eyes. I couldn't. He was snickering to Angela Reitman and pointing at me and my muddy beige pants. Angela was so mean, all she did was make fun of me even though we went to the same church.

I got my poem. I sighed. The last time I had tried to be funny was when I read my mom riddles when she was getting the divorce. But she already knew why ducks flew south and why the chicken crossed the road, and finally she just asked me not to bring the riddle book to the kitchen table anymore.

Miss Alexander asked if I was daydreaming again. When I shook my head she said I had to go to the front of the class. Sometimes I thought the teachers *tried* to embarrass you.

I read:

> "My lunch is not like other kids',
> With peanut butter and Cheese Whiz.
> Mine has pepitas in a bag,
> And other stuff that makes me gag.
> You know it's very hard to hock it,
> Who wants shrimp in a pita pocket?
> My cheeks are getting very gaunt,
> I threw away my crab croissant.
> Mom says, 'You didn't finish
> Your feta torte mixed with spinach!'
> I don't know what to say to her.
> You see, my mom's a caterer."

People laughed. Well, they were supposed to laugh. But it wasn't like it was funny. It was a laugh at a geek-wad poem.

Miss Alexander said, "Did you write that yourself?"

I let all the air out of my lungs and walked slowly back to my seat. I said, "Yessss."

She said, "Do you know the meaning of the word *gaunt?*"

I looked at her gaunt face and said in a low voice, "Very, very thin. Okay?"

Then we all heard the sirens. No fire drill alarm either. Everybody looked at everybody else. I tried to look puzzled and didn't say anything.

There was that buzzing sound that comes just before they are going to make an announcement over the school loud-speaker.

"Would all the children who used the school phone today please come up to the office?"

Fear chilled my skin. I raised my eyebrows at the other kids and shrugged. No way I was going to that office. If they figured out I was there, I'd just say I forgot.

Todd's eyes were on me. Too bad, I wasn't telling him anything. After a minute of buzzing silence, the loudspeaker went off. We moved on to the next funny poem, which was some dumb thing about a girl going to a mall in Denver and seeing a girl she went to kindergarten with and then they went and had ice cream.

I was wondering if Principal Hicks was still in the creek. I was wondering what I saw in the woods.

I couldn't keep worrying about whether the secretary was going to remember me, because it was time to go to art. I liked this class because once you learned what it was you were supposed to do, everybody left you alone. Even Mr. Jameson, the teacher, left you alone. He usually went in the back to cut mats for his own artwork. Supposedly the parents got mad that he was working on his own stuff when he should have been teaching us, but I really liked not having a teacher in the room. If we got too loud, he poked his face around the corner of the back room and gave us this fierce gorilla look. If we were really noisy, then he sent us back to our classroom. Nobody wanted that, because Miss Alexander would punish us with extra grammar work that nobody else in the whole school had to do.

Anyway, for the last two weeks Mr. Jameson had been teaching us how to cut designs into linoleum blocks that we were going to use to make prints. If you want to know how it will look in a print, hold it up in front of a mirror. Only nobody did that last part because then people would make fun of you.

We had art every three days. Last time we got to the part where we began to cut our designs into the blocks with X-Acto knives. Man, were they sharp! We'd been warned to be careful, not wave them around. Still, somebody always ended up getting cut and being sent to the office for a bandage.

We got to the art room. Mr. Jameson wasn't there.

Pretty soon one of those frazzled-looking substitute teachers showed up, a short, heavy woman with long, gray hair. She looked so scared, you just knew everyone was going to act up. Then I thought, wait a minute: she was in the office when I made my 9-1-1 call.

"Uh, class . . ." she began, "there seems to be a problem with your supplies. . . ."

Oh, boy. I could feel it coming. No linoleum cutting today.

Sure enough. The substitute said, "And if any of you

know where the bag of X-Acto knives is, please report it to the office. Now, please go back to your classroom."

"So is Mr. Jameson sick, too?" I asked the girl next to me. Too late I saw it was Angela Reitman.

"No, stupid," she hissed. "He was fired. The parents had complained so many times that they finally went to the school board and the superintendent. Principal Hicks was forced to fire him. He told the teachers at this big faculty meeting they had on Monday. Don't you know anything?"

"I thought Principal Hicks was sick, Miss Know-It-All."

"He got sick Tuesday, Arch-Barf."

On the way back to Miss Alexander the Gaunt's classroom, I thought about two things.

Number One: How did some kids always know what was going on? Did her mother tell her about Mr. Jameson being fired? How did she know about a monster faculty meeting on Monday?

Number Two: Why did my mother always expect the kids to be nice to me in school? When I came home she always said, How was your day? All bright and cheerful. And I was supposed to say, It was great, I'm so popular, smart, good-looking, and athletic. Everybody likes me. Instead I told her things that happened. For instance. One time a kid said, I bet you have lots of cavities. I said, Do not. He said, Do too. I said, Do *not*. He said, Prove it. So I opened my mouth. And he stuffed it full of grass.

If I told her the girls in my class called me Arch-Barf, my mother would get furious. When I was younger, she would call the parents of whoever said or did the mean thing. That made everything worse, of course, so I had to make her promise not to do that anymore. This whole year she's worried about me, but she didn't say anything. Still, it was in her eyes.

We got back to the classroom, and Miss Alexander started to write a grammar lesson up on the board. Everybody groaned. *Uses of the Subjunctive.* I wanted to write up next to it, *Who cares?* They weren't doing this in the other sixth grades. I knew, because I was in another class at the beginning of the year. They moved me over to Miss Alexander's class in January because the other class had too many kids.

"This isn't in the curriculum!" said Angela in a loud voice.

Whooee! Miss Alexander whirled around and squinched up her wrinkled-lunch-bag face. We all got out our pencils. We wrote, *As it were . . .* but nobody knew what that was supposed to mean.

My mind went back to Mr. Hicks. I wondered if the police had found him, if they were splashing around in the creek. And what I saw in the woods: Was it a person, an animal, or just something that didn't belong, like trash? When I tried to imagine it, nothing was clear.

Someone's eyes were on me. When I looked up, Todd was walking back from the pencil sharpener. He dropped the pencil when he got to my desk, leaned over, and said, "Sorry," in a rough whisper.

I pretended to ignore him, but it gave me something to think about while I was writing out all the places where you were supposed to use the subjunctive. Was he really sorry? *If he were . . .* ha ha. I sure wanted to tell him about what happened when I ran away from school.

When we were done with the subjunctive stuff, there were still twenty minutes left before the last bell. As always, it felt like forever.

Miss Alexander was looking around the room for something to do. She picked up a bunch of folders that we did at the beginning of the year. They had sheets inside—"A Time Capsule About Me." She doled them out as fast as could be.

On the sheet you had two lines for each question after your name. One you put down in September, one you were supposed to put down in May. I looked at mine—my name, age (eleven then, eleven now), what did my father do (he was still an ob-gyn doctor, which means that he helps women have babies), what did my mother do (that hadn't changed either).

Then you got into the more personal questions—what my hobby was (Dungeons and Dragons), who my best friend was (Todd Druckman—now I wrote *Maybe*), what was the best thing that ever happened to you (Christmas), what's the worst thing that ever happened to you (I wrote, *my parents' divorce* in the fall. Now I wrote, *being embarrassed by friends.*)

Ten minutes to go. I was thinking the clock must be broken or something. Then this note landed on my desk. It was from Todd. I sneaked a glance at Miss Alexander, but she was grading the subjunctive papers.

I opened it oh-so-carefully. *Where'd you go during recess? I'm sorry I called you a geek. I was mad because the band teacher made me wear my chewing gum on my nose through the whole class. I want to be friends again.*

I peeked at Miss Alexander and then at Todd. His eyebrows were raised.

I wrote, *I found the dead body of Principal Hicks in the creek.* Then I tossed the note back to him. Miss Alexander flipped a page but didn't notice what we were up to. A minute later the note came zinging back to me.

Cool! Can we go see it?

I thought for a minute. Angela was watching us, but I just made a face at her. I wrote back, *Yeah! I don't know if it will still be there. Can you sneak out and meet me at the school tonight? I'll take you to the spot.*

When my note back to Todd was in midair, Angela piped up, "Miss Alexander, they're passing no-otes!"

Oh, brother. My face got hot and red when Miss Alexander minced down the aisle and picked the note up off Todd's desk. She opened it and read it. Great.

Then she went back to her desk. What was she going to do, call the cops? No. She shuffled around and then put our note in an envelope. She said, "Todd and Archibald." That's what people always call me when they're mad. "I have bus duty and cannot escort you to the office. Therefore you may escort each other in taking this note down to the school secretary, please."

The bell rang. Todd and I marched down to the office with the envelope. We knew we had to go fast or we were going to miss our bus. In the hall we argued about whose fault getting in trouble over the note was.

When we got to the office, who was there but Mr. Jameson. Being fired from being an art teacher had made him look terrible. His black hair was sticking out all over instead of combed up in his usual wave. Most days he came to school dressed like Zorro in the old TV movies that Todd and I liked to watch: wide-collar white shirt, black pants. But in the last week he'd shaved off his mustache, and now he was wearing a smelly old blue sweatsuit. Miss Sloan was not at her secretary desk. Mr. Jameson gave us this questioning look.

"Hi," Todd said. "You sure look different."

"I'm here for my check," Mr. Jameson said in a flat voice I'd never heard from him before. "Where's the secretary? Where's the principal?"

It was the question about the principal that made Todd and me both gag and go speechless. There was lots of noise out in the hall, because all the kids were running to their buses. The phone in the office started ringing. Mr. Jameson stalked out.

I stuffed the envelope with the note in my pocket. If somebody asked me why I didn't leave it in the office, I'd say, There was nobody there.

Todd said, "Let's split."

As we were trotting out to the buses I remembered that we left our bags and stuff in the classroom. Too bad, get it on Monday. Miss Alexander would stare at me. She'd say, Why didn't you turn in the note you and Todd were passing?

And I'd say to her, *To whom was I supposed to give it?*

When I got home I tried to sneak past my mother and her friend Marla. I like Marla, but I wasn't in the mood to talk. Marla is my mom's best friend. Although she is heavy, I never think of her as fat. She's sort of heavy and soft. A human marshmallow, like. Anyway, Marla was married to my dad after he was married to my mom. My dad isn't really best friends with anybody.

My mom did not ask, How was your day? She took one look at me and started right in with, "Did you know about Principal Hicks being killed?"

"Gosh Goldy," said Marla, who winked at me. "Give the

kid a break. At least let him have a cookie or three. C'mon, Arch, look at what your mom just made." So saying, Marla offered me a plate of oatmeal cookies, and I took two.

My mom was dressed in her white double-breasted caterer's uniform, and she was wearing that pale brown makeup she thinks covers her freckles. She looked me up and down, then immediately spotted the rip in my shirt.

She said, "Are you okay? Want to tell me what happened?"

My mouth was full, so I shrugged. Then I said, "I'm fine. I fell on the playground." This was not exactly a lie. "So what happened to Principal Hicks?"

"Tom Schulz just called." This was the homicide investigator my mom was dating. Except she told me not to call it dating. "He said your principal was found in Cottonwood Creek near where it runs by your school. He said a tipper called from the school; they think it was a student. At one P.M."

"Huh," I said. "That's when I have language arts."

Marla said, "If you asked me," which no one ever had to do, "the person they should ask is Secretary Sloan the Sexual. I heard she and the principal were carrying on until a parent threatened to report him to the school board."

"Marla!" said my mom, and tilted her head toward me. Like I'd never heard about sex.

"Know anything about it, Arch?" asked Marla with a laugh.

My mother protested again. All I said was, "Miss Sloan chews gum all day even though there's supposed to be no gum in school."

But I was very interested in what they were saying. It would be more to tell Todd! The way to get adults to keep talking about their secrets is to pretend to be involved in something else. Then they think you're deaf. So I got out a piece of paper and began to draw a picture of some X-Acto knives.

Marla lowered her voice. She said, "Goldy, this is no joke. They were having an affair. What I heard was that he broke it off over the weekend. On Monday *she* more or less went public with it at a big faculty meeting. He had already fired the art teacher. Then he started in on that hag Alexander, teaching grammar that wasn't in the curriculum. And the Sloan slut announces, 'I'm not sure our own principal knows the difference between *lie* and *lay*, although he does *both*.'"

"Arch, what are you doing?" my mother demanded sharply. You see, she wanted to make sure I wasn't listening.

"Huh?" I looked down at my drawing. It didn't look like a very good collection of knives. I drew a balloon shape around them. "Drawing knives," I said. "A bag of them disappeared from the school."

Marla and my mother exchanged looks. My mother got up from the kitchen table and began to get out covered platters of food.

I said, "Where are you going?"

"Wedding on Lookout Mountain. I may be back late—" Before she could finish, the phone rang and she grabbed it. "Goldilocks' Catering, Where Everything Is Just Right!" Within three seconds her face fell. "Todd," she said sternly, "you know this is the business line—"

"Tell him I'll call back on the other line," I said as I grabbed my drawing and ran from the room.

He picked up the receiver before it had even rung one whole time.

He said, "He was stabbed."

"Oh yeah? How'd you find that out?"

"A neighbor who works on the rescue team told my mom."

I looked down at the drawing I had done. It looked familiar to me, even though I had drawn it right out of my head.

"Hey, Arch, you there?"

"Wait a minute." I kept looking at my drawing. It was one of those weird things like, I've been here before. I *had* seen this bag of knives I'd drawn. Only I thought it had been trash in Cottonwood Creek.

"We have to sneak out," I said, determined. "My mom

has a thing to cater tonight, so she'll be back late. I'll put a pillow in my bed so it'll look like me. Can you be at the school with a flashlight by ten o'clock?"

"Yeah!" he said. "Should I bring my dad's pistol?"

"No, you dummy! We're just going to investigate. It's not going to be dangerous."

At 9:15 my bed was stuffed with pillows, and I was clopping down Main Street in my high-top wading boots. I acted like a kid trying to catch up with his parents. There were still people walking down the sidewalks, most of them licking ice cream cones or trailing their dogs on leashes. I knew the easiest way to get to the place at the creek was to follow Main Street, which ran beside the water out of town. But I had to walk up Highway 32 to the school to meet Todd. Then we would cross the meadow together to the creek's other side.

I felt a little shiver of fear when I passed the high school. The high schoolers drive fast. They hate the elementary school kids. And there were no more people out; the sidewalk had disappeared when I made the turnoff toward the school.

At last I arrived at the orange door. Todd was shining his flashlight on some gorp he was eating. I only like the M & M's, so I turned down the handful he offered.

He said, "Did you bring a compass?"

"What do you think this is, a camping trip? I know how to get to the creek."

"Did you bring a knife?"

"Todd! For what?"

"I don't know. I brought one, though. Here, take the gorp. I saved you some M & M's. I brought some bandages and a first aid kit, and I don't have room in my pockets for all this stuff."

When I tried to shove the plastic gorp bag into my pocket, it wouldn't go. I put it into my other pocket, then wormed my hand down into my beige jeans pocket to see why it was so full. I pulled out an envelope.

"What's that, a map?" said Todd.

I opened it up, and Todd shined his flashlight on what was inside. It was a note.

Angela Reitman is a bitch and she wears falsies.

"Whoa!" said Todd. "Who were you sending that to?"

"It's not even my writing!"

"Well, do you have a map or not?"

I sighed and stuffed the paper back into my pocket. "Just turn your flashlight off and walk over to the traffic light. We don't want to attract attention. The streetlights will be enough to get us to the gate to the meadow."

"Oh, all right. You don't have to be bossy."

"I just don't want us to get in trouble. Besides, I have stuff to tell you." While we were crossing the street and walking past the houses that led up to the meadow, I told him about Mr. Hicks and the faculty meeting.

Todd said, "I guess he wasn't very popular."

When we got to the gate, the hinge made this horrible loud creaking sound when we opened it. All the dogs in the neighborhood by the school started barking at once. But dogs always barked in the mountains at night.

"Walk quickly," I said to Todd as we started along the muddy path.

Todd said, "I always think the knotholes in the trees look like eyes."

"Yeah, I know. Just shine your flashlight on the ground and don't think about it."

The wind whooshed through the trees. It was much louder than during the day. I looked back up toward the place where I had seen movement that afternoon. It was too dark to see anything. There was no moon, but millions of stars were twinkling. In the middle of the dark sky the Milky Way was shining like a highway of diamonds.

Todd said, "Should we sing?"

"Quit acting like this is Scouts!"

Pretty soon we were at the bank. We slid down the mud at exactly the place that I had come before.

"Is this where you found the body?" Todd whispered.

"No. But this is where I think the bag of blades is."

"Bag of blades! The X-Acto knives? Gross!"

I waded into the creek at the place where I had seen the litter. The water swirled around my feet. Even though I was wearing the waterproof boots, the water felt cold.

"Hey!" Todd whispered as loud as he could. "I thought I just heard some twigs snapping! Somebody's coming! Come back!"

"Oh, nobody's coming," I whispered back. "It's probably just a squirrel or something." I put one hand into the icy water and shined my flashlight with the other. The rock was there, but no bag of blades. Maybe the police had found it.

"C'mon, Arch, let's go see the body!"

I sloshed back through the water to the creek bank.

"Did you find the blades?"

"No. And I'll bet you anything they took the body, too, that's what—"

But at that moment we both heard crashing through the underbrush right near us.

"Flashlight off," I ordered Todd, but it was too late.

Above us, a tall figure in a Halloween mask shined a strong flashlight down on us. "Okay, boys," said this fake, deep voice. "Come up the bank and neither of you will get hurt. I have a gun."

We both started to turn, but then I said to Todd, "Run downstream 'til you hit Main Street! Go now!" When he started off, I threw my flashlight upstream so it made a loud splash.

As I hoped, the guy in the mask brought his light around to where the splash had sounded. By that time Todd was able to round a bend in the stream and race away.

"Get up here!" yelled the voice. The flashlight blinded me. "Now!"

I scrambled up the bank. When I got by the bushes, the light was still in my eyes.

"I'm not going to do anything," I cried. "I don't even know you!"

"If we can have a little talk, I'm not going to hurt you," he growled. "Or your mother, little boy. You see, I know who you are, and I can hurt your mother just like—"

"You leave my mother alone! You killed Mr. Hicks, didn't you?" I demanded. My heart was full of fear for my mom. I had to think of something. What, I still didn't know. Maybe I could throw M & M's at him. I said, "Why did you kill the principal?"

"Because he did the worst thing to me. Hey! Keep your hands away from your pockets!"

Don't worry, I wanted to say, Todd's the one with the knife; all I have is a note I didn't even write. . . . Wait a minute.

What's the worst thing that can happen to you? I had just written about that today. *When your friends embarrass you.* Or maybe when your boss embarrasses you? Like in a faculty meeting? When that boss ridicules something that's important to you? And something else I had written that day: a note to a friend, only that wasn't what I had taken down to the office and then stuffed in my pocket.

"Miss Alexander!" I shrieked as I lunged toward her. "I know it's you!" I bumped into her hard. She dropped the flashlight. When you surprise somebody, you can really whack them. She fell right over. I heard the gun land *plop* in the creek. Miss Alexander struggled, so I pushed her down the bank. She rolled in the mud, hit her head on a rock, and landed in the water. I jumped down next to her and pulled the half of her that had landed in the water out into the mud.

I didn't want her to drown.

Within ten minutes who should come crashing up the other side of the creek but Todd, my mother, and her boyfriend, Homicide Investigator Tom Schulz. I was holding a rock over Miss Alexander's head in case she woke up. She was breathing; I'd checked. If she woke up, I wanted to ask if she knew it was me when she'd been watching from the woods during recess.

"Oh, Mom!" I cried. I could hear my voice cracking. I guess I'd put off being scared.

"Archibald! How *dare* you stuff your bed with pillows?" She was still wearing her caterer's uniform. I could see the white cloth reflecting behind their flashlights. "I called Tom

Schulz right away. He said he'd listened to the 9-1-1 tape and thought it was your voice, and if you were missing, he bet he knew where you . . . Who is *that?*"

"That's probably our homicide suspect," came the deep, rumbling voice of Tom Schulz. I felt goose bumps. I could just hear satisfaction in his voice.

"Arch!" shouted Todd. "Are you okay? They were driving up the road when I was running down. . . . And you wanted me to go instead of you. . . . Why?"

I just smiled. Why? Because he was my best friend.

Angel on the Loose

Valerie Frankel

This town's been decent to me—no burglaries, muggings, rip-offs, or unwelcome come-ons (not many welcome come-ons either, for that matter). The Slope bends—Park Slope, Brooklyn, that is—but it doesn't break. For self-employed private dicks like me, the only things that break are our hearts (often), bank accounts (too often), and luck (not often enough). No case has cracked of late. Neither have my freshly manicured nails. Petal pink. The shade fits summer like the skin on a grape.

Kids are all over the Slope. School's out, but most of these homeboys are never in school anyway. I spread butter on toast at Savarin, my fav hash joint in the nabe, and flipped through the *Daily Mirror*. After a delicious perusing of Page Seven (the cheaply titillating city gossip column), I turned to the business section. Corporate layoffs have given new meaning to the phrase "ring around the (white) collar," and as I looked out the diner window onto Flatbush, I counted one, two, three hundred recently ejected suits sweating up and down the avenue, looking to adopt a hobby, a pet, something to whip the unemployment blues. I'm not working myself at the moment. That bothers me like a massage. Arthritic Mrs. Kiney, my regular waitress, warmed my mug. She pointed at the story I was reading ("Recession Reaches Nosebleed Heights") and squeaked, "Spago, Pokey and Shott lost it's biggest account last week. Two thousand got canned. A thousand more will probably go today." And SPS had been the hottest ad agency in New York City. I wondered how Mrs. Kiney knew about the firings. I wondered why she cared. "I've been having fits of loneliness," she added, and deposited herself in the booth across from me.

"Cheaper than shopping fits," I commented brightly.

"Easy for you to say, Miss New York," she said, and patted her massive hips. Mrs. Kiney calls me Miss New York for one of two reasons: The first is that I'm drop-dead gorgeous and might as well be a pageant princess. The second is that I embody all that is grisly, grimy, and hard about this city. I opt for the former. I've never asked to be corrected. My real name's Wanda Mallory. I'm on the unflattering side of twenty-five, not hard to look at, packed with good intentions, and confused by bad ideas.

"My Angel hasn't come home in days," Mrs. Kiney explained. "And I think I might curl up and die." She rubbed her joints, and her eyes got damp. I figured Angel was her kid, grandkid, or sexual plaything. She went on, "I know you're good at finding things. Your better half told me." She meant Alex Beaudine, my colleague and former main squeeze. We work at Do It Right Detectives in Times Square. I'm the owner; he gets paid just the same.

"My worse half needs cream," I said, waving my spoon.

"One more night without my Angel," Mrs. Kiney sighed wetly, "and I'll be another lonely old lady who wakes up to discover that affection and love are the only honest reasons to get dressed in the morning in this hell hole of a city."

I poked at my eggs. That my sunny, late breakfast had mutated into a sobfest over-easy didn't thrill me. And I'd been trying so hard to stop thinking about things that don't thrill me. "Wanda," Mrs. Kiney implored, "help me or live with the guilt you were born to nurture."

"How much?" I asked politely.

"We need to talk about that."

"I hate conversations that start with the word need." *Pro Bono Detecting* might as well be embossed on my business cards—if I had any. I made a mental note to get some printed up. "So what's the deal?" I asked. "Free breakfast for a year? Unsolicited gushings about my hair and my clothes?"

"I do love your hair." Mrs. Kiney wrung her arthritic hands. "If you bring Angel back safe and happy, I'll give you the firstborn."

"I thought your landlord had dibs on that."

"One of Angel's litter. She's due any day. That's why I'm so worried. The streets of Park Slope are no place for a pregnant kitty."

I, too, have a kitty. Her name is Otis. She's black as a hole and smart as a sock on the jaw. I picked her up on my way home from the ASPCA—my good deed for the decade—and have raised her like a mother wolf. I respect her enormously. She's the only woman I've ever known, including myself, who will tolerate bad treatment from no one. If I ever found Otis damaged, missing, or abjectly depressed, I'd have to hurt someone. I felt a rush of sympathy for Mrs. Kiney. We single girls in New York have to take care of each other.

"Got pictures?" I asked.

Mrs. Kiney scampered to the counter as best she could on her chunky gams. She returned with a photo album crammed with shots of Angel in a pillow bed, on the windowsill, playing with yarn, scratching furniture, yawning, preening, stretching, and licking herself shiny and clean. Each picture was dated, and some had cutesy captions (most obnoxious: "Angel with a dirty face"). And I thought I had a peculiar relationship with my cat.

I said, "She's very photogenic."

"I always thought she would've been a glamorous actress if she were born human."

"What if she were born, say, a guy?" I asked, genuinely interested.

Mrs. Kiney ignored me. "Think the photos will help?"

"What photos?" I smiled. She looked concerned. "Just

kidding," I said, and stood up, tucking the album under my arm.

Mrs. Kiney slipped my check into her apron. "Angel was last seen on my fire escape on Sterling and Flatbush. The address is written in the book." I headed out. "Wanda," she stopped me, "if you find out my Angel is . . . scratching a post in the sky, you can tell me. I want to know the truth. No matter how barbaric and sadistic it might be."

On that note, I split and walked the two blocks to my apartment. The sun was hot, the sky was clear. I'd planned to spend the day in bed. Otis leapt at me when I got home, her claws lovingly extended. I caught her and squeezed her and nuzzled her little face. She didn't seem to mind.

The first order of business on a working day was to shower. I, too, prefer to eat before I clean my paws. After my ablutions, Otis and I did what we call the Secret Morning Ritual. She sits in my lap and licks the shower water off my face, neck, and shoulders. It sounds cutesier than it is.

Towel wrapped turban-style around my luscious red locks, I placed calls to every veterinarian, pet shelter, ASPCA, and glue factory in Brooklyn. Every conversation went something like this:

Me: "Hello, kind sir. I'm calling about a lost cat."

Them: "Come down and look for yourself." Click.

My next move: Persuade my partner, Alex Beaudine, to check out all the sanctuaries for runaway cats on my list. I called him at his place on the Lower East Side in Manhattan. He said, "Heart of my heart," and then made a feeble attempt to bow out of working for no pay. Alex and his legs eventually agreed to journey to deepest, darkest Brooklyn only after I threatened to hickey my initials on his chest next time I caught him napping at the office. He knew I'd do it.

I got dressed and dropped Otis into the courtyard out back. There are three other black cats who live next door. Otis attempts to kick their butts on occasion. They weren't around that day, and she seemed disappointed. I went next to the stationery store. I Xeroxed flyers with Angel's puss and my number. Then I took to the streets.

On every traffic light post, storefront, and on a sprinkling of windshields, I taped a copy. I was puzzled. You'd think there'd be room on a telephone pole to pin a sheet of paper, but other people's notices about other lost cats hogged all the prime, eye-level space. Eventually completing my mission, I returned home. Alex was waiting on my stoop. He looked luscious as always in a Gap T and 501s. When all six feet of him unfolded upright to greet me, I flashed to the months we'd spent (and hours we'd passed) as lovers. The breakup wasn't mutual. He looked at his watch and then at me. He pushed some shiny brown hair off his face. So I forgot to leave him a note. So I'm an idiot.

"Why be on time when you can be twenty minutes late?" he asked.

"I was working. Dig my tan?"

"Tell me again about the hickey proposition."

"You wish."

I led him to my lair. I haven't completely abandoned the hope that Alex will start kicking himself for losing me. I brushed his shoulder by-accident-on-purpose and I walked to the answering machine. It was blinking. I pushed the button. "You've reached Wanda's Home for Unwed Detectives. Registration tax seasonal." Beep. "You better not be off having some meaningless sexual fling, Ms. I'm Not Around for the People Who Need Me." It was the voice of Santina Epstein, the fiftyish (fake) blonde beautician who lives upstairs. She's my landlord and surrogate mother. I mind every day, some days.

Alex said, "No wonder you were late."

"I wish," I said.

The message continued. "So I've got this friend, Mrs. Berkowitz from the salon? She lives around the corner. Her cat is missing and she's very upset. So I said to her, I said, 'Dottie, my downstairs neighbor is a detective.' This woman, she throws herself all over me. I almost died. Dottie, I love her, you know I do, she's big as a house. A shame—she has such a pretty face. So she says to me, she says, 'Santina—'" Beep. The message was cut off. I turned off the machine.

"Sweet mystery of life," I said to Alex. "Look at this." I

dropped the collection of phone numbers from neighborhood flyers on the butcher block island in my kitchen. "Ads for missing cats. All black. All in the neighborhood. All on the plump side."

"The owners or the cats?"

"Missing cat owners don't put their own photograph on a flyer, idiot."

"They do if they're searching for themselves."

"Only then in California."

"And parts of suburban New Jersey, I've heard." Alex absentmindedly flipped open Mrs. Kiney's Angel montage. He said, "When did you take all these shots of Otis? And who wrote these nauseating captions?"

"That's not Otis."

"Who else could it be?"

"Angel looks nothing like her. She doesn't have Otis's whimsical-yet-seductive whisker span."

"How could I have missed that?" Alex isn't a cat person. He could never understand. I took a second look at Angel scratching her ear. A layperson might think they look alike. They're both black, plump. Sudden terror exploded in my brain. I tore down the stairs and through the basement to my courtyard outside. Alex trotted after me.

I called for Otis. I used every pet name in my book (Bunnyhead and Special Love made her purr). She didn't come home. An hour later, she didn't come home. Alex went inside at the first sign of my voice cracking. I didn't go inside until I was sure it wouldn't crack again. He handed me a cigarette and suggested lunch. I stoked the smoke and agreed even though I'd eaten a few hours before. I don't usually seek comfort in food. But Alex was the only guy around. So my other option was out of the question.

We walked up Flatbush toward Antonio's Pizza Palace. The streets hadn't been swept for two days, and cigarette butts clogged the gutters. I tossed mine on the heap, and Alex scowled. My Otis was gone. I felt as crushed as gum under a boot. I imagined Mrs. Kiney's first moments of panic, and Santina's fat friend, and the dozens of other catless fretters in the Slope. Animal sacrifices and scientific experiments filled my thoughts. I couldn't contain a small sob. Alex, the thinking girl's hunk, didn't tell me everything would be fine. He knew better.

Or maybe it's that he didn't get a chance. No sooner had our feet hit pavement when a scream exploded from the Kibble4Kabookie store on my corner. We tore inside and found an elderly woman cowering in a corner, and the owner, kindly Mr. Moto, unconscious on the floor. Alex ran to him and checked his pulse.

"He's alive," Alex reported. "But this goose egg on his head won't hatch for weeks."

I asked the old lady what happened. She said, "I don't live around here and I didn't see a thing." Then she limped out the door.

Mr. Moto came to when Alex slapped his cheek. "The country people," he yelled. "They're coming to get me. Deliverance!" His eyes focused on me, and recognition set in. "Wanda," he said. "There's a pain where there once was a head."

"That's the traditional gift of the country people." Mr. Moto and I are old pals. I buy all my Fluffy Nibblées at Kibble4Kabookie—Otis won't eat anything else. The reminder of my small, furry friend unnerved me. I glanced quickly at the emptied cat food shelf by the fresh nip tree. I wondered if there was a connection.

"I had no bad Karma coming to me," Mr. Moto moaned. "I cleared that out last week when my wife left."

"Mr. Moto, who are the country people?" That was me. "And what happened to all the Fluffy Niblées?"

"I didn't have one drink, I didn't talk to a single woman. I barely left the store," he moaned. "It's been so lonely since she's gone."

"My heart bleeds. It doesn't show, but I'm bleeding."

Alex helped Mr. Moto to his feet. He teetered, but, resilient little guy, regained his balance quickly. "I only saw him out of the corner of my eye. One guy. He wore overalls and a red bandanna over his face." Mr. Moto wobbled to the register. "I had at least five hundred in here. And, so help my Karma, if one penny is gone, I'll kill." The machine popped open with a jangle, and Mr. Moto pored over the cash. He counted. We watched. Finally he sighed and shook his head. "It's all here."

"Don't let it get you down." That was Alex. "I know it's a bummer to give up a vigilante quest."

"Get out of here," Mr. Moto barked. "I'm locking up."

"We weren't here at all today," I said. "Be sure to tell the police about that stolen money. I hear you can write it off on your taxes."

"If I did that, my wife would come home pregnant."

We split. Mr. Moto promised he'd restock the stolen kitty grub. I remembered that I might not need the stuff anymore. I imagined Otis, lost, hungry, alienated by strangers, fending off vicious wildlife with her delicate little paws. The thought rocked my noggin, and I hallucinated a black cat in the Kibble4Kabookie's storefront window. I blinked, but it was still there. I stepped closer for a better look—I wasn't wearing my glasses. My phantom cat turned out to be a cardboard promotional cutout for Fluffy Nibblées of all things—a merciless tug at the heartstrings. Alex could tell I was getting upset again. He snagged me by the wrist, and yanked me away from the store.

We continued up the avenue to Antonio's. I scoured the streets for signs of feline life. Nothing. I stopped to check every dumpster, and Alex got annoyed, the heartless thug. I asked the pizza man if he'd seen my Special Love. He said no. The Sicilian looked decent, so I got a square. Alex didn't say a word to me while we ate, and I was grateful. I wondered if my detecting skills would be impaired by the crushing pain. I wondered if Otis was still alive. I shuddered and pushed my piece aside. I tooled outdoors to watch the street. The sun was still hot and the air was dry. Alex followed me out of the parlor. He popped the last morsel of pizza between his soft red lips. Even through my agony, I wanted to lick his eyebrows.

"Don't eat like that," I said.

"Would you prefer it if I fed my ears?"

"We need clues."

"I hear they go two for a dollar at the Army Navy store."

"Mrs. Kiney's place is across the street."

"Case the joint? Stakeout?"

"Garbage."

"Case the joint?"

"You heard me." Alex is anal-retentive. Like Joan Crawford, he gets mad at dirt. I've seen this. He has accused soot of ruining his life. And that was after he scrubbed the windows. "I'll wait if you want rubber gloves."

"Am I a man, or a coroner?" he asked, but I could see fear and disgust all over his adorable face. We traversed the avenue, located the appropriate cans, and plunged in with naked fingers. The goo I took for lo mein was thoroughly vile, but neat in a way, you know? Over my shoulder, I swear I heard Alex gag. He faux-coughed loudly to disguise it. On my third can, I hit pay dirt. And I don't mean a microwave oven.

"Pray, Watson. What fresh clue, this?" I asked, triumphantly.

Alex whistled. "It looks like Billy Joe Bob couldn't keep his pants on." I shook off the pair of overalls. Coffee grinds flew through the air, and a red bandanna hit asphalt. "What next?" he asked. "DNA testing? Print dusting?"

"I've got a sudden hankering for baklava."

"I could use a taste myself."

I flung the overalls back into the garbage, and we walked back down Flatbush to Savarin. A pale, middle-aged man nearly mowed me down on the way. He was pacing his three hundred pounds uphill. His wheezing revealed that he didn't jog often. What unemployed men will do to make themselves suffer.

Mrs. Kiney was still on her shift. A man with an expensive suit and a bald spot muttered to himself and to her at the counter. He didn't look familiar. Alex said he had to make a quick phone call. He said it was kind of private. I pretended I wasn't jealous. Hovering nearby to eavesdrop would have seemed too masochistic, so I sat down next to the grumbler at the counter. I dropped my elbows on the Formica—they made a clunk. I said to Mrs. Kiney, "The world is a cold, hard, unforgiving place."

Mrs. Kiney and the man nodded. They knew. The man grunted, "I've sweat. I've bled. My fluids are precious." He paused to shred a paper napkin. "Scum-sucking hyenas."

I asked, "What does a girl have to do to get a cup of coffee around here?" Mrs. Kiney propped a mug at my elbows.

The man reached for another napkin. On reflex, I checked for a wedding band—none. I wasn't interested anyway. He was too jolly for the likes of me. He said, "The ax is sharp. And the cut is swift."

"I'll take your word for it."

Mrs. Kiney squeaked, "This is Bert Jingle."

"Catchy name."

"He got fired today," she whispered.

"Jackels. Hyenas. Dirty, smelly, scum-sucking swine," he ranted. "They're nothing without me. Less than nothing. Negative nothing."

"He worked with my grandson, Georgie, at Spago, Pokey and Schott." The ad agency. So that's how she knew about the trouble there.

Bert stood abruptly and raised his arms to the ceiling. "French kisses for your kitty," he cried, and flung napkin confetti in the air.

"Maybe for your kitty," I said.

"That's the slogan Bert and Georgie were known for," said Mrs. Kiney while massaging her joints. She whispered, "SPS lost the account last week."

"Sucked us dry and spit us out like chaw," Bert raved. "I'll get those bastards."

"Now you sound like Georgie," Mrs. Kiney commented. "That is not a healthy attitude." She shook her head and wrung her hands.

"Georgie—my brother in pain," Bert lamented.

"He should be home soon," Mrs. Kiney assured him. To me she added, "He's been living in my basement since he lost his job. This has affected him so badly. His allergies are going haywire. And it's long past pollen season. I worry about that boy." She sighed and reached for my hand. "If Angel weren't lost, I could be more of a support. There's heartbreak everywhere."

Alex came over from the pay phone. He had a smug smile on his face—damn him. "No cat sightings yet, Mrs. Kiney," said my ex–better half. "Did Wanda tell you about Otis?"

"What happened to Otis?" she asked, concerned.

"When is your shift over?" I asked.

"A couple hours."

"I'll be back in half an hour with Angel."

"That's a horrible thing to say. Can't you see I'm hurting?" she asked.

"Half an hour." I downed the remainder of my coffee. Alex shrugged and checked his watch. We waved good-bye and took to the street.

Once on the street, Alex said, "I can tell by that stupid smirk that something's up."

"Likewise," I said. Alex blushed. "What's her name?" I asked. "Is she old enough to reach the elevator buttons?" Alex has a thing for younger women.

He said, "She voted in the last election."

"That explains the write-in for Mickey Mouse." Alex's eyelids twitched, and I knew I'd crossed the line between friendly jousting and malicious abuse. So I've got a big mouth. Better that than repression.

We walked the two blocks in silence. I accepted that Alex has a social life. And I know it's not my affair, but with the Otis caper solved, I needed to redirect my passions. Alex is my usual standby for that.

We buzzed Mrs. Kiney's brownstone. No answer. We banged on the door. Nothing. Alex suggested we climb up the fire escape. I said no. I was wearing a skirt (Donna Karan, black peasant—fitting for the Park Slope urban bohemian look). I asked him if he had his specialty set on him. He did, and used it to pick the door locks. His jimmying was completely visible to anyone who passed by on the street. No one tried to stop us. I was a little grateful, and a lot annoyed.

The apartment was cozy and sweet—doilies, crystal, and velvet galore. Mrs. Kiney'd been living there for twenty years and probably paid a pittance for rent. I wondered how she hobbled around without breaking anything. The door to the basement was in the kitchen. It was bolted from the inside. Alex was suggesting that we get a locksmith when I spotted the watering can by the windowsill. I filled it with hot water, and aimed the flow at the door crack. The tiny stream trickled downstairs (and all over the kitchen floor—I'd clean later). Sure enough, we heard a curse word from the basement followed by clomping sounds on the wood stairs. As soon as we heard the bolt slide free, Alex swung the door open and grabbed our culprit by the throat.

He said, "Whaddaya, whaddaya," and squirmed like a fish in a net. But he couldn't break free—Alex is so strong and manly.

"Georgie, baby," I said. "I'm the single, redhead detective your grandmother tried to fix up with you. Better than you ever imagined, no?" She had tried, by the way. At the time, I was freshly cut by Alex and I thought dating couldn't hurt. She showed me Georgie's picture. That's when I decided celibacy didn't sound so bad.

He wasn't grotesque, but the family strain of chunkiness was there. His eyes were watery blue, and his nose was red like a Christmas tree bulb. He sneezed and Alex released him. Georgie tumbled down the stairs—not his intention. We heard a thud and a moan, then a scurry and the sound of a thousand motorboats. We ran down after him. He was prone on the wood floor of the basement, a swarm of black cats licking and rubbing and climbing all over him. He sneezed again, and it sounded painful. I searched for Otis among the horde and couldn't pick her out. It stabbed me to think it—the cats all looked alike. And the basement wasn't even dark.

It was floodlit, in fact. While I picked through the dozens of cats searching for my Special Love, Alex said, "Mr. Moto might have something to say about this." I looked where he was pointing. A year's supply of Fluffy Nibblées crowded a corner of the room. Piled to the right were stacks of four other cat food brands and a case of Starkist Tuna. A white sheet hung against the back wall of the basement. On the floor sat five empty bowls. A video camera was propped in front of the whole set.

"Auditioning for 'America's Most Perverted Home Videos'?" I asked the still-swarmed Georgie. I don't think he heard me—his sneezes had advanced to seizures by that point.

He managed to utter, "The cats. The cats." I took the hint and pushed the gang of small, furry quadrupeds aside. I helped Georgie to his feet and guided him to a chair.

"I suspect you'll get the belt for this," I said. "Grandma's sympathetic heart got broken when Angel disappeared."

Georgie struggled to say his peace. "Seldane," he begged. "On the table." Alex brought the drugs over, and he gulped down some tablets. He took a deep breath and said, "You want an explanation."

"No, actually. I came here to get my legs waxed."

Georgie tried to speak again, but his sneezing fits, swollen eyes, and puffy flesh were too distracting. He choked out, "Spago . . . Fluffy . . . Evil."

"You're allergic to cats," Alex said, showing off his remarkable talent for stating the obvious. Georgie nodded.

"Let me take a whack," I started. "You got fired. You hate the world and everything in it. The only way to save your dignity is revenge. How am I doing?" Georgie blew his nose and nodded. "If Fluffy Nibblées hadn't left Spago, Pokey and Shott, you'd still have a job. The way you figure, the target for your plot is the food company."

His eyes were streaming. He coughed, "Death to Fluffy."

"The model for the ads is a black, chubby cat. You've got this nice video camera. This nice backdrop. Plenty of samples. Am I with you?" He blew affirmative. "You're trying to document that cats hate the stuff and would rather eat, say, some other cat food. Maybe a brand that needs help with their advertising." Alex whistled. I waved at him to stop. "So how'd the experiment go?" I asked. "Was Fluffy the big loser?"

He shook his head and managed to spit out, "No, dammit. They love the stuff"—sneeze—"That's all they want"—choke—"I hate them. Get rid of them." His face twisted for a second, and he looked even sicker. "I'm the big loser," he said, and I actually felt sorry for him.

"You're just out of work. Come on. You can't let this town break you," Alex encouraged. "And you're not a loser." Alex is always this way, supportive, helpful, assuring. Those are three of the reasons I fell in love with him. And I'd agree about Georgie—if Alex were right.

"He is too a loser," I said. So I'm a bitch. I stared at Georgie, in all his misery. "But I suppose he's suffered enough. Set the cats free and I won't tell your grandmother. They'll find their way home." He attempted a smile. "And take back the stolen food. Give it to Mr. Moto personally. Tell him Wanda sent you." Mr. Moto will like that. And maybe I'd get Fluffy wholesale.

Georgie struggled to his feet and opened the basement door that led to the street. He shooed the cats in that direction, but none budged. Could be a feline Stockholm Syndrome. Could be the abundant chow. Alex and I gave it a shot. A few ran out, but they snuck back in. Eventually we all agreed that Georgie would have to clear out the grub immediately. If the cats didn't leave then, he'd have to call all the numbers I'd collected and ask the hysterical owners to pick up their cats. That'd be easy. Picking them out of the crowd would be tougher.

Alex and Georgie left with about fifty pounds of Fluffy Nibblées, a few cats chasing after them. I hung around and tried to find Otis. For twenty minutes I hunted. Otis always comes when I call. She didn't that afternoon, and I felt rejected. Is her loyalty where the food is? Don't I give her everything she wants? And what of our special magic? I guess none of that mattered to a well-fed furball. I did ID Angel—our preggers friend. She was the roundest of the bunch. I wondered if Otis gained weight in the four hours since I'd seen her last. Slighted and confused, I went outside to sit on the stoop. I lit my second cigarette of the day. It tasted swell.

I checked my watch and debated calling Mrs. Kiney. She'll be horrified when she finds out. I watched a bunch of kids run in and out of the Korean deli at the corner. I wondered what they got away with. A few more cats crawled to the street. One jumped in my lap, and I rubbed its belly. A girl. She had a tiny patch of white in her armpits. I took a close look at her face. Orange eyes, check, chipped front tooth, check. And a whimsical-yet-seductive whisker span. I hugged her and squeezed her and kissed her little face. Otis didn't seem to mind.

The Ties That Bind

L. B. Greenwood

Like everyone else on Vancouver Island, Marcus had known that the summer had been quite amazingly hot and dry. Seemed every Victoria resident who stopped at the Gas'n'Eats complained about the damage the heat was doing to the area's famous gardens, and nearly every tourist complained, "I thought it *never* got this bad over here."

Still, the change in old Jack's place since Marcus had been out three weeks ago was a shock. Not that the deep lake was perceptively smaller, but the wild growth that ordinarily turned the hundred-odd acres into a gently rolling meadow had, in late August and with the weather now definitely cooler, already shifted to its autumnal mode. Even that low, bushy stuff (Marcus was no botanist) that ordinarily grew so profusely around the one end of the lake had contracted to a narrow, suffering strip.

The drought had done old Jack in too, for the well that he'd proudly proclaimed never failed had finally done just that, and he'd been forced to haul water up from the lake. He'd been carrying two buckets (both full, Marcus was sure) along the gravel path that wound up the hill to the house, lost his balance, and snapped one sparrow-thin leg just above the ankle. He'd broken bones before in his eighty-plus years, and knew at once the extent of the injury. Knew too that, fiercely independent though he was, this was one of those times when he had to have help.

So he'd bound his handkerchief around his leg and, with an ancient yard broom for a crutch, hobbled and hopped along the winding ruts that were his access to the road. He'd been found by a passing motorist—more and more traffic every day, with the valley becoming a virtual bedroom community for Victoria—and been taken in to the hospital.

He'd phoned Marcus from there, to ask him to see to Matilda, his old cat. Feed her good and leave some packaged stuff outside where she could get it, the old man had said in a pain-and-drug-filled voice, and she'd be okay until he was home. Which would be Sunday, day after tomorrow, or he'd wring the doctor's neck.

Oh, I can stay at your place until you're back, Marcus had said, no problem. Business at the Gas'n'Eats is as slow as molasses in January (an expression that he'd picked up from the old man, who'd spent his boyhood on the prairies). And, though Marcus hadn't said this, maybe a short spell of absence would help resolve his relationship (if it even deserved the name) with Dawn. Though he really didn't see how absence, or anything else, could do that.

"I don't want," Jack had concluded querulously, "any of my damn relations buzzing around the place while I'm gone, you hear me?"

"Didn't know you had any relations," Marcus had replied truthfully.

"Well, I have. Dolly's a bossy faggot. Paul's an old woman. Eddie's a scoundrel, and that last wife of his a shyster. Any of 'em show up, slam the door. Understand?" And bang! had gone the receiver.

Marcus had known Jack since shortly after he himself had started work a year ago at the small garage-cum-store-cum-café at the Crossings, ten miles out of Victoria. The old man had stomped in one day, furious because the bus service had been discontinued, and he'd had to accept a ride from some flibbertigibbet summer folk. "How'm I goin' to get in for me groceries if there bain't no bus?" he'd demanded, quite as if the deletion were Marcus's doing.

"If you could phone your order in," Marcus had begun, "maybe I—"

"Ain't got no phone. And don't want one, neither. Dolly'd be callin' me up ev'ry day to ask if I'd washed me neck."

"Maybe a neighbor—"

"Got none. Why I live far end've the valley."

"If you'd leave a list," Marcus had then suggested, "I could take the stuff out later on my way home. And bring a new list back for next time."

"Do that ev'ry month?"

"Sure. Long's I'm here."

"You one of these rattley young fools, be you?"

"I don't think so," Marcus had replied, honestly enough. Though he'd have been hard put to explain why, if he were neither rattley nor a fool, his only job at age twenty-seven was pumping gas for an ever-lessening number of hours a week.

The old man had shifted ancient striped braces on his frayed and wrinkled shirt. "How much you charge?"

This kind of question always made Marcus awkward, and, as usual, he'd mumbled in reply, "That's okay. Glad to help."

The result had been that he and Jack had become sort of friends. Marcus had even stayed at the old house on the lake now and then. Until Dawn had walked into his life.

Dawn: tall, slender, with waist-long straight hair of a dark blond, the most remote yet decisive girl he'd ever known. She'd arrived one day in the late spring, jumping from the back of a truck that had hardly paused, a knapsack on her back, a carryall in her hand, and entered the Gas'n'Eats for a hamburger and fries. These consumed, she had unhesitatingly carried her dirty dishes behind the counter and, while the astonished owner spluttered, added them to the crowded sink, and then washed, dried and put away the lot. In between she'd slipped off into the grocery and served three customers. By night she'd hardly spoken a dozen words to anyone, but she had a job.

Marcus had tried not to stare too openly, though his eyes seemed to follow her around quite beyond his control. At the end of the day as she slung her knapsack on her back, he had ventured hesitantly, "You got a place to stay?"

She had merely stared at him, hazel eyes like agate.

"I mean," he rushed on through a dry throat," I live in a cabin on the river, just the other side of the Crossings, and there's a shed. . . . It's not much, but we could clean it up a bit, and it's . . . private."

"Private," she had repeated coldly.

"No window. And I could put a lock on the door for you."

At that she had given a tight smile and, reaching one brown hand down to her worn boot, had let him see eight inches of narrow steel. Then she'd thrown her knapsack and carryall into the back of his Bronco, and had ridden in silence out to the cabin. He'd helped tidy the shed, and had been about to offer her blankets or supper or coffee or something, when she'd shut the door in his face.

Ever since, they had ridden together to the Crossings in the mornings and back in the evenings on those days when they had the same work hours. Otherwise Dawn hitched, flatly refusing to allow Marcus to drive her in or to pick her up. They shared food either had bought and either cooked on the little camp stove in the cabin's lean-to kitchen; they spoke seldom and never talked.

Marcus would occasionally ask if the soup needed more salt, just to get Dawn to say something; she never did even that much, and her answer was more apt to be a shake of the head than as much as a single word. All he knew about her was that she made small handicrafts, like sachets from flowers she had gathered and dried, which she peddled around the gift shops that abounded in and around Victoria. And that she'd turned his heart to mush.

Now he'd maneuvered around the bushy corner of the straggling driveway that led down to Jack's. Directly ahead and up a small hill was the near paintless old house, settling on its hams in the dead and dying wild grasses, a TV antenna at a rakish angle on the roof making an incongruous modern note. The redbrick well was near the top of the slope, the privy behind a heavy thicket of evergreens at the bottom. Just above it, in a little hollow, was a patch of that bushy stuff that grew near the lake, here a thick and luxurious tangle of stalks.

Parked in precise line with the sagging porch was a squat and mustard-coloured Mini, its state of spanking cleanliness rising above the poverty of bare tires and well-worn upholstery. All too obviously one of the relatives, whom Marcus was supposed to keep at bay, had jumped the starting gun.

Even as he stopped, the screen door sprang open, and a female version of the car popped out: no longer young, short and plump, dressed in well-pressed gray slacks and a patched red striped shirt, sleeves already rolled up and a bucket clasped in each firm hand. At her feet came marmalade Matilda, licking appreciative whiskers: if Jack didn't approve of this relative, his cat obviously did.

The woman started talking before Marcus had done more than set one foot on the baked earth. "You must be Marcus; Jack's told me about you. I'm his cousin Dolly, work as an aid at the Victoria General, saw him wheeled out of the operating room—he's doing fine—knew he'd be worrying about Matilda, so came right out. I was about to make a visit anyway, bring some cooking and do the place up again.

"Jack always grumbles at me, of course, but he never actually orders me off. Think he's secretly glad to see me, at least to see my pies. Not to mention my muffins." She laughed, cheerfully. "It was real good of you to come, Marcus, but you needn't stay—you've your job to think of, after all."

"That's okay, I've got a few days off."

"Well," Dolly hesitated, "you *could* fill these buckets for me, if you don't mind. The pump on the sink's useless; I suppose the well's gone dry. And no wonder after all the heat."

Marcus filled the buckets, helped Dolly move Jack's bed and wardrobe so that she could clean under and behind them ("Dear, *dear!*"), and washed the bedroom's walls and ceiling. (As Dolly said, even if they didn't look much different, now they at least knew they were clean.)

By then it was suppertime, and Marcus was only too willing to postpone all decisions about going or staying. He was blissfully involved with a slice of fresh blackberry pie when the unmistakable sounds of a car announced its approach, a vehicle of auditorally impeccable credentials and masterful proportions.

"That's never Paul!" Dolly exclaimed, leaning forward to peer out the window. "He's another cousin of Jack's—I don't believe it! Eddie. And his new wife, what's her name—Margo. They're in real estate, you know. Well, I'm not having this." She bustled out, belligerent purpose writ plain in every well-rounded inch, and Matilda marched at her heels, tail up.

Eddie was tall, dark, had no doubt once resembled Gregory Peck sufficiently to have been called handsome, and was still fighting a rearguard action against time. If his hair was decidedly thin on top, his sideburns were positively Elvis; if there was more flab on his middle than muscle on his limbs, his polo shirt and gabardine slacks were slate blue perfection. And his sandals might have been sported with pride by any Roman senator.

As for the car, it was all that the murmuring power of its approach had suggested. Dolly's Mini might be much cleaned and well polished; the gleaming black BMW looked above anything as plebeian as dirt.

Somehow the woman whom Eddie was gallantly helping out of the passenger side wasn't quite what was needed to complement the man-and-car ensemble. Certainly her makeup was à la Hollywood, her streaked bob every inch a coiffure, and the loose knit top in exact coordination with her ivory silk pants. But she was as old as Eddie, and, under the careless honesty of the setting sun, showed it. More, she was not slender, she was skinny, with the hard gaze of the ever aggressive and always unsatisfied, one hand even now fidgeting at the cowl neck.

Dolly greeted the newcomers on the porch, with the door shut firmly behind her. "Eddie, Margo—quite a surprise. Jack isn't here."

"That's why we are," Margo returned neatly. "When the hospital phoned—"

"They phoned *you?* Whatever for?"

"Because I *am*, after all," Eddie answered reasonably, "Jack's closest relative."

Dolly sniffed. "Nephew, that's all."

"Someone," Margo interjected, voice quickly sharp as her face, "is going to have to look after Jack's cat while he's in hospital. He thinks the world of that poor old thing—"

"Either of you ever stayed here?" Dolly inquired. "No, I didn't think so. So you don't know there's no bathroom."

"No—"

"You can take a dip in the lake, or you can haul water up, heat it on the stove, and haul it out again when you're finished: the well's dry, and I wouldn't trust the drain in that old sink. And behind those evergreens at the side of the house is a privy. If you even know what that is."

Eddie had obviously been struck speechless. Margo, though momentarily stunned, rallied much more quickly. "Jack needs us," she announced with demonstrable virtue, "and—"

Her final words were drowned by the hiccuping rattle of another car. Around the overgrown corner and down the ruts of the driveway came a gray Honda Civic, bumpers bent, hood dented, doors scraped, windshield scarred. A battered and rusty survivor of a car.

"Paul," Dolly observed, and opened the screen door. There was a note of . . . relief? perhaps even pleasure? in her voice. "I'll make some more coffee."

Jack, Marcus remembered, had labeled Paul an old woman. If so, he yet had the spunk to park his rust-nibbled compact right next to the ostentatious bulk of Eddie's BMW. Paul himself was of no more than middle height, saggingly thin, half-bald, wearing spectacles and a fawn-colored suit of far from recent vintage.

"Hi, Eddie," he commented in a flat, soft voice. "Thought you just might be headed this way. Saw your car go by."

"From your shop?"

"Right, Eddie. From the window of my gift shop. My *little* gift shop. On the outskirts of Victoria. Not a very good location, I admit, but the best I can afford. As Margo will, I'm sure, understand."

There was a lot going on here that Marcus didn't understand or like. He trailed after the three as they entered the house only because he didn't think he should leave without saying so.

"Nice to see you again, Dolly," Paul observed, giving her cheek a light kiss. "And this young fellow is Marcus, right? Jack's told me about you. Funny how concerned all the family is over an old cat, isn't it? Hi, Matilda," for she had followed him in and was rubbing against his leg.

Marcus hastily retreated to the Bronco to wait for a better time to announce his departure. The uncovered kitchen window revealed what could best be described as an animated discussion that went on and on, until finally Margo and Eddie slammed out to their car and returned to the house with small suitcases, Paul quietly removed a battered attaché case from his Honda, and a general parade to the biffy began. Then the kitchen lights went out; others showed, briefly, in the living room and upstairs, and all became quiet. Marcus had presumably been left to his own resources, to go or stay as he chose.

"Meow?" A brownish blur leaped into the back of the Bronco: at least Matilda welcomed his presence, and she, after all, was his reason for being here (well, at least his main reason). He'd stay until morning, he decided, opening his sleeping bag, until he was sure that someone was going to look after the old cat.

He made a trip to the biffy, noting with a small grin that it reeked of Lysol and Dolly's vigorous scrubbing. If he'd had any doubts as to why Jack's relatives had come flocking, the lights he could see sparkling all across the valley—everywhere but on Jack's place—would have given an answer. A hundred acres of rolling land, complete with a spring-fed lake, would be any developer's dream.

* * *

As always, she seemed to move without a sound, and as always, her very nearness disturbed him. Marcus woke to see Dawn, all silvered with the moonlight, heading with her implacable stride right toward him. For a few insanely joyous seconds he noticed only the knapsack on her back, and thought she'd come to join him. Then he saw the carryall in her hand and knew the truth: She was leaving. The shed, the Crossings, him.

Matilda had already leaped out, and he pushed the Bronco door wide. Afraid to say too much, he managed only a lame "Hi."

She set the carryall down, dropped the knapsack on top. "The hospital phoned the Gas'n'Eats. Jack can come home tomorrow if there's someone to stay with him. For at least two weeks, probably longer."

"Well," Marcus hesitated, wanting, and not daring, to ask if it made any difference to her what he did. "I've only been working part time, so maybe something—"

"Uh-uh." Dawn leaned back against the side of the car with a natural ease that Marcus could never imitate, Matilda purring against her legs. "Your job's gone, so's mine. The owner's sold to one of the oil companies. Be a filling station there in the spring. Maybe you could get taken on if you can hold out over the winter."

"So might you," Marcus urged hopelessly.

"Uh-uh. Not going to be a café or grocery."

"You still don't have to go."

She shrugged, face in deep shadow. "No job."

"We'd get by." No answer. "Where're you thinking of going?"

Yet another shrug. "On. Down the road. Anywhere."

Around the side of the house, obviously returning from the privy, came Margo. She had a flashlight whose downward beam revealed yards of billowing pink, and then, as she swept the light up to the steps of the house, a blazing snake of glitter around her neck, ending in a blinding medallion of shimmer on her bare chest.

Dawn became very still, Matilda dashed for the long grass, Marcus gasped, and Margo stopped abruptly. Her eyes raked the yard, her free hand yanking at the front of her negligee in a futile effort to cover those diamonds. Then, stumbling in her haste, she vanished into the house.

"Wow!" Marcus observed, most inadequately. Dawn, with one of her slight and dismissive shrugs, reached down for her knapsack.

"Look," Marcus said desperately, "you don't have to go *now*. It's late, you shouldn't be . . ." Dawn shot him a look that stopped him midsentence.

He tried again. "Let me run you into Victoria, or . . ." That, she didn't deign to answer with even a glance.

"You could at least stay the rest of the night here," Marcus exclaimed in exasperated frustration. "I'll sleep in the cab if you're afraid—"

What evil genius had made him say that? Of all the words he could have chosen . . .

Dawn threw her belongings into the back of the Bronco so hard that they bounced, and waited in icy silence until he miserably climbed in first. They lay down on the open sleeping bag, backs to the middle, as far apart as possible, and Matilda, being a sensible feline, didn't return.

Marcus didn't know if Dawn slept—she remained still and silent—but he certainly didn't.

The yard was bathed in late summer sunlight when Dolly flung the screen door wide and shouted, "Marcus! Get another bucket of water, will you?"

Without a word he moved to obey; without a word Dawn followed him. They washed in the lake, and each carried a full pail of water to the house.

The kitchen was full of the glorious smell of frying bacon and bubbling coffee; Dolly was at the stove, Paul setting the table. Marcus had started making awkward introductions when Margo and Eddie entered from the hall, Margo's cowl neck covering any hint of diamonds.

"This is my friend, Dawn," Marcus began again.

"Oh, surely not," Margo cut him off contemptuously, one hand fluttering at her throat. "She's got *significant other* written all over her."

That fired Marcus in a way that was to him as shocking as it was unstoppable. "More significant, at any rate, than you'll ever be, with or without your damn diamonds."

"You don't mean you wore those diamonds out here!" Paul's exclamation seemed to express genuine surprise, though the diversion was also very welcome to Marcus.

As was Eddie's hasty explanation. "We were getting ready for a real estate bash at the Empress when the hospital phoned. Too late to take the necklace back to the bank, so Margo decided she'd wear 'em. They're safe enough: she's never taken 'em off. Have you, love?"

"No, and I don't intend to," Margo agreed, her frosty eyes pointedly fixed on Dawn.

Who, in that deceptively gentle voice of hers, promptly delivered her message. Jack could come home tomorrow if there was someone to stay with him for at least two weeks, probably longer.

"I could close my shop," Paul began hesitantly.

"Nonsense, Paul!" Dolly shook a vigorous head. "You'd miss the last of the tourist trade, and you've little enough business as it is. I suppose I could take my holidays. . . ."

"And give up that Caribbean cruise you've already paid for?" Paul countered.

"There's no need of either of you sacrificing a thing," Margo interjected, her eyes aglitter with triumph. "Eddie and I can stay—no problem."

"Real estate business that bad, eh?" Paul's commiseration was patently mocking.

"One of us can always run back while the other stays with Jack." Eddie once more made a peace-offering explanation.

"So, you see," Margo topped it, *"we're* the only ones free."

"Not exactly," Dawn observed. "The Gas'n'Eats is closing, so Marcus is out of work. Me too," she added distantly.

"The perfect solution!" Paul exclaimed brightly. "Give Jack the one person he asked to come here, and help Marcus out too."

"Jack won't want any . . . superfluous *friends* around." Margo spoke with the full nastiness of the legally married.

"That's up to Jack, isn't it?" Marcus hardily interposed, all too encouraged by Dawn's comment.

"Exactly." Dolly slapped a heaping platter of bacon and eggs on the table. *"I'm* staying today, finish up the cleaning—"

"I could give you a hand," Dawn offered, "if you like." And her hazel eyes flicked a challenge at Margo. "Then maybe you could give me a ride into Victoria when you go."

"Glad to," Dolly replied briskly. "Marcus, I can use you too. There's water to haul up—*and* out—and furniture to be moved. The rest of you—" her eyes were on Margo "—can go any time, far's I can see."

"Just a damn minute!" Margo began.

Dolly cut her off. "Then why don't you and Eddie go into Victoria right after breakfast and see Jack? Ask him if he wants Marcus to stay, or you two."

After that, Dolly's excellent meal was consumed in such near total quiet that Matilda's bacon-prompted "Preow?" could be clearly heard from the porch.

Marcus surreptitiously saved a piece for her. At least, he thought dejectedly, he could make one female happy.

At midmorning, after a couple of hours of heaving furniture around and hauling water—clean in and dirty out— Marcus was dismissed by Dolly to go for a swim if he wanted. He looked a hopeful invitation at Dawn, but she, wringing out her scrub cloth, merely asked him to move his feet. So he crunched down the worn gravel path to the lake.

He was sitting on the beach, trying to enjoy the warm day, when Paul and Matilda ambled up.

"Any change," Marcus asked, with a jerk of his head toward the house, "back there?"

"Not that you'd notice. Dolly and I would be only too happy to leave you to care for Jack; Margo and Eddie haven't conceded an inch. But they aren't about to ask the old man for his opinion either."

"I suppose," Marcus said slowly, scratching Matilda's ears, "this *is* all about the property, isn't it?"

Paul pulled a wry face. "Plus the fact that Jack has no

closer relatives than the choice collection of pleasant personalities you've seen here. And the fact that we're all so damn tight-pinched that the thought of coming in for a piece of this is making our mouths water in a rather disgusting fashion."

"Even Margo and Eddie? A case of 'much wants more,' I suppose."

Paul took out a cigarette. "Let me tell you a little story, son. Eddie's been a salesman of some sort all his life—stocks, sports equipment, gent's haberdashery, boats, then real estate with Margo's firm. One of their less desirable associates went bankrupt in a rather momentous way and disappeared from the scene. Thereafter Margo started sporting those really spectacular stones, and Eddie that very lavish car.

"The rumor is that they acquired them for an infinitesimal amount of cash, with no difficult questions, including that of legal ownership, asked or answered on either side."

Marcus gave such a start that Matilda stalked off, indignant over a pulled ear. "So the necklace wouldn't be insured—no wonder Margo is guarding it so closely."

"What good is a girl like Margo without a bit of portable property?"

"You really don't like her much, do you?"

"I haven't much reason. My dad owned a jewelry store in the old part of downtown Victoria, been started by *his* father. I'd trained as a gemmologist and was off hiking in the mountains of Yugoslavia, my first holiday since I'd left school, when Dad died suddenly. His will left everything to Mom, and Margo got to her before I could even be notified.

"You know what's on the spot now? A gourmet seafood establishment. Our shop was on the waterfront, you see. By the time I made it home, Mom had had a stroke and spent five years in a nursing home. There wasn't a lot I could put into a new business; hence my little gift shop in the suburbs."

"And Dolly?"

"Nursed a cantankerous husband for twenty years, was left with nothing. Not even any kids. Only job she could find was as hospital aid. Getting ever closer to retirement and won't even have much of a pension."

"She seems . . . content enough, though. And good-hearted, the way she's come out here, and cooked and cleaned for Jack . . ." Marcus trailed off, realizing that that could be just to get into the old man's good graces. Though, if so, it apparently hadn't been any great success: Jack had labeled her a bossy faggot. And Paul an old woman. Still . . .

"Paul?"

"Yes, son?"

"You took Jack to the bank every month, didn't you? Because I asked him once if he needed a ride in, and he bit my head off: already taken care of, he said. And I think I've seen your old Honda go by the Crossings now and then."

"Oh, well, got to keep in with the old man, haven't I?"

"Then why didn't you get his groceries too?"

"Because the old coot wouldn't let me. I think he was getting lonely, enjoyed having you visit. You know why he finally had electricity put in a couple of years ago? So he could have a TV. A guy who'll do that isn't all that much of a hermit; he just wants his fellow beings on his own terms. Turn 'em off when he's had enough."

"How about Margo and Eddie? Haven't *they* even visited out here?"

Paul grinned. "Tried to, so Jack told me. More than once. He sent them packing each time."

"That's why they don't want to ask him if he'd like them to stay?"

"That's why: he'd pick you, hands down, and they know it. But if you weren't around, then my guess is he'd take Margo and Eddie rather than accept help that he knows would be pretty inconvenient from either Dolly or me. Or than stay in some extended-care ward. You figure on staying, son?"

Damn. "I don't know," Marcus mumbled, thinking and not wanting to say, *That depends on Dawn. If she goes, I go too. I've got to.*

"Yeah, I can understand. You know, I was married once.

Didn't work out, of course, but . . . I can understand. Especially after the sun goes down, and my shop is shut."

The noon meal was announced by Dolly's uncompromising yell of "Lunch!" The kitchen smelled lusciously like a bakehouse; Dawn was setting a plate of hot biscuits on the table, and returned to stand close guard over the oven. Marcus accordingly wedged himself onto the stool in the corner where he could unobtrusively feast his eyes on her unconscious grace.

Paul came in from the living room and was promptly ordered by Dolly, her plump hands assembling a salad, to take the dirty dishwater out. Paul obediently picked the pan out of the old sink and started for the door, to be met by the entering Eddie and Margo. And by Matilda, who, having danced neatly around Eddie, decided to shoot between the legs of Margo. She jumped, lost her balance, and grabbed at a chair. That upset, sending Margo into Paul, dishwater leaping from the pan.

"Ow!" Margo was clinging to the table with one hand and holding her ankle with the other. "That damn cat!"

"Here, sit down." Eddie had hastily righted the chair, now helped Margo into it and knelt at her feet. "Afraid that ankle's starting to swell, love. Got any ice, Dolly?"

"In the fridge," she said shortly, bent over, wiping up the spilled water. "Paul, for heaven's sake, put that pan back in the sink until after lunch. And, Eddie," who was dumping ice cubes into a towel, "hurry up. Don't you realize," as Dawn lifted a golden-topped casserole from the oven, "that's a soufflé?"

"Start eating, everybody." Eddie was wrapping the towel around Margo's ankle. "Be right with you in a jiffy . . . There, love, hold that on."

"I need a cup of coffee a lot more," Margo complained.

"Coffee for everybody, right?" Eddie asked courteously, and proceeded to pour it.

The soufflé was all that such a dish can be, the biscuits sinfully rich, the salad fresh and tangy. So delicious was everything, in fact, that the end of the meal was actually reached without a renewal of hostilities.

Then Margo said, abruptly and loudly, "Eddie and I are the only ones who can stay with Jack without serious inconvenience." She sent a glare swirling around the table. "You all know that's true."

"Marcus . . ." Dolly began, bridling.

"Wants to go with his . . . *friend*. Don't you?" Her narrowed eyes dared him to deny it.

Damn. "I don't always get what I want," he said quietly, not looking at Dawn.

Margo slammed her mug on the table, fingers of her other hand rising to her throat. "Now, just you listen to me—"

She broke off with a gasp that was close to a shriek. Marcus noted with amazement how her makeup was left stranded, like poster paints on newsprint, as the blood drained from her face. "My diamonds." Both her hands were scrabbling frantically at her neck now. "They're gone!"

"They can't have!" Eddie was already on his feet and on his way to her. "The clasp must have come undone, and—"

"Not that clasp," Margo whispered hoarsely, her eyes wide with panic.

"Maybe you didn't fasten it just right." Eddie was feeling down her back. "Stand up, it's got to be in your clothes somewhere."

But for all Margo and Eddie's increasingly urgent patting and shaking, no necklace appeared.

"When are you sure you had it last?" Dolly demanded.

"As I came in."

"Well, you tripped over the cat as soon as you stepped inside," Dolly summed up in commonsense fashion, "and sprained your ankle. You haven't moved from that area since, so the necklace isn't far away—can't be. Come on, everybody, start looking."

They did, and, Marcus observed with a sick jolt, they also kept an eye on one another during the process. No doubt that was unavoidable, what with the circumstances and the smallness of the space. The pairings of watcher and watched, though, were . . . interesting.

He looked at Dawn as often as possible because he always did. She, in turn, seemed very aware of Eddie. Paul had a corner of his regard that never wavered from Margo herself. She openly and accusingly glared at Dawn. Dolly seemed to be paying most attention to Paul; at least she ordered him from one place to another, suggesting that he look under the stove in case one of them could have accidentally kicked the necklace there, and telling him that there was no point in feeling in the cold dishwater because Margo had never been near the sink. Which was true enough.

As for Dolly, was anyone watching her in particular? Marcus couldn't tell. Or himself? he wondered with a start, abruptly realizing that he had to be counted among the suspects.

Suspects: That meant that he thought that the necklace wouldn't be found by their current efforts.

He was right, and the search soon petered out. For a few minutes the indefatigable Dolly drifted on from place to place, obviously struck by first one unlikely idea and then another—such as running the spoon vigorously through the small sugar bowl—but in the end even she had to concede defeat.

"Nothing for it," Paul finally said. "We've got to call the police."

"How?" Eddie asked succinctly.

"There's a phone at the Gas'n'Eats," Marcus suggested.

"And who's going to go in to make the call?" Paul asked, with a slow smile. "Margo?"

"We don't need the police," she snapped back, her face drawn with strain. "My necklace has to be still here, right here, in this room. Which we've searched. So now we search each other." Her eyes were battle-hard. "Dolly and the . . . girlfriend—" throwing a bitter sneer in Dawn's direction —"with me. Paul and Marcus with Eddie. Any objections?"

There weren't. The men trooped into the front room, leaving the women in the kitchen. And none of them found anything.

Marcus wondered if Margo had expected that they would.

He certainly hadn't, for, after all, they were all fully clothed in shirts and long pants, with sandals or sneakers. If a single diamond had been lost, possible hiding places would have been infinite; a necklace of the proportions of Margo's was an entirely different proposition. No one had even a shoe heel big enough to have held that necklace, and anyway, you'd have to be a sleight-of-hand artist to have used that kind of hideaway in front of everyone.

Of course, how did he know that one or more of the others mightn't be just that? And Eddie, Paul, and Dolly were relatives: could there be collusion between two, or even all three? Margo he was positive was innocent: her shock had been too genuine and lasting. And that Dawn, too, wasn't guilty. Because . . . because he wouldn't permit her to be. That was senseless? Then let it be senseless.

The silence in which they had assembled once more in the kitchen was again broken by Paul. "I'm going to the biffy. Anyone want to come to see I don't drop those sparklers down the hole?"

Nobody answered the gibe. Marcus began collecting the used coffee mugs, merely for something to do to keep him near Dawn. She carried the pan of dishwater outside and dumped it. Margo followed her as far as the porch, remaining there to smoke furiously and stare at them all through the window, Eddie standing morosely at her side. Dolly bustled about putting the food away, muttering, "Dear, dear," in a distracted way.

Then the kitchen was tidied, Paul had returned, Margo and Eddie reentered on his heels. Once more they all stood around, waiting for . . . what?

Again Paul first spoke. "Suppose, after dark, we put the lights out and use flashlights to go over the whole kitchen, inch by inch. If there's as much as a single stone even partially uncovered, it will leap out like a star. Like a garland of stars. Like a strip of the Milky Way."

Paul loves jewels, Marcus thought suddenly. Well, why shouldn't he? He *is* a trained gemmologist, after all. And therefore would know both the value of the necklace and how to dispose of it. He also had a deep and justified grudge against Margo. If he could be believed, of course . . . Dolly had little to look forward to (again, if Paul could be believed), and Dawn . . . was Dawn.

They had all agreed to Paul's plan, and went through what seemed to be an interminable afternoon. Though there was no good reason for any of them not to go for a walk, a swim, even a drive, they all stayed near the house. More, except for trips to the privy, near the kitchen. Dolly made cookies, apparently quite unable to do nothing. Paul sat at the table, playing solitaire with a dog-eared pack of Jack's; Margo and Eddie either smoked on the porch, or paced the yard immediately in front. Dawn sat belligerently on the steps, meeting Margo's gaze whenever it turned her way with eyes quite as hard and certainly as cold, and Marcus drifted miserably between her side and the kitchen.

At last dusk came, Dolly vaguely suggested supper, no one even answered. She made coffee, with which they toyed, and served her cookies, which they devoured, and finally the dark closed around them.

Eddie, Paul, Marcus, and Dolly all had flashlights in their cars, one was kept on the kitchen windowsill for night trips to the privy, and Dawn produced her own from her carryall. Thus armed, they put out the kitchen light and started the hunt, bumping heads and rears and poking sharp elbows into shadowy ribs in a way that would have been giggle-making if the occasion had been less serious.

As it was, there wasn't even a good false alarm to relieve the tension. The closest was when the beam of Marcus's flashlight picked up a weak and momentary shine under the table, caused by nothing more than the cellophane from a package of cigarettes.

At the end Margo shrilly demanded that they all go out and leave her to continue searching alone. Eddie seemed to assume that he would stay with her, and was almost hysterically ordered away; looking resigned, he joined Dolly and Paul on the porch. Dawn walked off around the side of the house, apparently headed for the privy; Marcus trailed across the yard to the Bronco to wait her return.

Which didn't come.

Eventually the kitchen ceiling light shone. A general exit and return from the privy started, without any sign of Dawn. The kitchen light went out, and those in the living room and in the upstairs bedrooms came on, briefly. The conclusion seemed inescapable: everyone, even Margo, had, however reluctantly, given up the search for the night and gone to bed.

Except Dawn.

Marcus climbed into the back of the Bronco, piled the carryall on top of the knapsack, and leaned against both. Dawn wouldn't, surely, just go and leave these behind: they contained the sum of her worldly possessions.

As far as he knew. Which wasn't at all far, was it? Only far enough that he would stake his life that, wherever she was, she didn't have Margo's damn necklace with her.

Who *had* taken it? And how? Presumably Eddie had been right: Margo hadn't fastened the clasp properly, and her ceaseless fingering of the necklace under her cowl top had brought it to the floor, sometime during lunch. Or just before lunch. At any rate, during a time when the small kitchen was full of them all, with movement all over the place. Marcus could remember nothing that was any help there.

There was something, though, nagging at the back of his mind. Some anomaly. Something he'd noticed earlier, soon after he'd arrived. Something to do with the dry weather . . .

Dead and dying vegetation everywhere, scant, short, stunted, sere. Except, of course, at the one end of the lake where that wild, bushy plant still flourished. And in that patch of it beside the house.

Marcus sat up abruptly. Why *should* that little hollow still be blithe and green? Not from the biffy, which was below. Not from the well, which was far above and also dry. Ordinarily the hand pump on the sink brought its water into the house; what, though, had Jack done with his household waste water?

Dolly had insisted that it be carried outside. Jack hadn't, Marcus realized with sudden excitement. He'd dumped it down the old sink, and the evidence of that was there in that patch of flourishing green. Flourishing because, in a simple gravity system, the drainpipe from that old sink ended there.

Somehow Margo's necklace had come undone and fallen to the floor. Someone had picked it up and, lifting the full dishpan of water a little, had slipped it down the drain. Letting that dishpan keep any of the others from even remembering the hole that was underneath.

Whoever it was wouldn't have dared retrieve the necklace yet, not while everyone was meandering around, going to and from the biffy. Whoever it was would wait until after dark. Until, like, about now.

Where was Dawn?

Marcus grabbed his flashlight and was out of the Bronco in a leap. There was enough moonlight still so that he could make his way across the yard and, once around the house, along the hard gravel path toward the biffy. He looked longingly toward that clump of green bushy stuff, but he resisted the temptation and slipped under the low-hanging boughs of the evergreens.

He didn't have long to wait.

The screen door of the house softly opened and shut: noises that didn't call attention to themselves by being too loud or the reverse, just the natural sounds made by a person considerate of others and conscious of the lateness of the hour.

The soft scrunch of footsteps followed, and a shape darker than the shadows appeared around the corner of the house. A change now in both sound and shape: the thief had stepped from the path to bend over that green-filled hollow. The beam of a flashlight jumped down, and as Paul had predicted, the diamonds at once showed their natural glory, like a fairy queen's tiara lost in the tangled stalks.

Marcus crashed out of the boughs, switching on his own flashlight as he ran. To catch, framed in its beam, the flying shape of Dawn, unleashed in a hard tackle that brought to a gasping heap that hunched figure. Eddie, the diamonds still glittering in one muddy hand.

For a moment they all remained still. Then Dawn leaped to her feet, and Eddie heaved himself into a sitting position.

"Margo's a bitch, you know," he observed, a trifle breathlessly. "A *royal* bitch."

"Whom you married," Dawn pointed out coldly.

"Yeah, well, real estate was the thing then, but you got to have a ticket to get in; Margo'd been at the game quite a while and suggested we join forces. The old—and monied —branches of Victoria still look askance at a man and woman's sharing quarters if they aren't legally hitched, so we did the deed. Just in time for the slump. I've got too many old matters hanging over my head, know what I mean? It's time for me to split, kids.

"So how about this?" He let the necklace dangle enticingly from his hand in the beam of the flashlight. "There's enough here for us all. Look, suppose I cut off the two sides—one for each of you—and keep just the medallion. Chance of a lifetime, kids. What you say?"

Marcus's "No way" blended with Dawn's expletive.

"You cut nearly through the string," she went on, to Marcus's great surprise, "before Margo ever put the necklace on last night, didn't you? Figuring the string would break soon, while she was putting on or taking off her wraps for the party. Maybe you'd even have been able to give it a little tug, help it come loose."

"You're pretty sharp, sweetheart, you know that? How'd you figure it out?"

"By not being the *sweetheart* of a slimebag like you. Necklaces like that don't have clasps that come undone readily, and Margo's the last woman to have been careless in doing it up. So you had to be behind it. Reason you were so concerned over her ankle: gave you a chance to scoop up the necklace, made her keep one hand holding that towel in place while she ate lunch. Kept her fingers away from her neck, gave you a bit longer. You popped the necklace down the drain while you were getting the coffee, didn't you? You aren't the kind to do that kind of favor for people. Not unless there's something in it for you."

"A fair enough assessment," Eddie admitted. "Now what, kids?"

Marcus glanced at Dawn; she gave a curt nod. "Hand the necklace over, Eddie, and we'll give it to Margo. Then you can get going. The faster the better."

"How do I know you aren't going to keep the whole thing?"

"You don't. It's just a risk you'll have to take."

The sound of a window being opened came from above. "Eddie? Where are you?"

"Oh, hell." Eddie tossed the necklace, a spiral of fire, to Marcus and scrambled onto his feet. "See you, kids."

"Not if we can help it," Dawn retorted.

The roar of the BMW soon briefly filled the night.

"Eddie!" This call was more urgent.

"We'll have to tell her," Dawn said with a small sigh.

"Just a minute." Marcus had been hit with a horrible thought. "Suppose she thinks *we* stole the necklace?"

"Stealing it so we could return it?"

"Maybe . . . you stealing it, my covering for you."

There was a long silence. "You'd do that?" Dawn asked slowly.

"Yeah, I'd do that. And more."

"No problem. Eddie's left the marks of those very distinctive sandals of his in that patch of mud. And besides, he's gone."

Of course: no problem. Except . . . *"You* aren't going to go. Are you?" Marcus had moved close to her. "Jack won't care if you stay; you could have the guest room."

"How'd you figure out what had happened?"

Trust Dawn not to answer him directly. At least she hadn't moved away. "That patch of green stuff: figured it had to be fed from that old sink."

"That green stuff is called broom. It's not native to the island, supposed to have been brought by a homesick Scottish bride."

"Funny how you can be homesick when you haven't even got a home."

"Especially when you haven't got a home," Dawn agreed quietly.

"Maybe—" Marcus slipped an arm around her; still she didn't move away "—we could sort of encourage Paul and Dolly to get together. I think they really like each other. I mean, if we were staying here."

"It *would* be great to have an oven again." Dawn leaned her head against his shoulder, and Marcus's heart nearly leaped from his body. "I made that soufflé, you know that?"

"It was a great soufflé."

"Not bad." Their lips met.

"Eddie! *Where are you?*"

This time Margo's yell came not from the window but from the back door. She was answered only by an inquiring "Preow?" from Matilda.

Nice Gorilla

Charlotte and Aaron Elkins

Tousled and sleepy, each facing in a slightly different direction, they sat on the sleeping shelves like great black lumps. Their huge, heavy heads drooped, their bodies slumped, their mysterious coffee-bean eyes stared at nothing. Lost in gorilla-reflections, they scratched themselves occasionally, or emitted a digestive rumble, or poked a listless finger in nostril or ear while they waited for their breakfast.

Pretty much like people first thing in the morning, if you ask me. Of course, these days you're not supposed to go around reading human attributes into animals, especially if you work in a zoo. "That's anthropomorphism, Fay," Dr. Treble would reprimand me, and shake his head, and stroke his neat little spade beard, and murmur, "Tut-tut." Literally. Henry Treble, the Sacramento River Zoo's director and my boss, was surely the only person in the world who actually said, "Tut-tut."

But tut-tutting didn't make it any less so. Gorillas were like people in a lot of ways. They were creatures of habit, for one thing, and once you established a routine with them, they got annoyed with you if you varied it. And since Fay

Novak is nobody's fool, you may be sure I went out of my way not to vary it.

Thus the morning greeting: the comfortable, long-established ritual that helped get them out of bed on the right side. With the traditional breakfast foods ready on the table beside me, I slid open the long, narrow Plexiglas window between the concrete-walled room that was their sleeping den and the concrete-walled corridor that was my office.

"So how's it going this morning, gang? Ready for some food?" The same words, the same quiet tone that I used every morning.

Every morning, five days a week, for well over a decade. It had been fourteen years ago that I'd shown up at the zoo's personnel office, looking for some volunteer work to fill the time after Teddy, my youngest, started school, and my husband, Bill, and I finally called it quits after eight years of the marriage made in hell.

Something in the Friendly Farmhouse, I suggested to the personnel director, where those tiny lambs and goats were. Or maybe the nursery, where those cute little infant tigers and finger-sized baby monkeys in diapers drank milk from bottles. This was received with a dismissive laugh. There were two openings, I was succinctly told: snakes and gorillas. Which did I prefer?

As you can imagine, that took some mental readjustment, but I finally decided in favor of the gorillas. For two years I was a two- and three-day-a-week volunteer. Then, when the gorilla keeper retired, I surprised myself by applying for the job. And Dr. Treble utterly amazed me by appointing me. So, without a second's hesitation, I gave up my half-time job as a lab technician—the occupation I'd trained for so long and diligently—and, at the age of thirty-six, stepped nervously into a brand-new job I'd never given a moment's thought to until two years before.

It was the best move I ever made. Here I am, pushing fifty now, totally content with my life, and without a shred of ambition. I've never applied for a promotion and never will. I'm just praying they let me stay right here for fourteen more years.

Nice Gorilla

At my call this morning, the animals rotated their heads to look with placid affection in my direction. They were hungry, naturally, but there wasn't any rush for breakfast. Gorilla troops always have a set order of precedence, and in all the ones I've seen, that order is always the same: The big dominant male gets first crack at the food—or the females, the bedding material, and anything else that strikes his fancy. Then, assuming there's anything left (which there always is, in a zoo), the others get their turn.

A couple of weeks earlier, Kendra Pederson had pointedly informed me that it wasn't that way in the wild, at least not as far as food went. In the jungle the foraging was democratic and noncompetitive, with no sexual or rank-order dominance. Wouldn't it make sense, she had rather pushily proposed, if I implemented such a system here in the zoo? Wouldn't it be more in keeping with the cooperative ethic of the bioclimatic systems approach that was the hallmark of late-twentieth-century zoo philosophy?

It had been one of my testy mornings, I'm afraid. Sure, that'd be just wonderful, I told her. And did she happen to have any ideas on how I might go about getting a five-hundred-pound male sexist gorilla to change his ways?

Kendra had stared disdainfully back at me. That, she told me, was the sort of thing she was used to hearing from the men. She'd expected more from me. And yes, as a matter of fact, she did have some ideas. Maybe I'd like to try gingerly putting one foot into the twentieth century and hear them out?

And maybe, I'd snapped back at her, maybe everybody would be happier if she just stuck to her research and let me do my job, which I'd been doing for almost fifteen years without her help, thank you, and without any complaints from the gorillas either.

Well, I'm sorry, but the damned woman had been getting on my nerves. This year's University Exchange Fellow, she was a comparative psychologist from the University of Michigan, and she was here on a grant to study stress in primates. So for the last three months she'd been skulking around taking notes on the apes and monkeys, with unwelcome emphasis on my gorillas.

Early on, she'd spent two entire days following me around with that notebook of hers, asking ten million questions and mostly curling her lips in a superior smile when I answered. If I'd ever spent two lousier days, I couldn't remember when.

That wasn't the worst of it. Twice now (twice that I knew about) she'd waited until after hours, when I wasn't around, and entered the gorillas' outdoor enclosure on foot—we are talking major no-no here—to sit behind a hillock and make observations at close hand. To get in, she had climbed over the waist-high chain link fence that separated it from the public viewing area, then used a rope to lower herself into the fifteen-foot-deep dry moat and to clamber up the inside bank. I had complained loudly to my immediate supervisor, Monte Holland, the curator of mammals, and Monte had very properly come down hard on her. This had not noticeably increased Kendra's warm feelings toward me.

That I could live with. What worried me was that she'd do it again anyway. Kendra was the kind of person who—well, the heck with her. Here came Mkoko, lord and master of the troop, for his breakfast. He was getting old now, almost twenty-four. His back, glistening with virile, silvery hair only a year or two ago, was dull gray now, and the massive muscles of his chest and belly that had bulked so formidably when I'd first come to the zoo hung slack and folded. But even in his prime Mkoko had worn his mantle with restraint, taking his due but not bullying and harassing the others the way so many dominant males did. I refer to gorillas, of course.

In response to my call he had pushed himself up from the sleeping nest of timothy hay he'd made on the floor—he'd never taken to the sleeping shelves the others preferred—and approached the barred window, pushing himself powerfully along on the callused knuckles of his fingers. He sat peaceably down in front of the window, loosely wrapped his arms around himself, rocked gently on his haunches, and peered searchingly up into my eyes.

"How's it going, old-timer?" I said.

Mkoko's response was a purring grumble from the back of his throat. "Contentment growl," Kendra had pedantically informed me when she observed it last week, as if I hadn't figured it out for myself after all these years.

When I returned the growl, expertly vibrating the air on the back of my palate (you learn some funny things in this business), Mkoko lifted a shaggy arm to the window. I briefly stroked the tips of the strange, smooth black fingers as protocol demanded. Then I placed a peeled orange on the palm of the gigantic hand, first checking to see that Edwin had hidden the morning dose of crushed aspirin in it. The aging gorilla was having arthritic joint problems, and the aspirin seemed to help a little.

Mkoko unhurriedly tucked the orange in his lower lip for safekeeping and put his hand up again. This time two bananas went into it. Satisfied, he grunted again, clutched the bananas to his chest with his hand, and with his remaining three limbs propelled himself back to his place. Once there, he turned his wide back and settled into an absorbed contemplation of the orange.

I smiled at his back. No, I wasn't about to try to get the poor old guy to change his ways at this point in his life. As far as I knew, nobody'd bothered to tell Mkoko it was the twentieth century.

With minor variations, the routine was repeated with the others. Kamila, the placid old matriarch; Utu, their four-year-old son; and two-year-old Beni, still too young to contain her morning exuberance, who hopped and somer-saulted around the den, grinning and mugging, and even scaling a tolerant Mkoko.

Last to come to the window was a shy, black-backed nine-year-old male on permanent breeding loan from the Cincinnati Zoo, who had yet to be accepted wholeheartedly into the group. Fred (apparently they had a different ap-proach to gorilla-naming in Cincinnati) would one day take over from Mkoko as leader, but first he had some maturing to do. Right now the old silverback could still make mincemeat of him, by force of personality if nothing else.

Fred was hardly the demanding type, but his morning tastes were discriminating; not oranges, or bananas, or monkey chow, but baked potatoes—in the jacket, if you please. I made sure there were some every day.

Fred grunted his appreciation and went galumphing back to his isolated corner, and I turned my attention to the one remaining animal. Mbinda, a big, nine-year-old female, was also on breeding loan, but from San Diego. If everything worked out as planned, she and Fred would eventually get a productive romance going, but things weren't looking good. The first time he had approached her—with honorable intentions, I'm pretty sure—he had gotten walloped on the ear. He'd run hooting to the far side of the enclosure, and he hadn't come within ten feet of her since. That had been two months ago, and I still wasn't sure how they were going to work things out. Or if.

But that wasn't what was worrying me now. Mbinda, who normally had a good appetite, hadn't come for her greeting and her bananas. She had propped herself sluggishly against a corner, torpid and apathetic. Her eyes were half-closed, cloudy.

"Hey, there, Mbinda, what's the matter, girl?" I called softly. "Look what I have for you." I waved a couple of bananas. Mbinda didn't even glance at me. She just waved a hand phlegmatically, as if batting backhanded at a fly, and went on with her vacant staring.

Concerned, I watched her for a while. Was she sick? More likely she was exhausted, and if so, it was her own damned fault. Always the most excitable of the troop, she had come unstrung at the commotion from the neighboring building the evening before. There, in what had once been the feline house, the elephants were being put up while the floor of their own quarters was repaired. Elephants being elephants, they were reacting with noisy displays of apprehension and unease. And Mbinda being Mbinda, she had fretted at all the stamping and trumpeting, and when the time had come for the gorillas to come indoors for the night, she'd gibbered petulantly and refused to go along.

Reluctantly I had allowed her to stay out all night. Not

that anyone "allows" gorillas to do anything. It's quite true that they are among the least aggressive creatures in the zoo, but they are also among the most powerful, and they don't seem to know their own strength. When they make up their minds to do something, nobody argues with them. Especially not the temperamental, self-willed ones like Mbinda.

It wasn't the first time it had happened, but before this she'd been as energetic as ever when she'd been let in the next morning for breakfast. Not now, however. I watched her with growing worry and irritation. Once more I tried with the bananas, then slid the window closed and walked the few steps down the corridor to the minuscule kitchen area where Edwin, having earlier gotten the gorilla's food ready, was brewing a pot of coffee and breaking out some doughnuts for human consumption.

"Edwin, Mbinda's not right. How'd she seem to you when you let her in?"

Edwin Pitkin was my Wednesday-Friday morning volunteer, a soft-spoken man of sixty who owned a small picture-framing business.

"Well, I'd say she was troubled," he said thoughtfully. "Brooding. Apprehensive. Distracted."

Edwin, need I mention, anthropomorphizes all over the place.

"Was she waiting for you?" I asked. "Did she want to come in?"

"Oh, yes. She practically fell in when I opened the door. I think she was sleeping against it. I'm afraid she didn't get much rest out there last night."

"Probably not," I said. "All the same, I think I'll give the clinic a buzz and have her listed on the morning rounds. Oh, hell, I'd rather wait till Sunday, when Maggie's not on duty, but I guess I better do it today."

Edwin was noncommittal on this. He poured us both mugs of coffee. "You know, it's not my place to say it, Fay, but Mbinda's problem is that she gets her own way much too easily. You really ought to make her mind, even when she doesn't want to."

Right, Edwin, good idea, I'll do that. "Mm," I said. "Coffee's good."

While Edwin left with a shovel to muck out the outdoor enclosure before letting out the gorillas, I called the vet's office. Standing at the wall telephone, I could see Mbinda through the window. She was slowly pursing and unpursing her lips, like a fish blowing bubbles, but otherwise she hadn't moved. I didn't like it a bit.

After I made the call, I sat down at the desk and began putting some notes about her in the daily keeper's report. Edwin, who was wearing his utterly noiseless cushion-soled shoes, came back in without my seeing him and touched my arm, making me jump.

"Whew! Edwin, I wish—"

When I saw his face I stopped. "What is it?"

"Something terrible's happened," he said in a strange, croaky voice. He was still holding the dung-smeared shovel. His face, which usually looked a smooth-skinned ten years younger, looked ten years older, drawn and ill.

"Outside?" I said. I could feel the hairs on the back of my neck stirring.

"Yes. It's . . . I think maybe you'd better . . ."

In a flash I was out of my chair, through the employee's door, and standing in the outdoor enclosure. It was deserted, of course, with the animals still inside, and at first I could see nothing the matter. The morning air was fragrant and cool, the grassy mounds and bare trees the gorillas spent their days among looked well-kept and inviting, the stream —wait, there was something wrong near the big dead climbing-tree in the center of the enclosure, where Mbinda had probably spent most of the night. It looked as if a bundle of old laundry had been dumped behind it, but a second glance told me that it hadn't. Bundles of laundry don't generally have feet, and this one had two of them; one in a sock and one wearing a Velcro-fastened sneaker that I thought I recognized.

Gingerly, keeping my distance, I started circling the tree. I could feel my breakfast, consumed two hours ago, change direction and start working its way up again. The body was all . . . funny; shapeless and awry, as if the limbs had been smashed. There were brown stains on the clothing.

I fully understood poor Edwin's condition now. I was damp with perspiration myself, and feeling sick, but I made myself look at the swollen, distorted face.

Then I shut my eyes and turned my face away.

Kendra Pederson would not be making any more unauthorized visits to the gorilla habitat.

"Has anyone *else*—" the way Lieutenant Weiss said *else* jerked me out of my daze; he was obviously repeating the question, and he was directing it at me "—been in the area this morning?"

"No. Just Edwin and me."

"You didn't touch her, did you?"

The thought alone was enough to make me shudder. "God, no. Would *you?*" The answer was so stupid, it made me start to laugh, which made my throat close up, which made me choke. In desperation I buried my face in the mug of hot, sweet tea that somebody, bless whoever it was, had made for me.

He regarded me with much the same expression he'd had on his face for most of the last hour. Lieutenant Weiss was about forty-five (when did detective lieutenants start getting younger than me?), and he was more like my old high school principal than my idea of a homicide detective. No chewed-on cigar, no world-weary, wise-guy manner. He had a receding hairline, a puddingy jawline, and an exasperated, now-I've-seen-everything manner, not that I could blame him for that. I kept expecting him to throw up his hands and say it out loud: "Now I've seen everything!" But he never did. Not so far, anyway. He just shook his head and wrote things down in his notebook.

There were five of us in the conference room of the Administration Building, sitting around the table: the lieutenant; me; Dr. Treble; Maggie Rice, our vet; and my supervisor, Monte Holland, curator of mammals.

Dr. Treble was not taking it well, but then, crises had never been his thing. If you want the truth, he had never been much of a director, and a lot of people, including some of the zoo trustees, were saying that it was past time for him to be replaced with somebody younger and more aggressive. I think the problem with him was that, even now, twenty years after assuming the directorship, he was first and foremost a scientist, and an old-fashioned one at that. He kept a very low profile when it came to the controversies that had to be faced in today's zoo world, preferring to bury his head in the technical details that should have been left to curators and keepers. The prevailing view of the staff, myself included, was that he was a nice enough old guy, but he was never there when you needed him, and always in your hair when you didn't.

"May I ask something, lieutenant?" he said. Until now he'd spoken hardly at all.

Weiss nodded. "Sure."

"Will you tell me why in the world this inquiry is being conducted by the Sacramento Police Department? Are you going to arrest Mbinda? Are you going to put her on trial? Tell me, is she entitled to an attorney at public expense? Are you going to grill her?"

Dr. Treble wasn't usually so caustic, but he could get a wee bit prickly when he was upset.

The lieutenant failed to appreciate the sarcasm. His mouth tightened. "Who would you suggest?"

"Well . . . well, of course, that's not really, not really my . . ." He brought out a folded handkerchief to dab at his beard, and his voice subsided into unintelligible mumbles. Sad to say, it was pretty typical behavior for him when he was challenged.

Weiss looked a little embarrassed by Dr. Treble's collapse. "Look, sir," he said more gently, "somebody's died pretty horribly out there. As of now, I don't see much doubt that this gorilla, Bindo—"

I brought my face up from the mug. "Mbinda," I said. If he was going to call her a murderer, at least he could get her name right.

"—this gorilla, Mbinda, killed Dr. Pederson. But when something as weird as this happens, we have an obligation to satisfy ourselves that there *hasn't* been a homicide—that is, that she hasn't been murdered by another person. That's what the crime scene crew is doing out there now. That's what I'm doing in here with you. The minute it's established, believe me, we'll be happy to bow out."

"Well, all the same," Dr. Treble muttered, unmollified. "I mean, really."

Monte Holland looked up from lighting his pipe. "What you say is only reasonable, Lieutenant," he said equably, his sturdy, sensible face wreathed in fragrant smoke. "How can we help you?"

This was Monte at his best. Commonsensical, logical, conciliatory, soothing. Also tranquilizing. He was, in fact, the dullest man I'd ever met. When he started talking, my eyes started glazing. It was rumored that he was about to be offered a prestigious research position with the Smithsonian, something I looked greatly forward to. Not out of personal animosity, you understand. But I kept dozing off in the middle of his weekly staff meetings. And since I have a tendency to make unbecoming sounds when my head tips over backward, it can get embarrassing.

"What you can do is answer a few more questions," the lieutenant said, addressing all of us. "I'll tell you the truth, I'm a little mixed up on gorillas. It used to be, they were the most ferocious animals in the jungle; if you went near them, you'd get torn apart. Now, everything I read, it says they're shy and lovable and good-natured. Well, which is it? Is Mbinda capable of doing something like this or isn't she?"

I sympathized with his confusion. In the old days, Frank Buck, Lowell Thomas, and a whole generation of adventure-writers made wild animals out to be a lot more ferocious than they really were. It made good copy. Nowadays, it's the other way around. Wildlife-writers tell us that sharks are misunderstood denizens of the deep, nowhere near as vicious as they're made out to be. Wolves are caring, loving creatures who don't bother you if you don't bother them, and are monogamous to boot. And gorillas are the gentle giants of the forest.

Well, that's all true enough, but just the same, you'll

notice that nobody goes down into the water to study sharks except from inside a steel cage that looks as if it could withstand a Cruise missile attack, and nobody's yet made close friends with a loving, caring pack of wolves . . . and nobody in his right mind walks into a gorilla enclosure with gorillas in it.

"Let me put it this way, Lieutenant," Monte said slowly. "The gorilla is the most robust and massive of all primates, and possessed of extraordinary strength. And there have certainly been attacks on humans by gorillas, although I don't personally know of any other documented cases that have resulted in death. On the other hand—"

Monte's speech tended to have a lot of *on the other hands*.

"—every reputable behavioral scientist who's studied them will tell you they're among the least assertive of all primates, and in a confrontation they'll generally retreat if given a chance. So the question isn't whether she's capable of it or not, because she certainly is, but whether she *did* it or not."

"Uh-huh," Weiss said. Was that a slight glaze on his eyeballs? "Well, tell me this: Would you say what happened to Dr. Pederson—the broken bones, the heavy bruising—is typical of a gorilla attack?"

Monte puffed thoughtfully on his pipe. "Actually, no. Gorillas do more bluffing than anything else. The few recorded attacks on humans have involved biting, or perhaps a swipe of the arm, maybe two swipes. No more than that—not that a mature gorilla's swipe couldn't tear a person's head off. But no, not this kind of brutal assault."

On the other hand, I thought. I sat up straighter, before I started dozing.

Monte also rearranged himself in his chair. "Now, on the other hand, all the great apes have frequently been seen to toy extensively with objects, to manipulate them, take them apart, throw them, and so on and so forth. Mbinda may have engaged in such exploratory behavior after she k— after Dr. Pederson's death. That could easily enough account for the, er, damage. Wouldn't you say so, Fay?"

Oops, almost caught me, but fortunately I was still more or less alert. "Well, yes," I said, "I'd agree with that."

With what? Had I just accused Mbinda or defended her?

Unsurprisingly, Lieutenant Weiss looked less than edified. He turned to Maggie Rice, our zoo veterinarian. "Any comment, Doctor?"

Maggie, sharp-faced and fretful, had been with the zoo for six or seven years, and at first she'd been a terrific zoo doc, with a tremendous rapport with the animals. Then, last year, while she was trying to examine an injured snow leopard that hadn't been properly restrained, she'd been badly mauled on the neck and shoulder. She'd had to go through months of therapy to get her left arm functioning again, but it still wasn't—and never would be—a hundred percent of what it was before.

When she came back to work, her attitude toward the animals had changed; she was afraid of them. Most animals are pretty good at picking up signs of nervousness, and it makes *them* nervous, and that is not good for the patient-doctor relationship that is so critical for veterinary work. I know that the gorillas had become uneasy around her, and now, if something was the matter with them, I preferred to wait for her days off if I could, when the substitute vet was on duty. But that wasn't always possible.

"What you have to keep in mind," she said, "is that we're talking about a wild animal here, an exotic, and the fact that it's been raised in a zoo doesn't change that. Its genes are still wild-animal genes, and no matter how kindly it's been treated, or how conditioned it's been to having human beings around, all of its instinctive aggressive and defensive behaviors are still there. No exotic animal can ever be considered wholly reliable," she said stiffly, and I knew she was remembering that leopard. "When it feels threatened or insecure, all bets are off."

"So you think she might have done this," Weiss said.

Maggie had never been a mincer of words. "Yes. I don't see that there's any other conclusion."

Lieutenant Weiss looked inquiringly at the rest of us.

"Uh, yes, I would have to concur with that," Monte said. Dr. Treble nodded too.

The lieutenant looked at me. "Mrs. Novak? You agree? You know Mbinda best. You've been closest to her."

That's right, I thought, rub it in. This was like asking a mother if she thought her baby boy, the apple of her eye, could really be the ax murderer who'd just chopped up forty-two people. Well, not quite, because I didn't confuse my charges with my children. I loved those animals, I worried about them, and sometimes I got fed up with them. But I knew they were gorillas, not people, and what Maggie had said was correct, even if she was speaking with a personal ax to grind. They weren't wholly reliable. They weren't answerable for their actions.

And of them all, Mbinda was the most uneven, the quickest to annoyance. Yes, I thought, if Kendra had barged in on Mbinda's space when she was already upset by the elephants and probably uneasy about being outside all by herself, if Kendra had accidentally frightened or flustered her, then, yes, Mbinda might have become enraged and attacked her. Anyway, what else was there to think?

"Yes," I said, barely getting it out. Notwithstanding all of the above, I felt like an utter louse. I was resentful and aggrieved too. Who knows, maybe I felt responsible, as if I should have brought Mbinda up better.

Mostly, uncharitable as I knew it was, I was angry at Kendra. If not for her staggering irresponsibility, Mbinda wouldn't be facing certain euthanasia, the zoo wouldn't be about to take a terrific battering in the media—and Kendra herself would still be alive. She had been scheduled to meet with Monte at 6:30 P.M. yesterday, an hour and a half after the zoo closed, to discuss her stress-research progress with him. But he'd told us that when she hadn't shown up by 6:45, he'd given up on her and left for home.

Now, it looked as if she was already dead by then. The rope—the same one she'd used before to get across the moat—still hung there, looped around a stump and a rock. According to the coroner, she'd been killed by heavy blows to the skull within two hours either way of 5:00 P.M. So she'd probably climbed into the enclosure a little after the five-o'clock closing time, expecting to be out by 6:30. Only it hadn't worked out that way. As far as I knew, she was still lying at the base of the tree.

Lieutenant Weiss snapped his notebook closed. "Let's go have a look at her," he said. "I may have some questions. I'd appreciate all of you coming."

A panicky knot tightened in my chest. "Lieutenant, I'm sorry, I just . . . I don't think I could . . ."

He surprised me by laying a gentle hand on my arm. "Hey. I'm talking about Mbinda," he said. "Okay?"

"Oh. Yes, sure. Sorry, I thought—"

"I know."

We walked the short distance without saying much. The zoo was open, but it was before noon on a weekday, so there weren't many people. The walkway that led to the viewing area at the outdoor gorilla enclosure was blocked with yellow tape. I could see a van and a police car near it, but I kept my eyes averted, even though I knew I couldn't see the spot where Kendra was from here.

Monte walked glumly beside me. "What a week," he muttered around his pipe. "Oh, my Lord."

His difficulties had begun on Monday when Kicker, one of our mandrills—those are the queer-looking baboons with the bright blue and red noses—had died, apparently from stress connected with its appearance the day before on "Animal World," a live television show that Monte hosted. Once upon a time, there had been many such shows, but they had faded out as people began to realize how much stress was put on the animals through disrupting their routines and carting them around to unfamiliar places with strange sounds and activities. Monte's program was one of the last holdouts.

As unlikely a TV personality as he might seem to be, he was actually pretty good in front of the cameras, and quite remarkable when it came to working with the animals; famous for it, in fact. Possibly it was that calm, reassuring, sleep-inducing voice, or maybe his own highly evident lack of fear, but whatever it was, he was successful at displaying animals that you didn't usually see under the lights in a television studio. Mandrills, for instance, who are probably my least favorite primates. They have ugly tempers, nasty canines, and a number of mannerisms not highly valued in polite society.

But with Monte in charge, this one had been decorous and cooperative. The show had gone well, but the next day the baboon had abruptly dropped dead. Unfortunately, it was the second time in a year it had happened, a young howler monkey having died after a show earlier in the year. With Kicker's death, Monte had immediately announced cancellation of the program, but he had been taking some flak over the affair since then.

The entrance to the work section of the gorilla area was at the end of a narrow, bleak concrete courtyard. Just inside the threshold was a shallow pan of liquid. Lieutenant Weiss started to step over it.

"Walk through it, please," I said. "It's disinfectant. To protect the gorillas."

He looked down at his shoes, then doubtfully at me. "They're clean."

I pointed at the pan. "Feet," I said. I was on my turf now.

After a moment's hesitation, he sloshed through it, and the rest of us followed suit. I closed the door behind us.

"Have you had a TB test in the last year?" I asked him. "What? No."

I went to a cardboard box on my desk and got out a surgical mask. "Then wear this, please. For the gorillas' protection."

"Don't worry about it, I'm not getting close enough to breathe on them."

Sternly I held out the mask. It was good to feel as if I was at least a little in control again.

He sighed and began to put it on, then looked suspiciously at the rest of us. "How come only me?"

"Everyone else has been tested," I told him.

He grumbled something, but tied it docilely behind his ears, and we all went to the Plexiglas window to look at the gorillas. I pulled up the blind I'd lowered to keep them from getting excited by the police who'd been using this area as their base all morning. The gorillas were calm, but growing a little restless now. They wouldn't be permitted outside, of course, until the crime scene work was finished.

"Which one's Mbinda?" Weiss asked.

I pointed. It had been four hours since I'd first seen her in the morning, and she looked better now, no worse than the others: lethargic, a little bored, a little at loose ends. With Mkoko dozing in a far corner, she had taken over his mound of hay and was sitting in it, examining her feet and yawning. She'd had no breakfast, I remembered, so she had to be hungry. She'd never have another breakfast, I thought abruptly. It was hard to sort out just what I was feeling. Not good, that was for sure.

"Fay," Maggie said in my ear, "I'll take care of . . . you know, arranging for . . . you know . . ."

"Putting her down," I made myself say. "Thanks, Maggie."

"It's funny," she said musingly, eyes on Mbinda, "the lab was just doing an analysis for Kendra, and now they'll be doing one on Mbinda tomorrow—on account of Kendra, so to speak. After the autopsy."

Autopsy. It seemed decidedly unfeeling to talk about Mbinda's autopsy with her sitting there in front of us, playing with her toes.

The lieutenant was speaking. "Does she—"

Mbinda must have heard his voice through the partially opened barred window. She lifted her head and looked at us without much interest, almost as if she were seeing through us. Then her eyes widened and jumped into sharp focus.

And all hell broke loose.

A gorilla's distress scream—I mean one in which the animal puts everything it has into it—is one of the most explosive sounds in nature. Fantastically loud and piercing, it starts without any buildup at all, right up at about 110 decibels. It paralyzes even those, like me, who have heard it many times, and for those not familiar with it, the instinct is for immediate flight. Lieutenant Weiss blanched and fell back a foot; the rest of us only an inch or two.

Mbinda jumped to her feet, then quickly dropped, cowering, to her haunches and kept on screeching, still staring wildly at us, her lips curled back over her teeth. The echoes bounced deafeningly off the concrete walls. The rest of the gorillas looked as startled as we were for a second, and then they started in too, Mkoko with a series of low, nervous hoots, and old Kamila, usually so tranquil, with a howl and a heavy, sidewise, bipedal dash across the floor, during which she blindsided poor, gentle Fred, who gave a panicky yelp and started hopping in circles himself, patting the top of his head, tossing hay, and chattering. The babies, Utu and Beni, got into it too, but over the rest of the din, we couldn't hear their squeals.

"This is my fault!" Maggie shouted. "I'm the one who's upsetting her. Remember, I had to knock her down with a tranquilizer dart in August, and seeing me has shaken her up all over again." Maggie looked pretty shaken up herself. "I'll get out of here and she'll quiet down."

She left hurriedly, and we waited for the riot to subside, but nothing changed. Mbinda was still cowering and screaming, and the others were taking their lead from her.

The lieutenant said something to me, but I couldn't hear a word. I slid shut the thick window, which helped, although we could still hear the yipping and hooting.

"Why is she doing that?" he asked. I could tell that his teeth were on edge from the noise. So were mine.

"I don't know," I said. "I mean, obviously we've upset her, but—"

I looked helplessly around for a clue, and my eye fell on a green-covered notepad that was standing up in one of the cubbyholes above my desk. "That's Kendra's!" I said. "Her field observation notebook. Mbinda must be associating it with her, and that's what's set her off—"

"That could very well be," Monte said. "Let's find out." He went to the cubbyhole, took out the notebook, and carried it a few steps to the side, out of the animals' sight. At once things began to return to normal. Mbinda's screams faded to a rhythmic *hoo-hoo-hoo*, and then, after a few seconds, to nothing. The others slowly settled down too.

"Jesus Christ," the lieutenant said, letting out his breath. "That's amazing. I never knew a gorilla had a memory like that."

"Oh, yes," I said. "They remember faces, objects—"

"Interestingly enough," interrupted Dr. Treble, who once again hadn't said anything for a while, "they seem to have a particularly good memory for unpleasant experiences. They can recognize a veterinarian who's shot them with a tranquilizer dart—something gorillas greatly dislike—months after the event, even if he reappears in street clothes, or with a hat on, or in sunglasses, say. Even through a window, so it's not the sense of smell, you see. Sometimes, if he's seriously hurt or startled them, they won't ever let him near them again. That's what Dr. Rice thought was occurring, I imagine."

"But it wasn't," the lieutenant said. "Occurring."

"No," Monte said slowly, looking at the notepad. "It was this she was reacting to. What happened out there last night—this must have brought it back." He closed the pad and shook his head. "Poor Kendra. Poor Mbinda. Lieutenant, may I leave now? I have a meeting I ought to attend, and I don't really think I have anything else to contribute."

"Nor do I," Dr. Treble said.

Weiss nodded. "Go ahead. And thanks for the help, both of you. I think what happened is pretty clear. I'll write up my report and get out of your hair."

They left together. I wished I could have asked to leave too, but I worked there.

The lieutenant sank into the old chair at my desk. "Guess you'll have to put Mbinda to sleep," he said.

"Yes."

"I'm sorry about that. You must get to like them."

"It's not your fault," I said shortly.

He shivered. "Cold in here. And damp. From all that concrete." He looked around. "Concrete, bars, Plexiglas." He patted the battered desk. "Crappy furniture. I feel like I'm in a jail."

I laughed for the first time that day. "That's life here in the zoo. The animals get to spend all day playing in the fresh air, and the keepers wind up behind bars. It used to be the other way around. How about some coffee?"

"Thanks. If there's fresh."

"It'll just take a minute. I could use some myself." I walked the few steps to the "kitchen" and started spooning coffee into the automatic's filter.

"Hey, wait a minute," the lieutenant called. "If that pad was where Dr. Pederson took notes, how come she didn't have it with her when she went into the enclosure last night?"

"Well, she left it behind yesterday afternoon, about three. It's not the first time. When she came back, after closing, the work area would have been locked and there wouldn't have been any way for her to get it."

"Oh. Hey, how did Mbinda react to it this morning when she saw it? Same way as just now?"

"She didn't. Never looked in my direction, just sat there like a slug."

"Oh."

I pushed the *brew* button on the coffee maker and came back to the desk, frowning. The lieutenant's questions had started me on a bizarre train of thought. Could it possibly be that . . .

"You know, I'd like to have another look at that thing," I said, rummaging in the mess on the desk. "Where'd it go?"

"The pad? I think Holland took it."

"He did? Damn. Maybe I can reach him before he goes to his meeting."

He hunched his shoulders. It was fine with him.

"And, Lieutenant—don't write up your report for a few minutes."

That made his eyebrows go up, but before he could answer, one of his detectives appeared at the door to report on the crime scene results.

Lieutenant Weiss pointed to the pan. "Wipe your feet in that, Pete. And put on one of those masks. For the gorillas' protection," he added firmly when the younger man made a face.

As they sat down to confer, I poured coffee for all of us, and went to the wall telephone to call Monte.

He was still in his office. Yes, he'd walked off with the pad, all right, and yes, he would drop it by on the way to his meeting.

I looked in my Rolodex for the number of our pathology lab, dialed, and asked to speak to my contact there.

"Bonnie, I understand you were doing some work for Kendra Pederson."

"Yes, she wanted some blood work on Kicker, the mandrill that died."

"Like what kind of blood work?"

"Just a minute."

I sipped my coffee without tasting it. My heart had kicked up a few beats, and it wasn't from the caffeine. I was on to something, I was sure of it now.

Bonnie got back on the line and began reciting a list of tests. One of them was the one I was waiting for.

"Chlordiazepoxide?" I repeated, hardly believing it. What level?"

"Um, let's see . . . wow, five milligrams per hundred milliliters."

"Thank *you!*" I said excitedly, and banged the receiver into its cradle.

Both men were watching me curiously. The lieutenant's mask was lifted so he could drink the coffee. "What's up?"

I leaned against the concrete block wall, arms folded, forcing myself to speak calmly. "We had a mandrill die this week after a TV show, presumably from stress. I just found out Kendra had the lab do some work on it."

He looked understandably befuddled. "And?"

"Five milligrams of chlordiazepoxide per one hundred milliliters of blood."

"Oh," he said. "Really?"

"Chlordiazepoxide is a benzodiazepine, Lieutenant."

"No! Think of that, Pete." He was getting that exasperated look again.

"A *tranquilizer,* Lieutenant."

123

I thought he'd understand then, but of course, he didn't know what I knew. I leaned earnestly on the desk. "Listen—"

Monte stuck his head in the open door and waved Kendra's notepad. "Here you go, Fay. Let me have it back when you're done. It should go with her papers."

I took the pad. "You bet. Monte, can you stick around a minute? I want to try something."

He scowled. "Well . . ."

"Just five minutes."

"All right, five minutes."

All three of them were looking quizzically at me. They could feel my excitement. No wonder; I was so nervous, I was hyperventilating.

I made myself take a deeper if not calmer breath, and walked to the window, the pad down low by my side, where the gorillas couldn't see it. I slid the window all the way open.

"Mbinda," I called softly.

She turned to look at me.

Slowly I raised the notebook to where she could see it. Lieutenant Weiss flinched before the coming pandemonium.

But there wasn't a sound. Nothing happened. Mbinda regarded me gravely, waiting to see if I was going to do anything interesting, such as offer her a snack. When I didn't, she went back to what she'd been engaged in before, which was the delicate exploration of her left nostril.

I heaved a ragged sigh and turned to the three men, shaky with relief. "There," I said huskily.

"There where?" the lieutenant shot back with irritation. "I don't get it." He looked at Monte. "Is that the same pad or isn't it?"

Monte blinked. "Well . . . of course."

"But half an hour ago you were telling me the sight of it drove her up the wall. Now she couldn't care less. What the hell is going on?"

Monte spread his hands. "I'm as confused as you are."

The lieutenant turned to me, just a little tartly. "This seems to be your show, Mrs. Novak. You want to tell us?"

"The notebook never upset Mbinda," I said.

They stared at me. Monte started to say something, but Lieutenant Weiss cut him off. "Now, look," he growled at me. "I was there. Here's the way it went: A: Gorilla is quiet. B: Gorilla sees notepad. C: Gorilla goes bonkers. D: Notepad gets removed. E: Gorilla is quiet."

"Not quite," I said. I was surprised to find myself beginning to enjoy this. "Taking away the pad didn't quiet Mbinda down."

"Lady, I was standing right there. The minute Dr. Holland here took that pad away from the window—" He stared at Monte, then back at me. "Are you saying—"

"That's right," I said. "Mbinda didn't calm down because she couldn't see the pad anymore, she calmed down because she couldn't see *him*—" I turned and spoke to Monte, thinking I owed that much to him. "Because she couldn't see *you* anymore. The pad never upset her in the first place. Just you."

Monte swallowed and tried to laugh, and I knew I was right. "Why in the world would she be upset with me? *I've* never tranquilized her."

That, I thought, was pretty bold, considering. "Yes, you have, Monte," I said quietly. "You shot her with a dart gun last night, after closing. That's what was wrong with her this morning. She was full of tranquilizer. I'm going to have her blood tested to make sure." I paused. "Chlordiazepoxide would be my guess."

That hit home. His eyelids fluttered. "And why would I do that?"

"Because that was the only way you could get away with putting Kendra's body in the enclosure with her. You killed Kendra, Monte."

"And why would I do *that?*"

"Because she really did show up for that 6:30 meeting with you, Monte, and she told you—" I was well out beyond what I knew for sure here, but I figured I might as well go all the way "—she told you that, as part of her stress research, she'd ordered a blood test on Kicker, and she found out that he'd been heavily tranquilized—that *you* tranquilized him, and it was probably what killed him. And probably what killed that howler a few months back. You tranquilized them all, didn't you? That was your secret, wasn't it? The reason all those animals were so docile with you. The reason you were always so fearless."

He managed a pallid smile for the lieutenant, but spoke to me. "I deny that emphatically and categorically. But for the sake of argument, let's just say it's true. Are you seriously suggesting I would murder someone over a thing like that?"

"A thing like that," I said, also for Lieutenant Weiss's benefit, "would destroy your career if it got out. There's no way the Smithsonian or any reputable zoo would want anything to do with you. So you had to—"

"This is patently absurd," he said sharply. "Lieutenant, are you going to stand here and—"

"It's easy enough to see if I'm right."

Monte's eyes swung back toward me. The pupils seemed very small.

"Just ask Mbinda," I said.

"Ask Mbinda!" he shouted. "Lieutenant, the woman is—"

"Go stand in front of the window," I said. "Let her see you. Without the notepad. See what she does."

"Ridiculous. I'm not about—"

Lieutenant Weiss cut in. "You refuse to do it?"

"Of course I refuse to do it. You have no conceivable right to—"

"Read him his rights, Pete."

After the detective had taken Monte off, Lieutenant Weiss poured both of us fresh mugs of coffee, and sat down at the tiny kitchen table with me.

He lifted his cup to me in a toast. "Not half bad, Mrs. Novak," he said with a slow grin of approval. "I swear, now I've seen everything."

I found myself giggling, not something I often do. "I was

scared to death," I said, and waited for the fit to pass. When it did, I swallowed some coffee. "Look, Lieutenant, you realize I have no way of proving half of what I said. Is this going to stand up in court?"

"It depends. Will Mbinda back us up? Will she have another fit if we show him to her?"

"I think so, but do it in the next few weeks. Do you mean you *can* force him to let her see him?"

"I don't see why not. We can set it up like a regular lineup. Bring in a few guys that look roughly like him, and see which one makes her go bananas." He laughed, an unexpectedly jolly sound. "A murderer being fingered by a gorilla. It's a first, I'll tell you that."

The mention of bananas woke me up. I hopped out of my chair and went to the cooler. "My gosh, what am I thinking of? She hasn't had anything to eat all day."

I got together a bowl of her favorite treats—peanuts, tomatoes, oranges, bananas—and took it to the window. This time getting her attention was easy. She came eagerly up to me. It was wonderful to see her looking herself again.

"Mbinda," I said, "I owe you an apology."

I put a few peanuts in her upraised palm and she started in on them at once.

The lieutenant was watching beside me. "You feed these things by *hand?*"

"Sure," I said. "Gentle giants, remember?"

I gave him a banana and an orange to give to her, and showed him how to stroke her fingers.

He did it gingerly, but when she started that relaxed, growling purr, he laughed again, delighted, and patted her fingertips.

"Nice gorilla," he said.

Take Care of Yourself

Janet LaPierre

Matt Riordan—born Mike Riley—sat at the end of the second row, where the graceful slouch of his long body and the attentive expression on his face would be visible to the woman behind the table.

Sabrina Shaw was finishing a cross-country book tour with three weekend appearances here in San Francisco, where she lived. On Friday evening, in one of the city's biggest bookstores where she played to a crowd, he'd stayed well back, to get a good look at her without himself being seen. Saturday afternoon, in a store only slightly smaller, he sat in the last row but fully upright, towering over most of his neighbors; unless she was one of those speakers who don't really look at their audiences, she must have seen him. And tonight, in this small but elegant neighborhood bookshop, he'd caught her glance twice. Good planning yields good results.

Not to get cocky now, Mikey, warned his inner voice. Intelligence as well as talent spoke from the novels of romantic suspense that were earning Sabrina Shaw fame and million-dollar advances; and intelligence was evident in her presentation of herself and her work.

So okay, she was smart. The shocker was the fact that she

was nearly as good-looking as the photo on her dust jacket, beautiful almost, with pale hair knotted softly back from a broad brow and elegant cheekbones. He read strong character in that face; the firm jawline reminded him of . . . of Edith, that's who. When on the prowl, Matt invariably found his lust quickened by small, dark women with heavy-lidded eyes and soft curls and soft, round bodies. But come time to get serious and he found himself seeking some stern Anglo-Saxon princess like this one. Maybe it indicated a formerly unsuspected strength of character on *his* part.

Sabrina had reached the last ten minutes of her talk, explaining why and how she had set her most recent novel in Seville. Discussion would follow, and then signing. In Matt's opinion, Sabrina was a pretentious name even for a writer; probably she'd chosen it early in reaction to the plainness of her real name, Martha. Martha Shaw, originally from somewhere in southern California, now Sabrina Shaw of San Francisco. Matt suspected she had another place as well, a hideaway out of the city; he hadn't located that yet, but if it existed, he would.

The talk came to its end, and he kept his posture easy and his expression calm while fidgeting inwardly through the questions. Finally Sabrina asked for one more, answered it briefly, and thanked her audience, who applauded and then began to line up with books in hand. Matt took a place near the end of the line; when his turn finally came, he handed her not only the just-purchased Seville book but a well-worn copy of *Liaison In Lisbon*.

Her professional smile took on a personal warmth as she saw this five-year-old volume, and she really looked at him as she asked his name for the inscription. "Bless you, an *early* reader. I'm very fond of this book in spite of the dreadful title. Didn't I see you last night?" she asked as she began to write.

"I had an appointment and couldn't stay to the end," he told her. "But I was interested in what you had to say; I've written a couple of thrillers myself."

Her face froze and he chuckled. "Oh no, I'm not looking for free advice. They were actually published, by this little paperback house. The poor editor who bought them, I think they took her out back later and shot her."

She laughed aloud at this, then finished her signature and handed him his books. "If you're not in a hurry, there's some fairly decent wine over there; the store owner is a friend."

A dozen people had gathered around the refreshments table. Matt chatted easily with other fans, raised his glass to the author when she joined them, and made space for her beside him. Finally the group began to disperse; Matt was gearing himself up to suggest a drink in the bar of the small hotel across the street when the bookshop's owner returned from answering the telephone and drew Sabrina aside.

". . . eleven o'clock to Seattle," said Sabrina, and Matt, attentive gaze fixed on the gray-haired woman who was speaking to him, tipped his head slightly and directed his very acute hearing across the room. Mumble mumble something, from the owner, and then ". . . pick you up in fifteen minutes."

Shit. He'd thought she was finishing her book tour tonight and would stay in the city for a while. And now he'd made contact, he couldn't afford to let go. As Sabrina returned to the dwindling group, Matt looked at his watch and sighed. "Damn, time got away from me again. Miss Shaw . . ."

"Sabrina, please."

"Sabrina, I really wanted to talk to you about Portugal; it's one of my favorite places. But I'd better hustle up a cab or I won't make the late shuttle to L.A. Look, please take my card; then if you feel like it sometime, you can call me and we'll meet for a drink." After a moment's hesitation, she took the card, then took Matt's extended hand and smiled up at him.

"Actually, I'm flying tonight, too, to Seattle," she told him. "An enormous limousine, compliments of my publisher, is collecting my luggage now and should be here in fifteen minutes. I'd be happy to give you a lift to the airport."

So you've come to this, picking up men at your own signings. Stretched out in her corner of the plushy limousine seat, Sabrina couldn't decide whether she was irritated with herself or just amused. She had noticed this Matt Riordan yesterday, of course she had: a head taller than anyone else, pale blue eyes narrowed attentively in that lean, dark face. There, she'd thought at once, the face of her next hero, have to be American this time because the face so clearly was; maybe a former spy or military man in, um, Greece.

He'd been a merchant seaman, he was telling her, and more recently had crewed on ocean-racing sailers. Sailed all over the world, one of the reasons he particularly liked her books. Obviously she had traveled widely, too.

It was a time she loved remembering and didn't mind sharing—Marty Shaw the footsore, enchanted explorer from college graduation on, working at whatever came to hand and then finally, magically, skinning out a living as a travel writer. She had lived, usually poverty-fashion, in nearly every major city in Europe, and some so small they didn't show on maps.

As she spoke she reminded herself comfortably that she had in her travels dealt with men of all kinds and colors, all or most preferences and perversities. No move this one made was likely to give her trouble. "Oh. I finally gave up full-time wandering for personal reasons," she said in response to his polite question. And left it at that, no need for him to know that she'd returned to California upon her mother's death, to provide temporary solace to her distraught ten-years-younger sister. For a moment she saw Birdie's wide brown eyes and outstretched, imploring hands. Not so temporary, it turned out.

"So you settled down and shaped your experiences into fiction. Which is what I tried to do," he admitted, "but you have talent and I haven't. I should be envious, Miss . . . Sabrina. But *Liason* gave my wife such pleasure that all I am is grateful. Portugal was the last place we went together, just before she got too sick to travel."

Sabrina measured this revelation for its manipulative intent, and then was ashamed. Thirty-eight years old and she had the pinched soul of an ancient cynic. There was no ring on the left hand he rested casually on the center armrest, but she could make out a faint, pale indentation high on the ring finger. It seemed clear that his wife had died. "Here we are," she said as the car pulled up to the curb. "Maybe we'll have time for a drink."

In the quietest of the available bars, she insisted on buying his scotch and water. She herself had a Bombay over the rocks, and listened to his memories of Portugal and inspected him, covertly she hoped. Early forties, she decided, and looking younger without giving the impression he was working at it. Springy dark hair, thick brows with that sexy little quirk at their outer edges, slightly uneven teeth. Either he exercised regularly or he simply had good genes; his body in narrow slacks and a tailored shirt was trim and looked hard.

Not so fast, she cautioned herself, and told him an anecdote from her own Portuguese days. He wasn't poor; the slacks were Italian, and probably the shoes as well. But he wasn't wealthy, flying on the cheap and wearing an inexpensive watch. For the duration of her drink she listened to him with pleasure, looked at him with even more pleasure. Then she rose in response to the loudspeaker, shook his hand, and strode off to the announced gate and her first-class flight.

Matt kept his eyes on her retreating figure until it was swallowed up in the flow of travelers. Excellent carriage; he liked that in a woman. Good body; maybe a little thin, but taut, not bony. And tall enough at probably five ten to look good beside him. Their entry into the bar together, his hand at her elbow, had drawn several admiring glances.

The bartender appeared, and Matt gestured toward his empty glass. He'd treat himself to one more single malt, in celebration of a job well begun. Then it would be back to beer for a while at least; Edith's money, which had looked like a fortune to him four years earlier, had simply . . . dwindled away. It was the shock of his last bank statement that had galvanized him into action; less than twenty thousand left, and he couldn't even remember where most of the rest had gone.

Cheers, he said silently to the figure in the mirror, and raised his glass in salute. Sabrina Shaw was cautious, as you'd expect an intelligent, experienced woman to be. But she had looked him over much more directly than he had dared do with her, and clearly she'd liked what she was seeing.

In fact, he thought as he took another sip of scotch, he'd had the distinct feeling that she was getting turned on as she inspected him. According to the maid at the Northpoint Condominiums, no man had actually lived with Miss Sabrina Shaw in the five years she'd owned her apartment; but she'd usually had one around, somebody who took her places and often stayed the night with her. Over time one man would disappear, to be replaced in short order by another, always attractive and frequently gray-haired. The señorita was between men now, the maid had said with a shrug as she pocketed the second of Matt's twenties. Last one hadn't been around for a couple of months.

The bartender appeared and cocked an eyebrow; Matt shook his head and laid two bills on the bar. Sabrina had never been married, a fact probably in his favor; most women approaching forty started to worry that they might have missed something. He'd give himself a month to get her into bed, and from the way she'd looked at him tonight, it wouldn't take that long. He'd allow three more months to get her to the church or city hall or wherever. He just hoped that Sabrina could be nudged into thinking of marriage without wondering also about her biological clock. As number three of nine little Rileys, he had seen enough babies to last him a lifetime.

Matt Riordan finished the last drop of his scotch, gave his mirror image a nod, and pulled a small notebook from his shirt pocket. Drink and tip, six dollars, he jotted. If he now took an airporter van rather than a taxi back to town, it would add up to a fairly inexpensive day. He was happy he'd decided to put Sabrina Shaw at the top of his list.

Matt had worked hard at being a good husband to Edith, exercising discretion about the occasional screwing around that was only to be expected when a man was so many years his wife's junior. Poor Edith; the fact that she had finally found him out was one of his few real regrets. Things would go better for everyone, he was sure, if he could land a younger, more attractive, wealthy wife.

It was Wednesday evening when Sabrina finally got back to her spacious apartment in its featureless modern highrise building. Her other residence, in the small north coast town of Port Silva, was a charming and eccentric Victorian, a quirky, odd-angled house surrounded by a large garden; in San Francisco she took quiet pleasure in plain white walls, wide windows, deep-toned, patternless carpets, and comfortable low couches. Nothing here called attention to itself; nothing even looked expensive except her music system, and of course the computer and attendant electronic gear in her workroom.

She stripped and showered, washing away the grime of travel and the friendly, attentive look she always put on for her readers. One day her face would freeze, the way her mother had threatened in her childhood that crossed eyes would. Never mind, it would be in a good cause: money and the resulting freedom.

As she pulled a long terry-velour robe from her closet, she reminded herself for the nth time that she should dispose of the other robe hanging there, James's dark plaid Pendleton. James, alas, was gone and not likely to return. She missed his civilized wit, and she missed his body in her bed; but once he'd realized she was absolutely serious in her unwillingness to marry him (or anybody at all! she'd wailed to his departing back), he had gathered up the few things he'd kept here and walked out.

Forgetting his damned robe. She opened the closet door again, plucked the robe from its hook, and rolled it up tightly. Into the wastebasket it went, and probably one of the maids could find a use for it. Although it would be too long for most men.

Um. Not for Matt Riordan, it wouldn't. She did like very tall men, liked the brief illusion of helplessness it gave her to look way up to somebody. She checked her watch, then stood before the mirror to brush her long hair, watching her face to see whether lascivious imaginings could be traced there. Riordan had turned up in her thoughts several times over the last few days, and in one X-rated dream as well.

Not only was he a hunk in a lanky kind of way, he was fairly near her own age, a nice change and maybe a sign she was finally growing up. Probably because her own father had disappeared from her life when she was eight years old, Sabrina had always been attracted to older men. Well, except for the occasional quick tumble in some foreign place where no one knew her, kid stuff and undignified and too dangerous these days anyway.

Riordan was not as smooth as James, had no Ivy-League or old-money patina. He was well traveled, however, and seemed well read. He was probably as attached to his own personal freedom as she was to hers. And the main thing was, he turned her on. Sabrina—*Marty* always inside her head, plain gangly bony Marty who was the despair of her petite, elegant mother—Sabrina often resented her own strong sexual appetites and the inconvenient need to have a man in her life. A therapist had told her she was compensating for her loveless childhood, a conclusion so obvious to any novelist that she'd promptly canceled her future appointments with him. Besides, it didn't help. Maybe nothing but old age would help.

She looked at her watch again and picked up the telephone to punch out the familiar numbers. Punctuality was one of Birdie's needs, and it was nice that she'd managed to get home in time. She hated to hold private conversations in public phone booths.

"Hello, love," she said softly into the receiver.

"Hi, Marty. Are you there in your apartment?"

"That's right, safe at home and getting ready to work hard."

Birdie giggled. "I look at the pictures of your apartment every day. I like this place better."

"That's good."

"But one of these days, maybe next month, I'm going to come to visit you in San Francisco."

"That's wonderful. I'll show you all around," Sabrina said gently. It was an irony whose edge had lost its bite to time that a born wanderer should have a younger sister who was the victim of severe agoraphobia. It had taken near-sedation to move Birdie from their dead mother's house in southern California to the Victorian in Port Silva. Once settled in there, she had gradually expanded her self-imposed prison to include the large yard behind its high board fence. But no further, not out the gate, not into the town. Never if she could help it.

"So tell me, what's blooming now?" Sabrina asked. Birdie was a magician with plants, and her beginning-of-summer garden would be weeks ahead of any others on the chilly north coast. Little, soft-voiced Birdie was fearless against pests, even including the occasional fence-jumping deer; she was strong as any farmer's wife from wielding mattock, hoe, and spade.

Birdie began a breathless recital of Latin names, most of which Sabrina didn't recognize. And there were robins, and hummingbirds, and a mockingbird who sang wonderfully and drove the neighbor's nasty cat to fury with cat imitations.

"Birdie, leave that cat alone. Promise me you'll do nothing more than throw something at it. A *small* something."

"But it makes these smelly messes just where I've prepared the ground . . . oh, all right," she said as Sabrina drew in a long breath. "I won't hurt the stupid thing. Are you coming soon?"

"Not for nearly a week, dear. Next Monday."

"Oh, right, it's on the calendar. I've been lonesome or something lately; I have these bad dreams, and then I wake up crying for Adele. I wish she was here, and you too, and we could all be a family again."

Sabrina made a noncommittal noise. Although she never permitted herself to quarrel with Birdie's sugar-coated memory of their mother, she refused to speak agreement with it. "Birdie, is Mr. Silveira bringing your groceries on Tuesdays and Fridays?"

"Oh yes, he brings them right up on the porch and rings the doorbell. He's a nice man. But that newspaper boy . . ."

"What about him?"

"He's such a sloppy thrower that some days the paper hits the fence instead of coming over. So I have to open the gate." She hissed in displeasure. "And reach out with the rake. It makes me so mad!"

"I'll call the paper for you," Sabrina promised. "Is there anything else you need?"

"I don't think so. Nothing I can't order, anyway."

"Good." Such were the advantages of a small town: people would deliver things, the doctor would come to the house (for someone like Birdie, at least), and neighbors accepted her oddness, keeping an eye on her without bothering her. "Birdie, I have to go now. Be good, take care. I love you."

"'Bye, Marty. Take care, I love you," echoed her sister.

With a long sigh, Marty Shaw set the phone down. She strode to the kitchen, opened a bottle of wine, and poured herself a glass. Sabrina Shaw, that's who she was. And somewhere in her travel purse was the card with Matt Riordan's phone number.

At seven minutes past three by the bedside digital clock, Matt Riordan pushed the down comforter aside, sat up ever so carefully on the edge of the king-size bed, and when there was no movement from his sleeping bedmate, got to his feet. This was the time she usually slept most soundly, and they'd sat up late over brandies the night before.

Now or never, he thought, and clenched his jaw against a panicky giggle as he crept to the door. Sabrina hated clichés. Sabrina hated commitment, Sabrina loved fucking. Loved sex, he amended, prudish Irish boyhood prevailing even as the grown man crept naked through his lover's dark apartment to violate her confidence. No, only her locks. No confidence.

The workroom door was closed but not locked. He was terrified that she'd wake and discover him, but there was no other way; she wouldn't give him a key to the apartment, wouldn't let him stay here on his own in the daytime while she was away. Or even when she was *here* if she was working. Matt banged his hipbone on the corner of the computer table and stifled a curse.

He closed the door, pulled down the dark blinds she used while working, and turned on the desk lamp, trusting the thick carpeting to prevent any telltale ray from escaping under the door. Sabrina Shaw was an easy lay, a skillful and exciting lover, but after three months, she still shied away from declarations of affection or any talk of a shared future. With his money dribbling steadily away, and the friend whose car and apartment he'd borrowed due back from Europe in six weeks, he was desperate to find his way into the secrets of her life, her real confidence. Otherwise, he'd have to cut his losses and move down the list.

The desk drawers were not locked, nothing there of interest but the silly little secret compartment containing the keys to the locked filing cabinets. This struck him as a surprising lack of cleverness in a writer of suspense.

Manuscripts. Contracts. Business letters. Folders marked variously: story ideas, cuts and saves, faces. Royalty statements and bank statements; a flip through the most recent bank statements showed nothing much, no revealing canceled checks. If Sabrina had a hideaway, and he was sure she did because she disappeared fairly regularly and without explanation for nearly a week at a time . . . if she had one, she apparently kept its records there.

A noise bristled the tiny hairs along his spine; he froze to listen, heard nothing, decided the sound must have been from the street. He had a sudden vision of himself here, naked and cowering, and humiliation washed over him like a blast of hot air. Damn the stubborn bitch! he said silently, and vowed to turn up something, anything, that would give him a hold over her and earn him some return for his time and effort. He yanked the last drawer out and found bills and receipts for this apartment. Fees, utilities, insurance, telephone, maid service, groceries from the market that delivered. Wait, he thought, and the hairs prickled again, pleasurably this time.

The telephone records were lengthy, calls made all over the country and abroad as well. But there were regular calls to a town in northern California, Port Silva. At least once a week, from here or by credit card from wherever she was. No, no calls the weeks he'd suspected she was hiding out. So she went to Port Silva.

He whispered the number to himself several times to settle it in his memory. What could she have up there, an illegitimate child? No, that was not something she would bother to hide, unless it was retarded and probably not even then, not tough Sabrina. A husband maybe? Or a lover who demanded secrecy? Didn't make sense; from these particular trips she always came home seriously horny.

He replaced everything as he'd found it, extinguished the light. Stepped out into the black hallway and crept shivering toward the bedroom. If she were to find out what he'd been up to . . . The noise he heard now was definitely from the bedroom, creak of bed and a low sound that might have been a word. He darted into the bathroom and flushed the toilet, waited a moment, and then stepped boldly into the hall, into the bedroom.

Sabrina lay on her belly, face turned away; she must have muttered in her sleep. He slid into bed with great care, praying she wouldn't wake. If she rolled over now and reached for his cock, she'd find nothing but a shriveled nub.

Matt had sautéed mushrooms and fresh tomatoes gently in a little butter, filling for the omelets. He was a much better cook than Sabrina, and he enjoyed doing it, especially since a maid came in later and cleaned up the mess. He turned an omelet out on a plate, set the plate under a warming light, put a dab of butter in the pan and then three lightly beaten eggs.

"You're a cheerful laddie this morning," remarked Sabrina from the table, and he realized with irritation that he'd been singing "Danny Boy." He hated that sappy damned song, his drunken father's favorite.

"Don't stop, you have such a nice voice. And I didn't know until last night that you could play a guitar." She smiled at him, and leaned her head against his arm for a moment as he set her plate on the table.

"I don't play well, just for my own pleasure." *There* was an unfortunate phrase, one he used too often and she, he suspected, understood too well.

"Are you going to work today?"

"This afternoon." Matt was tending bar in a nice small restaurant owned by a fellow he knew, a man looking for investors to help him expand. "But I don't think I'm going to buy in. Location's not quite good enough."

"Um," she said, and shrugged. Sabrina looked wonderful this morning, sunlight gilding her hair and warming her pale skin. "Well, I plan a hard day at the computer."

"Too bad. I thought we might go back to bed."

She met his glance and held it, a slow flush rising from the neck of her robe. Then she blinked and shook her head. "Can't. Sorry."

From workaholic Sabrina, that pause was an accolade. He still had her number, two ways. The color in her face increased her beauty and gave it an edge of vulnerability; anger of the night before forgotten, he thought maybe he actually loved Sabrina. "I've wondered," he said, "have you ever thought of having a child?"

"A baby?" She spat the word out as if it were a euphemism for an indecent act.

"Well. People do. Women do."

"Not a woman raised by a perpetual teenager who had three husbands and hated all other women including her own daughter." Her mother, Sabrina had learned when she herself reached puberty, considered the sex act messy and disgusting, something men demanded and a fastidious woman avoided whenever she could, any way she could. "If you're planning a litter, Riordan, you'll have to look for another bitch."

"Sabrina, I wasn't!" As she pushed her chair back and rose, he moved quickly and caught her, wrapping her close in his arms and brushing his cheek against her hair. "I'm sorry."

For a moment she rested against him. Then she stiffened,

straightened, and raised both hands to stroke her hair back. "No need; it has nothing to do with you. Shall I meet you for dinner tonight?"

"At the restaurant? Sure. Jen comes on at nine, and she can handle the bar alone on a weeknight."

"Good. Because I'm going to catch the red-eye to New York tomorrow night, to deal with a contract. And then I'll be away for a week."

"I'll miss you."

"Good." She stepped back into him, wrapping her arms around low to fondle his ass while delivering an open-mouthed kiss. "Then you just avert your eyes from the maid here, and keep your hands off that cute little Latino cashier at the restaurant. I have never learned to share."

Marty Shaw slid lower in the lounge chair, dropped the latest *Publishers Weekly* to the bricks of the small patio, and picked up her paperback copy of *Persuasion;* this held her attention for some ten minutes. It was hot on the north coast, as it often was in September; usually she enjoyed the change, but today she felt sticky and irritable.

They had not come to Port Silva to hide out, not at first. Marty had simply wanted a safe, attractive home for her sister, a place she herself could visit regularly without too much effort. But her reversion to her plain Marty Shaw self during the move, and Birdie's agoraphobia combined with a natural secretiveness, had granted them a blessed anonymity.

Not for much longer, though. Her last book but one, set in Florence, had made a brief appearance at the bottom of the best-seller list; the Seville book was already number eight and poised to climb. Port Silva wasn't so tiny that everyone expected to know everyone else, but eventually some of its twenty-five thousand inhabitants were going to recognize her.

The back screen door flew open and Birdie came trotting down the steps to head for the lettuce bed, colander in hand. No one would ever take them for sisters, thought Marty, as she did at least once every visit. Well, half sisters. Birdie was her model for the lusty peasant girl in any novel that called for one: barely five feet tall, with huge dark eyes and a tumble of lustrous black curls, her generous breasts and bottom emphasized by a tiny waist. Birdie had looked like this from about age eleven, and had suffered for it in ways the slower-developing Marty still felt both thankful and guilty for having escaped.

"Isn't it a gorgeous day?" Birdie called. "Don't you just love . . . all this?" She made a sweeping gesture that took in house and garden. When Marty didn't answer immediately, Birdie set the colander down and came across the grass. "Well, don't you?" she demanded.

"It's very nice."

"Marty, you look so skinny and tired. I put a bottle of your white burgundy in the fridge this morning, and I'm going to bring you a glass now."

If her burgeoning fame became local news, they would probably have to move, thought Marty sadly. That would be a dreadful ordeal for Birdie. Here she had her garden, the solitude she needed, and a few friends: a woman from the plant nursery, another who drove the library's bookmobile, and a retired schoolteacher who came to play gin or cribbage. How long would it take to find their like in another place?

"Here," said Birdie, putting a glass in Marty's hand. She sat down in a canvas chair with a matching glass. "The paella is done, but it can wait until the fog comes and cools us off. Marty, I think you should move up here to live. You could get regular rest and fresh air, and I'd be able to see that you eat properly for a change."

"I have to work, Birdie. We couldn't keep this place without an income."

"We could fix the attic over into a workroom. And I'd be very quiet and not bother you. Or is it that you have somebody in San Francisco that you like better than me?" she asked in a rush.

"Of course not, love. You're my best friend." Marty closed her eyes and thought of her big, white, quiet workroom. Her obedient machines. The muted hum of city traffic. And lest she feel selfish, she reminded herself, Birdie would actually be uncomfortable having to share her house on a permanent basis. "But I need my own place to work," Marty said. "How would you like to cook in somebody else's kitchen?"

"Ugh. Well, I'll go make a salad. You just relax and I'll bring you more wine in a few minutes."

And in San Francisco she had Matt Riordan, who couldn't handle two *weeks* in this little town. Matt was lazy, and probably truthful about himself no more than half the time. She suspected he might be a fortune hunter. But he was absolutely the best company she'd ever had in her life. He was funny, and cheerful, and so adaptable she was thinking about taking him along on her research trip to Greece.

In bed they were wonderful, two bodies that fitted together perfectly like matched halves of a new and magical creature. And the randy bastard had better not be out humping some dolly right now, she thought, cupping her breasts to contain their sudden ache. She wasn't sure she could afford Matt Riordan, but she wasn't ready to give him up.

A musical sound from the direction of the house: the doorbell. Birdie could get it, she decided, and drank the last of her wine. Birdie's fear was of going out, not of letting others in.

A short time later the screen door opened and Birdie put her head out. "Marty?" She turned to say something over her shoulder before coming down the steps. There was someone behind her, someone tall, still shadowed by the doorway.

"Marty, he says he's your friend, Matt Riordan. I asked him to stay for dinner."

Matt Riordan pulled up the hood of his blue sweatshirt and leaned out of the bus shelter to peer down the street. No sign of movement behind the tall fence, nobody out on the street in the soft morning fog. Sabrina—no, Marty in Port Silva; she'd made that absolutely clear. Marty Shaw.

Marty would be out soon, because it was almost 10:00 A.M., an hour later than the usual time of her run. She ran every morning, come rain or snow or goddamned earthquake; couldn't face the rest of the day otherwise. He pushed the hood back to leave his ears free, collapsed onto the bench, and fumbled a Tums into his mouth. Best paella he'd ever tasted, and he'd had to eat it under an ice-gray glare that wished him poison in every bite. His gut was going to be messed up for days.

Face it, Mikey. You made a very bad mistake. You may have just accomplished the biggest screw-up of your life. He'd bought this enormous bouquet of something and found the house and rung the doorbell, which got answered by this very tasty morsel he thought was a maid. And found out thirty seconds later that his Sabrina had turned into Marty, a skinny witch in old shorts and a ratty T-shirt. Hair pulled into two tight braids, big, ugly glasses instead of her contacts, and her eyes glaring through them like she was ready to peel his skin off in strips and enjoy the job.

He got up for another fruitless look up the silent street. Sat down again, shivering even though it wasn't really cold. Besides being mad at himself, and scared at what he was probably losing, he was pissed off at the sister, somehow the cause of this war between him and Sabrina, and, he suspected, getting a kick out of the whole mess. Or half sister, probably; Sabrina had said her mother had three husbands.

Whatever she, Birdie, was, she didn't seem much of a reason for all Sabrina's furious secrecy. A little odd, probably not too bright. Just sat there shoving food in her mouth, now and then snatching a quick look at him from big dark eyes. She was one of the round, soft ones, the kind you can't help wanting to put your arms around and cuddle. Especially those tits; be nice to get your hands on those.

He closed his eyes and cursed himself softly, pounding a fist on his knee. Here he was trying to think with his gonads as usual, and the best thing he'd had going in his whole life was sliding out of reach. Money aside, he and Sabrina were right for each other, as good a match as any two wary and battle-scarred veterans were likely to find. He heard the sound of an engine and turned quickly to look, pulling his hood up. The driveway gate was open, and as he watched, Sabrina's red Japanese sedan backed out and paused.

Oh shit, she'd looked this way. Had she seen him? He didn't think so; she was a careful driver simply checking for approaching cars. She eased the rest of the way out and drove off in the opposite direction, not looking back again so far as he could tell. The gate swung shut, pulled from inside.

Matt sat back down and drew several deep breaths. Okay, what he'd do now was go talk to the sister. Find out what Sabrina . . . better remember to call her Marty . . . what Marty had said last night after he left, after she ushered him to the gate and told him to get his ass out of town that minute and never interfere in her life again as long as he might be lucky enough to live.

Never mind, she didn't mean it. He'd ask dim little Birdie what her sister's mood was this morning, and what he could do to straighten things out. His best approach was to try to get her on his side by telling her he really loved Marty and wanted to marry her. If that didn't work, he'd by God think of something that would.

Sabrina Shaw started her car and backed slowly away from the edge of the headland. She had run and run, maybe five miles and then five miles back, keeping herself to an easy, ground-swallowing pace. Then she'd sat here for probably an hour, staring through her windshield at the fog, windows lowered so she could listen to the roar of the invisible ocean. Now she was going back to Birdie's house, to have a shower and shampoo and do her nails. And pack to return to the city.

Sabrina was tired of being Marty, tired of old clothes and no makeup and this grungy, boring little town. She was going to get out of here and go back where she belonged, and during the three-hour drive she'd decide what to do about Matt Riordan.

The run had cleared her head and blown away much of her anger. Last night Matt had insisted he loved her; she was sure at least that he wanted her. She knew she wanted him. Maybe it would work. Maybe she could find a companion for Birdie, someone to live with her or right next door and keep an eye on her so that Sabrina could truly travel again. With Matt.

She parked on the street and opened the front door to find the house dim and quiet. "Birdie?" she called, moving through the hall to the clean and empty kitchen, where the back door was ajar. "Birdie?"

The heavy fog was beginning to break up a bit here, into cottony clumps jostled by a sporadic wind so that the yard seemed full of silent, uneasy ghosts. Condensed drops fell from the towering monterey pine to the brick patio in steady progression, then in a scatter as the wind puffed. Hearing a clang, metal against rock perhaps, Sabrina peered more intently through the shifting gray to glimpse a figure at the back of the yard, where the roses were. No one but Birdie would think of gardening in a fog like this.

"Birdie, I've been called back to the city." Coward, thought Sabrina. "I'm going to shower, and then pack. If you finish out there, maybe you could put up a lunch for me?"

There was a muttered reply, sounding like assent. Leaving the door open, Sabrina shed her running shoes and peeled off her sweats to toss them on the washing machine before heading for the staircase and the big upstairs bathroom. She started up, then paused and turned to look at something draped over the newel post.

It was a blue sweatshirt, old and faded. With a hood. She shook it out and peered at the label inside the back. "L.L. Bean," and then "Riordan" in ink so faded as to be almost unreadable. For sailing, marked with his name because everybody on the crew had one.

"Matt?" What could he be doing here, after she'd told him, ordered him, to stay away? And where was Birdie? She ran for the door and stopped two steps short, suddenly aware that she was cold, that she was wearing only a jogging bra and a pair of briefs. "Birdie?" she called in a voice that creaked.

She gripped the doorjamb and watched something gather itself into solid form at the back of the fog, take shape and grow darker and move forward. *Spink, spink, spink* of water on the bricks, squeak of feet against wet grass. The spade was very long, but the figure carrying it was not, not tall. Birdie stepped free of the fog, its moisture making diamond-glitter in her hair and on her eyelashes.

"Birdie, my God! Where were you?"

"I was working. Marty, you should put some clothes on," she said in disapproving tones. She propped the earth-clotted spade against the house, then stepped inside.

"God, I was afraid you'd been . . ." As she moved to embrace her sister, something dangling from her own hand got in the way. A blue sweatshirt. "Birdie? Where did this come from?"

"That? I don't know, I think it's been around for ages."

Sabrina's head began to throb, and there was a metallic taste in her mouth. "Birdie. This has Matt's name in it. And he wasn't wearing it last night."

"Oh?"

"Birdie, was Matt here this morning?" Sabrina dropped the sweatshirt and took hold of the smaller woman's shoulders, to give her a shake.

"He said I shouldn't tell."

"I see." Sabrina blinked sweat from her eyes. "Well, he won't mind. So long as I'm not mad, and I'm not."

"You should be, Marty. He's not a nice man."

"Birdie . . ."

"He came here to see *me* because he knew you were gone." Birdie stepped back and crossed her arms over her breasts. "He wanted to be too friendly."

Oh, Christ, thought Sabrina wearily. Dumb bastard will never learn to keep his hands to himself. But he wouldn't have meant anything, just his being-a-guy pose. How could she have thought he might have harmed Birdie?

"He put his hands on me, Marty. He was going to make me do nasty things, the way Stepfather did."

"He was not! Birdie, Matt isn't like that." Sabrina heard the quaver in her voice and closed her mouth for a moment, then opened it to gulp a deep breath. The room seemed full of fog, blown through the open back door by a chill wind. Birdie looked oddly dark and old. "Birdie, where is he? Where did he go?"

"Nowhere."

Sabrina looked wildly around the room, then found herself staring at Birdie's outstretched hands, brown and strong and streaked with earth. Birdie spoke in a soothing, don't-worry voice. "He didn't go anywhere. I'm putting him by the roses."

The Last to Know

Joan Hess

═══════════

"Bambi's father was murdered last night," Caron announced as she sailed through the door of the Book Depot, tossed her bulky backpack on the counter, and continued toward my office, no doubt in hopes I had squirreled away a diet soda for what passed for high tea these days, in that scones were out of the question, and clotted cream merely a fantasy.

"Wait a minute," I said to her back. Although her birth certificate claimed we had an irrevocable biological tie, I'd wondered on more than one occasion if the gypsies hadn't pulled a fast one in the nursery. We both had red hair, freckles, green eyes, and a certain determination—in my case, mild and thoughtful; in hers, more like that of a bronco displeased with the unfamiliar and unwelcome weight of a cowboy with spurs.

She stopped and looked back, her nostrils flaring. "I am about to Die of Thirst, Mother. We have a substitute in gym class, and she's nothing but a petty tyrant, totally oblivious to pain and suffering. We had to play volleyball all period without so much as—"

"What did you say about Bambi's father? Was it some sort of obscure Disneyesque reference? Thumper developed rabies? Flower found an assault weapon amidst the buttercups?"

"I am drenched in sweat."

I told her where I'd hidden the soda, then sat on the stool behind the counter and gloomily gazed at the paperwork necessary to return several boxes of unsold books. The sales departments of publishing houses are more adept than the IRS at concocting a miasmatic labyrinth of figures, columns, and sly demands that can delay the process for months, if not years.

Caron returned with my soda and the insufferable smugness of a fifteen-year-old who knows she can seize center stage, if only for a few minutes. The reality that the center stage was in a dusty old bookstore patronized only by the few quasi-literates in Farberville did not deter her. "Not Bambi the geeky deer," she said with a pitying smile for her witless mother. "Bambi McQueen, the senior who's editor of the school newspaper. Don't you remember her from when you substituted in the journalism department?"

It was not the moment to admit all high school students had a remarkably uninteresting sameness, from their clothes to their sulky expressions. "I think so," I said mendaciously. "What happened to her father?"

"It's so melodramatic." Caron paused to pop the top of the can, still relishing her ephemeral power. "It seems he was having an affair with Bambi's mother's best friend. The friend showed up at their house, tanked to the gills and screaming at him for dumping her, then said she was going to go home and kill herself." She paused again to slurp the soda and assess how much longer she could drag out the story. "Pretty dumb, if you ask me. I met him when Bambi had a Christmas party for the staff, and I was not impressed. He's okay-looking, but he's got—had—this prissy little mouth, and he was forever peering at us over the top of his glasses like we were nothing but a bunch of botched lobotomies swilling his expensive eggnog."

"What happened after the friend said she was going to kill herself?" I persisted.

"This is where it gets Utterly Gruesome. Mr. McQueen

was really alarmed and followed her outside. She got in her car, but instead of leaving, she ran over him in the driveway and smashed him into the family station wagon like a bug on the windshield. She claimed her foot slipped, but the police aren't so sure." Caron dropped the empty can on the counter and made a grab for her backpack.

I caught her wrist. "That's a tragic story. Where'd you learn the details?"

"It's all over school. Bambi wasn't there today, naturally, but she called Emily at midnight, and Emily told practically everybody in the entire school. Emily's mouth should be in the Smithsonian—in a display case of its own." She removed my hand. "I have tons of homework, Mother. Unless you want me to like flunk out and do menial housework for the rest of my life, you'd better let me go to the library and look up stuff about boring dead presidents."

"I find it difficult to imagine your success as a cleaning woman, considering the sorry state of your closet and the collection of dirty dishes under your bed. By all means, run along to the library and do your homework. Afterwards, you may explore this new career option by cleaning up your room." Her snort was predictable, but I realized there was something that was not. "Where's Inez? Is she sick today?"

"I really couldn't say," Caron said coldly as she headed for the door. "I don't keep track of treacherous bitches."

I was blinking as the bell above the door jangled and the rigid silhouette of my daughter passed in front of the window. Inez Thornton was Caron's shadow, in every sense of the word. Not only did she trail after Caron like an indentured handservant, she did so in a drab, almost inanimate fashion that served as a perfect counterpart to Caron's general air of impending hysteria. Inez was burdened with the lingering softness of baby fat, thick-lensed glasses that gave her an owlish look, and a voice that rarely rose above a whisper, much less rattled the china. On days when Caron was a definitive raging blizzard, Inez was but a foggy spring morning.

And also, from this parting pronouncement, a treacherous bitch. "This, too, will pass," I murmured to myself as I bent down over the devil's own paperwork, determined to banish images of a splattered windshield until I could devise a way to convince a heartless sales department to restore my credit, however fleetingly.

That evening when I arrived in the upstairs duplex across from the lawn of Farber College, Caron's room was uninhabited by any life form more complex than the fuzzy blue mold on the plates under her bed. At the rate they were accumulating, full service for twelve would be available on her wedding day, saving her the tedium of bridal registration.

I closed the door, made myself a drink, and sank down on the sofa to peruse the local newspaper for the article concerning Bambi's father. On the second page I found a few paragraphs, thick with 'allegedly' and 'purportedly,' that related how Charlene "Charlie" Kirkpatrick, longtime friend of Michelle McQueen, had contributed to the untimely demise of Ethan McQueen. Ms. Kirkpatrick would be arraigned as soon as she was released from the detoxification ward of the hospital, and Ms. McQueen was refusing to be interviewed. Mr. McQueen was survived by his wife and daughter of the home, his mother in a nearby town, and a sister in California. The funeral would be held Monday at two o'clock in the yuppiest Episcopal church, followed by a graveside service at the old cemetery only a few blocks from the Book Depot.

I put down the newspaper and tried to envision Bambi. It was too much like seeking to pinpoint one buffalo in a stampeding herd, which was how I'd described the denizens of the hallways of Farberville High School when I'd been coerced into substituting for doddery Miss Parchester, who'd been accused of embezzlement and murder.

I gave up on Bambi's face and turned on the six-o'clock news. The death, accidental or intentional, was the lead story, of course, since Farberville was generally a dull place, its criminal activity limited to brawls among the students, armed robberies at the convenience stores, and mundane burglaries. Although the story struck me as nothing more lurid than domestic violence of the worst sort, the anchorman had a jolly time droning on while we were treated to footage of a bloodstained driveway and the battered hood of a station wagon.

Footsteps pounded up the stairs, interspersed with strident voices and bitterly sardonic laughter. Odds were good that it wasn't Peter Rosen, the police lieutenant with whom I'd become embroiled after a distasteful investigation involving the murder of a local romance writer. He was unnervingly handsome, in a hawkish way, and invariably maddening when he scolded me for my brilliant insights into subsequent cases. We were both consenting adults, and indeed consented in ways that left me idly considering the possibility of a permanent liaison. Dawn would break, however, and so would my resolve to give up my reservations about marriage, about dividing the closet, about facing him at breakfast every morning, about assigning him a pillow, and about relinquishing my life as a competent, marginally self-supporting single woman.

Caron stomped into my reverie, her eyes flashing and her mouth curled into a smirk. On her heels was a girl who was briskly introduced as Melissa-from-biology, who bobbled her head indifferently and allowed herself to be led to Caron's room.

"Can you believe Inez is actually spending the night at Rhonda's tomorrow?" Caron said, slathering the sentence with condemnation. "I suspected all along that she was using me so she could cozy up with the cheerleaders. I felt sorry for her because she's so nerdy, but that doesn't like give her the right to—"

Caron's bedroom door closed on whatever right Inez had dared to exercise.

Hoping that Melissa-from-biology was up on her tetanus shots, I made myself another drink, watched the rest of the news and the weather report, and was settled in with a mystery novel when I heard more decorous steps outside the door. I admitted Peter, who greeted me with great style and asked with the quivery optimism of Oliver Twist for a beer. His face was stubbly, and there were darkish crescents under his molasses brown eyes. His usually impeccable three-piece suit was wrinkled, and a coffee stain marred the silk tie I'd given him for his birthday.

Once I'd complied with a beer, I curled up next to him and said, "You look like hell, darling. Were you up all night with this tragedy in the McQueen driveway?"

He glowered briefly at the newspaper I'd inadvertently left folded to the pertinent page. "All night, and most of today," he admitted with a sigh. "Not that we're dealing with something bizarre enough to warrant a true crime novel and a three-part miniseries. The victim's midlife crisis resulted in his death, the destruction of the lives of two women who have been best friends since college, and who knows what kind of psychological problems in the future for the daughter. Married men really shouldn't have affairs." One hand slid around my waist, and the other in a more intimate direction as he nuzzled my neck. "Neither should single men. They should get married and settle down in domestic tranquillity with someone who's undeniably attractive, well-educated, intelligent, meddlesome, and incredibly delightful and innovative in bed."

I removed my neck from his nuzzle. "If you tell me about the case, I'll heat up last night's pizza."

"Are you bribing a police officer?"

"I think there are at least three slices, presuming Caron didn't detour through the kitchen on her way to the library," I countered with said child's smugness, aware that the way to a cop's investigation was through his stomach.

He fell for it, and once I'd carried out my half of the bargain, he gulped down a piece with an apologetic look, wiped tomato sauce off his chin, and said, "Charlie Kirkpatrick and Michelle McQueen met in college, where they were roommates for four years. Both eventually married. Michelle stayed here, and Charlie lived in various other places for the next fifteen or so years. They kept in touch with calls and letters, however, and when Charlie divorced her husband five years ago, she moved back here and bought a house around the corner from the McQueens. Her son's away at college, and her daughter's married and lives in Chicago."

"And?" I said encouragingly.

"She and Michelle resumed their friendship—to the point that Ethan McQueen began to object, according to the daughter. Charlie worked at a travel agency, and was always inviting Michelle to come with her on inexpensive or even free trips. They went to the movies, had lunch several times a week, played golf on Wednesday mornings, and worked on the same charity fund-raisers. Charlie ate dinner with them often, and brunch every Sunday."

"What was the husband like? Caron met him and dismissed him as prissy-mouthed judge, but she's of an age that anyone who doesn't fawn all over her is obviously demented."

"He was a moderately successful lawyer," Peter said. "He was past president of the county bar, involved in local politics, possibly in line for a judgeship in a few years. He played poker with the guys, drove a damned expensive sports car, patted his secretary on the fanny, seduced female clients, all that sort of lawyer thing."

"Including having an affair with his wife's best friend? Have I been underestimating the profession?"

"Michelle says she began to suspect as much about six months ago. She couldn't bring herself to openly confront either of them, although she did break off her relationship with Charlie. Said she couldn't bear to pretend to chatter over lunch when she was envisioning the two of them in a seedy motel room. Last night her suspicions were confirmed."

"What will happen to Charlie?"

"She'll be arraigned in the morning. The prosecuting attorney's talking second-degree murder at the moment, maybe thinking he can get a jury to go for manslaughter. There's no question that Charlie Kirkpatrick was in a state of extreme emotional disturbance; the wife was able to give us a detailed picture of what happened."

Peter put down his plate and tried a diversionary tactic involving my earlobe, but I made it clear I wasn't yet ready for such nonsense. Retrieving his plate, he added, "If the wife repeats her story on the witness stand, the prosecutor knows damn well he'll lose. We already know Charlie had more than enough alcohol in her blood to stop a much larger man in his tracks, and she was incoherent. We're subpoenaing records from her psychiatrist. What's likely to happen is that Charlie will plead guilty to negligent homicide, a class A misdemeanor. She'll receive a fine and no more than a year in the county jail, and be out within three months. If her lawyer's really sharp, she may end up with nothing more annoying than a suspended sentence and a couple of hundred hours of community service."

"Not exactly hard labor in the state's gulag," I said, shaking my head. "If she and Michelle were so close for twenty years, why would she have an affair with her best friend's husband? Unless she's completely devoid of morals, it seems like he'd be her last choice."

"The ways of lust are as mysterious as that charming little freckle just below your left ear," he said. In that I'd gotten as much as I could from him, I allowed him to investigate at his leisure.

Nothing of interest happened over the weekend. Caron continued to hang around with Melissa-from-biology, carping and complaining about Inez's defection to the enemy camp. The general of that camp was Rhonda Maguire, who'd committed the unspeakable sin of snagging Louis Wilderberry, junior varsity quarterback and obviously so bewildered by Rhonda's slutty advances that he was unable to appreciate Caron's more delicate charm and vastly superior intellect.

The extent of Inez's treachery spread like an oil slick on what previously had been a pristine bay: spending Friday night with Rhonda, shopping at the mall the following day, being the first to hear the details of Rhonda's Saturday night date, and actually having the nerve to tell Emily that she felt sorry for Caron for being a moonstruck cow over Louis.

As for the tragedy at the McQueen house, less and less was found worthy to be aired on the evening news or reported in the newspaper. The station wagon was impounded and the driveway hosed down. The arraignment was delayed until Monday, while the doctors monitored Charlie Kirkpatrick's condition, and the prosecuting attorney pondered his alternatives. Michelle McQueen and her daughter remained inside the house, admitting only family members and a casserole-bearing group of Episcopalian women.

Sunday afternoon I called my best friend, Luanne Bradshaw, and we talked for a long time about the McQueen case. Our relationship lacked a parallel, in that I was widowed and she divorced; but we did agree that it was perplexing to imagine being so enamored of a mere man that one was willing to throw away a perfectly decent friendship.

Monday morning took an ugly turn. Caron stomped into the kitchen, jerked open the refrigerator to glare at an innocent pitcher of orange juice, and said, "I want to go to the funeral this afternoon. You'll have to check me out at noon so I can come home and change for it."

"Why do you want to go to the funeral? Bambi's hardly a close friend of yours, and it didn't sound as if you were fond of her father."

"Bambi is the editor of the school paper, Mother. Everybody else on the staff will be there. Do you want me to be the only one who Can't Bother to be there for Bambi?"

"Does this have anything to do with gym class?"

She slammed the refrigerator door. "I am trying to show some compassion, for pity's sake! After all, I do happen to know what it feels like when your father's accused of having an affair and then dies. Everyone gossips about it. Poor Bambi's going to have to come back to school and pretend she doesn't hear it, but she'll know when all of a sudden people clam up when she joins them, and she'll know they're staring at her when she walks down the hall."

It was a cheap shot, but a piercing one, and I acknowledged as much by arranging to meet her in the high school office at noon. I was by no means convinced the tyrannical gym teacher was not the primary motive for this untypical display of compassion and empathy, but it wouldn't hurt Caron to suffer through a funeral service in lieu of fifty relentless minutes of volleyball.

Peter called me at the Book Depot later in the morning to

ask if I might be interested in a movie that evening. After I'd forced him to tell me that Charlie Kirkpatrick had been arraigned on charges of second-degree murder and then released on her own recognizance, I granted that I might enjoy a movie, and we settled on a time. I may not have mentioned that Caron and I were planning to go to Ethan McQueen's funeral, but it was nothing more than a minor omission, an excusable lapse of memory on the part of a nearly forty-year-old mind. I was attending it only because Caron was not yet old enough to drive, and I was unwilling to sit in the car outside the church, I assured myself. And perhaps I was just a bit curious to see the woman whose best friend had killed her husband. Prurient, but true, and a helluva lot more interesting than the stack of muddled invoices and overdue bills on the counter.

Nevertheless, I righteously waded through them until it was time to fetch Caron and go by the apartment to change into our funeral attire. After a spirited debate about which of us was to drive, the individual with the learner's permit flounced around to the passenger's side and flung herself into the seat with all the attractiveness of a thwarted toddler.

"Are things any better between you and Inez?" I asked as I hunted for a parking place in the lot behind the church. There were so many shiny new Mercedes and Beamers that it resembled a dealer's lot, but my crotchety old hatchback slid nicely into a niche by the dumpster.

"Hardly," Caron said, her voice as tight as my panty hose. "If she wants to spend all her time with Rhonda Maguire, I really don't see that it concerns me. Melissa may be dim, but at least she's loyal."

"Would it help if I spoke to Inez?"

"That'd be swell, Mother. She'll tell Rhonda and her catty friends, and I'll Absolutely Die. There's no way I could show my face at school ever again, and you can't afford one of those snooty, genderless boarding schools for the socially inept."

On that note, we went into the church and found seats for the requiem mass for Ethan McQueen, who was, according to the obituary within a pamphlet, a beloved son, brother, father, and husband. The church was crowded, and the only view I had of the grieving widow was that of soft brown hair and a taut neck. There were a lot of high school students present, and I caught myself wondering how many of them had gym class in the afternoon. It was not a charitable thought, but the mass was impersonal and interminable, and my curiosity unrequited.

"I can't wait to get out of these shoes," I said as Caron and I started for my car.

Her lower lip shot out. "We have to go to the cemetery. Everybody else is going, including the creepy little freshmen with acne for brains, and I don't want to be the only person on the entire staff of the *Falcon Crier* who's so mean-spirited that—"

I cut her off with an admission of defeat. We waited until the hearse and limousines were ready, and joined in the turtlish procession along Thurber Street to the cemetery. Parking was more difficult, and we ended up nearly two blocks from the canvas roof shielding the family from the incongruously bright sunshine.

"Over there," Caron muttered as she nudged me along like a petulent Bo Peep.

I looked at the family seated in chairs alongside the grave. Bambi was familiar; I had an indistinct memory of a simpery voice and well-developed deviousness. Her mother was rather ordinary, with an attractive face and an aura of composure despite an occassional dab with a tissue or a whispered word to Bambi and the white-haired matron on her other side.

We took our position at the back of a crowd of students, most of them shuffling nervously, the boys uncomfortable in suits and ties, the girls covertly appraising one another's dresses and jewelry. I was trying to peer over them to determine when the show would start when a hand tapped my shoulder.

"Hi, Mrs. Malloy," Inez whispered.

"Inez, how nice to see you," I said, then waited to see how Caron would react. She did not so much as quiver.

"This is Emily Cartigan," Inez continued with her typical timidity, blinking as if anticipating a slap. Emily nodded at me, arched her eyebrows at Caron's steely back, and drew Inez toward the perfidious Rhonda Maguire and a neckless boy wearing a letter jacket over his white shirt and dark tie.

I stole a peek at Caron, fully prepared to see steam coming from not only her ears, but also her nostrils and whatever other orifices were available. To my surprise, she had a vaguely triumphant smile as she gazed steadily at the dandruff-dotted shoulders of the boy in front of us.

The graveside service was brief, its major virtue. Very few people seemed inclined to approach the family, and those who did spoke only a word or two before fleeing. I could not imagine myself murmuring how sorry I was that the deceased had been killed by his mistress, and suggested to Caron that we forgo the ritual and go home to change clothes.

"I'll be there later," she said with a guileless look. "I want to stop by my father's grave for a few minutes and see how the plastic flowers are holding up."

"You do?" I had to take a breath to steady myself. "That's a lovely idea, dear. Would you like me to go with you, or wait in the car?"

"No, it may take a long time. I'll be home later, and then I've got to go to Melissa's house so we can like work on this really mindless algebra assignment."

She took off on a gravel path that wound among the solitary stones and cozy family plots enclosed by low fences, her walk rather bouncy for someone on what some of us felt was a depressing mission. As she reached a bend, she looked over her shoulder, although not at me, and disappeared behind a row of trees.

Car doors slammed as the mourners began to depart. Bambi sat talking to her mother, who shook her head vehemently. After a moment, Bambi shrugged and stood up, and escorted her grandmother to the baby blue limousine. The preacher handed Michelle a Bible, held her hand for a moment, and walked toward his car with the obligatory introverted expression of the professionally bereaved. Michelle remained in the chair, her hands folded in her lap and her head lowered.

I walked toward my car, wishing I'd tucked more sensible shoes in my purse in anticipation of the distance. The gravel was not conducive to steady progress in even moderately sensible low heels, and I was lamenting the emergence of at least one blister when I saw a figure partially shielded by an unkempt hedge. Despite her sunglasses and a scarf, I recognized her from an earlier newscast when she'd been transferred from the hospital to the county jail. I had no doubt I could confirm the identification when the evening news covered her arraignment in a few hours.

It was curious, but so was my accountant when I tried to report fanciful quarterly estimates. I reopened the Book Depot, sold a paperback to my pet science fiction weirdo, and tried to reimmerse myself in paperwork, but I was distracted as much by the idea of Caron visiting her father's grave as I was by the image of Charlie Kirkpatrick observing the graveside service from behind the hedge. I finally pushed aside the ledger, propped my elbows on the counter, and, cradling my face in the classic pose of despondency, thought long and hard about the nature of friendship . . . not only between Michelle and Charlie, but also between Caron and Inez.

A theory began to emerge, and I called Luanne. "Would you have had an affair with Carlton?" I asked abruptly, bypassing pleasantries when thinking of my former husband.

"Not on a bet. From what you've said about him, he was a pompous pseudointellectual with an anal-retentive attitude about everything from meat loaf to movies."

"Did I say all that?"

"I am astute."

"I am impressed with your astutity—if that's a word."

"Not in my dictionary. If that's all, I just received a consignment from Dallas, some really nifty beaded dresses. I need to inventory the lot."

I rubbed my face. "Hold on a minute, Luanne. What if Carlton had been more like . . . say, Robert Redford. Would you have had an affair in spite of our friendship?"

"And when he dumped me, drive to your house and run him down in the driveway? Is that your point?" I made a noise indicating that it was, and after a moment of thought, she said, "No, but I'd be seriously tempted. You know how I feel about blue eyes and shaggy blond hair."

"Even sprinkled with gray?"

"I assume you're making rude remarks about his hair, but I wouldn't mind if his eyes were sprinkled with gray. I must count beads. Talk to you later."

I replaced the receiver and resumed staring blankly at the cracked plaster above the self-help rack. Luanne had answered honestly. She wouldn't have betrayed me, although the leap from Carlton to Robert required the imagination of a flimflam artist and the thighs of an aerobics instructor. Ethan to Robert was equally challenging.

Some women would, and had done so since the monosyllabic hunter had run into his distaff chum posing coyly in a scanty mastadon stole. But those weren't the women who had deep and long-lasting friendships with other women. They lacked the essential mechanism to bond, and most of us had learned to spot them quickly and clutch our men's arms possessively when they approached to poach.

I hung the fly-splattered Closed sign on the door, locked up, and let myself out the back door. I then unlocked the door and went inside to find the McQueens' address in the telephone directory. I was still clad in funerary finery, and I hoped I would be inconspicuous in the crowd of lawyers, their spouses, and whoever else was there.

Nobody was there. There was not one blessed car parked out front, not one mourner visible in the living room window, with a cocktail in hand and misty stories about good ol' Ethan. Wishing Luanne were beside me to dissuade me, I forced myself to go onto the porch and ring the doorbell.

Bambi opened the door and gave me a puzzled look through red, puffy eyes. "You're Caron Malloy's mother, right? You subbed for Miss Parchester for a few days when she was trying to poison everybody in the teacher's lounge."

"Something like that," I murmured. "I came by to offer you and your mother my condolences. This has been such a terrible time for you, and all I can say is that I'm really sorry. If there's anything Caron can do for you . . . ?"

"She's like a sophomore," said Bambi, clearly appalled at the concept. "Thanks, but no thanks. Listen, it was nice of you to come by, and I'll pass along the message to my mother when she gets back."

"From the cemetery?"

"Yeah, she was afraid those howling reporters would be here, and she said she wanted to be alone while she tried to understand how . . . Charlie could have done what she did."

"They were really close friends, weren't they?"

"That's what's killing her, she says. They've stayed in touch since college. When Charlie was married, she and my mother didn't talk on the phone every week, but they called at holidays and wrote a lot and sent funny cards and stuff like that. We visited them when they rented a beach house."

"She must have been thrilled when Charlie moved to Farberville and they could see more of each other," I said encouragingly, telling myself I was allowing Bambi to express her grief and confusion—rather than interrogating her four hours after her father's funeral.

"I suppose so." Bambi stepped back as if to close the door, but I opted to interpret it as a gesture of welcome and came into the entry hall. "Like I said, Mrs. Malloy, I'll tell my mother you came by," she said with an uneasy smile, "but it's about time for me to pick her up and—"

I radiated warmth like a veritable space heater. "Of course it is, dear, and I know you're not in the mood for visitors. I'll be off in a minute or two. From what I've heard, your mother began to suspect the two were having an affair about six months ago." I clucked my tongue disapprovingly.

Bambi conceded with a sigh, unable to withstand the persistence of a dedicated meddler. "Right after they came back from a weekend at some bed-and-breakfast in Eureka

Springs, they stopped seeing each other. My mother just said she'd learned disturbing things about Charlie and didn't want to be around her anymore. I think my father was secretly pleased that she didn't call all the time or show up Sunday morning with cinnamon rolls and the newspapers. He seemed happier, but maybe it was because he and Charlie were—you know. Everybody in town knows, so why wouldn't you?" Her eyes brimmed with tears and her hands curled into fists. "Everybody at school knows, along with everybody at church and everybody at the goddamn grocery store! They probably knew the entire time." The tears spilled down her cheeks, but she ignored them with fierceness well beyond her years. "I guess that stupid saying is true—my mother was the last to know."

"One final question," I said despite the guilt that was gushing inside me and threatening to choke my despicable throat. "Were you here the night of the . . . accident?"

"No, I was over at Emily's house cramming for history. My mother usually won't let me go out on school nights, but this time she did on account of how it was the midterm exam. She was supposed to pick me up at ten, but Emily's father had to tell me what happened and drive me home."

"Why don't you rest, Bambi? I'll drive over to the cemetery and bring your mother back." I patted her on the arm and left before she could protest, if she intended to do so. She was more likely to be so relieved at my departure that she was unable to get out a single word.

I parked beside the stone wall girding the cemetery, stuck my fists in my pockets, and walked up a path tangential to the canvas tent. I made an effort to keep my face lowered, although I doubted Michelle would recognize me—since we'd never met. I was not surprised to see two women seated on the grass, legs crossed, hands flickering as they talked. Nor was I surprised to hear laughter. After all, these were two old friends with a history that spanned twenty years. They'd shared stories of married life, of children, of financial woes, of vacations, of triumphs and disasters.

They froze when I veered at the last minute and stopped in front of them. "Charlie Kirkpatrick and Michelle

McQueen?" I inquired politely, if rhetorically. "I'm Claire Malloy. I own the Book Depot, and my daughter, Caron, works on the school newspaper with Bambi."

I studied their faces; neither had the glint of a predatory woman incapable of female friendship. Michelle was pretty, if not beautiful, and there was a gap between her front teeth that indicated she was not obsessed with perfection. Charlie had cropped dark hair, a wide mouth, and a longish chin that reminded me of Luanne, especially when she was tired.

These women were tired, but I would be, too, if I'd been propping up a facade for six months, culminating in what amounted to premeditated murder.

"Why are you here?" asked Michelle.

"A better question," I said, gesturing at Charlie, "is why is she here? Isn't she the woman that took advantage of your friendship to have an affair with your husband and then run him down in the driveway?"

Charlie winced. "I came by after the funeral to try to explain what happened to Michelle. Having an affair with Ethan was the lowest, vilest thing I've ever done in my life. I'd been deeply depressed all winter, drinking too much and thinking too hard about how empty my life was. It's taken five years for the divorce to sink in, and once my son left for college and I had the house all to myself, I fell apart."

Michelle squeezed her friend's hand and said, "I knew you were unhappy when Chad left, but I had no idea how bad it was. Ethan must have sensed your vulnerability and moved in like a vulture, just like he did with his clients, such as that woman who was brutalized by her husband and the poor girl last year whose husband and baby were killed in a car wreck." She grimaced. "I'm sure there were others, but I was naive, and he was adept at lying."

"And you were always the last to know," I said as I looked down at her watery eyes and white face. "I wish I believed it, but in this case, Ethan was the last to know, wasn't he?"

"To know what?" Charlie said, then exchanged a quick look with Michelle.

"To know he was having an affair with you," I said. "The plan is very good, by the way. Two old friends stop seeing each other when one suspects the other of the affair. The husband purportedly breaks it off, and the mistress storms the house in a drunken rage and manages to kill him in the ensuing scene. Why, with the wife to testify, the mistress might get off with only a few months in the county jail—or even working weekends in a crisis center or a nursing home. In the meantime, the grieving widow collects the insurance money and bravely faces the future with a daughter who'll be away at college in a year. What were you two planning to do?"

"Buy a bed-and-breakfast," Charlie admitted in a low voice. "The one we stayed at in Eureka Springs is on the market."

"And travel during the off season," added Michelle. "Ethan refused to go anywhere that didn't have at least one championship golf course, which ruled out most of the planet. Charlie found a great deal on a two-week trip to France, but Ethan wouldn't even open the brochure. I was so excited about bicycling and hot-air ballooning through the chateau country, and all he did was shake his head and mention that damned resort on Hilo we've been to every year for the last decade."

I sighed. "I don't know what will happen now. I'll have to tell the police what I know, but it's up to them to prove it."

Michelle smiled serenely. "There's a paper trail of motel receipts, dinners for two on nights when I was visiting his mother, long-distance calls to Charlie, credit card invoices for expensive gifts that never made it home."

"I've been seeing a psychiatrist," Charlie contributed, "and I was so overwhelmed with guilt that I had to tell him about the affair. He's been very worried about my rages and occasional suicide attempts. In the last few months, his service has logged quite a few hysterical midnight calls."

Michelle rolled her eyes. "You'll never get those blood-stains out of the bedspread, dummy. You're dying to get the sofa recovered, but you have to slit your wrists in bed."

"I am so confused," Charlie said, then started to laugh.

Michelle leaned against her, her laughter lilting despite the proximity of her freshly planted husband, and looked up at me with a grin. "Please forgive me—it must be the shock. But if you could see this hideous mauve sofa . . ."

I turned away and took several steps, then looked back at them. "A friend in need, huh?"

They were already lost in a conversation of bicycles and passports. I walked back to my car and drove home, imagining a scenario in which Luanne would risk a jail sentence, albeit a short one, to murder an inconvenient husband in exchange for a trip to France. It was easier than I'd anticipated. I refused to allow myself to ponder the inverse position.

When I arrived home, I went to Caron's door and was about to knock when I heard her say, "I can't tell you my source, Louis, but I swear on last year's Falconnaire that Rhonda has a date with Bruce this Friday while you're at the Southside game. All you have to do is call her the next morning and ask why she was seen at the drive-in movie with him, and why the car windows were steamier than a sauna." There was a pause. "I can't tell you, but my source is very, very good. We just thought you'd be interested, that's all. I've got to work on this really mindless algebra assignment, so 'bye!"

As I lowered my hand, I heard Inez's muted laugh. It was nearly drowned out by Caron's cackles of victory. Shrugging, I went to the kitchen to fix a drink, then got comfortable on the sofa and reached for the telephone. I should have called Peter to tell him what I'd learned, but I found myself automatically dialing Luanne's number. After all, a good friend deserves to be the first to know.

Henrie O.'s Holiday

Carolyn G. Hart

The pieces clicked into place just before the rose red sun made its swift plunge into the darkening tropical water. One moment I was sitting on the terrace—not quite wishing a prompt end to my suddenly less-interesting vacation—and the next I was tingling with excitement, an old hound responding to scent, quite convinced that I was present at murder in the making.

Obviously, during the past few days—despite my absorption in Jimmy—I'd been cataloging facts, making assumptions, assaying character, drawing conclusions.

It was as clear to me now as the crimson splash of the Caribbean sunset that Frank Hamilton—boyish, diffident, appealing Frank—intended to murder his wife, Winona. His much older wife, Winona.

"Mrs. Collins?"

I realized, from the tone, that Alice Korman had spoken several times.

"Yes, Alice." I turned a little in my chair and smiled at the dainty blonde from Montana.

"They said your husband had to go back to the States. An emergency. I'm so sorry." She peered at me with sympathetic blue eyes. "Is there anything we can do?"

Such a nice young woman. Earnest. Full of goodwill. And, at the moment, I wished she were back in Montana. I wanted to move closer to the Hamiltons. Much closer.

I suppose I dealt a bit summarily with Alice. "Jimmy isn't my husband."

"Oh." A bright flush flared in Alice's cheeks. Not the last wash of the sunset.

I grinned. Alice apparently was one of the benighted millions who believes sex ends at fifty. And assuredly by sixty. No way, José. Neither Jimmy (Jameson Porter Lennox Jr. to the readers of his rapier-sharp investigative books) nor I would ever see sixty again. But, over the last decade, both of us widowed, we'd met several times a year in various resorts for R&R (rest and relaxation in military parlance, and we all know the most zestful and relaxing of human pursuits). As in most endeavors, from bicycle riding to bedroom romps, the more you do it . . .

"Oh, I'm sorry. I didn't mean—" She lifted a hand to her mouth, overcome with embarrassment.

"Quite all right. And kind of you to offer. But there's nothing anyone can do. A family matter. He'll be fine." My smile had slipped away. I'd driven Jimmy to the airport that morning so he could fly back to Maryland in response to a despairing call from his daughter, Rachel. I doubted his arrival would help. But I understood why he went. Call it loyalty. Call it love. Call it foolish. But call it decent.

So there was nothing I could do at this moment—a hostage to my carved-in-cement airline ticket for three more days—to help Jimmy and his daughter. But perhaps I could help Winona Hamilton.

As I'd expected, Alice, her face still beet red, fled the terrace as soon as possible, murmuring something about dinner and clothes and her husband, Burt.

Under cover of the fairly boisterous cocktail-hour bonhomie among the tourists whose lives would briefly touch for a week at the Crystal Lagoon resort, I was able to focus on the Hamiltons, the spring/autumn honeymoon couple from Peoria, Illinois.

I'd noted them at once upon my arrival. Honeymoon

couples are certainly the norm on St. Thomas, but this was a couple with a difference, unashamedly fiftyish Winona whose warmth made every stranger a friend and whose merry brown eyes sparkled with eagerness, and young (late twenties?), slim, tousle-haired, shy Frank, who glanced often and eagerly at his wife, seeking approval.

Tonight was no different. They sat close together on a wicker sofa, holding hands, murmuring occasionally.

Then Charlene Sandler, her chestnut pageboy shining in the flare of light from the hurricane lamps, strode briskly across the terrace, confidence in every line of her lithe, youthful figure. Her slightly husky voice—I had the sense it evoked quite different responses in her listeners depending upon sex—could be heard by all present. "Frank, I missed you at the scuba diving this afternoon."

Frank shot her a look of such irritation that I noticed it immediately, then he darted a sideways glance at his wife. Winona's cheerful face was still for a moment; then, ignoring Charlene, Winona stared determinedly out to sea.

Charlene could scarcely have announced a fact more interesting to me. I decided to deal myself in.

Leaning forward, I addressed Frank. "I suppose Mrs. Hamilton's close call yesterday took the fun out of scuba diving?" Actually, since I'd been present, Winona had never been in any real danger. The facts were simple. Five Crystal Lagoon guests were diving in some fifty feet of water from a raft moored near an upthrust of rocks out in the crescent-shaped bay. Lillian Brewster, co-owner of the resort and a certified dive instructor, was supervising. Jimmy and I rented resort equipment. Winona and Frank brought their own. Charlene Sandler rented. The Hamiltons went over the side first, followed by Jimmy and me. When we were about forty feet down, Jimmy, true to his nature, headed for an enticing grotto. I swam after him, but slowly, fascinated as always by the swirl of aquatic life around me, a curious barracuda, a sea turtle that must have been young when Darwin explored the Galapagos, a fist-size fish that glowed green and rose and yellow.

The water around me suddenly rippled.

I turned and realized at once that Winona's air supply was gone. She was flailing wildly, beginning a too-fast, panicked rise. I gave a massive kick with my flippers and reached her in time. Grabbing her arm, I yanked once hard. Terrified eyes bulged behind her mask. Calmly I offered her my octopus, the spare regulator available on every tank. She grabbed it, and finally sense prevailed. After all, she must have practiced this maneuver fifty times when she'd learned to scuba. I was concentrating on Winona. As long as she remained calm, she was safe. Jimmy swam close. He gave me the circled thumb-forefinger, good-going sign. As for Frank, he was swimming away, unaware of the drama behind him. Winona and I, both breathing from my tank, ascended slowly. We hadn't been down long enough that a decompression stop was needed. We broke the surface and swam to the raft. Winona clung to the ladder. Charlene and Lillian hurried toward us. As Winona gulped in air, still frightened, Frank came up. When he heard his wife's choking report, he embraced her. "Winnie, God, how awful . . ." His voice shook. I felt relieved from duty and went back down, glad to resume my dive. So I didn't know what had ensued when the Hamiltons regained the raft. I could make up for that missed opportunity now. I looked directly at Winona. "What caused the malfunction of your equipment?" I'd asked questions for one newspaper or another for more than a half century. I am difficult to ignore.

"The pressure gauge was broken. I checked before I started down and it registered three thousand psi, but all of a sudden I ran out of air." Remembered panic flickered in her eyes.

It is terrifying, even when you know what to do, to run out of air.

Charlene frowned. "Was the gauge broken?"

Winona glanced at Charlene, then looked away as if the sight hurt. Charlene was slim, but definitely curvaceous. The pink halter didn't cover much of her firm, rounded breasts. Her shorts were short. She'd dropped into the chair next to Frank's, and her lightly tanned body was a young man's dream.

Hmm.

"It must be." Frank's voice was just a little high. "Before we left the States, I took everything to our dive shop and had them go over it. They must have missed it."

I gave him an unwavering stare. It had demoralized much stronger men than he.

"I'm going to give them hell when we get home." It would have been more impressive if his voice hadn't quavered.

I didn't shift my gaze. The gauge could have been rigged. "Accidents happen, don't they?"

"God, if it hadn't been for you!" He gave me such an emotionally charged look, I was startled. "It's horrible to think what could have happened. If it hadn't been for you . . ."

"It turned out okay," I said briskly. Then I arched an eyebrow. "But that's Winona's second close call. Isn't it?"

Did I imagine that the silence at our end of the terrace was suddenly strained? A raucous peal of laughter sounded from the group around the bar.

"I don't know what you're—"

Charlene interrupted Frank. "That's right!" she exclaimed, giving me a sharp, swift look. "On Monday Mrs. Hamilton stumbled over that skateboard on the steps coming down the hill."

Resort cottages in St. Thomas cling to steep, rocky, sharply shelving terrain. At some points, the steps connecting the various levels of the resort skirted steep drop-offs. The island of St. Thomas is the cliff-gashed top of a sea mountain. Roads are narrow and twisty, gouged into the mountainside. Gradients range from steep to steeper. It takes a good heart and strong legs to climb the steps, and in fact, the resort keeps a minivan going up and down the hairpin roads during the day to spare the guests undue exertion. But almost everyone chooses to walk—carefully —down the steep steps from the upper cabins to the resort center and the dining area.

I'd heard about Winona's early morning fall at lunch on Monday. The hero of the hour was Bob Humphrey, a huge young man. Fortunately for Winona—and a disappointment to Frank?—Humphrey was jogging up the steps, getting in shape for ski season, when Winona stepped on the misplaced—or quite carefully placed?—skateboard. The skateboard was traced to a sandy-haired little boy who loudly denied having left it on the steps. He kept saying, "I left it down by the pool, Mom. I know I did." I, for one, was ready to believe him.

Winona said good-humoredly, "Children aren't perfect. That's what I tell my son now about his little boy."

Charlene leaned forward. The halter gaped wider. Frank stared briefly at the cornucopia offered, then averted his eyes.

"So you have a son, Mrs. Hamilton." Charlene's lips parted in a silky smile. "How old is he?"

Winona's face reddened. She looked at Frank, then jumped up. "I'm going upstairs." Her eyes blinked rapidly, hiding a spurt of tears.

Frank scrambled to his feet. "Wait, wait, I'm coming, too."

Such a devoted young husband.

I was damned hungry by the time the Hamiltons approached the dining room that night, but my patience was rewarded. I was standing half-hidden behind a palm. When they passed, I waited an instant, then sped after them. When I caught up, just before they reached the doorway, I called out cheerily. "I'm in luck tonight. I was held up by a call from the States and thought I might end up eating alone. How nice that you've just come down. Let's ask for that lovely table out on the end of the terrace, the one where you feel you can see halfway to Miami."

I beamed at them.

As I'd expected, they were no match for untrammeled effrontery. Besides, Winona's good nature precluded rudeness. Soon we were sipping cocktails and studying the menu. I noticed—and so, of course, did Winona—that Charlene, gorgeous in an apricot sarong, sat nearby at a table for one. Frank didn't glance her way once. Which was a dead giveaway. There wasn't a man in the room unaware of

Charlene, and that included the waiters. Despite her surface patina of tanned healthiness, there was an underlying edge of sensuality that couldn't be missed.

I was my most charming, lightly regaling them with episodes from my past—with an emphasis on crime coverage. I chatted about Dolly Foster, who'd killed three husbands and four children with arsenic before anyone became suspicious, and discussed the puzzling case of Joseph Timmons, the high school football coach in Dallas who walked out of his last class one May afternoon and was never seen again, and my theories as to what happened, and recalled sultry Astrid Bruno, who was convicted of murdering her husband though she claimed a witch had done it, and why I thought she was telling the truth.

If I do say so, I had their attention. One can't talk about the most elemental human passions without eliciting interest, because even the most staid and boring humans harbor violent emotions. Think about it.

"Dear me, Mrs. Collins, you've led a very exciting life." Winona finished her last bite of swordfish, grilled with lemon, and winked at Frank. She was in high good humor this evening, even willing to put up with war stories from an old newshound. "But don't you find it upsetting—to deal with people like that?"

I raised an eyebrow. "People like what?"

"Why, all these criminals you've told us about. Isn't it depressing?" She reached out a plump hand to pat my arm sympathetically.

Frank watched her adoringly. Then he turned to me. "Winona's the most understanding person in the world."

I glanced at Winona. Surely he'd overdone it now—

But she simply smiled back at him, and you would have thought this table was the honeymoon center of the world, it exuded such tenderness.

But I was determined to break through that cocoon of ignorance. "All these people I've told you about were solid, middle-class churchgoers, who paid their bills and helped their neighbors out when they could. Interesting thing is, most murderers are very ordinary people. That's why we always get quotes from their friends about how shocking it is, how unbelievable, that so-and-so was a really nice person." I speared a pimiento and said briskly, "Most murders are committed by people we know, people you'd never suspect of murder. What's even more certain, lots of murders are never detected."

I had Frank's attention. He had started to raise his cocktail glass, but he slowly replaced it and stared at me. "Never detected? What do you mean?"

"Accidents. Funny thing, how so many accidents aren't accidents at all." I met his gaze directly. Was that a flicker of panic in his eyes?

Winona fingered her wineglass. "That's dreadful. It would be so awful," her voice dropped, "to think someone you trusted, someone close to you . . ."

I studied her with interest and irritation. Had it not yet occurred to her to question her own "accidents"? Obviously not. Well, the week wasn't over. I still had time to get her attention. But for the moment, I had one more task to accomplish. I managed it as I spooned into my dessert. Peach melba, my favorite. "Is there anything special on tap tomorrow?"

Winona clapped her hands together happily. "Oh, yes, I can't wait. I'm driving up to a bird preserve. Did you realize . . ."

I learned a great deal about tropical birds, their habitats, interests, adventures, and predilections, and found her a fascinating, vibrant conversationalist. I also learned that she was going alone in their rental car—"Frank? Oh, Frank's a sleepyhead. I can't think of any reason he'd ever get up at four-thirty."

"Not for birds." His glance at her and his meaning was so clear that she blushed.

I complimented her on her willingness to negotiate the hairpin roads since, as an American, she wasn't used to driving on the left as is the custom on St. Thomas.

She gave me a dazzling smile. "Why shouldn't I? I've never been afraid to try anything."

* * *

175

I would have been a good cat burglar. There's something in me that loves the midnight dark and the feeling of a world at rest—and vulnerable. After the cabaret closed, I slipped down the steep steps to the narrow, dark path alongside the sea. The Hamiltons had long since said good night. I wondered idly if they'd had sex. It should surely have followed his unmistakable declaration. But I had much more to concern me, and I was eager for the silence of late night to fall.

It was close to 2:00 A.M. when I climbed back up the cliffside. The parking area near the main lodge was quiet and dark, as I'd expected. I always carry a pencil flash, so I had no difficulty finding the Hamiltons' rental car, a blue Ford Fairlane. I also have a useful key chain medallion which has the innocent appearance of an oblong photo frame. (My late husband Richard's picture, bareheaded and smiling, in the bow of a PT boat.) Recessed in the frame are several small but exceedingly effective tools: a knife, a screwdriver, and a lock probe.

It took less than five minutes to puncture all four tires beyond repair.

The next morning I drifted casually through the parking lot as the young man from the local garage fastened the tow chain to the front of the Ford. I was pleased to see it was being towed. I'd thought that would be likely. (Four new tires demand wheel alignment.)

"William?" I inquired.

He shook his dark head. "Edward."

"Sorry. Did they remember to tell you to be sure and check the brake fluid?"

Of course, no one had.

But it never occurred to Edward to question instructions from an old lady who spoke with authority.

That afternoon it came as no surprise to me when I called the Allenson garage and learned that the Ford had no brake fluid. If Winona Hamilton had driven down the corkscrew road that morning . . .

* * *

The office was small, poorly lighted, and smelled like cheap cigarettes. A small crucifix on the back wall was the only adornment. The man behind the desk—Police Lieutenant Cyril Nelson—had listened without expression as I introduced myself and related the attempts on Winona Hamilton's life and her boyish husband's obvious awareness of another, much younger, woman.

Nelson was a big man, barrel-chested, blunt-faced. His blue suit was crumpled and shabby, his white shirt too tight, his necktie loosened and skewed to the left of his chin. The smoke from his limp cigarette wreathed an impassive dark face.

I concluded and he said nothing. My chin probably jutted out a trifle. "You can check with the garage."

Wearily Nelson stubbed out the remnant of cigarette. He flipped open a slim telephone directory. A blunt finger ran down the column. He dialed and asked for information about the rental car. He listened, his face inscrutable, said thanks, hung up. Then his brown eyes surveyed me.

I knew what he saw, a late-sixtyish woman with dark hair silvered at the temples, a Roman coin profile, and a lean and angular body poised to move, always poised to move.

That, of course, was the basics of what he saw. But I knew without asking the lens through which he viewed me. An American tourist, an old woman. Alone. Probably starved for attention, sexual and otherwise. Beginning to suffer the delusions of old age. A lost thimble had to be stolen. Conversations between strangers across a room indicated collusion and danger. Imagining plots at every turn, directed, if not at myself, then at another older woman.

I realized that I should have to call upon a young police friend in the States to vouch for me. I didn't like it, but this was no time for me to stand on pride. Winona Hamilton's life was at stake. "Lieutenant Nelson, please call Lieutenant Don Brown of the Derry Hills, Missouri, Police Department. He will tell you I can be trusted."

A tiny smile pulled at the corners of his wide mouth. At another time and place, I thought I might like Cyril Nelson very much.

"I am certain, Mrs. Collins, that you are indeed a woman of good reputation in your city. And I applaud your concern for your fellow American, Mrs.—" he glanced down at his notes "—Mrs. Hamilton. Unfortunately—or perhaps very fortunately—I see no evidence here of crime. The skateboard?" He shrugged heavy shoulders. "I have three sons. I watch every step I take in my drive. It, too, you understand, is steep and dangerous. And the scuba equipment? Sports equipment often—"

"Malfunctions." I interrupted impatiently. "Of course. But surely the loss of brake fluid is another matter."

He tapped the notebook with his pen. "Ah, yes. The loss of the brake fluid. Because of damage to the power brake proportion valve block." He closed the notebook. "You have driven much on our beautiful island?"

My eyes narrowed. "Some."

"Then you know, Mrs. Collins, our roads are rough. There are many rocks." He pushed back his chair, heaved six feet two of muscle to his feet.

Our interview was over.

The resort sparkled in the late afternoon sunlight. Not a cloud marred the azure sky. The water was as smooth and clear as green glass. I found Winona Hamilton reading—a travel guide to the Andes—on the middle terrace.

She looked up and smiled happily.

I looked about.

She answered the unspoken question. "Frank's gone for a dive. I know all about getting back on the horse, but I'm in no hurry."

And, I thought dispassionately, she'd rather die than appear again in her swimsuit in the presence of Charlene.

"How was your trip to the bird sanctuary?" I dropped into the chair beside hers.

She shook her head in disappointment. "I didn't get to go. Perhaps tomorrow. But it was the most surprising thing— the tires on our car were slashed! I wonder if it's because we're Americans?"

"I doubt it. Probably just some boys up to mischief. So you've had a quiet day. No more accidents?"

"Hmm? Oh no, very quiet." Accidents, real or engineered, were far from her thoughts. She was busy planning a trek to the Andes and oblivious to the currents of desire swirling around her.

I went down to the beach after I left Winona. I found an empty hammock among the palm trees, one with a good view of the raft. I watched Frank and Charlene engage in what was obviously a sharp, short, violent argument. It was not, I felt certain, a confrontation between strangers. Clearly they knew each other well. Had Charlene's presence at the honeymoon resort been prearranged? Maybe he'd asked her to come—a side dish, so to speak—and maybe she found seeing Winona as his wife too galling. Maybe she was telling him she was through.

Whatever it was, when Frank flung himself from the raft and swam furiously toward shore, I decided to retreat. I knew the situation was explosive. The rest of the day, I managed to be near Winona Hamilton. Just in case.

At dinner, I stopped by their table. I couldn't quite manage a gush. Too out of character. But I beamed and chattered. "Do you know, I've been thinking about Peoria. I have an old friend who lives there. Used to work on the paper. I'll have to tell her all about you two. She never misses a copy of the paper, so I know she'll keep me up-to-date on my holiday friends." Would Frank take it as intended? WARNING—Don't think I will miss an "accidental" death after you get home.

I was nearing the end of my holiday stay. Should I warn Winona outright?

She would never believe me.

What really irritated me was her total lack of perspicuity. At one point, Charlene came over and asked Frank to dance, and when he started to stammer a refusal, Winona smiled and told him to go ahead.

As I walked up the steep steps to my cabin, I was oblivious to the beauty of the tropical night, the sweet scent of the flowering shrubs, the rustle of coconut palms in the offshore breeze. Time was running out.

Each cabin at Crystal Lagoon is quite separate and private, clinging to the rocky mountainside, secluded in thick brush, but with a lanai looking out to sea.

Quite idyllic.

I unlocked my door and turned on the light. The furnishings in the combination bed-sitting room were spartan but comfortable, a coffee table and straight chairs, a sofa, two easy chairs, a queen-size bed. I showered and stepped out in time to hear the ring of the telephone.

Wrapped in a towel, I grabbed up the receiver.

Jimmy's voice—so far away, yet so clear—made me smile. "Henrie O., I miss you." (Henrie O. is the nickname given to me by my late husband, Richard. He always said that I packed more surprises into a single day than O. Henry ever did into a short story. Rather gallant of Richard, I always thought.)

"Jimmy, I'm having a hell of a time!"

"Oh?" That single syllable packed a lot of questions.

"No, Jimmy. Not another man. Murder."

"Christ, Henrie O., what's up?"

I told him.

"I'll catch the next—"

"No. I can handle it."

A pause, then a swift "I know. I just hate to miss the excitement."

He reported on Rachel's problems, the kind that don't have easy answers. I didn't try to give him any. But I said I'd be in touch.

He didn't waste time warning me to be careful. His last words were "Give 'em hell, Henrie O."

I was still smiling when I propped up the pillows and sat on the bed. Movement at the periphery of my vision attracted my attention. I looked toward the wall above the small, adjoining kitchenette. A slim green lizard skimmed toward the ceiling. Nature's best insect removers. I put on my reading glasses and picked up the carafe of water from the bedside table.

I've faced danger many times.

Small-arms fire.

Bombs.

Mobs.

Storms—at sea, in the air.

I stared at the milky swirl in the water. The hair on the back of my neck prickled.

A moment later, I poured some of the water into a shallow dish and placed it on the lanai. I closed the door, then watched and waited. Soon the stone lanai swarmed with life, lizards, tiny crabs, a black snake. A brown toad's tongue flickered into the liquid.

It wasn't fun watching the toad jerk backward, writhe, and die, but it was as clear an answer as I've ever had.

I was the quarry.

Five minutes later, I slipped away from the lanai, my destination an unoccupied cabin two levels above. The locked door was no barrier with the help of my key chain. I didn't turn on a light here, of course. I did take the precaution of placing a chair beneath the knob of the door and balancing a broom against the sliding doors to the lanai.

There were plenty of empty cabins. I could safely spend the remaining nights undetected. I never underestimate an enemy.

Fully dressed, I slept lightly because my mind was engaged, considering alternatives. By dawn, I had a plan. (Later, my young police friend in Missouri would demand to know why I hadn't taken the carafe to Lieutenant Nelson. That was simple. Why wouldn't Nelson believe I'd poisoned the carafe myself? It was not, as Don Brown claimed rather bitterly and, I felt, altogether unfairly, that I was proving I had the soul of a buccaneer and the instincts of a barracuda.)

In the safety of daylight, I returned to my cabin. The freshly washed, empty carafe sat on the table next to the bed.

How disappointing it must have been for my visitor. An unmade bed without an occupant. The assumption, of course, would be that I'd not drunk water at bedtime and had departed for an early morning walk. There would be no reason to suspect that I knew I was hunted. Fine. That gave me an edge.

I ate an especially large breakfast and enjoyed every bite, greeting everyone on the terrace cheerily. I went into Charlotte Amalie soon after. I wasn't concerned about Winona's safety. She was safe as long as I was alive. So it was a relaxed outing on my part, though it took several hours to round up all the items I needed, including a nylon rope and pitons. One of the essentials, a hand-size tape recorder, I had with me, of course. I never travel without it.

That afternoon I utilized the siesta hour, but I didn't assume Frank was resting. I took no chances. Once dressed in my new hiking boots, long-sleeve shirt, and slacks, I took a circuitous approach to the top of the cliff and Point Cagle, the highest elevation within the resort boundaries. Just short of my goal, I wormed through foliage to settle on a low limb of a banyan tree. I waited a full thirty minutes to be certain I was unobserved.

When I was sure no one was about—except a cold-eyed turkey vulture that circled and circled above—I scouted out the rim of the cliff. The view was spectacular, a sheer drop of some three hundred feet to sharp-edged rocks washed by the surf.

Richard enjoyed mountain climbing, and we did a lot of it, so it wasn't difficult to drive the pitons in place and work my way six feet down the cliff wall. I threaded a short line through the last piton, then climbed back up, removing the other pitons as I went. I hid the loop of rope at the top beneath a clump of rock plant. Then I looked down one more time at the boulders so far below and the waves crashing over them.

As the sun began its plunge into the west, I joined the convivial group around the bar. Two new honeymoon couples. Some businessmen from Miami with women who clearly were not their wives. My own particular honeymooners beamed with happiness. I watched cynically. Frank obviously had spent the afternoon delighting Winona. She radiated contentment, satiety. I tried to understand a man who could juggle sex and murder and still have the face of a choirboy. It was only when he looked toward Charlene that his eyes turned wary and still.

I ordered a margarita—it's the salt I love—and proceeded to wax lyrical about the beauties of St. Thomas.

"My vacation's almost over. And there's only one thing I haven't done."

Ramona, the bouncy brunette who doubled as entertainment director and tended bar during the cocktail hour, gave me a bright, encouraging smile. I suppose Ramona's job description included a passage on dealing with the elderly.

I spoke to her, but clearly enough for all to hear. "I haven't watched the sunrise from Point Cagle. So that's what I'm going to do in the morning. At sunrise. To see the world come alive—oh, I can't wait."

"That's a hard climb," Ramona said doubtfully. "And the edge of the cliff's all crumbly. Uh—Mrs. Collins, maybe I'd better go with—"

"Certainly not," I retorted briskly. "When, my dear, was the last time you were up at dawn?"

"Dawn," one of the Miami bimbos declared, "was meant for birds."

This initiated a round of ribald commentary. Winona Hamilton pretended she hadn't heard. Charlene gave her a disdainful glance.

I took a deep drink of my margarita. I'd earned it. Everyone knew the old lady was going to be on top of Point Cagle at dawn.

And the edges of the cliff were crumbly.

I stayed in a different unoccupied cabin that night. I was determined that I, not my opponent, should pick the playing field. I doubted the carafe was poisoned again, however, or any other assault planned there. How much easier to shove a helpless old lady off the top of a cliff with crumbly edges. Of course, if Frank were truly smart, he'd drop his plan to murder Winona—at least in the foreseeable future. But the determination to remove me argued an implacable resolve to murder Winona—soon.

I reached the top of the mountainside shortly before dawn. The dancing spot of my flashlight announced my arrival. I wore a loose cotton dress, stout shoes, and (one of yesterday's purchases) a fluffy, cream-colored cotton shawl. Shawls are not a part of my wardrobe, but a shawl was essential. It hid the belt and pouch around my waist.

Without doubt, my foe was already in place. Perhaps in the thick cover of that clump of firs, perhaps among the low-lying limbs of the banyan. I was alert for the scrape of a shoe, for the rustle of foliage. Although I gave the appearance of leisure, I went directly to my spot.

Here was my moment of greatest danger. But I counted on my adversary's caution. There would be time given to be certain I was alone, that no one else was about. That gave me time to stand at the edge of the cliff, to give a sharp little cry of vexation as I dropped my flash, to bend down to retrieve it.

That done, I was ready.

I knew as the pink streaks of dawn turned bright and the sky was transformed from pearl to rose that I was silhouetted against the horizon.

A rattle of stones announced the arrival of my pursuer.

I half turned and looked toward the trail.

And felt a flash of anger. Dammit, what on earth had possessed *her* to come—and how was I going to get rid of her?

Charlene Sandler walked toward me.

I tried desperately to think of a way to deflect her, send her back down—

As I've said, I've faced danger many times.

But this time death was walking toward me.

"Nosy old bitch, aren't you?" A tiny giggle hung in the air. Obscenely. "Older even than Winona." Her face sharpened with hatred, making her ugly. Ugly, obsessed, and dangerous.

Charlene stopped a few feet from me. "How could he marry *her*? It makes me sick! I couldn't believe it when he left me." She stared at me, her eyes uncomprehending. "He left me for her. And she's old, old and ugly."

"Not too old," I said sharply, "and not ugly."

I felt a surge of irritation with myself. Not only had I misread the evidence there for all to see—Frank's adoration, real and deep, for his wife—I had been guilty of rank sexism and the kind of prejudice against age that I spend a good deal of my time combating.

Yes, a young man could love an older woman.

Yes, a young woman could be driven to pursue a past lover, in a frenzy to destroy the woman who had supplanted her.

And yes, I was facing a far more dangerous adversary than I'd expected. But all I had to do was lead her on to talk, record her plans to kill, and I would save not only Winona, but Frank.

"It's obvious Frank adores Winona. If anything happens to her—"

A vicious smile twisted Charlene's face into an almost unrecognizable mask of hatred. "Oh, it's going to happen to her, you old bitch. I'm going to kill Winona. She's not going to have Frank. Frank belongs to me. In fact—" she placed arrogant hands on her hips "—I'm going to kill her tonight. An overdose of Valium—because she's so upset by your accident!" Her chuckle was warm and satisfied.

It was the laughter that fooled me.

I didn't expect death to strike with laughter in the air.

So, despite all my preparations, I was caught by surprise.

Charlene lunged at me.

Her hands, palm out, slammed into my right shoulder.

And over I went.

I had intended to fake the strike, the way a movie hero fakes taking a punch.

Instead, a numbing pain seared my right side, but my gloved right hand, hidden in the folds of the shawl, tightened on the nylon rope I'd looped around my wrist as I

185

picked up the dropped flashlight. So I banged over, yes, but my lifeline held, though I slammed hard into the side of the cliff.

I braced myself against the cliff wall and checked the belt looped around my waist. The pouch held the tape recorder —all was well there—and the pitons and hammer I'd need to climb back up the cliff.

"Goddamn you." Charlene peered over the cliff edge. "Why didn't you die?" she screamed.

"Not my time yet," I called up cheerfully, though my shoulder ached like hell. Still, I was flush with adrenaline. "Checkmate, Charlene."

But acceptance of defeat requires rationality.

Charlene leaned over the cliff edge, reaching down, down, trying to grab at me.

And the crumbly edge gave way.

I barely had time to flatten myself against the cliff face as she hurtled by. She plummeted past me, her angry scream turning to a shriek of horror.

I pounded the pitons into the cliff automatically, then removed them once past, a task done so many times over the years that I could do it without thinking. My breathing was ragged, I admit, as I pulled myself back over the lip of the cliff. I dropped the pitons and hammer into the pouch, looped the rope around my waist, then used the shawl to cover it. No one questions how an old lady wears a shawl.

Of course, I had the recording. I could well have made the whole affair public. But why tarnish two lives? Charlene's acts were hers; Winona and Frank didn't deserve the misery and unnecessary guilt that would result from public disclosure. Let them remember their honeymoon with joy.

So I made my decision. I adopted a suitably shaken and shocked expression when I heard the sound of running feet nearing the top of the trail. Although understandably distraught, I would manage to give a clear account of the dreadful accident. So unfortunate—the treacherous, crumbly edge of the cliff.

Night Visitor

Audrey Peterson

Over his breakfast, Ian MacDougal, employee of Finch Investigations, Ltd., scanned the morning newspaper, skimming past the usual dicey international crises, past the current hints of scandal among the royal family, and on his way to the soccer results, when he was stopped short by an item on an inner page.

"Ealing Woman Found Dead," read the caption, followed by the information that the body of Mrs. Enid Hackford, of number 62 Mardale Road, had been found by a neighbor. The victim appeared to have died by strangulation. The husband, Mr. George Hackford, was "assisting the police with their enquiries," invariably a euphemism for "He's our chief suspect."

"Now what?" MacDougal asked himself. "Do I tell the police what I know? I'll let Finch decide."

What MacDougal knew about the Hackfords of Ealing went back to the day a month or so earlier when he reported in to the London office of Finch Investigations. Waiting by the receptionist's desk for his chief to be free, he saw the door to the inner sanctum ajar and heard Finch's voice on the phone. "MacDougal? Yes, that's the one—eccentric chap, quotes poetry right and left. Otherwise, a good man."

Then the chief's voice called out, "Send in MacDougal when he arrives."

With a wink at the young woman behind the desk, MacDougal tapped on the door and went in.

Unabashed, the chief said, "Ah, there you are, MacDougal. Here's one for you. Chap suspects his wife's having a nocturnal visitor whilst he's away."

Ian MacDougal reached across the desk and took the folder held out to him. Sitting with knees wide apart, body bent halfway to the floor, he scanned the top sheet of the form.

"Surveillance to start at eleven P.M. Bit late for the lover to arrive, eh?"

"That's why I thought of you, MacDougal. You don't mind the night work."

" 'The night has a thousand eyes, and the day but one.' "

Finch rolled his eyes upward and sighed. "Yes, yes, quite right, I'm sure. Well, then, chap's name is Hackford. The address is there. He travels for a firm that makes household gadgets—electric this and automatic that. On Mondays to Thursdays, he stops over at various hotels along his route and comes home to Ealing on the weekends. Any questions?"

The deep lines across MacDougal's forehead didn't move.

"No, sir. Looks to be a routine obbo, eh?"

"I see no problems. Just ring in your report in the mornings."

"Righto, gov'nor. I'm off, then. As Alfred, Lord T., would say, 'Some work of noble note may yet be done.' "

Finch sighed again and picked up the ringing telephone on his desk.

Shortly before eleven o'clock that evening, MacDougal pulled his nondescript Ford Escort into a spot between two cars, across the road from the Hackford residence, number 62 Mardale Road, one of a row of terraced houses like thousands of others that had sprung up in the suburbs of Edwardian London. MacDougal noted that while the ground floor of the house was dark, a light showed behind the draperies of an upstairs window.

Glad of the still mild October weather, he settled down with his thermos of tea. A patient man, he didn't find the waiting the agony that some of his fellow operatives complained of. On his retirement from the Metropolitan Police, he had enjoyed filling his time, not to say his pocketbook, by taking odd jobs for Finch's bureau. Long a widower, his son off in America doing something clever with computers, MacDougal was free to come and go as he liked.

At midnight, no one had approached number 62, and MacDougal knew that no access was possible except from the front. His scouting earlier in the day had shown that, like most terraced houses, the back gardens here were bounded by a wall giving onto identical backs of houses facing the street behind.

By one o'clock his supply of tea was getting low, and he decided to abandon ship for the night. This was a Tuesday. Two more chances this week for the visitor to turn up. And MacDougal drove back to his flat in Shepherds Bush and slept until nine.

The next night gave him his first sight of the man. At ten minutes after eleven, as MacDougal noted in his log, a chap approximately five feet nine inches tall, slight build, blond hair falling to his shoulders, wearing jeans and a black leather jacket, turned the corner of Curry Lane, five houses down, and walked quickly along Mardale Road. At number 62, he opened the gate, closing it carefully behind him, and, producing a key, let himself into the house.

Quite a regular, thought MacDougal. She doesn't have to come down to let him in. Fear of the neighbors noticing, no doubt. As he watched, no light appeared on the ground floor, but a few minutes later, the light upstairs went out and the house remained in darkness.

Soon after midnight, the man emerged, walking briskly down the road and around the corner. MacDougal started his motor and moved slowly along, turning left into Curry Lane. No sign of the man.

At the next crossroad, he swung the car around and crept slowly back toward Mardale Road. Now he heard a motor start up behind him, but by the time he turned again, the car was gone.

"Early days," MacDougal murmured. "I'll catch him next time round."

But on the Thursday, the nocturnal visitor didn't turn up, and nothing further was done on the weekend as hubby was presumed to be at home.

Back at his post on Monday evening, MacDougal was unable to find a parking spot opposite number 62 and settled for one farther down the road from Curry Lane but still offering a clear view of the house, even through the misty rain that had persisted all the evening.

At a quarter past eleven, when the night visitor turned up again, the pattern was the same as before. In a few minutes the upstairs light was extinguished, and shortly after midnight, the man slipped out the front door and down the walk.

This time MacDougal was out of the car and on his feet, walking briskly down the opposite side of Mardale Road and crossing into Curry Lane only seconds after his quarry had turned the corner. But the man stepped quickly into a car and sped away before MacDougal could get a look at the license plate, obscured as it was by the rain and the darkness.

"'Vanished like a guilty thing surprised,'" MacDougal muttered in exasperation.

The Tuesday evening produced no sign of the visitor, but on Wednesday he turned up, only this time a light appeared on the ground floor after the man entered the house. Then, as before, the upstairs light went out.

When the man emerged, MacDougal followed on foot and watched as the man stepped into a black taxi that had obviously been instructed to wait. Without turning on its headlamps, the taxi moved quickly away, but not before MacDougal noted its number.

"Got him this time, gov'nor," he reported on the telephone the next morning. "The cabbie can tell you where he dropped his fare, and Bob's your uncle."

"Good work, MacDougal. Carry on."

But an hour later, the head of Finch Investigations rang back. "It's all off, MacDougal. We found the cabbie and learned the fare was dropped in front of Marks and Spencer's in Ealing Broadway. When I rang up and gave the client the info, he says very good. He knows enough now to have a bargaining point with his wife if it comes to divorce, and that's all he wanted. Many thanks to all, and he's sending in the check today."

A month or so later, MacDougal had pretty much forgotten the Hackford surveillance, as other assignments had kept him occupied. Now, reading of the murder of Mrs. Enid Hackford, his first thought was that since hubby knew of the night visitor, he may have gone berserk and strangled his wife in a fit of jealous rage. But if so, why did the man wait a month before taking action?

In any case, his chief could decide whether to inform the police. As MacDougal reached for the phone, it rang.

"MacDougal?" It was Finch himself. "You remember the Hackford surveillance in Ealing last month?"

"Yes, sir. I've just seen the item in the news."

"Right. Well, I've had a phone call from the CID. It seems Hackford has an alibi for the night in question, but he's told them about his wife's night visitor and says that chap may be the one that killed her. They want you to go round and report what you saw."

At the Ealing police station an hour later, MacDougal was asked to wait until Detective Chief Inspector Wilson, who was leading the investigation, was ready for him.

He took a chair next to a statuesque redhead whose dress clung becomingly to bosom and hip. Early thirties, he guessed. Not a lady to be trifled with, from the set of her mouth.

"You here for the Hackford case?" Her voice was pleasantly husky.

MacDougal nodded.

"They'd better not try to pin it on George. He couldn't have done it. He was with me that night."

Murmuring a noncommittal "Mmm," MacDougal averted his gaze from her flashing eyes and stared at the floor.

"You see," she went on, "his wife had a bloke of her own—he's the one they want to find."

Before MacDougal could frame a reply, an officer appeared, calling, "Miss Stone, please. Miss Joyce Stone."

With a "Ta, ta," the redhead rose and followed the officer into another room.

Five minutes later, MacDougal was taken to the incident room, where Detective Chief Inspector Wilson asked for a full account of the visits to the Hackford residence by the blond man in the leather jacket.

"Right. Now, here's the problem. Hackford is loaded to the teeth with motive. He and his wife had substantial insurance policies made out to each other. He's been shacking up, as the Yanks would say, with his alibi lady for some time past, so her word may not be worth a hill of beans."

" 'A tale told by an idiot, full of sound and fury, signifying nothing.' "

"Eh? Ah, yes. Well then, on the night in question he was at the White Lion hotel in Guildford. Nobody at the hotel can verify Hackford's presence—or absence—during the wee hours of the night. It's certainly possible for him to pop up to Ealing, strangle the wife, and get back with no one the wiser. But a jury learning of the wife's night visitor is going to have good cause for reasonable doubt. Defense will say it could have been a lover's quarrel.

"But here's an odd thing. Most of the prints in the house belong to Hackford or his wife, bar a few here and there that could be a workman or a onetime visitor. Now, it's possible the night caller didn't leave any prints, if he spent most of his time in bed. The bathroom, had he used it, would have been cleaned in the normal course of events. But it still seems odd not to have found some evidence that he was in the house."

Wilson's phone rang, and while he talked, MacDougal, legs apart and head halfway to the floor, sat in a trance.

When Wilson had rung off, he said, "All right, MacDougal, thanks for coming in."

Still bent over, MacDougal raised his head. "What does this man Hackford look like?"

"Just an ordinary sort of chap. Why do you ask?"

"About five foot nine, slight build?"

"Yes, about that."

"I see. About the size of the night visitor, eh?"

"So what does that mean?"

"It just occurred to me that a man could fix up a nice alibi for himself. He could dress himself up, have himself followed, and after disposing of the wife, he could lay the blame on a mythical lover that doesn't exist."

"Bit farfetched, isn't it?"

"As the Bard says, 'There are more things in heaven and earth, Horatio, than are dreamt of . . .'"

"Yes, yes, I daresay. Well, look here, we've got Hackford in another room. Why don't you have a look? I'll have him brought in."

Presently an officer came in, escorting a dark-haired man wearing a pin-striped suit and a worried frown. Passing MacDougal, they went to a desk where a few words were exchanged, then went back out of the room.

"Well?"

"I couldn't see the man's face, you understand, but the height and the slight build are the same. I could testify to that, but not to much more."

"I see. At least it isn't ruled out, eh? Right then, MacDougal. You'll probably be called at the hearing."

And so it proved. George Hackford's solicitor asked for a full committal hearing, hoping to have the charges dropped by revealing how scant was the evidence of the police against his client.

When the case for the crown had been presented, the defense called the hotel manager, who confirmed that George Hackford was indeed booked at the hotel on that date and had been seen in the dining room as late as nine o'clock in the evening and again at breakfast.

He was followed by the alluring Miss Joyce Stone, whose

ringing tones matched her powerful physique as she testified that Mr. Hackford had been in her presence during the entire course of the night in question.

MacDougal's evidence went as he had expected, describing the nightly visitations at the Hackford residence in Ealing, and confirming for the prosecutor the possible resemblance of the man to the accused, despite his disguise.

The magistrate's decision appeared to MacDougal to be touch and go, but in the end he did commit Hackford to trial, at the same time granting him bail until that date.

Outside the courtroom, MacDougal walked out into the icy air of early December and headed for the nearest pub. As he ordered his pint, he heard a voice at his elbow and saw the anxious face of George Hackford peering into his.

"Mr. MacDougal? Excuse me, sir, I wonder if I might have a word with you?"

"At your service."

Hackford ordered a double whiskey and led the way to a table in a far corner. Holding his glass in trembling hands, he took a sizable gulp of his drink. "I'm desperate, Mr. MacDougal. I've got to talk to someone, and at the hearing just now, you seemed a decent sort of chap. You see, the police are right. I *was* the man you saw going into my house."

MacDougal raised a hand. "Perhaps you'd best stop right there, Mr. Hackford. If you're going to confess to this murder, I have no legal privilege to your confidence."

"But I *didn't* kill my wife! The thing is, if I tell them the truth, I'll really be in the soup. They'd never believe me. If I tell you the whole story, will you advise me what to do?"

"As the good book says, 'Examine me and prove me: try out my reins and my heart.'"

Hackford blinked. "How's that? Oh, yes, to be sure. Well, then, my wife and I were married for ten years. It had never been what you might call the grand passion, but we jogged along well enough. In the fifth year, she was expecting a child and we were both pleased about that, but when she miscarried, she had an operation, and children were now out of the question.

"About a year ago I was given the territory I have now, and that's when I began stopping over during the week. I could have come home from most places in the evenings but would never make it back through the morning traffic. Enid didn't seem to mind that I was gone. She had her job during the day, and one or two neighbors often dropped in of an evening. Then she watched the eleven-o'clock news on the telly and turned out the light at twenty minutes past, regular as clockwork.

"That's how I timed my visits as I did. But to go back a bit, about eight or nine months ago I met Joyce—Miss Stone—and we hit it off like a house afire. When I was in Guildford, where she lives, she would stay the night with me, and I'll tell you, MacDougal, I didn't know it could be like that, if you know what I mean. Soon she would come to me at other stops along the way, or I would go back to Guildford to her place when it wasn't too far. At first I thought it would be just a fling, but I soon found I was hooked good and proper."

MacDougal cleared his throat. "As with Cleopatra, custom did not stale her infinite variety?"

"You've got it in one! So it went on for a while, but then Joyce started talking about getting married. That was a bit more than I had bargained for, and I pointed out that if I abandoned my wife, she could demand a good chunk of my salary. Then Joyce came up with the plan that you know about. If I could show that Enid had a lover, it would help the cause, so to speak. At first I balked, but Joyce is a determined lady, and in the end I went along with it.

"At first it all went off as planned. As I slipped into the house, I could hear the telly upstairs, and I simply stepped into a small room under the stairs that I use as my office and waited till the telly and the light went off. Enid was a sound sleeper, and after a suitable interval, I walked out again.

"But on the third visit, I banged into a table, and she must have heard, because she called out, 'George, is that you?' and I could hear her coming down the stairs. I snatched that blond wig off my head and stuffed it into a drawer of my desk, switched on the light, and pulled out some papers, calling out that I'd forgotten some reports I needed for the next day.

"And then, MacDougal, something happened that was the last thing in the world I expected. She was wearing a sheer nightdress, and she came straight up to me and put her arms around my neck and kissed me. It had been a long time since we—well, you understand. I thought she'd lost interest, and I expect she thought I had too. We walked up the stairs with our arms around each other, and well—it was like being young again. We both laughed and talked about how it had been on our honeymoon, all those years ago. I don't know how to describe it . . ."

MacDougal smiled. "Like Browning's thrush, you recaptured that first fine careless rapture?"

Hackford's pale face lit up. "That's it! We read that poem in school, but I never thought it would have any meaning for me. Well, after that, everything changed. I found I had gone off Joyce. For a long time I had been fed up with her pushing and her nagging, but I wanted to let her down easy. I told her I wouldn't go on with the night visitor plan as it wasn't fair to Enid. She argued, but when she saw I wouldn't budge, she gave in. Then, after a time, I told her the divorce was off. She did cut up rough at that, but then she calmed down and said she would see me at the hotel at Guilford the following Wednesday and we could talk it over.

"I agreed, and when she came to my room, she was all smiles. Fixed me a drink, said she loved me too much to make me unhappy. I'd never seen her that way before. She said I looked tired, and she tucked me up in bed, saying we could talk about our problems in the morning. To my surprise, I fell asleep almost at once and had the best night's sleep I'd had in weeks. In the morning she was just the same, telling me not to worry and everything would sort itself out."

"And that's the night your wife was murdered?"

"Yes! Sometimes I think I'm going mad, MacDougal. I *know* I didn't kill her, but then who did? The police said there was no sign of a break-in. She must have opened the door to whoever it was."

MacDougal pondered. "Mr. Hackford, I understand your wife's life was insured for a substantial amount?"

"Yes. We took out mutual policies at the time we thought we were having a child. I'd never given it much thought since."

"Did Joyce—Miss Stone—know about the insurance?"

"Joyce? Let me think. Yes, I did mention it once. But you don't mean . . . ? She was in bed with me all that night."

"Was she? I suspect there was something in your drink that gave you that inordinately sound sleep."

"Oh, Lord! I see what you mean. But she couldn't have. Enid was strangled, and I read somewhere that women never use that method to kill someone."

"It's rare, indeed. But a very strong woman, like Miss Stone, who wants to make it appear as a man's crime—yes, it's entirely possible."

"I do see your point. The police would believe the killer was the mysterious night visitor. Then, with Enid out of the way, Joyce was sure I'd end up marrying her. If she'd kept on with her winning ways, I expect I would have done. But if she did kill Enid, how would we ever prove it?"

"I'll have a little chat with the detective chief inspector."

When questioned, Miss Joyce Stone denied ever having entered the Hackford residence, but an unidentified handprint inside the front door of number 62 Mardale Road, and two fingerprints on the underside of a table near where the body of Mrs. Hackford was found, proved to be hers.

It soon became clear to MacDougal that his own role in the solution of the case had been conveniently forgotten. The press were loud in praise of the fine work of the CID, but no mention was made of Ian MacDougal.

With a shrug and a wry smile, MacDougal reflected, with King Lear, that ingratitude was indeed a marble-hearted fiend.

Homebodies

Barbara Paul

Annie broke her arm the day before they were to leave, trying to drag a trunk down from the attic. The trunk got away from her and bounced once off her forearm on its unaccompanied journey down the stairs.

"Why didn't you call me?" Jake demanded. "You shouldn't have tried it by yourself."

"Oh, you live so far away, and I didn't think it was that heavy," Annie explained. "Don't fuss so, Jake."

"What did you need the trunk for anyway? We were just going for the weekend."

"Mama wants to borrow it. She needs an extra one."

Jake thought the accident meant their trip was off, but Annie wouldn't hear of it. She'd rescheduled all her Friday clients (Annie was a speech therapist) just to make the trip, and make it she would. So she was wearing a blue canvas sling on her arm and a brave smile on her face when he picked her up early Friday morning. Jake wedged the bone-crunching trunk into the back of his car and they were on their way.

Jake wasn't as sanguine about the trip as Annie. It wasn't the best of conditions for meeting her family; they were going to a funeral. Annie's grandfather had died, the nearest thing to a patriarch her extensive family had had. Jake would have preferred the introductions to take place under less gloomy circumstances, but no sooner had the two of them agreed to marry than Annie started talking about taking him home to meet the folks. Then word came that Grandpa Kirkland had died.

Home was a town called Wrightsville, which Jake had been only vaguely aware of before he met Annie. Annie said everyone from both sides of the family had been born there, Kirklands and Pooles alike. She wanted *their* children to be born there. Jake had said *Ah* and *Um* and coughed discreetly. Annie went on that people liked to make jokes about returning to the Old Homestead, but it was heaven having a place to run to when you needed it, a place where you knew you would always be welcome.

They reached Wrightsville shortly before noon; the funeral was at two. "The house is an architectural nightmare," Annie warned with a laugh, "but inside it's roomy and comfortable." Jake saw what she meant as he pulled into the driveway. The house had been added on to many times, with no particular attention paid to matching the styles of either the earlier additions or the original structure. Most of the extensions had been tacked onto the rear, where a once spacious backyard had provided the most room for expansion.

Jake followed Annie to the kitchen door, where cries of *Annie!* and *Mama!* rose as Annie jerked the door open with her good arm. Then she and a large woman wearing a neck brace were hugging each other, and the latter was calling out, "Annie's home!" Jake stood holding the door and watching other people crowd into the kitchen.

Then both women pulled back, looked at each other, and said, "What happened?"

"Whiplash," said Annie's mother. "You?"

"Broken arm."

"Aw, baby. Does it hurt much?"

"Yes," Annie admitted. "But I have pain pills. Uncle Tedward! Cousin Bette! And Young Malcolm!" More hugging.

With a smile, Annie's mother reached out a big hand to Jake, still self-consciously holding the door. "You must be Jake—come in, come in! I'm so glad to meet you at last. We'll sit down and get acquainted properly once this business is finished."

By *this business,* Jake assumed she meant the funeral. He said, "I'm sorry about your loss, Mrs. Kirkland. It's hard, losing a father."

"Why, thank you, Jake. We're all going to miss having Grandpa Kirkland around. But he was my husband's father, not mine. And call me Mama Sue—it's easier that way. Annie, take Jake around and make sure he meets everybody."

Easier than what? Jake wondered.

"Come on!" Annie sang out, clearly enjoying her homecoming.

"Did you bring the trunk?" Mama Sue asked.

"It's in the car—Jake will get it later."

Jake followed Annie from room to room, pursuing a labyrinthine path he wasn't sure he could retrace on his own. At least three generations were in the house, from old folks to running children. The mood was surprisingly cheerful, as if they were all gathered for a family reunion party instead of a funeral. Jake met Aunt Dottie, Young Herbert, Grandma Kirkland (the new widow), Brother William, Malcolm Senior (who, oddly, had an ear missing), Cousin Oliver, and a number of others whose names he desperately tried to remember. There was even a Sister Kate—*whose* sister, Jake couldn't quite figure out. But he understood why Annie's mother said calling her Mama Sue would be easier; there were also a Mama Marcie and a Mama June.

Jake's stomach growled; it had been a long time since breakfast. "Uncle *Ted*ward?" Jake said questioningly to a distinguished-looking man wearing an eyepatch.

"My name's Edward, so of course I was called Teddy," the man explained pleasantly. "Somehow that eased over into Tedward as I grew older. I'm so used to 'Uncle Tedward' now that at times I forget what my real name is."

Jake looked around for Annie; he seemed to have lost her.

"Uncle Tedward, I wonder if you could point me toward a bathroom. We were in the car for five hours and—"

"Say no more, my boy. This way." Uncle Tedward led him to a narrow door opening off a landing separating two floor levels by only one step each way. Behind the narrow door was a rather spacious old-fashioned bathroom.

When he came out, Jake looked for Annie again but still couldn't spot her. He shook hands with an old man called Grandpa Poole, who peered at him myopically and murmured something that sounded like *Oh yes, June's boy,* and then wandered away. Jake's stomach growled again. He stopped a child running by, a little girl with a Mickey Mouse Band-Aid across her nose, and asked her to take him to the dining room; on his first trip through, he'd spotted a sideboard there loaded with sandwiches.

The girl led him to the food and then darted off. Jake helped himself to a tuna-fish sandwich and was chewing contentedly when a man about Jake's age stepped up to the sideboard and looked over the sandwiches. He glanced at Jake and said, "You must be The Fiancé. I'm Young Malcolm." He held out his left hand.

"Jake Dietrich," Jake said, shaking his hand awkwardly.

"Sorry about the left hand, but . . ." Young Malcolm held up his right arm to display the wrist splint he was wearing. "I don't know why, but funerals always make me hungry."

"Um. Tell me . . ."—Jake couldn't bring himself to call the other man *Young Malcolm*—" . . . do all these people live here?"

"In Wrightsville, you mean?" Young Malcolm asked around a mouthful of corned beef.

"In this house."

"Oh, no. Most of us have homes elsewhere, but a lot of us will be staying overnight. Kate and I are going to stay."

So Young Malcolm was married to Sister Kate. "A long drive back?" Jake asked, making conversation.

"We live in Meade."

Jake had never heard of Meade. Just then one of the Mamas came up on the other side of him and started building a Dagwood sandwich—Mama Marcie, Jake remembered. She looked at what was left of Jake's tuna-fish sandwich and made a *tsk-tsk* sound. "Is that all you're eating? Here, try some of these artichoke hearts. Uncle Tedward made a special sour cream dressing for them." She scooped two big spoonfuls onto a plate.

"Thank you," Jake said, not mentioning that he hated artichokes. As he took the plate from Mama Marcie, he noticed half of her left forefinger was missing.

She saw him looking and gave a rueful laugh. "I did it to myself. I was watching 'General Hospital' and chopping mushrooms at the same time and . . . well, I guess I got a little careless."

Jake's stomach turned over.

"Papa Ross told you that was going to happen," Young Malcolm said.

Jake put the artichokes down and said, "I, uh, I've got to go get a trunk out of the trunk."

"I'd offer to help, but . . ." Young Malcolm held up his wrist splint again.

"That's all right," Jake said hastily. "I can manage."

"Nonsense," Mama Marcie said, and then raised her voice. "Somebody here want to give The Fiancé a hand in moving a trunk?"

Several voices answered in the affirmative, and Jake picked out the healthiest-looking of the volunteers, a teen-aged boy who seemed to have all of his body parts intact. The two of them went out to the driveway and wrestled the trunk out of the car. Back in the kitchen, the boy said, "Where do you want it, Mama Sue?"

"Oh, down in the basement, dear, thank you."

Jake found himself on the wrong end of the trunk going down the narrow, poorly lighted stairway, but they made it to the bottom without mishap. Then, just as they were moving the trunk against a wall, the boy dropped his end; Jake barely got his foot out of the way in time.

"Hey, good reflexes!" the boy said blithely.

Jake muttered something under his breath and headed back up to the kitchen. There he turned to the boy and said, "Er, thanks for your help, ah . . ."

"Cousin Rathbone." The boy gave him a cheery grin and headed back toward the dining room.

Jake turned to Mama Sue. "Did he say 'Rathbone'?"

"Yes, dear. His name's Basil, but no one calls him that. It's a kind of joke, you see." She and Uncle Tedward were busy putting meats in the oven to finish roasting while they were all at the funeral. "Why don't you go find Annie?" Mama Sue asked. "It's time we were leaving for the cemetery."

Jake found her in the rear living room (the house had two) talking to the little girl with the Mickey Mouse Band-Aid on her nose. "And you mustn't run around during the funeral, Little Marcie," Annie was saying earnestly. "All you kids—you mustn't run."

"Mama already told us that," Little Marcie said.

"Well, I'm telling you again. No running! Now, scoot." The child ran away as fast as she could, and Annie turned to smile at Jake. "Time to go?"

Outside, the family's automobiles were parked all up and down the street; still, Jake wondered if there were enough to accommodate so many people. But before the mob on the sidewalk could start getting in the cars, a big Greyhound bus lumbered by, belching black smoke over everyone. "This is too much!" Malcolm Senior said. "I say we get a lawyer."

"No," a woman Jake couldn't identify chimed in, "we need to go to city council and get an ordinance passed."

"The bus station's only a block down that way," Annie said to Jake, pointing. "They could just as easily route their coaches along Mansmann Boulevard, but they send them through this residential area instead. They say it saves time."

Malcolm Senior snorted. "Eleven minutes! It saves them eleven minutes exactly. And we get stuck with the noise and the fumes. Well, we'd better get going." Everyone seemed to head for whatever car was nearest.

"Er, should I drive?" Jake asked.

Only Cousin Rathbone heard him. "Hey," he yelled, "do we need The Fiancé's car?" Replies of *No* and *Plenty of room* floated back.

Jake followed Annie into the backseat of someone's
Buick, taking care not to bump her broken arm as he settled
in. A fat man sat wedged behind the driver's wheel, need-
lessly revving the engine. The straw-haired woman sitting
next to him turned and smiled. "It's so good to see you
again, Little Annie."

"And it's good to see you, Cousin Philippa. It's been a
while." Then she noticed the expression on Jake's face and
explained, "I was always called Little Annie to distinguish
me from Mama's sister. I was named after Aunt Annie."

"Who died just last year," Cousin Philippa added with a
sigh. "We all miss her."

The fat man behind the wheel pulled the car away from
the curb. "Damned stupid way to go, if you ask me," he
muttered.

"Now, William," Cousin Philippa said.

Brother William, Jake remembered, and asked, "How did
she die?"

"She shoulda had that old furnace replaced years ago,"
Brother William growled.

"It blew up?" Jake asked, alarmed.

"Oh no, nothing like that," Annie said. "My, you are
jumpy, Jake."

Cousin Philippa said, "Aunt Annie's house had a big
old-fashioned coal furnace, and during the winter months
she or Uncle Weldon had to go down and shovel in coal
three and four times a day. One day last winter Aunt Annie
evidently tripped over the shovel or something, and she fell
headfirst into the furnace. Just the top half of her, you
understand. It was a shock for Weldon to find her like that,
ashes from the waist up." She smiled apologetically. "Aunt
Annie always was a bit clumsy."

"Damned stupid way to go," Brother William repeated.

Jake didn't have another word to say the entire drive.

The funeral was to be a graveside ceremony. The cemetery was a large one, beautifully kept. Only five chairs had
been placed by the grave, for the nearest of kin. Everyone
else was expected to stand—including Mama June, who
Jake was mildly surprised to see, was on crutches; she'd been

seated when Annie introduced her back at the house and Jake had noticed nothing wrong. The five chairs were occupied by Grandma Kirkland, one middle-aged woman, and three middle-aged men, one of whom was leaning heavily upon a cane. The widow and her four children. It struck Jake that he'd not yet met Annie's father; he must be one of the three men sitting with Grandma Kirkland.

The minister began to speak, and Jake quickly concluded that either Grandpa Kirkland had been the saintliest mortal ever to walk on the face of the earth or the minister was the biggest liar he'd ever come across. Jake stole a look at Annie; her face revealed nothing of what she was feeling. Cousin Bette started snuffling into a handkerchief. The kids got fidgety as the minister droned on, but on the whole they were well behaved. Once Grandpa Poole told the minister to speak up, but that was the only unusual thing that happened.

When the minister finished his hyperbolic eulogy, Grandma Kirkland stepped forward and scattered a handful of soil over the closed coffin. One by one, her four adult children followed suit. The coffin was not lowered into the ground; that would be taken care of after the family had left.

"I've never actually seen that done before," Jake said to Annie as they walked back to Brother William's car. "The scattering of soil on the coffin, I mean. I suppose that's why the coffin was kept closed."

"Not really. It was just that the remains were in no condition to be viewed," Annie replied.

"A long, wasting illness, was it?"

"No, Grandpa Kirkland was a robust old man until the day he died. Didn't I tell you? He slipped and fell under a street-cleaning machine—all those big brushes and things? Poor Grandpa, he didn't have a chance."

Jake's head was reeling. He could hear the others talking in the car on the way home, but he tuned out.

Brother William's car was one of the last to get back. As they parked, they could see everyone milling around another car, which now sported a crumpled fender and a smashed grill. "Of course," Jake said light-headedly as he got out of the backseat. "Naturally." Cousin Oliver was holding the back of his neck and grimacing; Jake watched as Mama Sue took off her neck brace and handed it to him.

Suddenly Jake needed a drink; he needed one badly. He left Annie gawking at the semiwrecked car and headed into the house. He found his way to the dining room, where the sideboard had mysteriously been cleared of food. But there had to be something to drink. "So where's the hooch?" he asked aloud.

"It's down here," a tiny voice answered him. Jake looked down to see Little Marcie pulling open one of the doors of the sideboard to reveal at least a dozen bottles of liquor.

"Child, you are an angel in disguise," Jake said, pulling out a bottle of scotch. Little Marcie giggled and ran away.

By the time the others started drifting in, Jake was working on his fourth drink. Annie walked in and spotted Jake; she sat down and put a gentle hand on his knee. "Are you all right, Jake? You look as if something's wrong."

"Oh, I'm awright, awright!" he said, slurring his words. "In fact, I jus' may be th'only one here who *is* awright." He finished off his drink. "No broken bones, no missing body parts." He thought a moment. "No, wai' a mint. Cousin Bathbone is awright. Nothin' wrong wi'him."

Annie laughed. "Cousin *Bath*bone?"

"Yeah. Rasil Bathbone. He's okay."

"Yes, he does seem in good shape, doesn't he? I guess he's completely recovered by now. Oh, Mama June—wait, let me take those crutches." She went to help the older woman.

Jake fixed himself another drink.

"Going to City Council won't stop the buses," Malcolm Senior was saying, fingering the scar on the side of his head where his ear used to be. "They'll take two years just to put the matter on the agenda."

"Well, maybe we do need a lawyer," Aunt Philippa conceded.

"Speaking of lawyers, where's Mr. Cahill?" someone asked—Aunt Dottie, if Jake remembered correctly.

"Should be here by now."

"Hey, Mama Sue, when do we eat?" Brasil Muthbone.

"Ask your Uncle Tedward—he's doing the honors."

"Just as soon as the will's read," Uncle Tedward said.

"Uncle Will?" Jake asked tipsily. "Papa Will? Brother Will?"

Nobody paid any attention. "Why don't we ask Mr. Cahill to sue the bus people for us?" Aunt Dottie asked.

Brother William shook his head. "Cahill isn't a trial lawyer, and it may go to trial."

The one called Young Herbert said, "Isn't The Fiancé a lawyer?"

Every head in the room turned toward Jake.

"'M'nengi'eer," he mumbled.

"He's an engineer," Annie translated.

"Well, maybe Cahill can recommend someone."

"Too bad The Fiancé isn't a lawyer."

"Jake," Jake said thickly. "M'name's Jake."

Grandpa Poole nodded at him pleasantly. "June's boy."

Just then a young woman Jake would have sworn he'd never laid eyes on before appeared at the door to announce Mr. Cahill had arrived and was ready to read the will. Everyone got up and trooped into one of the two living rooms—*How'd they know which one?* Jake thought woozily as he weaved after them.

He and Annie found an ottoman they could share by sitting back to back; the other furniture in the room was soon filled, and various cousins and uncles and the like had to lean against the walls or sit on the floor. "Annie," Jake said over his shoulder in a low voice, "which one's your father?"

"Why, you met him, Jake. He's the one with the cane. That's Papa Ross."

Jake stared at the man with the cane. "I dint meetum."

Annie sniffed. "You've had too much to drink."

Jake didn't answer but turned his attention to the lawyer. Mr. Cahill, it so happened, was built like a linebacker; but the appearance was deceptive. The lawyer had a prissy way of speaking that was totally at odds with his bone-mangler looks, and he probably would have been ineffectual in a courtroom. He seemed to be in a hurry. *Wants to get out of here before somebody drops a piano on his head,* Jake thought gloomily.

"Are we all here?" Cahill asked, and then without waiting for an answer: "Good. I will now proceed to read the will." He cleared his throat. "'I, Donald Clarence Kirkland, being of sound mind and body, have decided to dispense with the usual legalistic horseshit that nobody pays attention to and get straight to the point. This is how the loot is going to be divided.'"

The first part of the will seemed to be what everyone expected, an equitable division of property and money among the widow and the four surviving children. Jake noticed the family listened to this part with barely concealed impatience. It was when Cahill got to the disposition of personal property that everyone perked up.

It seems that Grandpa Kirkland was a collector, or perhaps *accumulator* was a better word. The old man's choices of who-got-what were as arcane as what he'd actually left behind. Teenaged Cousin Rathbone's mouth fell open when he heard he'd been bequeathed an eight-by-fourteen Art Deco wall hanging depicting a stylized sunset in the Florida keys. Cousin Philippa grumbled audibly at the news that Grandpa had left her his antique Highlander bagpipe. Grandpa Poole wondered out loud what he was expected to do with a Carrara marble faun.

"'To my granddaughter Annie Kirkland, who never read a word of Charles Dickens in her life,'" Cahill intoned, "'I leave my collection of first editions of Dickens's work.'"

"We read *Great Expectations* in school," Annie said defensively.

"'And my beloved sloop, the *Pandora,*'" Cahill went on, "'goes to my nephew, Edward Poole, in the secure knowledge that he will maintain her in the high style the old girl deserves.'"

"Uncle Tedward!" Young Malcolm exclaimed, unbelieving. "Uncle Tedward gets the *Pandora?*"

Uncle Tedward fiddled with the strap of his eye patch. "You were expecting the boat, Young Malcolm? I'm sorry if you're disappointed, but Grandpa Kirkland promised it to me long ago."

"What's going on here?" Young Malcolm shouted. "I spent every free minute of the past two years taking care of that tub, and Grandpa told me he'd leave it to me when he died!"

"I hate to tell you guys this," Aunt Dottie spoke up, "but Grandpa Kirkland promised *me* the *Pandora.*"

"It doesn't matter if he promised it to every member of the family," Cahill said testily, "he left it to Tedward and that's that. May we get on with it?"

As he went on reading the will, the grumbling grew more open. "Diamond cuff links?" Cousin Oliver complained. "Nobody wears cuff links anymore!" Mama Sue was amazed to learn she now owned all her father-in-law's deep-sea fishing gear. By the time Cahill was finished, the only one who looked happy with his inheritance was a twelve-year-old boy to whom Grandpa Kirkland had left a lifetime subscription to *Smut* magazine.

"That concludes the reading of the will," Cahill said, trying to make himself heard above the hubbub. "If you have any questions . . . ah, no, I suppose not. Well, then. Don't bother—I'll see myself out." Jake was the only one who noticed him go.

"Why did he leave me his Lincoln?" Mama Marcie asked the room at large. "He knew I didn't drive."

"I'll swap you my Burger King shares for it," Young Herbert offered.

Mama Marcie looked interested. "What are they worth?"

"Don't know. Let's check the market listings." They went off in search of a newspaper.

"Does this always happen?" Jake was losing his buzz; he sounded almost sober.

"Just about," Annie said with a smile. "You know what I think? I think Grandpa Kirkland deliberately made his bequests as inappropriate as he could, just to give everybody a good time swapping and bargaining. Did you hear what he left Little Marcie? A set of power tools."

Jake shook his head. "Kind of a bad joke for Young Malcolm, though. He really wanted the *Pandora*."

"I know. But last year when Grandma Poole died, she left him a Matisse everybody else wanted. Things even out." She paused to turn down Mama June's offer to swap her high-density television/entertainment center for Annie's first editions. "It'll be all right, Jake—you'll see."

Then it was time to eat—real food this time, not snacky stuff like sandwiches and artichoke hearts. Mama Sue was sitting this one out, gladly turning her kitchen over to Uncle Tedward and a few helpers. Uncle Tedward placed a big roast on the sideboard next to a steaming turkey; "I like to cook," he said to no one in particular. It was grab-and-sit dining; Jake loaded a plate with meat and potatoes, took a cup of strong black coffee, and looked for a seat at the enormous dining table, now rapidly filling up. He squeezed in between Brother William, the fattest person in the room, and Cousin Bette, the skinniest. Jake drank down his coffee and went for another; he wanted all his wits about him with this bunch.

Young Malcolm hadn't given up on the sloop. "What'll you take for the *Pandora,* Uncle Tedward?"

"Ah, I've forgotten what Grandpa Kirkland left you."

"The duelling pistols. You've always admired those."

A laugh. "But not enough to give up the *Pandora* for them."

"I meant in addition to cash."

Uncle Tedward chewed his meat thoughtfully. "I don't think so. But you're welcome to come for a sail whenever you like."

"That's not the same thing," Young Malcolm muttered.

"No, it isn't," Uncle Tedward agreed cheerfully.

"You want to buy the deep-sea fishing gear?" Mama Sue asked him.

"I might. Let me think about it."

Little Marcie had sold her power tools to Malcolm Senior and was now trying to buy Mama June's high-density television. Jake listened to the dickering with amazement;

Mama June was making no allowance at all for the fact that Little Marcie was a child, thumping a crutch against the floor in a vain attempt to intimidate her. Annie swapped her first editions for an empty lot in a rundown section of Wrightsville. "It'll be worth something someday," she said optimistically.

It had been a long day and Jake was tired, but he persuaded Annie to go for a stroll before turning in; he needed to get out of the house for a while. They wandered past the bus station, now closed down for the night. Jake cleared his throat and said what was on his mind. "Annie, I'd like to go back to the city tomorrow. We could leave early and be back by noon."

She looked hurt. "But why, Jake? We came for the weekend—it would be rude to leave on Saturday morning."

"Do you really think anyone would miss us?"

"Of course they'd miss us! Did something happen? Why do you want to leave?"

Because your relatives are a bunch of kooks with no idea of personal safety. "I'm uncomfortable, Annie. I don't fit in here."

"Oh, Jake!" She stopped and gave him a hug, pressing her arm cast against his back. "I know the family can be overwhelming at first, but give yourself a chance to know them a little better before you bail out. They're good people."

"Yes, they all seem nice." *Nice and dangerous.* "But I truly would like to go home."

She sighed. "Ah, but you see, I *am* home. How about a compromise? We'll leave early Sunday morning instead of waiting until late afternoon. You can stick it out one more day, can't you?"

It was Jake's turn to sigh; she looked so hurt, he didn't have the heart to insist. "All right, Annie. One more day."

For a few minutes they hung on to each other there on the deserted sidewalk and then turned and walked back to the house. Jake said good night and went upstairs. He was sharing a room with Cousin Oliver, who spent a good forty-five minutes trying to figure out how to sleep in Mama Sue's neck brace before giving up and taking the thing off.

Jake was awakened the next morning by Annie's hand on his shoulder and her urgent voice in his ear. "Jake, wake up! Something terrible's happened. Get up and get dressed." She went over to the next bed to wake Cousin Oliver.

Jake swung his feet to the floor. "What's wrong?"

When she was sure they were both awake, Annie said, "There's been an accident. I'm afraid Uncle Tedward is dead. He slipped on some grease on the kitchen floor and cracked his head against the corner of the table. Mama found him when she went down to start the coffee."

"Ah, *hell!*" Cousin Oliver said, and got out of bed.

"Hurry, Jake," Annie urged, and left them to get dressed.

Jake pulled his clothes on quickly; in a daze he followed Cousin Oliver downstairs. Most of the family were gathered in the dining room, some crowded into the doorway that led to the kitchen. *I don't want to see this,* Jake thought, and was horrified to find himself elbowing his way to the front.

Uncle Tedward lay sprawled on the kitchen floor, the back of his head a bloody mess. The grease was shiny on the tiled floor—it looked like turkey grease—and the corner of the table had blood on it. Papa Ross stood leaning on his cane with one hand and patting Mama Sue's shoulder with the other. "He was going to fix us all breakfast," she sniffled. "All I had to do was the coffee." Jake looked at Uncle Tedward and thought: *Just how badly did Young Malcolm want that damned boat anyway?* And immediately felt ashamed.

Cousin Philippa said, "Shouldn't we take him upstairs or cover him up or something?"

"No, no," Papa Ross said hurriedly. "We promised Sheriff Fleming that the next time something happened, we wouldn't touch a thing. He was quite adamant about that."

"Did you call him?"

"Yes, he's on his way."

Jake still hadn't exchanged a single word with Annie's father, but this was hardly the time to introduce himself. He eased over next to one of the two double-doored refrigerators, being careful to avoid the grease on the floor, as more members of the family crowded in for one final look at poor dead Uncle Tedward. From a distance came the sound of a siren. "Here's the sheriff," someone said unnecessarily.

Sheriff Fleming came in the back way, took one look at the mob in the kitchen, and ordered everybody out; no one budged. The sheriff was almost as fat as Brother William, and he was followed by a younger man with bulging eyes and broad features that gave him an unfortunate resemblance to a frog. Sheriff Fleming jerked his thumb over his shoulder at the frogman and said, "M'new deputy. Name's Harrelson. Now, let's see what we got here."

The sheriff hunkered down beside the body but didn't touch anything. He looked at the grease on the floor and examined the corner of the table where Uncle Tedward's head had hit. "You figure he slipped in the grease and hit his head?"

"That must be what happened," Papa Ross said.

Deputy Harrelson was studying the floor. "That's an awful lot of grease. An *awful* lot. How could he miss seeing it?"

"He had only one eye, Deputy," Aunt Dottie said in a tone of mild reprimand.

"Still, that's an awful lot—looks as if somebody just took a roaster pan full of grease and sloshed it all over the floor."

A murmur ran through the family. "You can't be suggesting murder!" exclaimed the quavery voice of Grandma Kirkland, the new widow; it was the first time Jake had heard her speak.

Malcolm Senior snorted. "Damnfool way to go about murdering someone. How could the killer be sure it'd work?"

"He wouldn't have to be," Deputy Harrelson said earnestly. "It'd be easy enough to finish off the job—a piece of pipe or a wrench would do the trick."

"Ugh!" said Annie. Somebody gagged.

Sheriff Fleming got up and walked over to drop a heavy hand on his deputy's shoulder. He lowered his voice, but not enough so that every word wasn't audible to the others in the kitchen. "Harrelson, you're new here and you don't know this family—but *believe* me when I tell you it was an accident. Don't go looking for crimes where there ain't none. Now, why don't you go get the camera out of the car and take pictures of all this here?"

Deputy Harrelson looked disappointed but did as he was told. Jake stared at the floor. The deputy was right; it was an awful lot of grease. He couldn't make out any skid marks, any disturbed surface that looked as if it had been caused by a slipping foot. Could the grease have been thrown on the floor *after* Uncle Tedward had died? The sheriff was looking the other way; Jake quickly bent down and dabbed at the grease. He sniffed his fingers; turkey grease, all right.

Sheriff Fleming stepped gingerly around the grease over to Mama Sue and Papa Ross. "The coroner's gone hunting for the weekend, and there's no way to get hold of him. I'm going to call Detweiler's Mortuary to come get Uncle Tedward and keep him till Monday morning."

Mama Sue sniffled. "We always use Sandler's Funeral Home."

"Yes'm, but Mr. Detweiler, he has a couple of those deep-freeze units, you know? So's to preserve Uncle Tedward until the coroner gets a look at him on Monday. Y'unnerstand."

Just then Deputy Harrelson came back with the camera, and this time everyone did have to leave. In the dining room, Jake asked Mama Sue what she usually did with leftover turkey drippings.

"Sometimes I save the stuff for soup," she said, "but usually I just throw it out. It's not all that tasty, you know, and not really very good for you. But remember Uncle Tedward did the cooking yesterday. He might have saved the grease."

"But what would he have been doing with it this morning? Wasn't he fixing breakfast?"

"Who knows what he was up to? Uncle Tedward loved to experiment—maybe he'd thought up some new recipe for eggs."

"Eggs cooked in turkey grease?"

Mama Sue made a face. "It doesn't sound too likely, does it, dear?" With an apologetic smile she changed the subject. "I think it would be simpler if we just sent somebody out to get our breakfast. Oh, Young Herbert!" she called across the room, and moved away. Evidently a death in the family wasn't reason enough to skip breakfast.

Jake sank into a chair at the dining room table and buried his face in his hands. What a *godawful* weekend. He sensed rather than saw someone sit down next to him. "Not the best way to meet the family, is it?" a voice said.

He looked up to see Young Malcolm scratching his nose with his right hand. "You're not wearing your wrist splint," Jake said.

Young Malcolm looked at the palm of his hand as if some explanation were written there. "I don't think I need it anymore. It *feels* all right." He flexed his wrist a couple of times.

"What happens now?"

"Well, I guess we'll all be staying on for another funeral. This is Saturday morning . . . Monday, I'd say. No, wait—the coroner has to examine the body on Monday. Tuesday, then. I'm going to have to call my boss."

Jake was thinking he would *not* have to call his boss, as he fully intended to hold Annie to her promise to leave early Sunday morning. He was sorry about Uncle Tedward, but Sunday morning he was *out of here*.

Jake felt uneasy sitting next to Young Malcolm; he excused himself and went looking for Annie. When he found her, Jake drew her out on the front porch away from the others. "Uncle Tedward didn't have time to make a new will," he said to her, "so who gets the sloop now? Who inherits?"

Her eyebrows shot up. "It looks as if Young Malcolm's going to end up with it after all."

It was the answer he'd expected, but he still didn't understand. "Isn't he Malcolm Senior's son?"

"He is, but . . . well, Uncle Tedward was a widower. He had only one child, a daughter, and that's Sister Kate."

Jake nodded. "And Kate is married to Young Malcolm. That would do it, all right."

Annie looked at him oddly. "Jake, what are you thinking?"

He took a deep breath and told her his suspicion that the turkey grease had been spilled on the floor deliberately, to make Uncle Tedward's death look like an accident. "And with Young Malcolm so hot for the *Pandora* . . ."

She was horrified. "Jake, are you out of your mind? You think one of us . . . would kill another one of us? You don't know what you're saying!"

"Annie, I know it's only—"

"You don't know anything! You look at a spot of grease for ten seconds and you conclude Young Malcolm is a killer!" She was near tears. "That's a dumb murder weapon anyway —turkey grease!"

"It's a false clue," Jake corrected. "Annie, try to calm down—"

"Don't you tell me to calm down! You come here to my home, you accept our hospitality, and right away you decide we're not good enough for you and you want to leave! And now you come up with this stupid theory—"

"Dammit, Annie, if you'd only *listen*—"

A new voice interrupted them. "Come on, you two, don't fight. Not now." Brother William stood filling the doorway to the porch. "Save it for later."

Angrily Annie pushed past him and went back into the house. Jake heaved a big sigh and sank down sideways on the top step, leaning his back against one of the porch pillars. If Annie didn't believe him, who would?

Brother William wheezed as he lowered his considerable bulk to the step next to Jake. "Lovers' spats always seem to be a part of it, but now isn't a good time."

"I know." Jake used the pillar at his back to scratch an itch.

"You'll make it up. Annie's a good girl." The fat man looked for a softer spot on the step, couldn't find one. "It's about time we had a wedding in the family again. It's been a while. Of course, Carolyn *almost* got married last year."

Who the hell was Carolyn? "They called it off?"

"No, they had the church and the minister and the bridesmaids and about a million guests invited—everything was all set up. Then two nights before the wedding, Carolyn and her fella—Ryan, his name was—they drove up to Lookout Point. Local lovers' lane, you know. Anyway, Carolyn and Ryan were getting in a little last-minute premarital smooching when the car brakes gave way." Brother William made an over-the-cliff motion with his hand and arm. "Carolyn got out with only a few bumps and bruises, but poor Ryan was in traction for six weeks." A sigh. "Then Carolyn broke the engagement. She said he was unlucky." He shook his head. "It really was too bad. Ryan sounded like a nice fella."

My god, it's contagious! Jake fought off a wave of hysteria and fixed on something Brother William had said. "What do you mean, Ryan *sounded* like a nice fella? Didn't you know him?"

"Nope. Never met 'im. The time the wedding was scheduled, well, we couldn't make the trip. Philippa had both legs in casts then, all the way up to her hips."

I'm not going to ask, Jake thought, *I am definitely NOT going to ask.* "What happened?" he asked.

"She fell off a hang glider. A woman her age! You'd think she—hey! What are you doing that for?"

Jake was banging his head against the pillar.

Forty minutes later, Jake was finishing off his cold Egg McMuffin and nursing a headache. The men from the mortuary had come and taken Uncle Tedward's body away; Sheriff Fleming and his underappreciated deputy were long gone. Young Herbert and a man Jake couldn't put a name to came in with cardboard boxes filled with breakfast food. While they were all eating, someone suggested that maybe The Fiancé would take care of clean-up. They were including him in the family chores now; wasn't that nice.

Jake went to the kitchen for a plastic garbage bag and stared at a greaseless floor and a bloodless kitchen table; somebody had taken care of *that* clean-up quickly enough.

He went through the house collecting paper cartons, cups, napkins, leftover food, thinking all the while that maybe Annie was right. Maybe he'd jumped to a big conclusion from very skimpy evidence.

When the plastic bag was full, Jake took it out back to the garbage cans, all eight of them. And all eight were full. Hold on—the one on the end might still have some room. He started pulling out the smaller plastic bags to make room for his big one and came across something wrapped in newspaper. Curious, he opened it . . . and found a wrist splint. Young Malcolm's wrist splint. Why did he throw it away—why not just save it for the next time? Then Jake noticed the splint was stained, and it felt greasy. He sniffed at it. Turkey grease.

Jake's mouth fell open when he realized he was holding evidence in his hand, evidence that would at least place Young Malcolm in the kitchen at the time the grease was sloshed/spilled/poured onto the floor. Garbage cans forgotten, Jake ran back into the house to look for Annie. No: she'd just get mad at him again. And this was *evidence* he had, for crying out loud; best go straight to Sheriff Fleming with it.

The nearest phone was in a hallway separating the two living rooms. Jake looked but couldn't find a phone book. He was asking directory assistance for the sheriff's number when a hand reached from behind him and broke the connection. Jake watched in horror as another hand took the stained wrist splint away from him. "I don't think you want to make that call," Young Malcolm said tightly as he grabbed Jake by the upper arm. "Come on."

It's the first time I've ever been grabbed by a murderer, Jake thought idiotically. "Wh-where're we going?"

"Out back."

Jake was not a big man; Young Malcolm, unfortunately, was. Jake could put up only token resistance as the other man propelled him out through the back door. There was enough backyard left to accommodate an outdoor stone grill; Young Malcolm pushed the wrist splint into the ashes.

Do something! Jake thought. Scared to death, he neverthe-less made a grab for the splint. Young Malcolm stopped him simply by picking up a long-handled cooking fork and cracking him across the knuckles. Then Uncle Tedward's killer calmly pulled out a cigarette lighter and set fire to the wrist splint. "Should have done that in the first place," he muttered.

The rubberized parts of the splint stank, and Young Malcolm had to keep relighting the fire, but eventually Jake's evidence burned away as he watched. His arm hurt where Young Malcolm was still gripping him. "Could you let go of me now?"

"Not until I'm sure you understand something." The other man looked at him closely, as if trying to see into Jake's mind. "Without the wrist splint," Young Malcolm said, "it's your word against mine. Which one of us do you think the family's going to believe? Hell, even Sheriff Fleming would take my word over yours. Without the splint, you've got nothing."

The weapon, Jake thought desperately, *there has to be a weapon.*

"And if you're thinking of looking for a weapon, I'll save you some time and tell you it's right there in the kitchen— already inspected by the sheriff and cleaned up by Mama Sue. I just bashed his head against the corner of the table. That's all it took."

Jake was trying not to throw up. "How could you do it? How could you . . . you took a life . . . all because of some stupid boat?"

"Because of a promise," Young Malcolm said earnestly. "We take our promises seriously in this family, and Grand-pa Kirkland promised me the *Pandora.* And Uncle Tedward knew it! He knew it all along. He should have refused the bequest in favor of me." He paused for a moment. "You know, I'm very fond of Annie, and I'd hate to see her lose her husband before she even marries him."

It took a moment for Jake to get his heart out of his throat. "Are you threatening me?" he asked, suddenly a tenor.

Young Malcolm considered. "Yes," he said. "Just remember—what I did to Tedward, I can do to you. *Do you understand?*"

Before Jake could answer, Mama Sue opened the back door and called to them. "You busy, fellas? I need some help."

As they started back to the house, Young Malcolm muttered under his breath to Jake, "Remember."

As if I could ever POSSIBLY forget.

"It's Grandma Kirkland," Mama Sue said as they entered the kitchen. "She's got it into her head that she wants to pack up all of Grandpa Kirkland's clothes right now, for the Goodwill people. I'm sorry, Jake, I wouldn't have had you take the trunk down to the basement in the first place if I'd known . . . I thought she'd wait awhile. But she's got her mind made up."

"You want us to bring the trunk up from the basement," Jake said dully. "Malcolm and me. In the basement."

"If you don't mind, dear."

"Of course we don't mind," Young Malcolm said smoothly, pushing open the door to the basement and holding it so Jake would have to go first.

Jake told himself he was being foolish, that Young Malcolm wouldn't do anything with Mama Sue right there in the kitchen. He picked his way down the narrow stairs and grabbed one of the trunk handles. Young Malcolm could see he was nervous . . . and did nothing at all to relieve the tension. *Maybe he likes having someone afraid of him,* Jake thought.

Once again he was stuck on the wrong end. Young Malcolm backed his way up the stairs, letting Jake bear most of the weight a few steps farther down. *All he has to do is let go of his end . . .* Jake pushed the thought away.

"Dammit!" Young Malcolm exploded. "Someone shut the door." They edged up to within two steps of the door; Young Malcolm balanced his end of the trunk on his knee and groped behind him for the doorknob.

Suddenly the door swung open, catching Young Malcolm's half-turned shoulder. Both men yelled as they lost their purchase and started an unstoppable tumble down the steps. Jake felt his ankle go *crunch* and let out a scream as both the trunk and Young Malcolm rolled right over him. *It's true,* Jake thought dizzily, *you really do see stars.* He looked up to the top of the stairs; Little Marcie was standing there holding the door, a look of innocent surprise on her face.

Jake tried to move and ended up screaming again as the pain shot up his leg. Even so, he'd fared better than Young Malcolm. The other man lay at the bottom of the stairs with his head at an impossible angle; the broken neck and staring eyes told Jake that Young Malcolm would be committing no more murders.

"That's the second dead body I've seen today," Jake said, and passed out.

The first thing he saw when he opened his eyes was the brace around Cousin Oliver's neck. Jake closed his eyes and burrowed deeper into the bed. *Go away.*

"How ya doin', sport?" asked Oliver's friendly voice.

Jake opened his eyes again. "Better than yesterday."

Cousin Oliver grinned. "Glad to hear it." He went out to the top of the stairway and called down, "He's awake!"

Jake cautiously moved his legs; the cast on his broken ankle was heavy. Much of Saturday was a blur. He remembered the hours in the hospital, hours when he felt safe and cared for—feelings he had never previously harbored about hospitals. He remembered telling how Little Marcie's unexpected opening of the basement door had started Young Malcolm and the trunk rolling down the steps. He'd told the story to the family, to hospital officials, to Sheriff Fleming. Deputy Harrelson had started asking questions that made it clear he suspected Jake of engineering the accident . . . until the sheriff shut him up. Jake no longer considered the deputy underappreciated.

He felt a surge of gratitude toward Little Marcie; the child had unknowingly solved his problem for him—and perhaps even saved his life. Right now he wanted to get Annie to talk a taxi driver into taking them all the way back to the city;

and the sooner they started, the better. Jake glanced at the window and was surprised to see how high the sun was. The pain pills the doctor gave him had completely knocked him out; he'd slept straight through the night and most of Sunday morning.

Mama Marcie was the first up the stairs in response to Cousin Oliver's announcement that Jake was awake. "Oh, I'm not going to ask you if you're feeling better, because I can see you are! Here, let me fix your pillow."

Jake let her. "Mama Marcie, I hope your daughter isn't, well, I hope she doesn't feel guilty about what happened."

"My daughter?" Mama Marcie looked puzzled. "Rita's in Alaska."

Rita? "I meant Little Marcie."

"Oh, Little Marcie's my niece. And no, she doesn't seem to feel guilty. We think she doesn't understand it was her opening the door that made Young Malcolm lose his balance. And nobody's going to tell her, right?"

"Absolutely right."

Then the others started trooping in—Mama Sue, Aunt Dottie, Cousin Rathbone, a few faces Jake still had no names for. Even Little Marcie came in; she stared big-eyed at Jake for a moment and then ran away. "William and Papa Ross send their regards," Cousin Philippa said. "Stairs are kind of hard for them."

"How's Malcolm Senior doing?" Jake asked.

"About as well as could be expected. We're planning a double funeral for Tuesday. We think Uncle Tedward and Young Malcolm would have liked it that way."

Jake was sure Uncle Tedward would have hated it. He looked over the crowd; the one face he wanted to see wasn't there. "Where's Annie?"

The others all exchanged furtive glances and left the explaining to Mama Sue. "She's gone back to the city, Jake. She took your car keys and left about an hour ago."

"What?"

"Try not to get excited, dear. Annie said she had a client early Monday morning she didn't want to put off—you know how conscientious she is about her speech therapy thing. And since you were in no condition to travel . . . well."

Panic hit Jake from several different directions. "She left without me? You let her go alone? That's a five-hour drive, and she has a broken arm! She'll wreck the car! She'll kill herself! She didn't even *tell* me she was going!"

Aunt Dottie sighed. "Annie said you'd fuss."

"She's perfectly capable of making the drive," Mama Sue said soothingly. "Annie said tell you she'd call your boss and explain. And she'll be coming back next weekend to get you. So you just take the week to recuperate, and before long you'll be good as new."

"She left me here?"

"Where better? Cousin Oliver is going to be right there in the bed next to you in case you need anything during the night. And the rest of the time you'll have all of us looking after you—you'll never be alone. This is where you belong, dear. You're part of the family now."

Never before had mere words struck such a chill in Jake's soul.

Mama Sue mistook the look of terror on his face for fatigue and started shooing everybody out. "Get some rest, and after a while I'll send up a nice tray. And don't you worry about a thing, Jake. We're going to take care of you." She closed the door gently behind her.

They all wandered downstairs into the front living room. "How's he doing?" Papa Ross asked.

"He'll be all right," Mama Marcie said. "A little upset because Annie left without saying goodbye, but he'll get over that."

"Lord, I hope so," Brother William wheezed. "We need a wedding in this family."

"We ought to take that trunk out and burn it," Cousin Rathbone said. "It got Annie and The Fiancé both. And Young Malcolm too, in a way."

"It's hard to believe," Aunt Dottie said sadly. "First Grandpa Kirkland, then Uncle Tedward, and now Young Malcolm. All gone within a week."

"Yeah," said Cousin Oliver in a tone of awe. "Three

deaths in one week! That must be some kind of family record, isn't it, Mama Sue?"

She thought back. "I do believe you're right. Papa Sherman and Uncle Mike and Sister Pamela all died in the same month, but this is the first time we've had three in one week."

"A family record," Young Herbert agreed. "It could have been four, you know. The Fiancé came pretty damn close."

"Strange fella, that Fiancé," Brother William remarked. "Doesn't talk much."

"There he goes," Little Marcie said in her tiny voice. Cousin Rathbone joined her at the window.

The last they saw of him, Jake was heading down the street toward the bus station, stumping along as fast as Mama June's crutches would carry him.

Happiness
Is a Dead Poet

Sharyn McCrumb

The first thing Rose Hanelon did at the Unicoi Writers
Conference was to commandeer the reservation clerk's
typewriter, and change her name tag from "Guest Author"
to "Nobody in Particular."

It wouldn't work for long, of course. By the end of the
Welcoming Reception, the conference organizers would
have introduced her to enough novices for word to get
around, and she would spend the rest of the conference
listening to plot summaries of romance novels (surely
superfluous, since romance novels *had* only one plot);
dodging poets carrying yellow legal pads; and trying to look
sympathetic while housewives explained why they were only
on Chapter One after four years.

You had to go, though, she told herself, as she took the
green-tagged room key and trudged off in search of an
elevator. Agents and editors often turned up at these conferences, apparently under the delusion that a weekend's
confinement in a motel outside the state of New York
constituted *travel*. These people could be useful. She always
waited until two days into the conference to talk business
with them, because by then they had been so steeped in
novice-babble that she seemed brilliant by comparison.

Rose did not get the opportunity to feel brilliant as often as she thought she deserved, which was perhaps another reason to attend these regional conferences. Being hailed as a literary lion by *Writers Market* junkies compensated for the well-bred scorn she endured more or less regularly from the college English Department, to which she did not belong. She and several of its faculty members sniped at each other with less than good-natured derision over their respective literary efforts.

The opinion in Bartleby Hall was that Rose was not worthy of serious consideration as a writer, because she wrote "accessible" fiction. That is, she used the past tense, quotation marks, and plots in her books, rather than venturing into their literary realm: experimental fiction of the sort published by the "little" magazines. These tiny, subsidized (sometimes mimeographed) journals paid nothing, and were read chiefly by those planning to submit manuscripts, but they counted for much in prestige and tenure.

Rose didn't have to worry about tenure. She was the college director of public relations. (The English gang pronounced her job title as if it were something she did with no clothes on.) For her part, Rose professed not to want a job teaching semicolons to future stockbrokers, and she often said that the English Department would give a job to a Melville scholar any day, but that they would have never hired Herman Melville. Still, the steady trickle of disdain ate away at her ego, and she often threatened to write a "serious and pretentious novel" just to prove that she could. So far, though, time had not permitted her such an indulgence. The time that she could steal away from her job, her dog, and her laundry was spent producing carefully plotted mystery novels featuring a female deputy sheriff. Her works had not made her a household name, but they covered her car payments and inspired an occasional fan letter, which was better than nothing. Certainly better than writing derivative drivel for years and then not getting tenure.

This weekend's conference was as much as she could manage in the way of career development. She could practice her lecturing style and sign a few books. Besides, the setting was wonderfully picturesque: a modern glass and redwood lodge on Whitethorn Island in Lake Adair. The choice of site was an indication that the conference organizers believed the myth about writers craving solitude. Apparently it had not occurred to them that the likes of Emily Dickinson wouldn't be caught dead at a conference in the first place. Rose often wished she were rich enough to be temperamental, but since this was not the case, she had learned to cope with the world. The place looked pleasant enough to her, and she had quite enjoyed the boat ride over. All in all, Rose was feeling quite festive, until she remembered what writers conferences tended to be like.

It was a regional conference, devoted to all types of writers, without regard for merit or credentials. All that these people had in common was geography. Rose had decided she needed the practice of attending such a small, unimportant conference. If it went well, she could work up to an important event like an all-mystery convention. Being nice to people was not a thing that came naturally to Rose Hanelon, despite her job title. Public relations at the university simply meant generating puff press releases for anyone's slightest achievement and minimizing the football scandals with understatement and misdirection. Even a curmudgeon could do it. Thus her need to practice charm. After a few minutes' observation of her fellow attendees, Rose began to think that she had set herself too great a task for her first venture in celebrity.

The other guests waiting for the elevator were smiling at her, having noticed that the name tag of "Nobody in Particular" had the gold star for "Program Guest." They glanced at one another, trying to guess what this dumpy little lady with the bobbed hair and rimless spectacles could be an expert in. She did not look benevolent enough to be in Children's books. Children's book editors were popularly supposed to resemble Helen Hayes or Goldie Hawn. Perhaps she was an agent. No one knew *what* an agent would look like.

Rose in turn noticed that the gawkers' name tags were pale pink, signifying aspiring romance novelists. Would-be mystery writers had name tags edged in black, and western writers had a little red cowboy hat beside their names. Rose wondered what symbol would indicate the poets. Not that a mere notation on a name tag would be warning enough, she thought sardonically. Amateur poets ought to be belled and cowled like lepers, so that you could hear them coming and flee.

This thought made her smile so broadly that one of the pink tags actually ventured to speak to her. "I see you're one of our program guests," said the grandmotherly woman in lavender.

Rose nodded warily, edging her way into the elevator. The doors slid shut behind them, turning the elevator into an interrogation room until the third floor, at which stop Rose planned to bolt.

"Are you an editor?" the plump one asked breathlessly.

"No." Editors were like ghosts; all novices talked about them, but very few had actually seen one. "I'm a writer," she admitted, noting that her stock with them had dropped considerably.

The novices exchanged glances. "Not . . . Deidre Bellaire!"

"No. Rose Hanelon." *And you've never heard of me,* she wanted to add.

Their faces looked blank, but at least they did not begin to thumb through their programs in search of her biography. The elevator creaked to a stop, and Rose hoisted her bag out into the hallway.

"A published writer!" the lavender lady called after her. "How wonderful! Well, we're here to take Deidre Bellaire's workshop in writing romance novels. Tell me, what's your advice for writing a romance novel?"

"Try sticking your finger down your throat!" said Rose, as the metal doors closed between them.

Jess Scarberry eased through the front doors of the hotel, balancing a small canvas bag, containing his weekend wardrobe, and a large leather suitcase, containing sample copies of his mimeographed poetry "magazine" *The Scarberry Scriptures*, and 137 assorted copies of his own books—softcover, $5.95. Scarberry liked to call each volume a "limited edition," which indeed they were, since he could only afford to print a few hundred copies at a time, and these would take years to sell.

He looked the part of a poet, Walt Whitman variety, with his short gray beard, well-worn Levis, and chambray work shirt. *A man who gets his inspiration from the land*, his appearance seemed to suggest. But if Jess Scarberry heard America singing, the tune was "How Great Thou Art," directed admiringly at himself, in a chorus of feminine voices.

The fact that Scarberry neither had, nor wanted, any male followers was evident from his books, which all had titles like *Shadows in the Mist* or *Rivers of Memory*, and from the poems they contained, which were all variations on the idea that the poet was a lonely wanderer occasionally seeking refuge from the cruel world in the arms of love. His photo on the back of each book showed a pensive Scarberry, wearing a sheepskin jacket, and leaning over a saddle that had been placed atop a split-rail fence. The biographical notes said that the Poet had been a working cowboy, an ambulance driver, a tugboat captain, and that he was an honorary medicine man of the Tuscarora Indian tribe. His most recent occupation—literary con man and jackleg publisher—was *not* mentioned.

Scarberry cast an appraising glance around the hotel lobby, sizing up the livestock at what he liked to think of as a literary rodeo. During the weekend, he would bulldog a few heifers, rope and brand some new Scarberry fans, and collect enough of a grubstake to keep himself in Budweiser and wheat germ until the next conference.

As he approached the registration desk, he remembered to walk a bit bowlegged, suggesting one who has left his horse in the parking lot. He hoped the twittery ladies near the potted palm had noticed him. When he finished registering, he would go over, personally invite them to attend his workshop ("The Poetry of Experience"), and graciously allow them to buy him dinner.

"May I have a new name tag?" asked the tall young woman at the conference registration table. The fact that she had just torn the old one in half suggested that this was not a request.

Margie Collier's felt tip-pen poised in midair, while she checked the registration form. "We spelled it right," she declared. "Connie Maria Samari. S-A-M—"

The woman winced. "I only use one name," she said. "Just *Samari*." Samari . . . a lilting word that conjured up images of Omar Khayyám, and jasmine-scented gardens, but prefaced by "Connie Maria," the word sank back into an ordinary Italian surname, containing no romance at all. With all due respect to her Italian grandmother, Connie Maria felt that being called "Samari" would be a definite advantage to her career as a poet.

With only a small sigh (because she was used to humoring eccentrics), Margie Collier took out a new name tag and obligingly wrote "Samari" in large capital letters. "There you are," she said with a friendly smile. "I suppose you write Japanese haiku?"

Samari's response was a puzzled stare, until half a minute later, when enlightenment dawned. "That is *not* how my name is pronounced!"

Several ego-encounters later, Margie Collier looked up at a registrant, who had signaled her presence simply by the shadow she cast on Margie's paperwork. The awkward-looking young woman in an unflattering black plaid suit looked faintly ridiculous clutching a bud vase of red carnations. Margie found herself thinking of Ferdinand the Bull. "Those flowers will look nice in your room," Margie remarked, hoping that the woman wasn't planning to tote them around during the conference. She looked in the collection of Poet badges just in case, though.

"They're not for me!" said the young woman, blushing.

"They're for John Clay Hawkins. For his room, I mean. I'd like to pick up his name tag, too, if I may."

Margie frowned. "Are you his wife?"

"Certainly not! I am his graduate student. My name is Amy Dillow, and I also have a name tag. Dr. Hawkins will be arriving sometime this afternoon, and I wanted to make sure that his room is ready, and that the copies of his books arrived, and I'll need his name tag and a copy of the schedule."

When Margie Collier, still trying to make sense of this, did not reply, Amy sighed with impatience. "Dr. Hawkins," she explained, "is *required reading.*"

By whom? thought Margie, but she only smiled, and began to search the desk for the requested items. Some people thought that being rude was the first step to becoming a writer. She found Hawkins's name tag—not surprisingly—filed in the Poet section. *Really,* she thought, *these male poets seem to attract groupies like maggots to a dead cat.* She couldn't see what all the fuss was about. Margie's husband, a football coach at the junior high, often said that writing—and reading, for that matter—was women's work, and secretly she agreed with him. Give her a middle-linebacker any old day, instead of these peevish, sensitive artistes that didn't know *spit* from *come here.* Her idea of a real writer was Deidre Bellaire, who was just as sweet as peach jam, and she outsold those poet types by ten thousand to one, so that ought to show them, with their literary airs!

The first scheduled event for the Unicoi Writers Conference was a get-acquainted cocktail party, in which all the attendees met in the Nolichucky Room and either asked or endured the Writers Conference Litany: *What name do you write under?—Where do you get your ideas?—Should I have heard of you?* Outside, a raging thunderstorm lent the appropriate literary atmosphere to the setting. Rose Hanelon decided that the next person who came up to her and said, "It is a dark and stormy night," was going to get a cup of punch in the face.

Now she had retreated into a corner, clutching a plastic cup of lukewarm strawberry punch, with nothing but a glazed smile between her and a plot summary. She had long since lost the ability to nod, but the droning woman had yet to notice. Every so often she would pat her crimped brown curls (*as if anything short of barbecue tongs could have moved them*, thought Rose). "And then," said the aspiring author, prattling happily, mistaking silence for interest, "the heroine gets on a train and goes to New Hampshire. Or do I mean Vermont? Which one is the one on the right? Well, anyway, meanwhile, the hero has decided to go mountain climbing on a glacier. Do they have glaciers in New Hampshire? Well, it doesn't matter. Nobody's ever been there. So he goes to a psychic to, you know, see if it's going to be okay—what with his wooden leg and all, and—"

"Excuse me," said Rose. "Could I ask you something? If I give you two eggs, can you tell me if the cake will be any good?"

The narrator blinked. "What? The cake? What cake?"

"Any cake," sighed Rose. "You can't judge a cake from two eggs, and you can't judge a book from a plot summary. A bad writer can ruin anything. Just write the book and shut up." She stalked off in the direction of the hors d'oeuvres, but her way was blocked by a bearded man in a fringed buckskin jacket.

"Hello, little lady," he beamed at her in a B-movie twang. "You wouldn't happen to be an editor, would you?"

"Why do you ask?" Her eyes were glittering, the way they always did when people said words like "shortie" or "pulp fiction."

"Why, I just happen to have a new chapbook here that is Rod McKuen and Kahlil Gibran all rolled into one. I'm Jess Scarberry." He paused, waiting for cries of recognition that were not forthcoming. "I'm going to be doing a reading from it at eleven tomorrow. Why don't you come?" He beamed at a serious young woman in horn-rimmed glasses who was standing near Rose. "And you, too, of course, ma'am."

"I'll keep it in mind," said Rose, edging past him as she

reached for a cheese cube. Jess Scarberry wandered away in search of other victims.

When he was out of earshot, Amy Dillow snickered. "I can't believe he thinks anybody will come to his stupid reading," she sniffed. "John Clay Hawkins is lecturing that hour on the poetic tradition."

"Really?" Rose wondered what else was going on at that hour. Flea-dipping seemed preferable.

Amy nodded, eyes shining. "He's been published everywhere! Even the *Virginia Quarterly Review*. And John Ciardi once called his work *well crafted.*"

"That silver-tongued devil," murmured Rose.

"I'm doing my dissertation on Dr. Hawkins," Amy confided. "I think Sylvia Plath and Philip Larkin are just too overdone, don't you?"

"Well, that's because people have heard of them," said Rose. "I suppose you'd have a better chance of getting a professorship as a Larkin scholar than as a Hawkins expert. Still, it must be useful to be able to discuss the symbolism of the poetry with its author."

Amy looked shocked. "Oh, I wouldn't do that! What would he know about that? He just writes them. It's up to us scholars to determine what they mean. But I do see quite a bit of Dr. Hawkins. I'm sort of working as his volunteer secretary, too. I just hate to see him wasting his time on anything but his Muse."

Rose grunted. "I wish somebody felt that way about mystery writers."

"That's him over there," whispered Amy, pointing at a silver-haired man with a shiny blue suit and a leathery tan. The substance in his glass did not look like fruit punch. He was surrounded by several other men—an unusual occurrence for a male poet at a writers conference. Even Amy seemed to feel that the phenomenon warranted an explanation. "Those other men are also regional poets. That young one in the leather jacket is Carter Jute, and the gaunt, elderly one is Mr. Snowfield. And there's the guy in the cowboy outfit who just invited us to his poetry class. I don't know who he thinks he is."

Rose smiled in the direction of Jess Scarberry, talking shop and, no doubt, chapbooks with the academic gentry of his field. "That," she said solemnly, "is the *poet lariat.*"

Meanwhile in the Poets Corner, John Clay Hawkins was smiling genially as the discussion of poetry went on around him. He had already sized up Scarberry as a con man poet, but he wasn't particularly offended by it. After all, was an iambic pentameter sex life really so much worse than what poor old Snowfield did—using his lackluster lyrics to evade teaching freshmen, and as an excuse for pomposity with other members of his department? Young Jute, he decided, was going through a phase, probably on his way to becoming a William Faulkner clone. He had already acquired the drinking problem, and he seemed to revel in the "inaccessibility of his work," as though being incoherent made him smarter than anybody else. Hawkins sometimes wanted to say to these people, *"All babies are incoherent, but they grow up. That is the principle difference between an infant and a poet."* But he never did say anything so unkind. Other people's folly didn't really annoy John Clay Hawkins; they all seemed very remote.

Mostly he was tired. His career as a poet had begun while he was in graduate school when he had written a slim volume of poems commemorating the marriage of his old roommate, Norman Grant, to a cheerleader named Lee Locklear. The poems were tastefully obscure, so as not to resemble the bawdy limericks usually offered by groomsmen on such occasions. He had meant them as a gift, since he couldn't afford so much as a shard of the expensive china pattern the couple had chosen, but the old roommate had been a literary type himself, and flattered by this poetic tribute, he had sent copies of *Grant and Lee's Union* to *The Carolina Quarterly* and to various other prestigious southern publications. The editors of those august journals, not apprised of the coming nuptials, assumed that the verses were a retrospective of the Civil War, and they were published to considerable acclaim in several magazines. The LSU Press brought out the entire collection the following year, and it won an obscure prize thanks to the presence of an LSU man and a Civil War buff on the panel of judges. After that, John Clay Hawkins found that people took it for granted that he wanted to continue being a poet, and to his surprise, he found that he was rather good at it, so he kept writing. Long after Mrs. Lee Locklear Grant had dumped old roommate Norman Grant for a Wachovia Bank vice president, Hawkins continued to receive writing fellowships, and to spend a good part of his nonteaching time lecturing at various universities. After twenty years of unfailingly patient workshops and well-performed readings that people actually understood, Hawkins found himself enshrined in academic hearts somewhere between Robert Frost and Yoda the Jedi Master of *Star Wars*. He bore beatification with quiet dignity, and went on writing simple, beautifully phrased poems about rural life. Sometimes, though, hearing the same old questions for the hundredth time that day left him feeling unutterably weary.

He turned to smile at a twittery woman who was tugging at his elbow. "Tell me," she said, through Bambi eyelashes, "Where do you get your ideas for a poem?"

An elegant woman also bent on speaking to him had overheard this remark. "Poets get ideas everywhere," she snapped. "That's what makes them poets!" Having thus frightened the church bulletin versifier out of the fold, the dark-eyed young woman offered her hand to John Clay Hawkins. "My name is Samari," she purred. "I also write verse."

"You must meet Carter Jute," Hawkins murmured, recognizing an example of his colleague's taste in women.

The woman ignored his ploy. "I especially wanted to speak to you. I have found the ranks of scholarly poetry to be rather a closed circle. . . ." She glanced over at Jess Scarberry and shuddered delicately. "With good reason, perhaps. But I do think I have a special gift, and I'd like you to read my work and to suggest some places that I could send it."

As often as this trap had sprung shut on him, John Clay Hawkins had not yet devised a foolproof way to get out of it.

He tried his first tactic: the Aw Shucks Maneuver. "Oh, I just buy *Poets Market* every year, and send 'em on out to whoever seems to like my sort of work," he said modestly, studying the tops of his shoes.

"Yes, but you're a *name,*" Samari persisted. "I'm not. It would really help if you'd recommend it. Then I could say that *you* told me to send it to them."

Hawkins studied the jut of Connie Maria Samari's jaw, and the sharklike glitter of her eyes, and he recognized the Type Three Poet, the Lady Praying Mantis. In relationships she eats her mate alive, and professionally, she is as single-minded as Attila the Hun. Struggling would only prolong and embitter the encounter. Worst of all, he actually had to look at her work. A simple "Send it to Bob at *Whistlepig Review*" would not satisfy her. She wanted a diagnosis based on a reading. "Well, bring it along later," he sighed. "I'll be in my room—406—after eleven. I'll look at it then."

As she moved away in search of other prey, Hawkins remembered that he had also promised to have drinks with Jute, Snowfield, and Scarberry after eleven, and he had promised interviews or consultations with two other novices. Fortunately, Hawkins was a night person, and his lecture wasn't until eleven. Surely, he thought, there must be quicker forms of martyrdom.

Rose Hanelon, who went to bed with the chickens (exclusively), had been sound asleep for several hours when the pounding on her door called her forth from slumber. Groping for her eyeglasses and then her terry cloth bathrobe, she stumbled toward the door, propelled only by the thought of dismembering whoever she found when she opened it.

"Miss Hanelon?" An anxious Margie Collier, looking as if she'd thrown her clothes on with a pitchfork, fidgeted in the doorway. The sight of a glaring gargoyle in a dressing gown did little to calm her. "Did I wake you?" she gasped. "I mean . . . I thought you writers worked late at night on your manuscripts."

"No," said Rose between her teeth. "I'm usually out

robbing graves at this hour, but it's raining! Now, what do you want?"

"I'm sorry to disturb you, but since you are a mystery writer, we thought . . . Oh, Miss Hanelon, there's been a murder!"

"How amusing for you." Rose started to close the door. "These little parlor games are of no interest to me, however."

"No! Not a murder game! A real murder. Someone has killed John Clay Hawkins!"

"That is too bad," said Rose, shaking her head sadly. "He wasn't my first choice at all."

Eventually Margie Collier's urgency persuaded Rose that the matter was indeed serious, and her next reaction was to ask why they had bothered to wake her about it, instead of calling the local police. "They aren't here yet. Besides, we thought they might need some help," said Margie. "The people at this writers conference are hardly the criminal types they're used to."

"No, I suppose not. They're the criminal types *I'm* used to." She stifled a yawn. "All right. Give me ten minutes to get dressed. Oh, you might as well tell me about it while I do. Save time. What happened?"

Margie sat down on the bed, and modestly fixed her eyes at a point on the ceiling while she recited her narrative. "About midnight, a woman named Samari went to Dr. Hawkins's room to show him her manuscript—"

"I've never heard it called that before—" called Rose from the bathroom.

"She's a poetess." Margie's tone was reproachful. "She knocked, and found the door ajar, and there he was, slumped in his chair at the writing table. Someone had hit him over the head with a bottle of Jack Daniels."

"Was it empty?"

"I believe so. There wasn't any spilled on the body. Ms. Samari came and got me, not knowing what else to do."

"An empty whiskey bottle." Rose wriggled a black sweater over her head. "Dylan Thomas would probably approve of that finale," she remarked. "There. I'm ready. If you insist on doing this. I'll bet the police shut down this show the minute they get here."

"Maybe so," said Margie. "But that won't be until sometime tomorrow. The storm is too bad to take a boat across. And they won't risk a helicopter, either."

"What? We're stuck here? What if somebody becomes seriously ill?"

"I asked the hotel manager about that. He said there's a registered nurse on the staff. Actually, she's the dietician, but in an emergency—"

"Never mind. I guess I'm elected. Let's go investigate this thing."

Margie brightened. "It's just like a mystery story, isn't it?"

"Not one that my editor would buy."

Although Rose Hanelon wrote what she liked to call traditional mysteries, she was well versed in police procedure, first of all because she read widely within the genre, and secondly because the town house adjoining hers belonged to a police detective who liked to talk shop at his backyard cookouts. He particularly enjoyed critiquing the police procedurals written by Roses's fellow authors. With no effort on her part, Rose had assimilated quite a good working knowledge of law enforcement. She wondered if it would serve her well in the current emergency. Probably not. People had to cooperate with police officers; but they were perfectly free to ignore an inquisitive mystery writer, no matter how knowledgeable she was about investigative procedure.

"Do you think you'll be able to solve the crime?" asked Margie, who was scurrying along after Rose like a terrier in the wake of a Saint Bernard.

"I doubt it," said Rose. "The police have computers, and other useful tools for ferreting out the truth. Paraffin tests; ballistics experts. If Joe Villanova had to use his powers of deduction to solve cases, he'd be in big trouble. He's a police officer; lives next door to me. He'd probably arrest me for even trying to meddle in this case. Too bad he's not here."

"Oh, but you've written so many mysteries!" said Margie. "I'm sure you know quite a bit."

"I can tell you who I want to be guilty," Rose replied. "That's what I do in my books."

"Do you want to examine Mr. Hawkins's body?"

"No. I'm not a doctor, and I don't want to get hassled for tampering with evidence. Let's just go and badger some suspects, shall we?"

Margie nodded. "I asked the hotel manager to put the poets in the hospitality suite."

"I hope they didn't bring along any manuscripts," muttered Rose. "The very thought of being cooped up with a bunch of bards gives me hives."

"It seems strange, doesn't it, to think of poets as murder suspects. They are such gentle people."

Rose Hanelon raised her eyebrows. "Have you ever been in an English Department?"

The door to the hospitality suite was open, and the sounds of bickering could be heard halfway down the hall. "I think we should just conduct a memorial service in Hawkins's scheduled hour tomorrow," Carter Jute was saying. "It would be a nice way to honor his memory. I wouldn't mind conducting the service."

Jess Scarberry, the poet lariat, sneered. "I'll bet you wouldn't mind, Sonny, but remember that I'm also scheduled to do a reading at that hour. You're not taking away my audience for some phony displays of grief."

Connie Samari, mothlike in a red and black polyester kimono, toyed with her crystal earrings. "I suppose we could all write commemorative poems in honor of John Clay Hawkins," she murmured. "Read them at the memorial service."

Snowfield held up a restraining hand. "Just a moment," he said. "I think that I am the obvious choice for regional poet laureate, now that Hawkins has shuffled off the mortal coil. In light of that, the hour ought to be spent introducing people to my own works, with perhaps a short farewell to Hawkins." He shrugged. "I don't care which of you does that."

The poets were so intent upon their territorial struggles that they did not notice the two self-appointed investigators watching them from the doorway. What, after all, was a trifle like murder compared to their artistic considerations?

Amy Dillow, Hawkins's graduate student, glared at the upstarts. Two spots of color appeared in her pale cheeks, and she drew herself up with as much dignity as one can muster when wearing a pink chenille bathrobe and bunny slippers. "I am appalled at your attitudes!" she announced. "John Clay Hawkins was a major poet, deserving of much greater recognition than he ever received. The idea of any of you assuming his mantle is laughable. I will conduct Dr. Hawkins's conference hour myself. I have just completed a paper on the symbolism in the works of Hawkins, and it seems logical to read that tomorrow as we pause to consider his achievements."

Rose Hanelon strode into the fray, rubbing her hands together in cheerful anticipation. "Well, this won't be hard!" she announced. "It sounds just like a faculty meeting in the English Department."

The poets stopped quarreling and stared at her. "Who are you?" Snowfield demanded with a touch of apprehension. He didn't think any major woman poets had been invited to this piddling conference. Anyway, she wasn't Nikki Giovanni, so she probably didn't matter.

"Relax," said Rose. "If anybody called me a poet, I'd sue them for slander. I'm not here to replace Caesar, but to bury him. He was murdered, you know."

Amy Dillow sighed theatrically. "Now he belongs to the ages."

Margie Collier, ever the peacemaker, said, "Why don't I get us some coffee while Miss Hanelon speaks to you about the murder. We thought it might be nice to get the preliminary questioning done while we wait for the police." She hurried away before anyone could raise any objections to this plan, leaving Rose Hanelon alone with a roomful of egotists and possibly one murderer.

The poets sat down in a semicircle and faced her with varying degrees of resentment. Some of them were sputtering about the indignity of being a suspect in a sordid murder case.

Rose sighed. "I always find this the boring part of murder mysteries," she confided to the assembly. "It seems to go on for pages and pages, while we listen to alibis, and tedious contradictory accounts of the deceased's relationships with all present. And in order to find out who's lying, I need access to outside documents detailing the life and loves of the victim. Obviously I can't do that, since we're storm-bound on this island."

"Perhaps we could tell the police that Hawkins committed suicide," said Carter Jute. "That would protect us all from notoriety, and it's very correct in literary circles. Hemingway, Sylvia Plath."

"We *could* blame it on Ted Hughes," said Rose sarcastically, "but that wouldn't be true, either. You'll find that the police are awfully wedded to facts, as opposed to hopeful interpretation. They will investigate the crime scene, get fingerprints off the bottle, and that'll be that."

"Surely the killer would wipe the fingerprints off the murder weapon?" said Snowfield. He reddened under the stares of everyone else present. "Well, I've read a few whodunits. After all, C. Day Lewis, the English poet laureate, wrote some under the name of Nicholas Blake."

"Never mind about the murder!" said Carter Jute. "What are we going to do about Hawkins's time slot tomorrow?"

"Yes," said Rose. "Why don't you discuss that among yourselves? And while you do, I'd like to read that paper on the life and works of John Clay Hawkins. Do you have it with you, Ms. Dillow?"

Amy Dillow stood up, and yawned. "It's in my room. I'll get it for you. But why do you want to read it now?"

"It helps to have a clear idea who the victim was," said Rose.

"Oh, all right." She shuffled off in her bunny slippers. "I haven't proofed it yet, though."

In the doorway she nearly collided with Margie Collier, who was returning with a pot of coffee and seven cups. She set the tray on the coffee table, and beamed at Rose Hanelon. "Have you solved it yet?"

"Not yet," said Rose. "It's easier on television, where one of the actors is paid to confess. Real life is less tidy. This lot haven't even decided what to do with Hawkins's hour yet."

"Well, you could read John Clay Hawkins's last poem," said Margie. "The one he was writing when he died."

"He was working?" said Rose.

"Yes. I looked at the paper under poor Mr. Hawkins's hand when we examined his body. Of course, we can't remove the actual paper from the room. I'm sure the police would object to that, but I did make a copy while I was waiting for the hotel manager to arrive. Would you like to see it?" She fished a sheet of hotel stationery out of the pocket of her robe and handed it to Rose.

"Read it aloud!" Snowfield called out. The others nodded assent.

"Oh, all right," grumbled the mystery writer. "I knew you would find some way to turn this into a poetry reading." Holding the paper at arm's length, she squinted at the spidery writing, and recited:

"There's this guy.
his name is Norman
and he's sitting in a white room.
he's sitting in a white room,
but you might as well call it
white death.
Norman is holding death like
a white peach to the window
and turning,
turning death
like the dial of a timer
in the white light of the sun.
death begins to tick.
Norman puts death down
and stares with his white eyes
at the white wall.
his shadow is white and moves
without him around the white room.
then death goes off."

She lowered the paper and blinked at the assortment of poets. "That is the most stupid and pointless thing I have ever read. Do any of you bards get any meaning out of that?"

Jess Scarberry shrugged. "Shucks, ma'am, these professor types don't have to make sense. If you don't understand what they write, they reckon it's your fault."

Snowfield scowled at him. "It seems clear enough to me. Hawkins was obviously contemplating his own mortality. Perhaps he had a premonition. Keats did."

Rose Hanelon rolled her eyes. "Keats had medical training and symptoms of tuberculosis. I'd hardly call that a premonition. I should have thought that if Hawkins foresaw his own murder, he'd have gotten out of there, rather than sit down and write a poem about it. Still, with poets, you never know."

"Who's Norman?" asked Margie with a puzzled frown.

"A metaphor for Everyman," said Carter Jute.

Connie Samari snickered. *"Everyman.* How typical of the male poet's arrogance! And I think that poem stinks!"

"I expect it's over your head," said Snowfield.

Amy Dillow returned just then with a sheaf of dot-matrix-printed papers. "Here's my thesis on Hawkins. It isn't finished, of course, but you may find it helpful."

"A polygraph machine would be helpful," said Rose. "Reading this is an act of desperation. But it will have to do. Pour me some of that coffee." She settled down on one of the sofas and began to read, while the bickering went on about her.

Carter Jute handed a cup of coffee to Amy Dillow. "It's such a shame about poor old Hawkins," he said. "By the way, Amy, do you have a copy of his current vita?"

"Why do you ask?"

Jute gave her a boyish smile. "Well, I was thinking what a void his passing will leave in literary circles. There were certain editorial positions he held, and workshops that he taught year after year—"

"And you thought you'd apply for them?" Amy Dillow looked shocked.

"He'd want someone to carry on his work," Jute assured her.

Connie Samari laughed. "And heaven forbid that his honors should go to someone outside the old-boy network, right?"

Margie Collier looked dismayed to be caught in such a maelstrom of ill will. She had always thought of poets as gentle people, wandering lonely as a cloud while they composed their little odes to nature. "Why don't we all try to write a poem in memory of poor Dr. Hawkins?" she suggested. "Does anyone do haiku?"

Rose Hanelon looked up from her reading. "You say here that Hawkins was married."

"He's divorced," said Amy.

"From whom?"

"A librarian named Dreama Belcher. They didn't have any children, though."

"Just as well," muttered Snowfield, shuddering. "Imagine what the progeny of someone named Dreama Belcher would look like!"

"What became of her?"

"I don't know," said Amy. "Nothing much, I expect. She didn't have the temperament to be married to a poet."

"She preferred monogamy, I expect," said Samari. "I've often thought that male poets were reincarnations of walruses. Can't you just picture them up there on a rock, surrounded by a herd of sunbathing cow-wives?"

Jess Scarberry reddened. "It's understandable," he said. "Poets need inspiration like a car needs a battery. If you're writing love poems, you need something to jump-start the creative process."

Rose Hanelon ignored him. "Walruses," she echoed. "That's interesting. So John Clay Hawkins was . . . er . . . Byronic. That could have been hazardous to his health. Especially if one of his girlfriends objected to his philandering. Are any of his conquests here?" She peered at Amy Dillow with a glint of malicious interest.

The young graduate student blushed and looked away.

"Certainly not!" she murmured. "I was solely interested in his work."

"Don't look at me," said Connie Samari. "I met him for the first time tonight. And he definitely wasn't my type."

"Yes, but if you went to his room to discuss your poetry, and he made a pass at you, you might have killed him by accident, trying to fend him off."

"If I had, I would have called a press conference to announce it," said Samari. "I certainly wouldn't have fled the scene and denied it."

Jute and Snowfield, seated on either side of her, unobtrusively edged away. Jess Scarberry crossed his legs and whistled tunelessly. Rose Hanelon went back to reading the thesis.

"Would anybody like more coffee?" asked Margie nervously.

After a few moments of uneasy silence, the poets returned to the topic of Hawkins and the professional repercussions that would ensue.

"Wasn't he set to do a guest professorship in Virginia this summer?" asked Snowfield.

"Probably. I know he was slated to write the introduction to the Regional Poets Anthology," said Samari. "Had he written that?"

Amy Dillow shrugged. "Not that I know of."

"I was thinking of applying for his slot at Breadloaf," mused Carter Jute.

"There'll never be another John Clay Hawkins," Amy Dillow assured them. "He was the greatest poet of our region."

"Oh, come now!" Snowfield protested. "You ladies always say that about a good-looking fellow who reads well."

"Oh, don't be such a dinosaur!" said the graduate student. "I loved Hawkins's work before I even knew what he looked like. He's one of the few original voices in contemporary poetry. The fact that he was a drunk and a lecher is neither here nor there."

Rose Hanelon was wondering if Detective Joe Villanova

was awake at—what was it?—4:00 A.M. Probably not. He wouldn't be much better at this than she would, though, with no forensic evidence to go on. "Oh, well," said Rose. "Even if I don't figure out who the murderer is, all of you will be too exhausted tomorrow to commit any more murders, no matter which of you is guilty."

Carter Jute consulted his watch. "Gosh, that's right! We all have to be on panels tomorrow. Or rather—today. And we still haven't decided what to do with Hawkins's hour."

The others stood up, yawned and stretched. "Long day," they murmured.

"Wait! I'm not finished!" Rose was still rifling through the clues. "Is anyone here named Norman?" she asked in tones of desperation. "Does anyone know Hawkins's ex-wife?"

They all shook their heads. "Sorry we can't help, little lady," drawled Scarberry.

"Wait!" said Connie Samari. "We never decided what to do with Hawkins's hour!"

"Ah! Hawkins's hour. I will be taking that," said Rose Hanelon with a feral smile.

By skipping breakfast, Rose managed to get three hours sleep before the conference sessions began, but she still looked like a catatonic bag lady. Five cups of coffee later, she had recovered the use of most of her brain cells, but she was still considerably lacking in presentability. When she ran into Joe Villanova, helping himself to doughnuts at the coffee break in the hall, he did a double-take, and said, "If you'll lie down, I'll draw chalk marks around you, and ask the coroner to take a look at you."

His next-door neighbor managed a feeble snarl. "Buzz off, Villanova. I'm solving this case for you. Come to the next lecture in the Catawba Room, and you'll see."

"You don't mind if we continue doing the fingerprinting and the suspect interrogations in the meantime, do you?"

"Not at all. So glad you could finally manage to come."

"Hey, I'm not risking my neck in a helicopter for a guy who is already dead. Listen, when you do this lecture of yours, don't violate anybody's rights, okay? I have to get a conviction."

Rose looked up as a gaggle of silver-haired women walked by. They were wearing Poet name tags, and they seemed to be earnestly discussing onomatopoeia. "I don't suppose you could arrest all of them, Joe," she said. "We have quite a surplus of poets."

The Catawba Room was packed for John Clay Hawkins's hour. Some of those present were groupies of the distinguished and handsome poet, and they had not been informed of his death. Others had heard that a mystery writer was going to conduct the session, and attended in hopes of hearing a postmortem. All the poets were there in force in case Rose Hanelon didn't use the whole hour. Scarberry, whose session had consisted of three elderly ladies, adjourned his group, and joined the crowd in the Catawba Room. Villanova, with a ridiculous smirk on his face, sprawled in the front row with his arms folded, waiting for Rose to make an idiot of herself.

Rose surveyed the sheeplike faces, and wished she'd had time for another cup of coffee. "Good morning," she began. "I have come to bury John Clay Hawkins, not praise him. As you know, our featured speaker was murdered last night with an empty bottle of Jack Daniels."

"Those who live by the sword . . ." muttered Samari from the front row.

"Even now the police are measuring and photographing, and doing all that they can to collect the physical evidence to convict the killer. I used another approach—the examination of motives. Who would want to kill a poet?"

A suppressed whoop of laughter emanated from the romance writers contingent in the back of the room.

"Precisely," said Rose. "Who *wouldn't* want to kill a poet? But why this particular poet, when there are so many more annoying and less talented specimens around? Besides, in this case, the suspects were all poets themselves, or people well acquainted with John Clay Hawkins as a human being."

Hawkins's fellow bards glared up at her from their front-row seats.

"The main motive that occurred to me was professional competitiveness. Hawkins, as a well-known minor poet, had a number of workshop engagements, editorships, and other poetic plums that everyone else seemed to want very badly." Rose nodded in the direction of Jess Scarberry's waving hand, acknowledging his objection. "Yes. Except for Jess Scarberry. No one would give him any literary recognition, not even if he was the last poet on earth. But I doubt if he minds. He's in the game to pick up women and sell chapbooks, and he can do all of that without any academic recognition. If he killed Mr. Hawkins, it would have to be for more personal reasons. I didn't find any.

"That left Samari, Snowfield, and Carter Jute, whose personal attributes suggest that poems are made by barracudas. I didn't even have a favorite suspect among them. So I read Amy Dillow's thesis about John Clay Hawkins. And I read the last poem of Hawkins himself. Bear with me."

She read the poem in clear, measured tones to the startled audience. "At least it's timely," she remarked. "I wondered why Hawkins was thinking of Norman, and if in fact he knew anyone by that name." Rose held up Amy Dillow's thesis. "It turns out that he did. His old college roommate Norman Grant, interviewed by Ms. Dillow here as a source for material about Hawkins's early years. I called Norman Grant, and read him the poem."

"Since you had no address, how'd you find him on a Saturday morning?" Villanova called out from the front row. He was obviously enjoying himself.

Rose smiled. "Professional connections. I called the PR director for his alma mater, who is a colleague of mine. She looked him up in the alumni directory. Anyway, I called Norman Grant, and read the poem to him."

There was a murmur of interest from the audience.

Rose shrugged. "He said it made no sense to him, either. But then he said Hawkins's poems never did make sense, as far as he could tell. People just read them, and assigned them meanings. He said John Clay used to joke that once a critic found one of your works profound, then anything else you ever wrote would be analyzed to death. Didn't matter what it was. He said John Clay was getting pretty tired of all the pretension, and the old-boy network of you-blurb-my-chapbook-and-I'll-publish-your-poem-in-my-literary-magazine. He said it was the Mafia with meter. He said that Hawkins was talking about quitting the poetry business and coming to work with him. Mr. Grant is a crop duster in north Georgia."

"He's lying!" Amy Dillow called out. "He was always jealous of Hawkins's success. Norman Grant flunked English!"

"He told me that, too," said Rose. "He said they used to laugh about it, because John Clay Hawkins wrote his papers for him that term. Now, assuming Hawkins was planning to quit poetry, there would be no need for the other poets to do him in, but that still leaves one very clear motive." She pointed to Amy Dillow. "If Hawkins renounced poetry, your graduate career would have been ruined, wouldn't it? You couldn't very well make your literary reputation on an ex-poet who was never widely recognized to begin with. Besides, dead poets are so much more respected than live ones. Look at Sylvia Plath: famous for being dead."

Amy Dillow jumped to her feet. "He had no ambition!" she cried. "He wouldn't apply for the right fellowships, or curry favor with the really important critics. I had to do something! His work really had potential, but he was holding back his own reputation. I did it for scholarly reasons! I had to kill him so that I could devote myself to the legend!"

Rose's jaw dropped. "You did?" she exclaimed. "You mean *you* did it?"

Amy Dillow nodded. "I thought you had figured it out."

"No," Rose blurted out before she thought better of it. (It had been a long night.) "I was just using that theory for dramatic effect, building up for the big finish. You see, Norman Grant also told me that Hawkins's first wife, Dreama Belcher, is still a librarian, but now she writes romance novels as Deidre Bellaire. I assumed she had done it."

A wizened figure in rhinestones and green chiffon stood up in the back of the room, waving her fan. "I killed the bastard off in eight Harlequins and three Silhouettes," she called out. "That was enough. Got it out of my system."

Joe Villanova's shouts of laughter drowned out the polite applause from the mystery fans. Rose Hanelon shrugged. "My editor will want me to change this ending."

The Jersey Lily; or, Make Me Immortal with a Kiss

P. M. Carlson

"Blow winds! and crack your cheeks!" I reckon Shakespeare was thinking of February in Chicago when he wrote that. I huddled into my deep blue traveling cape with the Langtry hood, hoping I was not going to have to pawn it too. I was out of work, out of money, and pining to get back to my friends and family in Saint Louis. But so far, 1883 was not a very encouraging year for an actress who'd been anointed the Bernhardt of Missouri only a few short months ago.

I turned onto Michigan Avenue and saw a throng of people surging about the entrance of a dry goods store. Curious, and realizing that a crowd would shield me from those notorious winds, I wriggled my way to the front, and heard one excited lady exclaim, "Here she comes!"

Several people looked my way, but the lady cried, "In the store!"

I followed her gesticulating finger. A tall, elegant man leaned out the door of the dry goods store and said, "Make way, please!" Those of us in the first row obligingly pushed back against those behind us, despite their complaints. The man held the door, nodded to someone inside, and crooked his arm. A dainty gloved hand was placed on it. Proudly he led out the most beautiful woman in the world.

A little gasp of admiration ran through the crowd; and I'm bound to admit, she was indeed a dish for the gods. She was perhaps an inch taller than I, with a figure that was at once full and willowy. She had a queenly bearing that brought harmony to every graceful move. She wore a rich pearl gray suit, a lustrous fur neckpiece, and a beautiful feathered hat with a veil that didn't quite hide her lovely auburn hair nor the sweetly sensuous curve of her lips. She was the Prince of Wales's celebrated mistress, at once royal and scandalous. She was Lillie Langtry, the Jersey Lily herself.

She was also the reason I was stranded penniless in Chicago.

The crowd was not awed for long. As she stepped forward on her escort's arm, a man at the rear sang out, "Hey, Lillie, give us a kiss!" Another cried, "Take off yer veil! Let's see yer face!" There were more shouts, and the crowd began to shove me from behind.

The man with Mrs. Langtry scowled and stepped forward confidently, but only a few people gave way. Someone, still shouting about the veil, snatched at it. Suddenly hands were everywhere, tugging at her hat, her gloves, her fur. The neckpiece came off, and the hat was snatched away and dismembered. I glimpsed her eyes, a perfect violet in color but full of consternation now. The man with her was shouting and striking out with his cane at the greedy arms around them. The cries of the throng became wilder. I dodged back into the dry goods store and watched through the window. In a moment a squad of police appeared and began tapping people with their nightsticks. The policemen surrounded Mrs. Langtry and her escort, and bustled them away amidst catcalls from the disappointed crowd.

I studied my reflection in a window to make sure my blue velvet bonnet with pink ostrich plume tips had not been damaged in the fray. Then I adjusted my traveling cloak, which was falling a little askew because I'd had to push it aside hastily when I tucked Mrs. Langtry's fur neckpiece under my bustle.

Why, how can you think such a thing? Of course I planned to return it! But you wouldn't want such an elegant adornment to fall into the hands of one of the ruffians in that crowd, now, would you?

Besides, I reckoned Mrs. Langtry owed me a trip to Saint Louis.

She was staying at the Grand Pacific Hotel. I presented myself at the desk half an hour later and explained in my best British accent that I was an old friend of Mrs. Langtry's secretary, Miss Pattison. The clerk was of the opinion that I should leave a note, so I obligingly scribbled something indecipherable onto a card. "I'm only in Chicago for the day," I explained. "Please deliver it soon, or Miss Pattison will be displeased." I wandered over toward the staircase while the clerk rang for a bellboy. It was a simple matter to follow the boy upstairs to the correct floor. In fact, I let him go on alone to Miss Pattison's office, because it was immediately clear that Mrs. Langtry's door was the one surrounded by reporters. Most of them were interviewing a somber police sergeant about the near-riot, but one dark-haired little fellow with small eyes and a snout very like a possum cast a sideways glance in my direction. "You'll never get in, my sweet!"

I looked at him haughtily.

He handed me a card. "Well, if you do, I'll give you fifty dollars to get me in too! Here, I'm William Thorpe."

Of course, I considered the offer; but it seemed unlikely that he had the fifty dollars any more than I did, and my Aunt Mollie always encouraged me to collect all I could in advance. So I presented my own card with a note to the forbidding manservant at the door, and in a few minutes was allowed inside. Jealous whispers sizzled behind me. "Who is she?" "Is she with a newspaper?" "Look at the red hair! Maybe she's a relation!"

Mrs. Langtry was standing in a large rose-and-white room behind the entrance gallery. She appeared surprisingly unflustered for someone who had just been mauled in the streets, but I remembered her reputation for being imperturbable. Her auburn hair, caught in a graceful loop on the nape of her neck, was a shade darker than mine, and her skin was creamy, unfreckled, and unscarred. She looked me over with a trace of puzzlement as the maid announced, "Miss Bridget Mooney, ma'am."

Mrs. Langtry said, "How do you do. Dominic said you were a lady."

"I am; but as yet untitled, alas," I said.

The beautiful lips curved in a small smile. She knew the same was true of herself. "You're saucy. Are you a reporter? A ghastly woman reporter!"

"No! I am not a reporter, ghastly or otherwise. I was tutored by the greatest actress of her time, the illustrious Mrs. Fanny Kemble."

This news did not seem to hearten her. "Oh, I see. You're an actress! And of course, you're going to ask for a favor, and of course, you don't really know anything about my fur neckpiece. Please, take yourself away right now."

I stood my ground. "You're right, Mrs. Langtry, I'm here to ask a favor of you. But in exchange, I can restore your lovely neckpiece."

She inspected me carefully. "You're blunt, Miss Mooney. I rather like that. Very well, what price are you asking?"

"A job and passage to St. Louis."

"Isn't it possible for someone tutored by the famed Mrs. Kemble to find her own job?"

"Yes indeed, Mrs. Langtry! I was touring as Portia and Ophelia, and doing very well, too, as far as Milwaukee. Last year, as Juliet and Lady Macbeth, I was hailed as 'the Bernhardt of Missouri.'"

"Were you." Her smile was skeptical.

I thrust my rather worn clipping at her, and she arched her eyebrows. "Goodness, you're right!"

"Yes, Mrs. Langtry. I don't lie."

I know, I know, perhaps I exaggerated my honesty just a bit, because it's true that sometimes a girl has to stretch things, so as not to make trouble.

She looked up from the clipping, smiling again. "And just what happened to the profitable Portia and Ophelia after Milwaukee?"

"Our troupe came to Chicago, and was bankrupted. You see, Mrs. Langtry was playing Chicago too."

"Ah." She looked me over again and came to a sudden decision. "Very well, Miss Mooney. You may be an understudy until we reach St. Louis."

"Oh, thank you! Thank you so much, Mrs. Langtry!"

She picked up a pen and, in a large, looping hand, wrote out a little note explaining my new status. "Give this to Charles, fourth door on the right." She picked up the note and tapped her other hand with it. "Now, as to my fur piece—"

I withdrew it from my bustle, smoothed it, and handed it to her with a little curtsy. "I'm much obliged, Mrs. Langtry."

"Yes, you are much obliged, my saucy Miss Mooney!" She smiled. "I could turn you in as a thief, you know."

"Why, Mrs. Langtry! It fell off in the fray, and I merely retrieved it for you!"

She laughed and handed me the note. "No doubt. Be off, Miss Mooney! And if there's any more thieving, I'll toss you off the train myself!"

"Good-bye, Mrs. Langtry, and thank you."

I started for the door. A maid passed me, going in to Mrs. Langtry, carrying a note on a silver salver. A moment later I heard a gasp and the maid's anxious voice. "Madame! Madame, let me help you sit down! There, there!"

I looked back to see Mrs. Langtry sinking white as marble into a chair, sighing, "Thank you, Alice—oh—"

I ran back to her side, pulling out my bottle of smelling salts. "Alice! Get Madame a glass of water!" I exclaimed imperiously.

Alice scurried away while I applied the vial to Mrs. Langtry's perfect nose. She gasped, "Enough—thank you, enough!" A touch of color came back into her cheeks.

I picked up the note, which had fluttered to the floor. It was written in midnight blue ink on cream-colored paper. "Mrs. Langtry," it said, "thank you for your gift. Your niece will continue to enjoy good health and privacy if you bring a similar gift to the harness room of the Southern Hotel stables, St. Louis, at 2:00 A.M. February 6. Bring it in person."

Could it be? Could the perfect Mrs. Langtry be a victim of vilest extortion? My heart went out to her. I knelt beside her chair, folded the note, and handed it to her. "Mrs. Langtry, is there any way I can help you?"

"Oh, Miss Mooney, I'm torn in two! This threat to my—my niece—but my every move is watched by the reporters! I do not even have the privacy to send a cable to learn if she is truly threatened! I can only continue to accede to the blackguard's demands!"

"There were earlier demands?"

She took a deep breath, passed a hand over her eyes, and sat up straighter. "I mustn't say anything more. Miss Mooney, please, I was feeling faint. You must disregard what I said."

"Mrs. Langtry, I believe we both understand the ways of this world. I, too, have a little—niece." The violet eyes were alert now, not quite believing. I explained, "I provide her with a home in St. Louis. She is the reason I stooped to this brazen assault on your goodwill."

Mrs. Langtry looked into my eyes and unexpectedly reached out to squeeze my hand. Then she smiled coolly at Alice, who was hastening back with the glass of water. "Thank you, Alice. I am much better—just a dizzy spell. Please help the others at the door. Miss Mooney will stay with me."

I realized that the clamor outside in the corridor had increased. But Lillie Langtry's attention was on me. She said, "Miss Mooney, it is a rare consolation to enjoy such heartfelt understanding from a stranger, when even my husband is ignorant of the truth about my little niece. But you do see that secrecy is the most important service you could perform for me."

"And you for me, Mrs. Langtry."

"Yes, of course."

"But I would help if I could."

"I don't see—oh, Oliver! Whatever is the matter?"

I turned to see a lanky fellow with sandy hair and pale eyes rushing in. "Lillie, I just heard you were attacked by a throng of ne'er-do-wells! How dreadful for you!" He was impeccably British, with a deep, theatrical baritone. "What ghastly ruffians they are in this country!"

"It's those same ruffians who buy tickets and pay your salary," she said crisply. "Miss Mooney, may I present my fellow actor, Oliver Coleman?"

He managed to kiss my hand without once taking his eyes from Mrs. Langtry. "But your safety—dearest Lillie, we must protest!"

"Oliver, I am quite capable of deciding for myself what is to be done."

"She is! And you'd better get out now!" came an angry new voice, American this time. A tall, well-built young man was striding in. And I declare, he was a treat to the eye! He had expensive clothes, snow white linen, a diamond stick-pin, and gold cuff links. "Oliver, you're upsetting Mrs. Langtry!"

"I am extending my sympathy for her unpleasant experience!" huffed Oliver.

"And I say you should leave her alone!"

"Freddie, Oliver, let us not fuss, please." Mrs. Langtry's voice had a steely undertone. The two men looked at her sheepishly. She continued, "Miss Mooney, may I present Mr. Fred Gebhard, my—bodyguard?" There was the tiniest twitch at the corner of her lovely mouth.

Of course, I recognized his name from the newspapers. I gave him my hand and murmured, "Delighted." And I was delighted, yes indeed. One is always delighted to meet handsome young millionaires, even if they have already been claimed by the most beautiful woman in the world.

"Miss Mooney," he said. "An understudy, I presume? Well, your height is good, and your hair. But I must warn you that Mrs. Langtry has not yet missed a performance." He kissed my hand with warm enthusiasm, despite the dazzle of the present company.

I said, "Of course, I am completely at Mrs. Langtry's disposal. But I trust the need for an understudy will never arise, as Mrs. Langtry enjoys glowing good health."

Mrs. Langtry had been looking at me with half-closed eyes ever since Freddie Gebhard had mentioned my height and hair. Surely she, of all women, could not be jealous! But suddenly she said, "On the contrary, my health is fragile just now. Miss Mooney, please remove your bonnet for a moment and come here."

She was standing before a pier mirror. I untied my bonnet strings and joined her. For a moment we studied our images in the tall glass, and I began to get an inkling of what she was thinking. My hair, though a shade lighter, was already arranged in the "Jersey Lily" style. And I found myself standing proudly, squaring my shoulders and tilting my chin to a more classic angle. Unfortunately no amount of tilting could get rid of freckles or scars.

Mrs. Langtry nodded slowly. "We're not likely to do better," she mused, and turned back to the two men. "I desperately need a rest," she told them. "Miss Mooney is going to help me. I will rest quietly in my railroad car, and with your help, Miss Mooney shall meet the St. Louis public for me."

Freddie was instantly solicitous. "Lillie, darling, I didn't know! You poor dear!"

Oliver burst in, "Darling Lillie, why didn't you tell me? We can cancel, or—"

"No!" She almost snapped the word. "I am earning lots of lovely money, and don't intend to stop."

I agreed wholeheartedly with her sentiments. But Freddie said, "Money! Lillie, I could—"

"No, Freddie. I know you could, but I wish to do it myself. You and Oliver may both help. You must attend Miss Mooney as a bodyguard, so that the dear people of St. Louis will believe that they are in fact seeing me. Oliver, you must convince the rest of the troupe to remain silent about the deception. Otherwise there will be no choice but to cut the salaries." She glanced at me and said, "The same is true for you, Miss Mooney, although as the Bernhardt of Missouri, you should have no difficulty convincing people that you are an actress."

Well, that was true enough. For all the Jersey Lily's beauty and fame, no one claimed that she could act. "A pretty elocutionist," said the critics.

"Won't your friends recognize you?" Freddie asked me.

"The only roles I've played there in recent days are Lady Macbeth and Iago's wife," I said. "My Rosalind was done in Kansas City. Besides, people see what they want to see."

"But, Lillie, are you seriously ill?" Freddie turned to her, looking very handsome and concerned. "Did that rabble this morning bring this on?"

She shrugged prettily. "That, and the long strain of bearing with Henrietta Labouchère."

"Henrietta!" Both men snorted in disgust.

I asked, "Should I know who Henrietta is?"

"A termagant!" cried Oliver.

"A jealous virago!" said Freddie.

"She was my drama teacher," Lillie said to me. "And very helpful at first, I daresay. But she became very possessive once we reached these shores. Freddie offered to show me New York when we arrived there, but she wanted me to be rehearsing all the time."

Well, I thought that possibly Henrietta's point was well taken, judging from the reviews; but it did not seem prudent to say so in this company. Oliver said, "She was domineering, and had no talent of her own."

"She was ruling your life!" Freddie declared.

"Yes, we had a falling out," Lillie said mildly. "Now, Oliver and Freddie, do promise to keep our secret from the public! If I can rest for a few days, I'll be fine again. Oliver, promise me?" She took his hand and looked into his eyes.

"Oh, yes!" He cleared his throat, and added, "Of course, Lillie. Would that I could do more!"

Freddie was on his knees before her, looking very gallant. "You have my solemn promise too!" he cried.

She took his hand also. "Thank you," she said in a sweet, husky voice; and I knew that secrecy was assured more surely than it could have been with scores of legal documents.

I said, "I hope you will pardon my audacity, Mrs. Langtry. But as I understand my assignment, it involves more than the performances in St. Louis. It involves playing Lillie Langtry herself to the press, and on necessary public occasions, until your health is restored."

Lillie understood me. "You want more money."

"My understanding is that in addition to the travel expenses, your producer is paying you sixty-five percent of the gross." Backstage, our troupe had been abuzz about that amount. Most famous actors were fortunate to earn fifty percent.

"But I must pay the salaries of the company," she pointed out.

I inclined my head in agreement. "Still, while you are resting in your private railroad car, it seems to me that I should receive sixty-five percent of your share."

"Bridget Mooney, that's preposterous!"

"Yes, Mrs. Langtry." I smiled at her. "So is the assignment."

"Well—I suppose it would add to your incentive—"

"That's true, too, Mrs. Langtry."

"I'll do it on one condition."

"What's that?"

"That you call me Lillie, Bridget. You are a woman after my own heart!"

We clasped hands warmly, and I said, "Thank you, Lillie. Of course, it goes without saying that I will need some of it in advance."

She burst out laughing and said, "Freddie?" Casually he pulled a hundred dollars from a roll and handed it to me. Don't you agree that millionaires are perfectly splendid?

Then Lillie shooed out Oliver and Freddie and the servants like so many chickens, and the two of us set to work transforming my freckled Irish prettiness into her Jersey beauty. We mixed greasepaint to match her creamy coloring. "How did you get this little scar, Bridget?" she asked as she rubbed some onto my cheek.

"My little niece's father was a violent man."

"He must have been a ruffian!"

"No, no, Lillie! He was a gentleman, as near to royalty as

we've ever had in Missouri. But from time to time he was violent."

She finished my face and began to darken my lashes. "So you, too, know a prince. A violent one. Does he continue to trouble you?"

"He was killed. Shot by one of his closest friends."

"Oh dear, a violent death too. And did you love him very much, this prince?"

"I loved what he brought me. Riches, excitement, romance."

"Yes," she said. She had stopped working on my face and was studying me with that beautiful violet gaze. "Yes, Bridget, we are alike, you and I. Riches, excitement, romance—those are the things my little niece's father brought me. And he helped conceal her existence from the world and from my drunken, estranged husband, who would raise a scandal if he knew. Tell me, how old is your little niece?"

"Seven months. How old is yours?"

"Not quite two years."

"We'll keep them both safe, Lillie."

Well, we had a good cry together, the imperturbable Lillie and I, and then we finished painting my face. I looked lovely, though you understand I was still not Lillie's twin. But from a distance, wearing a veil and one of her Parisian dresses with some padding in the hips and corset, only a good friend could tell the difference. The most difficult task was learning to move the way Lillie moved. She was at once queenly and lissome, and it was difficult to imitate in a tight-laced, padded corset.

Lillie had a scrapbook of clippings, and I began to study it so I would know her opinions about America, Shakespeare, fashion, beauty tips, and so forth. One opinion was obviously missing. "Suppose they ask about the Prince of Wales?" I asked.

"Oh, Bridget, you must be very, very discreet! The slightest whiff of public scandal, and I will lose his favor."

"I'll do my best. But they may ask."

"Of course they will, they always do! So I become

suddenly deaf. I smile encouragingly at some other reporter."

"And if they accuse you of something scandalous?"

"My dear friend Mr. Gladstone pointed out that a public person is frequently attacked and slandered. Never reply to your critics, he said. Never explain. You will only keep alive the controversy."

So I was ready, with the help of Freddie and the troupe, to become Lillie Langtry for the public. But even Freddie and the actors were not aware of the deeper level of our plan. In fact, Lillie would not be resting in the bedroom of her private railroad car, as Freddie and the others would believe. She would remain in Chicago, wearing dark, shabby clothes and a black wig. Her faithful servant Alice and I were the only ones who would know that Lillie was not on the train. Thus, safe from Freddie and anyone else who had no right to know about her niece, Lillie could cable her mother on the Isle of Jersey to find out what had happened to the little girl. Lillie would then re-join us in St. Louis in time to meet the extortionist at the Southern Hotel.

Meanwhile, I would go ahead in splendor, playing Lillie Langtry in addition to Lillie Langtry's roles. I would not have to ride in the coach with the other actors and the common passengers. I would travel in the private railroad car that Lillie's friend Diamond Jim Brady had acquired for her use. It was called *The City of Worcester* and sported a living room, three bedrooms, and a private bath. The best bedroom would be kept locked, and Alice and I would turn away Freddie and the rest of her colleagues, explaining that she needed her rest. The troupe would help me deceive the public; Alice and I would deceive the troupe.

And wasn't it a ripping railroad car! I bounced on the bed, and opened all the cunning little drawers in the cabinetry, and ran the water in the bathroom. Alice watched with an amused smirk. Outside, the February landscape rolled by, rainy and gray, but inside it was all warm luxury.

After a few hours I put on my Langtry padding and paint, as well as a hat with a veil, and went into the next coach. It was filled with Lillie's actors and servants and stagehands.

When I appeared, the actress who played Phebe the shepherdess called out, "Miss Lillie! Are you feeling better, then? Oh!" She clapped her little hand to her mouth.

Pleased, I said, "Thank you, Mary, I am better." I kept my voice sweetly modulated, as Lillie did. "I hope to arrange a rehearsal on the Olympic Theatre stage as soon as we reach St. Louis. Would that be agreeable to everyone?"

"Yes, Miss Lillie!" There was a chorus of approval.

Oliver Coleman had done his job well. I smiled at him. "I'll arrange to speak to the reporters soon after we arrive also."

"Are you sure you are well enough, Lillie?" he asked with convincing anxiety.

"If it will increase the receipts, I'm well enough," I said firmly. There were shouts of "Hear, hear!" amongst the actors.

Suddenly someone in the aisle touched my arm. "Mrs. Langtry," he said. I looked up and saw the possumlike face of the reporter I'd met in the Grand Pacific Hotel in Chicago.

"Yes?" I said distantly. My heart was galloping. He was only two feet away.

"Mrs. Langtry, my—my newspaper is eager to know your opinion of—of Chicago."

"A splendid city, filled with strength and vigor," I replied.

"Vigor?" he asked, and licked his lips. He seemed nervous, almost shy, unlike his chipper self in Chicago, where he'd called me "my sweet." He added, "Are you unhappy about the crowd that destroyed your hat?"

What would Lillie say? I said, "I was sorry to lose the hat, but pleased to see the enthusiasm the people demonstrated."

His small, dark eyes were fixed on my mouth with a strange expression. I was worried—my mouth, I thought, was similar to the Jersey Lily's, and required only a small adjustment in the upper lip. Why was the little reporter staring at me so? I said nervously, "Do you have any more questions, sir?"

"Oh. Oh, Mrs. Langtry, it is true! We Americans are

enthusiasts. I for one have read everything ever written about you, and crossed the Atlantic to see you cantering in the park with the prince." He peered soulfully through my veil, and suddenly I recognized the expression and almost laughed out loud. Lovesick! This short, marsupial fellow was infatuated with the dazzling Lillie Langtry!

I said kindly, "What is your name, sir?"

"Oh. Thorpe. William Thorpe. Here—here is my card, Mrs. Langtry, if you would be so kind as to accept it." He thrust the card at me with trembling fingers.

Just then Freddie entered the far end of the car, saw me speaking to Thorpe, and came striding up the aisle waving his silver-headed cane. "Sir!" he exclaimed. "You've been told not to have anything to do with Mrs. Langtry!"

William Thorpe flattened himself against one of the seats to let Freddie by. "She—she was kind enough to answer my questions."

"Well, it's over! Mrs. Langtry must conserve her strength!" Freddie offered me his expensively clad elbow and led me firmly out of the coach toward my own.

"Is there a problem with Mr. Thorpe?" I asked him once we were on the platform.

"He's a pest. He's been after Lillie since New York. He buttered up Henrietta for news. He even bribed the hotel staff to let him into my rooms to try to convince me to get him an interview with her. As though I had influence!"

"Well, it's his job, I suppose."

Freddie snorted. "Well, it's my job to protect Lillie from people like him! He has no business in that car!"

"I'll try not to encourage him. But sometimes it's easier to say a few words to newspapermen, so they don't invent their own."

"That's what Lillie says," he admitted grudgingly as he opened the door of *The City of Worcester*. Alice was in the sitting room section, and he added anxiously, "How is she, Alice?"

Alice shook her head sadly. "She needs rest, Mr. Gebhard."

"Blast it! I'd hoped—well, she's right, of course. Do tell

her I've been asking." Freddie flopped into one of the overstuffed chairs and stared out at the damp landscape.

"I'm certain she'll send for you when she is able," I soothed him. "She's very fond of you, Freddie."

"Oh, do you think so?" He looked at Lillie's bedroom door, as calf-eyed as little William Thorpe. If he'd known that Lillie was still back in Chicago, he would have run back to her on foot. Poor Lillie was right—she could never send a private cable with so many eager swains attempting to help. Freddie continued, "She is so—not cool, how can I say it? Warm and cool all at once. I would think she cared only for my money—except that she won't accept my help to leave the stage!"

"Well, goodness, Freddie, I wouldn't either! I love the stage! But I wouldn't despise your money. It's one of your attractions. Though you have many others."

"Perhaps." Freddie sighed. "Oh, Bridget, I just don't know if I have a chance or not! She invites me to be her bodyguard—and then locks me out!"

Well, it would have been lovely, and profitable, to take dear Freddie into my arms to console him. But I knew that in the long run Lillie could be a more loyal friend than he, or a more implacable enemy. So I resisted temptation and said, "Freddie, you're still new in her life. Allow her some time. Now tell me what I should say to the reporters, to ensure good receipts."

"I don't know," he said listlessly. "She usually doesn't have to worry about it. Oscar Wilde meets her ship, or someone speaks against her in the U.S. Senate, or Henrietta storms out, or she's mobbed in the streets—there are plenty of headlines. And if news is slow, they print something about the blasted Prince of Wales."

I nodded slowly. Poor Lillie—the merest whiff of the existence of her little niece would be headlined all over America. She was not rich. Her drunken husband had gone bankrupt, but would not give her a divorce, and even with an admirer like Freddie temporarily at her feet, in the long run she had to depend on her own resources. As long as she walked the narrow line between respectability and scandal, people would buy tickets just for a glimpse of her. But with half of society already snubbing her, any indiscretion that tipped the balance—especially if it caused the Prince of Wales to withdraw his friendship—would tumble her into disrepute and ruin.

So I had to be extremely circumspect. But hang it, I had no intention of allowing those receipts to fall off when sixty-five percent of her share was to be mine.

Freddie went moping off, and after a moment I sent Alice for Oliver Coleman. The lanky actor appeared quickly but seemed disappointed that it was I and not the true Lillie who wished to see him.

"She needs her rest," I told him. "Oliver, she trusts you, and I must ask you some questions. First, as an actor, what is your opinion of my impersonation?"

"Not half-bad, Bridget! The walk isn't quite right yet, but the voice and appearance are excellent. Now, of course, I'm not saying that you are precisely—uh—"

"Of course not," I said tartly. "Nevertheless, I daresay I am playing Lillie better than Lillie could play me."

Oliver laughed. "I daresay."

"Now, Oliver, you were in England with Lillie. Tell me about Henrietta Labouchère."

"A terrible woman! Lillie is usually so strong. I can only think that she was ill when she fell under her influence."

"Is Mrs. Labouchère vindictive? Is she likely to write threatening letters?"

"I wouldn't be surprised. But it's too soon. I saw her to the boat myself! Has Lillie received such letters?"

"I have no idea, Oliver!" I said blandly. "I am just trying to account for Mrs. Langtry's exhaustion after Henrietta left. Lillie strikes me as a very healthy person."

"As healthy as she is beautiful!" Oliver's eyes looked suspiciously calflike too.

Well, I was beginning to tire of all these men falling at Lillie's feet when she wasn't even there, and I was. I snapped, "Come now, Oliver, time for a lesson! Help me learn to walk the way she walks!"

As we approached St. Louis, I drew Alice aside. "We must

part for a few days, Alice. I must move into Mrs. Langtry's suite at the Southern Hotel. The troupe has been splendid about supporting my impersonation, but we must continue to deceive them. They must all believe that Mrs. Langtry is here in *The City of Worcester* with you. You must be alert as ever and prepared to turn them away."

"Yes, madame. I'll turn away reporters as well."

"Good, although if we succeed, the reporters will come to me at the hotel. Well, keep the servants with you; I shall make do with Freddie and the hotel staff. Oh, and Alice, I must borrow a cap and apron from you."

I moved into the Southern Hotel, a magnificent edifice that had always been beyond my means. It had a splendid rotunda, and beautifully appointed rooms, and an efficient staff, except that one of them unaccountably lost a bottle of Lillie's scent, and I had to send to Alice for another. But all in all, my aunt Mollie would have approved of the way Mrs. Langtry had arranged her life. She knew how the quality lived, yes indeed.

I set the staff to work organizing a meeting with reporters two hours hence, followed by a rehearsal on the Olympic Theatre stage. Then, as Lillie Langtry, I asked the hotel staff to turn away all callers, pleading the necessity of a nap. But I didn't sleep. Instead, wearing Alice's cap and apron, no makeup, and a low-down Irish accent I'd learned from Papa, I curtsied my way past the unsuspecting guards at the door and went to my friend Hattie's cottage to see my little niece.

She was the dearest little creature ever, my niece. She had blue eyes and two wee teeth and the most cunning little nose and ears. We giggled and cooed at each other. I bounced her on my knees, and rocked her, and she very nearly chewed off the string of Alice's apron. Too soon, it was time to return.

As I rode back, I vowed that if I ever found the skunk that threatened Lillie's niece, I'd make him pay. That's about the lowest, cruelest thing a body can do, threatening a little niece.

The freckled Irish maid went back into Lillie's rooms at the hotel, and half an hour later the creamy-skinned, elegantly appareled Lillie Langtry descended to the rotunda to speak to the reporters, carrying a lily snatched hastily from a large bouquet that had been sent to her rooms. The interview went very much as Lillie and I had rehearsed—most of the questions concerned how she liked Missouri, and I only had to ignore a few about the Prince of Wales. But it occurred to me as the hotel staff escorted me away from the still eager reporters that nothing exciting had come up. No Henrietta Labouchères had stormed off, no Oscar Wildes had met the train, no ragtag crowds had snatched off my hat. We would get pleasant little mentions in the newspapers, but not the kind of attention Lillie usually received. And since the Olympic Theatre management had told us that, while tickets were selling well, there were still many left, something had to be done before tomorrow night's opening.

I paused and indicated to the hotel staff that I wished to speak to Colonel Cunningham, a highly moral reporter for the *Globe-Democrat*. My possumlike admirer William Thorpe and the other reporters cast angry glances at this favored fellow as he hurried to me. I stepped close to him and lowered my voice. "Colonel Cunningham, I must go to rehearsal, so I cannot speak now. But I admire your newspaper. Please come to my room tomorrow morning at nine, and we can arrange an interview."

He looked astonished. I smiled sweetly and tapped his chest with my lily. "And don't let anyone stop you, Colonel Cunningham!" Then I turned and glided swiftly away to rehearse.

Afterward Freddie escorted me back to the hotel, but he was clearly eager to pay another vain call on the empty bedroom in *The City of Worcester,* where he thought Lillie rested, so I asked him to visit me early the next morning. Once he'd gone, I became the freckled Irish maid again, and tripped away for a nice chat with Hattie and a lovely nap with my little niece.

I know, you're right, of course. My Aunt Mollie taught me that it was not safe for a young lady to travel the streets of St. Louis at night unprotected. But I can hit a squirrel at thirty yards with my excellent revolver, once the property of Jesse

James himself. It was the second-best thing Jesse ever gave me. So you see, I was protected.

Before dawn, I returned to the hotel. I bathed, applied my Jersey Lily greasepaint and Jersey Lily scent, and donned a dazzling peignoir that Lillie had provided. When Freddie arrived, he blinked. "Oh, excuse me, Lil—uh, Bri—uh, Lillie. I'll come back later."

"No, no, Freddie!" I smiled warmly. "Do come have breakfast with me. It's been lonely."

"You're a damned attractive woman," he said, coming in with no further ado.

We settled ourselves at the breakfast table in the sitting room, and I'm bound to admit that it made a scene from a lovely dream: flowers, crystal, silver, delicious rolls and marmalade, the most beautiful woman in the world, and the handsomest young millionaire. We discussed Lillie's health, and then Freddie's racing stable, and Freddie himself, and soon he fell under the spell of the flowers and the peignoir and laid his hand over mine. "You are lovely, damn it!" he exclaimed.

And that was the scene Colonel Cunningham saw when he pushed his way past the protesting maid and burst into the sitting room. He halted at the sight of us. "Mrs. Langtry!" he gasped. "What is the explanation of this?"

I donned my cool Lillie gaze. "Colonel Cunningham, please leave us, sir."

"Mr. Gebhard! What is the explanation?"

Freddie exclaimed, "The lady told you to leave us!"

"What am I to say to my readers? Sir, madam, this has every appearance of the vilest immorality!"

Well, that was unfair, don't you think? Freddie was fully and expensively dressed, and my peignoir concealed more than my ball gowns. In any case, we were not the least bit vile. On the contrary, we were ethereally elegant. But Colonel Cunningham was appalled.

Freddie, of course, was becoming angrier by the moment. His beloved Lillie was being insulted, and he could not explain that she was not even present. I laid a restraining hand on his arm and said, "Let us not fuss, Freddie." We listened to Colonel Cunningham rant on for a few minutes, but I refused to answer and managed to keep my sweet, hot-blooded millionaire from boiling over. When the colonel finally retreated, though, Freddie exploded.

"Damn him!"

"Oh, hush, Freddie. You know that Lillie wouldn't have spoken to him."

"Maybe not. But if he does anything more, I'll crack his skull!"

Freddie, at six feet and probably two hundred pounds, might be able to do so, although I knew that Colonel Cunningham, as a military man from Missouri, was sure to carry a pistol. I said, "Do take care, Freddie. Lillie wouldn't want you to be rash."

Colonel Cunningham's blistering attack on Lillie was published that same afternoon. She was immoral, he said. Fred Gebhard was her partner in sin. The citizens of St. Louis should boycott the theatre.

Freddie was furious. I restrained him while I could, but the minute I left for the theatre, he went down to the rotunda to smoke a cigar, or so he claimed. Unfortunately, Colonel Cunningham was there. I'm told that Freddie shouted, "Sir! You are an infamous liar!" and advanced on him, waving his stick. Cunningham backed away, one hand slipping into a side pocket in a way anyone from Missouri would find ominous, but Freddie, undaunted, kept shouting and waving his stick until at last the police came and removed Cunningham from the premises. Oh, I do wish I had been there! It must have been a dandy cockfight!

In most respects, Freddie was performing his part well. There was a beautiful lily bouquet in my dressing room. I picked up the note that came with it. "To Lillie," it said, "from your devoted Freddie."

But then I frowned. His note was written in midnight blue ink on cream-colored paper.

The next morning, an emissary from Cunningham arrived to challenge Freddie to a duel.

"No, Freddie," I said. "Absolutely not. We must never

respond to criticism. It's Lillie's own rule, and a very good one."

"I want to shoot the infamous liar!" Freddie shouted.

"Of course you do. But if one of you is killed, Lillie's career will be ruined."

"It's already ruined, isn't it? There's going to be a boycott!"

I smiled. "On the contrary, Freddie. The manager tells me that the controversy has created great interest. We're sold out for the run."

My financial difficulties were solved for the time, if I could keep Freddie from the duel. But then a fresh worry presented itself. A cable addressed to Lillie Langtry was delivered to my hotel room. "Dear Lillie, I'm devastated to say that due to the Mississippi flooding, I cannot reach St. Louis in time for our prearranged meeting about the ruby brooch. I hope you and the others can arrange the business without me. The family is safe." It was signed, "Mrs. L. L. Prince."

So it was up to me to meet the extortionist! It was not a comforting thought, because any extortionist who knew Lillie well enough to mention her niece was likely to know her well enough to see through my impersonation. I sat down to have a good think.

Who could it be? According to Lillie, no one knew about her little niece, not Freddie, not even her husband. It seemed impossible that an American could find out without visiting the isle of Jersey. But why would any of her British troupe engage in such cruel extortion? She didn't pay well, but as I well knew, some troupes were paid nothing at all. I wondered about the angry Henrietta; but she had been escorted onto the ship home. I sighed. There were not enough facts to make a good guess.

Last time, Lillie had said, the extortionist had been content with a brooch. This time he wanted Lillie there in person. I found this ominous. A mind cruel enough to threaten a little niece, even falsely, might be cruel enough to consider abduction of Mrs. Langtry herself, for vile enjoyment of her personal charms or for ransom from Freddie or even the Prince of Wales. I realized I would have to be extremely careful.

Just before 2:00 A.M., I tucked the ruby brooch Lillie had mentioned into my bustle pocket, smiled at the porters dozing outside Lillie's door, and glided swiftly along the hall and out to the stables. The night groom snored just inside the door, an empty whiskey bottle on the floor beside him. The stabled horses shifted and stamped as I entered, and I saw that the hasp on the harness room door had been pried off, though the door was closed. I knocked gently; but there was no answer, so I pushed it open. Inside, a small lantern spread a warm glow over the stored saddles and bridles. The room smelled of leather and saddle soap. But no one was there. Was I to leave the brooch without further instructions? Hesitantly I placed it on a bench.

A moment later there was a soft knock and I whirled to face the door. "Come in," I said.

Freddie closed the door behind him and bounded across the room to me. "Lillie! At last! I've waited so long for this moment!"

"Freddie!" I exclaimed. "But—but—" Hang it, he was a millionaire! It wasn't a brooch he wanted from Lillie.

"But what? You told me—" His face fell as he realized who I was. "Oh, damn!"

Whatever else we might have said, we were interrupted by the door bursting open again. A huge revolver appeared, and a man's voice hissed, "Sir! You are a cad! Lillie, I'll save you!"

"Why, thank you, sir, but—"

The revolver advanced into the room, followed by the possumlike snout and small, shiny eyes of the lovesick reporter, William Thorpe. "Your designs on Lillie are vicious and immoral!" Thorpe said.

"Liar!" Freddie exclaimed. "I wish to marry her!"

He took a step toward Thorpe, and I grabbed his sleeve. "Freddie, don't be rash! He has a gun!"

"And I'll use it!" crowed Thrope. "I'll rid you of this pest, Lillie!"

I said graciously, "Mr. Thorpe, I thank you for your concern. But Mr. Gebhard and I were merely conversing. If I wish to be rid of him, I myself will ask him to leave."

"No!" He flicked a frantic glance in my direction, but the revolver held steady on my millionaire. "You need me! You have been unable to dissuade him! I'll rescue you, Lillie!"

Well, hang it, this scene was not working. We were reading from three different scripts, it seemed. And though I thought Freddie's version had the most appeal, Thorpe held the pistol, so I switched to his. "Mr. Thorpe, I'm so very glad you came," I said soothingly, stepping toward him. "But you have already rescued me, you see. Do you know what would give me great pleasure, right now?"

"Oh, yes! You are grateful! You wish to—to kiss me! 'Make me immortal with a kiss!'"

From the corner of my eye I saw Freddie's hands clench, but I continued soothingly, "Of course, Mr. Thorpe, that is exactly right! But first I would find it a great pleasure to hold the gun on the despicable Mr. Gebhard myself. Please allow me!"

"No! No, I'm supposed to hold the gun! He's threatened you!"

"You infamous liar!" Freddie burst out unwisely.

William Thorpe smirked. "Lillie can decide who the liar is when she looks in your suitcases and finds the brooch she gave you last time!"

"How do you know what's in my suitcases?" Freddie demanded.

"Hush, Freddie," I said, trying to regain control. "After all, the extortion note was written on your notepaper."

"Yes, yes, yes!" Thorpe cried, delighted at my acuity.

Freddie looked at me in disbelief. "You believe this fellow?"

Thorpe answered gleefully, "I am her rescuer! I know all her problems! I know everything about Lillie!"

"He's visited London to see me canter in the park," I told Freddie. "He's seen the Prince of Wales."

At the mention of the prince, Freddie's look darkened. So did Thorpe's. Thorpe muttered, "Yes, the Prince of Wales.

And Louis Battenburg. And Edward Langtry. All unworthy of you, Lillie! And now this worm of a fellow!" He gestured at Freddie with the revolver.

Freddie was about to explode. "You are the worm, sir! To make such vile innuendos about a virtuous lady!"

"You say virtuous? And are your plans for her virtuous? No, she needs my help, my poor Lillie! You are like all the others! You are trying to drag her into the mud! I've been to the Isle of Jersey, too, and I know—"

Idiotically courageous, Freddie hurled himself at Thorpe. The sound of the gunshot rang through the little room. Freddie fell on top of Thorpe, and blood gushed onto the plank floor. Freddie looked at it, astonished, and then his eyes glazed over.

I sighed, adjusted my bustle, and gave Freddie a good sniff of my smelling salts. "Freddie! Are you all right?"

"I'm—I'm bleeding," he gasped. He struggled to a sitting position, staring at the gaudy red stain on his lovely white shirt.

"It's Thorpe's blood, you silly goose," I said.

"Thorpe's? But he was aiming at me!"

Well, I've never had much ambition to be the leading attraction at a trial, so it seemed best to keep the truth from Freddie. I said, "You must have knocked his arm aside when you tackled him, and he shot himself."

"Oh. Oh, yes, that must have been it!" Freddie seemed pleased with himself.

"It might be best to arrange to dispose of the body, Freddie."

"Yes. You're right. And I'd best rid myself of this clothing too." He stood up to begin his errands.

"And of course, we keep quiet about all this," I reminded him. "You know how Lillie hates fuss."

He looked a trifle disappointed. It would have been a fine story to tell at his club. But he admitted, "Yes, you're right."

"Freddie, why are you here? Did you, too, get a note?"

"Yes. I believed it was from Lillie. It smelled like her."

"I see. So Thorpe sent notes to both of us. He must have been the one who hooked some of Lillie's scent while I was moving into the hotel, to sprinkle on your note. And he must have stolen some of your notepaper when he bribed his way into your rooms in New York. He was quite mad, Freddie, less a reporter than a fanatic admirer. He wanted to show Lillie that you were a despicable cad, and to rescue her from you."

Freddie was puzzled. "But why?"

I shrugged. "So she would be grateful. So she would make him immortal with a kiss. Now, hurry, Freddie. It's up to you to save Lillie from this scandal."

He bustled off to look for his efficient manservant. I picked up the brooch and started out too. Then I paused and looked back at the poor little body on the floor, and blew it a kiss.

I know, I know, he didn't deserve it. He was thoroughly mad and cruel and low, and he'd threatened her little niece, and was about to shoot a perfectly splendid millionaire.

But hang it, I've done foolish things for kisses too. And I'd already made him immortal. Might as well finish the job.

The Jersey Lily left for Memphis at the end of the next week. I stood by the tracks just outside of town, richer by thousands of dollars—enough, perhaps, to become an actor-manager like Lillie, with my very own troupe and one hundred percent after expenses. Lillie had also given me half a dozen Parisian gowns in gratitude for saving Freddie and keeping him out of the duel. It hadn't been hard, really, once I reminded him that he fainted at the sight of blood.

In my arms I held my little niece. The locomotive puffed by us, and the other cars, and finally *The City of Worcester,* shiny and elegant as a jewel. I waved, and my little niece cooed and mimicked me, and I saw the most beautiful woman in the world looking out the window, fluttering her handkerchief at us and then dabbing at her eyes as she rolled away.